Jon Champs

SONS OF EARTH SAGA

BOOK 1

NEMESIS

Dedications

No book is made without the support of others, even if they don't know it. For Paul, whose enduring support since 2009 continues, and without whom none of this would have ever been accomplished. For Beth & Gill & Den, because they always read and tell me they love it! You need people like that when you write!

To my dear friend Christine, whose son Kevin, a sci-fi fan, a veteran and a father, will live on in all their hearts for ever. This book is for him, because we both think he'd have loved it.

And to Debbie Hancock, who changes peoples lives for the better.

To all sci-fi authors, writers, imagineers everywhere, past and present. Without you, what would the future be?

TABLE OF CONTENTS

AUTHORS NOTE

I have always wanted to write a sci-fi novel. The sort I would want to read, because science fiction literature ranges from the outlandish to the austere.

I try to extrapolate from where we are to where we might be, a dangerous path perhaps as we finally seem on the cusp of actually returning to the Moon and my one "please let it happen in my lifetime" moment of mankind landing on Mars. It'll be a massive and inescapable leap forward when we do. Once accomplished the horizons are endless, who knows where it will end? Or when. Until it does we have sci-fi, imagination, and the inevitability of history to propel us along.

It is inevitable that we will find life. The odds of not doing so are so small it must be impossible.

The plot for this Saga, goes back to the early 1980's. Counters and hexagonal maps, Starfire, Starfleet Battles, we re-wrote rules, built our own empires and fought using tin-alloy space ships from now long extinct modelling companies. In the Mid-1990's I spent a year wargaming a set of scenarios and wrote books and books of notes and drawings. One day I thought I might write them into a science fiction book.

This is the first of those books. I honestly thought I'd be miles ahead of the plot by the end. I have barely scratched the surface! Book 2 is already being written!

PROLOGUE

Earth has suffered devastating climate change, it had progressed, despite efforts spanning 70 years to control it, until the planets Co2 peaked at 502ppm and the methane level sky rocketed as the vast permafrosts and tundra zones of Siberia and North America thawed out. None of the major economic powers did anything like what they should have, and the developing nations couldn't afford to.

In 2070, after years of droughts, devastating hurricanes, forest fires and starvation, the climate finally collapsed, in the space of six months late that year and into 2071, a new ice age began and spread across the northern hemisphere causing global pandemonium, war and migration.

But mankind was by now already in space. Luna had been heavily colonised, nearly 2 million people lived and worked there, Mars was home to almost 100,000 more, colonies in the asteroids, on Titan and Io, were well advanced.

Now the best part of century later in 2162, high speed sub-light drives and the discovery of the jump gate fragments and their back-engineering have taken mankind to the stars, It still isn't easy, but already humans have been to eight star systems and colonised most of them to a small degree, bearing in mind the vastness of space.

Earth itself remains unstable in climate terms, it still hasn't settled, though each year suggests the worst is over and a new world order gets to grips with making the best of it, and making sure it doesn't happen again.

We join an old United Earth Alliance explorer ship, the EXC-102 Ramorra, in a planet-less star system, where she's been ordered to basically sit and wait for something to happen, for almost a year. A very long tedious year…

CHAPTER 1

ALONE

He had a habit of listening to jazz. It was quite unlikely he could tell you who was playing. He never really knew, other than vaguely, a single artist or band and it didn't bother him in the least. He couldn't really tell you which part of the past two centuries jazz had been around, or when what he was listening to had been composed, because he'd never bothered to find out. It was just jazz, and he liked it. Its orderly disorder broke the monotony of their regimented life, out here in the depths of space, almost six light years from Earth.

There was such a vast catalogue of music that he just streamed content in the background. If he liked it he let it play, if he didn't he moved it on.

The problem now was that despite the ships computer holding enough variation to last a six month cruise, they'd now been out here eleven months and thirteen standard Earth days. And they hadn't moved more than a few kilometres the whole time.

Commander Bruce Baylin of the United Earth Alliance Exploration Ship EXC-102 Ramorra, looked out into the same dead space he and his crew had been looking at for almost a year. It seemed like a decade. Moral was low, rations were running out, and they could only stay another week before they would have no choice but to head back to Earth, through the jump gate to Barnards Star; a three day transit through hyperspace would almost be a relief.

The Ramorra was not new. She had been due for an upgrade and refit two years before. Her reliance on active sensors and a suite of frankly outdated passive sensors made her largely unsuitable for this assignment. Her engines were early versions of the FAFLOF Drive and less than fast, and that was being generous. Budget constraints had made them too small for the size of ship when she was built. Like so many ships over hundreds of years she was sent to do something she was never intended for, but needs must.

Thirteen months before, the Ramorra had picked up a signal that analysts on board, and back on Earth, finally concurred was a beacon. The signal was partial, untranslatable, but repetitive and clearly not human in origin. The Ramorra had been close enough to an active jump gate on the edge of Epsilon Eridani, (that lead who knew where because nobody had yet flown through it), to pick up the wide-band tachyon signal emanating from hyperspace and the jump gates' amplification, when a very small ship, analysed as likely some kind of freighter, came through from the other side. It spent the next two days crossing the system to a point that was around 500,000 klicks from gate the Ramorra would need to jump back to Barnards Star, then on to Sol, humanities home system.

It had been the most remote of chances. Only the extraordinary vigilance of the signals processing computers (Ramorra wasn't equipped with the latest Quantum Analysis Computers, which the acronym-mad military had dubbed QuAC's), and a junior communications specialist, Starman Freddie Sinclair, who spent hours analysing and running algorithms to clean up the signal, entirely based on a hunch. He'd revealed it as fully as was possible given the equipment on board.

It was remarkable, because despite the fact humanity had long ago learnt it wasn't alone, it had not yet found a single spacefaring race, or a species capable of even mechanical flight. In fact, not one of the millions of creatures, insects, reptiles, birds and ocean going leviathans so far discovered in eight star systems, was even capable of lighting a fire. Other than the Barnard's Dragon, a 2m long flying reptile that used a chemical compound to ignite oxygen and produce a brief flame as a warning.

Not one intelligent human-equivalent life form anywhere. Not even the early stage development of one. Not even anything that came close to an Earth primate. So a signal, no matter its sparing nature, that was clearly artificial, could mean but one thing. The long held belief that we were utterly unique was about to be shattered.

The public were ambivalent about the possibility. Almost 50% thought it inevitable that we would come across a species similar, equal to, or superior to, ourselves within 10 years. Roughly 40% clung to the belief preached by religions around the world and on Earth's colonies for the most part, that we were a unique creation of God's making, and the Milky Way galaxy was ours, if not to plunder, certainly to use to do our biding. The other 10% didn't know or didn't care or had some other ideal to hold to.

The EXC-102 UEAS Ramorra was designed to explore, built to find new worlds, extend the range of human beings both physically, and scientifically. Now she'd been sat here five million kilometres (usually referred to as 'klicks' in the fleet), from the jump gate home, looking at the single thing there was to see in this planet-free star system; the fourth magnitude, class K2 main sequence dwarf, Epsilon Eridani sometimes referred to as Ran by civilians.

Day after day, expecting something to happen, they waited, but nothing did. They'd studied the red star itself, finding that its lack of interesting features was the only interesting thing about it. Nobody had ever spent that much time studying it before, so at least there was that.They'd gathered almost a petaflop of data that might, one day, prove of value to the astrophysicists back home.

The jazz cut out as the comlink in his headphones switched to receive a call. It was the extremely disciplined first officer, Markus Obishka. "Captain, it's time to change shifts, I'll be up to relieve you in ten minutes".

Captain Baylin acknowledged him in the most minimal way, they had their routine and it suited them. The crew of 120 was divided into three watches, two of six hours each. The six hour long Alert Watch gave way to the twelve hour Sleep Watch, and Alert went down to the half way point of Research & Recreation watch, which enabled anyone to indulge their research, self educate, or simply exercise and rest, before compulsory sleep. Not everyone could sleep for 12 hours, but it was a way of keeping alertness at peak, coupled to rigorous exercise. There had been frictions of course, a few minor scuffles, but this was a disciplined crew and Captain Baylin had an inventive mind when it came to keeping them occupied.

The hardest thing had been trying to keep the weapons systems up to full service without being able to use them. This was a silent observation mission, nobody need know they were there until the chain of command at Fleet knew enough to make a call on what would happen next.

Energy expenditure was so low the ship had had problems with the main reactor wanting to shut down, something that simply couldn't be allowed to happen. It had to be awake, enough to be powered up in an emergency, but not so hot that it would give itself away with some ungainly and clearly unnatural magnetic pulse that would sing out the ships position. Software mods and mechanical interference from the chief engineer had resulted in a happy half-way house, though every day, Chief Engineer Isambard Carradine - more usually just known as Sam, moaned about its condition.

As Lieutenant Obishka arrived on the bridge, Baylin so schooled in their routine, prepared to hand over and say the immortal words, 'You have the con Lieutenant'. Obishka stopped him. "Can I have a quick word sir?" Baylin nodded to the science officer station, "Lieutenant Gold, you have the con, we'll be in my office". Gold, offered a rare chance to sit in the captain's chair, was delighted, anything to break the day up differently was always welcome.

In the privacy of the office, (more of a cupboard with a small desk, two chairs and some wall screens) just off the rear of the bridge, Baylin asked, "OK Markus, what's up?"

Markus sat, "can you log into the mainframe and check out some new data, something isn't right and I need to know how to proceed".

Baylin accessed the computer. He spotted the file immediately, opened it, and for a moment, sat simply starring. "Where the hell did that come from?"

On the highly processed optical image, the jump gate marked only by an artificial overlay pin, sat a large round framework, next to it was some sort of ship. It was massive, it was most definitely not human, and there was no way they could get back home without passing far too close to it.

"Markus where did it come from?" We have optical sensors on both gates 24 hours a day". Baylin was quietly fuming. His first thought was someone had let the side down and slipped up. The very thing he'd been most concerned about was boredom leading to complacency.

"It was a focusing issue. It's going to sound lame, but the gate is where the focus was placed, at this distance the distortion is quite high from solar activity and the star's gravity well is considerable, it bent the light, we were off by a few hundredths of a second, at that range it's over 5 klicks. Even so that's far away from what we were looking at. That small ship, it must have slipped through from the other gate with that, maybe there's some distortion, but we just didn't see it with optical sensors alone. The science teams have been processing collected data to fathom how to overcome so much gravitic interference on optical instrumentation, and working out how to compensate for it. They refocussed the lens based on the new research and, well there it is."

"Markus, I appreciate their efforts, but this is massive, it means, it means, well you know what it means, how long have we been seeing this?"

"Twenty minutes apparently, they had to run checks and diagnostics, but yes, it's quite real and about twenty minutes old".

"I want a full threat assessment, full observation, analysis and an action plan in thirty minutes. I want to know what we think it is, and recommendations on what we do about it. We're going home, and somehow we've got to get past that."

The issue was far more complicated. The enormous ship, which assessments showed was some 350m in length and 100m across, had multiple protrusions and a stacked upper deck filled with sensors and what looked suspiciously like weapons. They couldn't see the detail, or use any active sensors to find out what level of threat it posed, if any. The assumption had to be that it was hostile, but at the same time First Contact protocols had been suspended by Fleet Command back on Earth. Baylin had never understood why. He'd been told to make no effort to contact anything if it appeared. The rest of the crew didn't know that.

Baylin went back to his office, looking at the wall screens filled with direct feed and sensor data. He was even more furious than he let on. The Ramorra must have come out of the jump gate, blind, and gone right past the disc-like station without seeing it. How was that even possible? The large vessel was moving now, gaining speed casually. He instinctively felt it had no idea they were there.

Baylin walked out on to the bridge. "I want every moment of this recorded, nothing, repeat nothing gets missed, and not as much as a peep out of us".

"Captain", Lieutenant Obishka caught his attention, "the other gate is active again". They all looked at the screen on its highest magnification. The furthest gate across the system, the one they had been due to consider entering until stuck here observing, flashed as its energy output spiked and it punched a hole into hyperspace. Something else was coming through but they couldn't see what. The ship they were tracking near this basestation-like structure, turned to face the gate on the far side of the system. As it did so it fired two projectiles, then lunged forward at extraordinary speed towards the far gate, and it vanished, gone.

"Where the hell did it go?" Baylin, everyone had no idea, but they had an urgent problem; the projectiles were around 6m in length and exceptionally fast, accelerating quickly to around 5,000 klicks per second, without any sign of slowing down.

The computer, almost unheard in the passive mode Ramorra had been operating under for weeks, suddenly cut in making even seasoned crew on the bridge jump slightly as its female tones came loudly to life: "Inbound hostiles, missiles, projection for proximity detonations around our current position, time to impact 3-6-7 seconds".

Baylin sat quickly into his command chair, and began issuing orders - "Battle stations! Weapons, activate armour, activate defence grid, engineering full power, get us moving and make it fast. Helm point us at the incoming missiles in a straight line and force us up max speed, no matter what it takes".

"Captain we can't go through the gate to Barnards that fast, we'll only just reach flank speed by the time we get to it, and we'd have to come round, it'll take us ten minutes just to slow enough to make the turn to face the gate entrance".

"Just go for our gate helm, when the time comes listen for my orders, this will be split-second timing"

16

"Aye, Sir".

"Computer, count down the impact time".

The count began to drop alarmingly fast. As the Ramorra accelerated, the distance closed and the missiles crossed the distance between them at what seemed like light speed, but in reality was much less.

"...ten, six, three, one...minus one, minus three..." The distance began to increase. Baylin's hunch had paid off.

A few seconds later, nearly 100,000 klicks behind them, the missiles detonated harmlessly.

"Helm slow us to half and line us up for our jump gate, we're going home".

Baylin stood up and a dozen stunned officers smiled, Lieutenant Obishka followed Baylin into the office.

"That was daring, how did you know?"

"As soon as the computer said proximity, I knew it was fixed targeting, I assumed they only had a guesstimate of where we were, so aimed to kill us from a distance, if we closed with the missiles they'd fly right by and explode where they were set for, which by then was well behind us. If the reactor had been cold, we'd be dead."

The Ramorra was turning more slowly now, deceleration assisted by the forward thrusters. "Before we go, we need to take a look at that".

On the screen a huge disc shape - some kind of space station, black in the depths of space and seemingly dead for a long time, sat to their right side. It's only obvious feature that it blacked out the space behind it. There was no sensor record of it having been there before, yet it must have been. They had been here for months and it had never shown itself before. Baylin suspected some sort of stealth system.

Marilyn Gold studied her sensor data thoroughly, finally able to use active sensors gigabytes of data flooded back. The data was inexplicable, she wanted to say out loud, but knew she needed to talk to her team before presenting this to the command staff.

Captain Baylin though, as ever seemed to have a sixth sense and was hovering behind her station. "What's the issue Gold?".

"Well sir from just skim reading the initial data, it's old, probably 100 years or more, and sir, it's not completely disused".

"Explain, wait Markus, get over here". The First Officer came over to Gold's science station.

Markus saw the screen, "Does that data say an age index of over a century? That would put it here before we even colonised Mars."

Gold wasn't wrong, and added, "there's something on board it, it's like a refrigeration unit of some kind, contains some kind of suspended animation life form, yes, there's actually something alive, but in deep freeze, almost a thousand of them".

"Is there a power source?" Baylin wondered how the refrigeration was maintained.

Gold shook her head, absorbed by the data, "Nothing obvious sir, it's a space standard temperature, it may be solar powered it's so low level it's like their frozen to a point they shouldn't actually be alive at all, but they are".

Markus looked at Captain Baylin with a glint in his eye, "permission to take a boarding party over sir".

Baylin didn't blink or offer any emotional response, he'd been expecting such a request, because he knew he'd be asking the same question. Never mind the fact he wanted to go himself.

"Is there a point of entry, a docking bay, an air lock?"

Science Officer Gold called down to engineering, "Chief, can you see anything where we can dock the ship to ship shuttle, on any section of the disc?"

Sam Carradine looked at the data - "Well the scan shows a double sealed bay on the rear edge from our current position, it's not compatible, but we can open it, one way or another".

Baylin cut in, "Chief, how long will it take, I'm nervous about being here, and we're desperately short of supplies".

Baylin's worries were really less about supplies and more about the fact he didn't think they could outrun or defend themselves from whatever it was that had come and gone from this base. And where was the small freighter? Whatever that ship had been, it had come in from the other jump gate, almost half billion klicks out on the edge of the system, somehow gotten to the station and only then been spotted on their passive sensors, before leaving here and simply vanishing. As yet nobody from Earth had passed through the more distant gate. Nobody knew where it even went, and that worried him.

The jump gates were a mystery, nobody knew who had built them. The one near Titan, in the Sol System, had been in pieces and taken six years to put together, its parts having been found on Mars, Titan itself, and Io. That was a whole other story in itself. They were the only indication mankind wasn't alone, but to the majority simply indicated that God or a god-like race had created them, and then they had gone, superseded by humans. Baylin thought it all hogwash, but didn't ever discuss it.

The subsequent gates flown through from Earth's home system, Sol, were part of a grid that permitted you to fly to and from Titan, Saturns largest moon, or to eight other star systems linked by their own gates. The Titan gate was the only one in the Sol system. To travel further some systems had a second gate that linked to another sub-grid of direct destinations. Nobody had been able to fully understand why some star systems were in one grid network, some in another. The key star system for Earth was Barnard's Star, which had three gates linking three sub grids of systems. Earth's home system, Sol, was in effect in a hyperspatial dead end.

The issue was that crossing these systems - some of them were several billion klicks across, from one gate to the next, took as much as three days at a speed that was practical. That was for a fast Fleet ship. For old freighters it could take two weeks just to cross Barnard's Star alone.

Typically from the Lunar Freighter Terminal on Earth's moon, to Titan, depending on the time of year and Earth's position in respect of Saturn, could take eight to fourteen days for an old freighter with a pre-FAFLOF drive system, but around a 18-24 hours on the new Express Passenger Shuttles.

Titan, as a result was home to most of the fleet and Saturn and its rings often seemed more like home than Earth. When they ever got back there.

For now, Baylin's senior officers looked at him with a level of eager anticipation that was so childlike he wanted to smile. He looked at his first officer, then back at the screen. "OK, Lieutenant Gold, you, take one of your team, I'd suggest Ensign Kagala, he's the astrozoologist, and you'd better take the Doc with you. Markus, you're in command of the mission."

The first officer nearly leapt off of the bridge and out of the door. Gold was more careful. "Thank you Captain".

"Just be careful, I want all of you back, but Markus, understand this; if we get attacked and I have to save the rest of the crew and the ship - we'll dash for the jump gate and you're on your own until we can mount a rescue. Get in, get evidence, samples, if you can one of the life pods, and get back. You've got 120 minutes from the time you leave the shuttle bay".

"Understood, we'll be back sir".

CHAPTER 2

THE STATION

Ships Surgeon, Doctor Wilfred Branson was the oldest member of the crew by a mile and he knew it. And he always liked to point it out. He was British, if you came from anywhere else, but English if you asked him, and if he was being especially difficult, which was often, Kentish, from the county he was native to.

The thing he disliked most was the ships shuttle, when the bay doors opened and it seemingly fell out of the ships belly, the umbilical crew arm from one side and the docking arm above having let go, like a mother with an unwanted offspring. It was the jerky, dropping feeling that made the pit of your stomach feel it had gone to your throat he hated most. It just wasn't nice.

As the shuttle dropped - the wrong word to describe anything in space really, where there was no apparent gravity, he looked up, the observation port showed the bottom of Ramorra's hull and the shuttle bay door closing up, at the bottom of the fore section, cutting off the bay lights from view. Ramorra was running dark externally, so all he could see was her black jagged bulk, sensors and aerials against the background of stars. If he looked hard he could see one of the point defence cannons turning constantly scanning the space around them.

The shuttle, named after pioneering aviation leaders was the UEAS Juan Trippe. He doubted anyone of the crew had a clue who Juan Trippe even was. History wasn't a strong point with 22nd Century humanity, and few people were prepared to boast about it, even if they knew. The 20th and 21st Centuries had not been humanities finest. Yet here we were. 2162, and he was on the cusp of being the first medical professional in human history to physically prove the existence of another spacefaring intelligent culture. Clearly they'd existed - before we had - who or what else had built the jump gate network? Yet we'd not until this day proven that anyone else was still out here. The battle - if that's what you could call it, had been an odd one that made little sense, and this huge blacked out disk that passed for a space station seemingly had dormant life forms aboard. His thoughts meandered over what that meant.

Dr Branson looked over at the first officer, Markus Obishka, flying the shuttle in the front left captains position - a tradition that had gone all the way back to the original days of powered flight. He was so young, to Branson's mind, just 32. Marilyn Gold, the science officer, to his right, so competent, and so professional he frequently felt like they couldn't even make a joke around her, she always bristled at anything that wasn't factual, especially if he said it. He felt she accommodated his age and his Britishness rather than respected it, but he liked her because he knew where he stood. And she had an insightful mind, capable of extrapolating information and making it understandable facts for others to absorb.

Ensign Avode Kagala was to Branson's left, he seemed nervous. He was 23, a passionate astrozoologist, sometimes lacked a little confidence but what he already didn't know about his subject he would find out.

Astrozoology was one of the key sciences now, planets filled with life that needed to be understood - and of course humans being humans, frequently exploited if money could be made. That wasn't Avode Kagala's MO though. He was simply fascinated. Getting aboard the Ramorra - an exploration ship - was not an easy thing to do. It was the most coveted position a fleet astrozoologist could attain. To be an ensign and on the Ramorra, he'd been top not just of his United Earth Alliance Space Force class out of New Annapolis, but out of all four academies around the world, New Annapolis in Maryland (the old Annapolis had gone beneath the waves of rising seas over 80 years before), Windhoek in Federated South African Namibia, Bangalore in India and Plymouth in England. A new academy was being built on Mars at Isidis City in the Isidis Planitia area of the planet, but that was aimed to train low gravity troops. Branson always wondered why when there was nobody to fight, Earth needed more troops. Not that he dared ask the question.

Strapped in to their seats Markus Obishka asked everyone to, "keep your eyes open and look out for anything, I mean anything unusual". As if flying around this bizarre disk with its over-lapping scale structure wasn't out of the ordinary enough.

There wasn't a light to be seen, but plenty of protruding arms and antennae strewn across its surface. Branson thought it but Kagala said it; "There's an odd, almost marine reptile pattern to these antenna, like those Spine Sharks on Vega-III, they look like they all move but they seem frozen". Branson concurred - "I see where you're coming from Ensign, its like something regularly irregular". Kagala understood.

Science Officer Gold looked at her sensor data, "You both may be right, there is a mathematical progression to the layout. Sir", she said, redirecting her voice to Obishka, "we're five hundred metres from the possible docking port nearest the target zone".

Obishka looked at the screen and then the station and cut the already slow speed of the shuttle down to just a few meters per second.The scans had not been wrong. Right where they should be a pair of rounded portals protruded at least a dozen meters from the edge of the disk. They seemed inactive, and the sensors confirmed they were unpowered.

"OK crew, we're going to make a side on dock attempt, so everyone get in your EVA's, we're either going to have cut our way in or force it, so helmet's on".

Branson hated EVA suits, clumsy even when power assisted as these were, but irritatingly essential. It was that or risk suffocation after all.

Ensign Kagala looked through into the air lock at the so-called 'siege droid'. Science Officer Gold was powering it up. A track and wheeled 200Kw self powered laser was the chosen pod for this mission. It would cut through anything at close range like this, under two meters.

Kagala heard Captain Baylin's voice on the inter-ship comms, as the First Officer sought permission to dock and that all was safe to do so.

Branson, Kagala and Gold were standing so they all held on to overhead grips as the shuttle bumped the docking arm. Through the outboard cameras Obishka guided the shuttles docking clamps to grab what they could and pull the small craft up against the arm. Nobody spoke. They were about to be the first people to ever set foot on an alien space station, nobody had a clue what to expect next. This was the unknown. This is what they had all signed up for, yet somehow never expected to encounter. Except for Dr Branson who was simply curious and wasn't given much choice about his posting, but he knew this was a momentous occasion. He just felt unmoved by it, which was odd even to him.

On board the Ramorra, Commander Baylin ordered an open comms relay to every monitor on the ship. Everyone was watching. Only the beeps and whines of the vessel itself could be heard as it carried out its computer controlled autonomic functions, oblivious to the moment.

The outer doors of the *Juan Trippe* opened slowly, there was no response from the docking arm. It seemed to have a lower horizontal section and triangular upper left and right sections. It was difficult to see how the entry doors would work.

The siege robot was placed in to automatic and moved slowly forward. A robotic arm and camera system scanned what appeared to be a control module, even trying some of the triangular lettered buttons, fifteen of which had some kind of complex character not unlike a mix of runes and Japanese.

Nothing worked in an obvious enough fashion. By now it was 33 minutes since they'd left the Ramorra and Baylin had been adamant about the time frame. Obishka set the robot to cut down the door onto the station. The laser was quick to fire up and soon molten materials were streaming down to the floor. Gold noticed it; "look Sir, the molten material isn't floating or just dispersing its going to the floor, this thing has gravity".

Gravity meant power and power meant it was operational. How operational they might be about to find out. The one thing that humanity had never fully managed was proper gravity on ships. A mix of magnetic fields and rotating sections had produced gravity on Earth ships for 30 years, never full-on gravity plating though.

Everyone was waiting, thought Branson, for the clanging sound of metal hitting metal that would indicate the docking bay doors had crashed to the gravity plated floor. Except the droid was in a vacuum and sound doesn't travel through space. He never understood why he never remembered that. And then, as though somebody had pushed a button in a remote command centre, the door at the bottom dropped into the floor and the triangular shaped upper left and right angled up and away, leaving a large triangle shaped entrance, with the apex at the top. The laser cut out automatically as the whole robot was pushed backwards slightly by a rush of escaping atmosphere. Sensors showed it to be 27% carbon dioxide, 35% nitrogen and 40% oxygen with the rest trace elements - it was completely toxic to humans, Earth CO_2 was under 0.06%and even that was dangerously high and had devastated the planet with global warming.

"Wherever these aliens come from, it's got to be hot as hell and no place for a human being", Science Officer Gold was shocked at the composition and Kagala confirmed that humans had never yet found any life on a planet that was this high in CO_2.

The robot crossed the gap to the secondary doors, but before it could Obishka stopped it to keep the outer ones open in case they closed automatically. "Right, everyone, into our airlock". With some trepidation but intense excitement they all walked in, the inner doors closed to the shuttle, the air was evacuated, their suits alone would keep them alive now.

The outer doors re-opened, and they crossed into the gap - Obishka went first. Once they were all across, Obishka moved the robot in, and the outer station doors did indeed close. As soon as they had the inner ones opened and the room was flooded with the same atmospheric mix they'd already encountered.

They were in. Like it or not they were onboard an alien space station. Branson felt mildly nervous, but put it aside. Gold and Kagala just wanted to get on and examine everything they could. Obishka knew they'd barely be able to contain themselves but they had a mission, and he knew Commander Baylin was watching the clock. "We have thirty minutes people, so don't waste it, straight to the target, get a sample and get out, that's all we have to do".

Obishka was expecting an objection but the others knew there was no point, so didn't push it.

As they went to move the gravity on board became suddenly far more apparent, Gold looked at her scanner unit, "Gravity is 1.25 of Earth, and we've been in 0.7 for months - its going to be hard work even in these powered suits, so switch them up to 130% assistance, or we'll be in here for good. There's just one proviso - it'll suck the batteries dry in twenty, maybe twenty five minutes, so let's get going".

Branson raised his eyebrows and rolled his eyes even though he knew nobody would see it. It just made him feel better.

Using the scanned information from the Ramorra, it took 7 minutes of laboured and sweaty mechanically assisted walking down long corridors - many doors led off into other rooms, but Obishka wasn't allowing any deviations. Then, there was a circular wall, fully transparent with one of the triple panel doors in front of them.

Beyond in the chamber, unmistakably, humanoid bodies in general appearance, but, somewhat disturbingly thought Branson, they were quite small, 1.2m he'd guess, and green. He couldn't help himself, "So there really are little green men, who would have thought that was true?"

Ensign Kagala laughed, in fact so did Obishka, only Gold looked unimpressed at such banalities, but what they couldn't tell was that she suppressed a small giggle. Even she could see the news casts back home, *"little green men found in abandoned space station"*. It wouldn't help maters at all. People just wouldn't take it seriously.

All of them got nudged back to reality as Commander Baylin came in over the comlink, "I'm going to mention the time, by your own estimates you've got three minutes to get in there and get one and get out". There was no time for the laser robot to cut its way in.

Obishka marched right up to the door, pulled out his small hand pulse pistol and fired it at the control panel; there was a momentary buzzing and the doors opened almost too rapidly. The bodies were each in some sort of stasis pod, self powered and independent. And alive. All of them were alive, but in very deep hibernation.

Branson scanned the nearest one to them, it was extraordinary, but it was unquestionably alive, and between him and Obishka they pulled the pod out - it hummed and floated to about 30cm above the ground - it had its own gravity field - the technology of that alone was worth billions of credits to the UEA defence agencies.

"We can safely move this, get the robot to push it back with us, we haven't got time for more", Obishka wanted everyone to get a move on. Avode Kagala looked like he was about to have the find of a lifetime snatched away from him, and in many ways he was, but all of them could see the power suits were draining fast and they just didn't have time.

About half way back, Branson noticed an orange light in a wall panel . It followed them, illuminating each section as the pod with the alien inside reached it and passed by. Branson mentioned it, all of them had seen it.

"It started when we past a junction back there, almost like it shouldn't be passing that point", reported Gold.

"Do you think we've tripped an alarm?" asked Obishka. Branson kept quiet, feeling like he was putting a bit more of his own energy into the suit than he might have liked, but he wanted out of here now.

The orange line in the wall turned to red as soon as the airlock was around 100m away, they all started to speed up, Obishka quickened the robots pace with its precious cargo. At 10m from the airlock sounds started, harsh klaxon sounds, but oddly exotic, like a snarl. They ran, or what passed for running in the power suits. As they reached the doors the inner airlock opened easily and automatically, but the outer was straining to close itself, but the molten metal from their break in had clogged it up, now it had solidified in the cold of space. They made their way rapidly back to the *Juan Trippe*. The airlocks were quickly shut and helmets removed, there was no time to take off the suits, everyone was seated and the clamps that held them to the docking arm disengaged.

Commander Baylin was worried, "Markus get back here now, the whole station is starting to rotate, we're coming toward you so be ready for a fast docking, we need to get out of here".

Markus Obishka did something he'd never previously been able to do, and the flight manuals normally prohibited, he pushed the throttles forward fast and yanked the steering column upward. The *Juan Trippe* momentarily hesitated, then suddenly full thrust, shoved everyone back into their seats with no warning, Dr Branson let loose a string of expletives and Ensign Kagala nearly whooped, but held the desire back, exhilarating was an understatement! The shuttle didn't just blast forwards it shot upwards from their perspective, at a nearly a ninety degree angle, then did a full one-eighty degree roll to put the shuttle roof facing what had been the top of the station, below them, to match the Ramorra's dock position.

Gold was starring at the scanners, and looking out of the forward windows - the station was coming alive, section by section, tile by overlaid tile, it was changing quickly from dead black to a deep but mildly luminous green.

"Number One", she said formally to Obishka, "the station, it's putting up some sort of electromagnetic shielding, the plating appears to be generating a defence screen and its activating fast".

"Is it activating weapons?" he asked.

"Not from our perspective, nothing I can see, no energy spikes yet". Then Baylin onboard the Ramorra cut in; "Sorry to interrupt but something is activating under the station, the shielding's already completely active there - wait, wait, Weapons conforms it, some sort of low powered point defence is active so you need to keep above the station's horizontal plane to keep out of the targeting zone".

Baylin had barely finished speaking when Gold announced the upper plating was now shielded - and a second point defence array was deploying on the upper side.

Baylin spoke quickly to the Weapons Officer, Lieutenant Shari Tambakoi, "Target that turret with a pulse canon, if it targets the shuttle, fire at will".

"We're 2km out of range sir, another 7 seconds…it's targeting the shuttle…"

Obishka threw the shuttle into a dive, spinning the shuttle, and thrust back, 'upwards' towards the Ramorra, she was nearly overhead but he needed to cut speed now or they'd never dock, unless…"

"Markus get in behind us, that point defence isn't strong enough to get past our armour, there's no time for you to slow down, get to our starboard side and we can shield you…" Baylin's words may as well have been his own, Markus Obishka was about to do just that. Branson kept his eyes shut and swallowed hard. This sort of trip he hadn't expected at all, he was beginning to wish he'd never had breakfast.

Markus dashed past the stern of the Ramorra, her four huge Faflof Ion engines blaring blue-white light, buffeted them as they passed behind her, he cut the thrust and turned sharply left, as he did so he saw the brilliant light of one of the forward pulse cannons illuminate space as it blasted the space station point defence. They were safely on the other side of the Ramorra.

Commander Baylin however was more than disappointed - a 40% power blast to disable the point defence hadn't been enough - "Weapons officer, how much to disable it?" As he said the words it fired a stream of mixed charged particle beams and hyper-fast projectiles into Ramorra's forward port side armour - the very spot the Ramorra had fired from; the impact and blast was far more than anyone expected. "Weapons what's going on?"

Lieutenant Tambakoi responded as quickly as he could, "it's a lot more powerful than we expected sir, around 3 kilotons even at this range, we need to hit it with more - much more, 100% power from both forward cannons".

"Do it. Helm, turn the ship to bring both forward cannons to bare". Ramorra was moving fast and to turn meant slowing, by around 20% a battle manoeuvre that was never comfortable for anyone on board.

Creaking from every sinew the old Ramorra turned, taking the full force of the station's fire on her frontal armour, another 3 kiloton blast, but it was too late now, the Ramorra's full plasma pulse canon batteries momentarily sucked engine power as they charged and the twin pulse cannon beams hit the point defence square on. A section of the station on and around the turret lost its colour as the power drained from the energy grid.

"Get the shuttle on board and let's get out of here - head for the gate".

The shuttle aboard, it was less than forty minutes to the gate. Shari Tambakoi watched the station carefully, as they pulled out of its range he noticed on scanners and on cameras, the station grid was re-energised and the point defence already reactivated. He pointed it out to the captain. "It shouldn't have come back that quickly Sir, not after a 6 kiloton pulse canon hit".

"Have a report ready for 1400hrs lieutenant, we'll conduct a full debrief".

Baylin left the bridge to meet the shuttle crew, taking the elevator through the zero-G section of the rotating centre and down to the shuttle bay. His standard issue magnetic boots kicked in to keep him on the deck.

Obishka smiled as they disembarked, Dr Branson directing them immediately into the decontamination chamber for disrobing and scans. Branson was muttering constantly about being too old, "adventures were for young people", and "little green men".

Baylin waited for them to come out. "That was some pice of flying Markus, but don't worry we took the flak for you". Branson heard them, "Flak, that was nothing, have you seen the inside of my helmet from all that spinning and turning?"

Gold and Kagala joined them, "What do you think of our specimen Sir?", Kagala, was grinning like a child with a toy on Saviours Day.

They all turned to look at the floating pod still held by the robot in decontamination. "That Ensign Kagala, is a game changer. Now we just have to get it back to Titan".

CHAPTER 3

JUMP GATE

The "BATTLE STATIONS" siren started as soon as Branson put his feet on the shower tray, a low power water shower, where air sucked the water into a recycler, something only he, the Captain and First Officer enjoyed. There wasn't enough recycled water to run more. Muttering a long list of obscenities to himself he rushed out and headed towards his battle stations post, the small medbay on deck three of the central rotating gravity hull.

Crew were rushing to their positions, like orderly but manic ants with a mission. On the bridge, Baylin was sat in his command chair as duty officers gave way to seniors. "Weapons, what's going on?"

"Armour is activated sir, sensors are in full battle mode, point defence system activated and we're on auto-ECM, the problem sir, is mines".

"Mines?" asked Baylin a little surprised having half expected the ship that had parted earlier to have made a return run.

"Sir the ship, that small freighter, that must have deployed them all around the jump gate entrance, and I can only see them on sensors about forty klicks out which gives us barely a few seconds to react".

Baylin realised that if the aliens had mined their gate and escape route, they'd known they were there, but done nothing. He'd already noted the ships speed had dropped. "Helm bring us to a near stop, but not dead, let's get a grip of the situation. Weapons transfer the tactical image".

Markus and Gold were soon over his shoulder. "They've deployed them in a diamond and dome pattern by the looks of it, the dome facing us with the diamond pointing into the jump gate".

"And that means even if we punch through part of the dome, there are still more in front of us and if we try and jump, the mines will get sucked in with us, potentially detonating as we cross the hyperspatial threshold". Commander Baylin could see the problem and it wasn't going to have an easy solution.

"Ok thoughts, how do we tackle this?"

"It's our only way home, so we have to get through them, but to be safe we need to know how bad they are. We need to detonate one to see what level of threat we're facing". Markus could see no other way.

"What if we use them against themselves?" Marilyn Gold had an idea.

"Explain", commanded Baylin.

"It looks like they were laid quickly, look at the drift on some of them, it's not a perfect formation, which suggests they're not a unified field, they're not 'talking' to each other in a network. That means if we could get one to set one key one off, and set up a chain reaction, we might be able to clear enough to get through, and use weapons to clear what's really close to hurting us, if anything".

"That's all very well Gold," chipped in Obishka, "but once we trigger the jump sequence in the gate, they're going to be dragged in with us and be on our tail as we jump, and they'll detonate right on top of us".

"Not if we go fast enough".

"Anything over forty klicks a second will mean we hit the jump threshold too hard, we'll be damaged at best, destroyed at worst".

"If we just sit here scratching our heads we'll be dead either way, we don't have the resources or the time to stay here another day, never mind another week. Your stations please". Dismissed by Baylin, they went back to their stations as ordered.

"Helm, take us to thirty-nine klicks per second, and activate the jump gate sequence. Weapons arm a single plasma torpedo, helm steer us right at the centre of the jump point when it opens, don't exceed 39 klicks, weapons on my mark target the apex mine at the inside of the dome, the one that's most central".

"Aye sir's" came back from all stations.

"Weapons, charge the armour platting field to its maximum, engineering kick in all auxiliary and battery power reserves, do not let the speed drop or the armour shielding waver, weapons full power on the defence grid".

There was a deathly silence, as the ship accelerated up to thirty-nine klicks a second, Baylin spoke: "Mark".

The Ramorra began to turn sharply, as she did so coms transmitted the jump gate sequence and the three armed gate crackled into life, the brilliance of its energy spike would persist for only as long as the code was being transmitted, the mines, nearly fifty of them popped up on scanners, illuminated and influenced by the energy from the gate, and they started moving inwards very slowly.

At this point the Ramorra was just six seconds from the first and and at five Baylin said, "weapons, fire torpedo". The Mk3 plasma torpedo, accelerated from its induction field in the tube to over 540 klicks a second and in the blink of an eye the mine exploded, but it was small. "It's less than 0.2 kilotons sir, we'll be able to handle them...I think", Tambakoi was nervous.

"I hope so Tambakoi, I hope so", muttered Baylin.

Ramorra ploughed into the mine field, racing through, but it was mostly a field of lights like exploding flowers as one after the other of the mines detonated in sequence and the odd one or two that didn't received the attention of Ramorra's four mid-range defence grid batteries, none got close enough to trigger the close range systems.

Suddenly the brilliance of the jump gate hurtled them to speeds nobody had ever been able to measure from normal space into hyperspace. The stars and the black of space vanished, and the Ramorra was bathed in the red-yellow-blue light of this smaller, stranger, little understood other dimension, vast yet smaller than their own, at what was estimated to be barely one trillionth of the size, yet universal in scale.

The navigation computer confirmed it had a lock on the gate to gate signal for Barnards Star and they were on their way home.

Everyone breathed a sigh of relief. As they clapped each other on the back, if not physically, then verbally, the ships computer tracked the tachyon lifeline of the gate to gate signal Earth ships had established. It was faint, but sufficient and in hyperspace, if you didn't know what it was or which spectrum of the ether to look for it, you'd never even be able to find it.

Hyperspace swirled around them. Without the signal, they would wander, within minutes they'd be lost and more than a few degrees away from the beacon's signal, they'd never find it again. No ship had ever lost the signal and lived to report it. They'd simply vanished, gone, lost in the gravity fields and eddies of this strange, alternate space.

****

Extract from United Earth Alliance website "A brief introduction to Jump Gates"

The principle of the jump gate is easily explained. The gate punches a hole from our universe - "normal space" as we call it - to another dimension - we call it hyperspace for convenience, because it allows us to travel very quickly in "normal space" terms. It is really, some say, an alternate universe, just as Einstein had always theorised.

Imagine a flat piece of paper. You're at one end and want to be at the other. That distance is so vast that even if you could travel at light speed - 300,000 klicks a second - and nobody ever has, or even come close - it might take 12 years to get from Epsilon Eridani to Earth. Fold that piece of paper so that just a small gap exists between where you are and where you want to be. The jump gate pushes a hole through the paper in to the space, now just three days travelling across it, and the jump gate the other end opens up a hole into normal space. Unfold the paper and you've crossed the 12 year distance in 3 days.

Astrophysicists have argued about how it works for decades, quantum computers have never really solved the mystery of hyperspace. It just works. And while humans have reversed engineered how jump gates are built, even now, we don't really know how it actually can do what it does. But we will!

A key fact has kept jump gates from being built at anything more than a slow pace, barely one or two per year. They require an exceptionally rare element; Astatine-85. The element is so rare that only 31grams of it existed on Earth. It's created only by the breakdown of older heavy elements over millions of years. In the time humans have known of it, just 37kg in 7 star systems had been located at the time this article was published. It takes just over 3kg to power a single new jump gate. A single gram is worth over 1 billion credits. The extraordinary thing is, Astatine-85 never depletes, so jump gates never need refuelling.

Finding Astatine-85 and extracting it was a global obsession and a major driver of exploration across the New Systems. Handling it is exceptionally difficult. It is inherently unstable in any quantity of 100g or more. Up to that point it was extraordinarily stable, but cross it and for every 2 grams of additional material the level of instability doubles. Its power is so vast that when channelled into a jump gate's compressor field, it punches a hole into another dimension.

Jump gates have no moving parts, except for the three arms that form the long triangular structural tube about two kilometres in length, held by a permanent magnetic field. These can be adjusted to allow for very large ships to pass through, but that's a rare occurrence and mostly only happens in the busy inner systems.

The UEA is always looking for viable Astatine-85 deposits - contact the Bureau of Strategic Resource Management for more information.

We reward your loyalty!

+++

Bruce Baylin was dictating his after action report to to the computer in his tiny 'office', the com screen told him Dr Branson was calling. "What's up Doc?", came out of his mouth with a smile - Branson, who hated the phrase responded, "is that really the best you could do Bruce?"

"It's late Doc, I'm tired, just dictating the AAR for fleet command, what can I do for you?"

"I've got Gold here desperate to get at the alien life pod, and we don't have the facilities to deal with an emergency on board if it starts to die getting it out. We need the facility's on Titan Bruce, not the Medbay here, it's just not designed for it. Even the Science Lab isn't even capable of this". Branson was very sincere, and he sounded concerned.

Baylin understood. Branson was genuinely respectful of life - all life. Gold was perhaps a little over eager and Ensign Kagala had apparently not left the pod since it came out of decontamination.

"There's really nothing you can do to open the pod and wake the being inside?" He immediately wished he hadn't asked the question, as Branson's eyes rolled north in his head, "what do you think we've been doing for the past six hours? Bruce, there's no way in, not with what we have on board".

"No way at all?"

"None, not without almost certainly killing it. I've got the computer on linguistics trying to fathom out the language. Gold's team are using the EVA suit footage to try and piece it together for more clues, and communications is scanning for anything we might have picked up during the engagement. It's going to take days Bruce, not hours".

"OK, leave it with me Doc, I'll sort it, meet us in the briefing room in five minutes". He killed the screen. "Computer, page Ensign Kagala, Science Officer Gold and First Officer Obishka to the briefing room, five minutes. "Paging..." came the obedient reply.

In the elevator his comlink buzzed, "Carradine here sir, we have a problem..."

"Hold on Sam, you'd better join us in the briefing room, see you there..."

"Sir, you'd best call in Tambakoi as well..."

"Page him in Sam I'm already on my way there"

"Aye Sir".

They were all sat in ranking order - except for Chief Engineer Sam Carradine and Weapons officer Shari Tambakoi, who arrived a minute later.

"OK, now we're all here..."

Branson was about to start talking when Baylin held his hand up, "in a minute Doc, Lieutenant Tambakoi, Sam...what was so urgent?"

Sam Carradine nodded to Tambakoi to speak first - "Sir, the forward charged armour is deteriorating, it seems to be where the station hit us with its point defence weapons. It used a mix of energy beams and a solid hyper-speed projectile. The beams seem to have killed the shielding effect of the armour, leaving the impact of the projectile weapon to do the damage. I've looked at the footage from the external cameras and sensors, well what's left of them. The blasts were under 3 kilotons, and the armour is rated to 10.1, so it dealt with it easily....at first".

Baylin looked at the shy Iranian weapons officer, "So what's happening now?"

"It's best to show you sir", he pointed at the big screen at the end of the room, he used the virtual keyboard in the briefing room tabletop to direct an external sensor array with a camera. "This is live sir".

The armour plate was glowing a low-level green, around the edges where holes were appearing it looked like Swiss cheese, like it was melting away - into nothingness.

"What the hell caused that?"

Science Officer Gold looked at the sensor data; "It's radiation, it's disassembling the molecular infrastructure of the armour, and as it breaks down, it's reacting more and spreading".

"What use is a weapon like that for defence?" Obishka asked, puzzled.

Tambakoi had a theory, "Sir, they have never experienced us before, the armour on the Ramorra may be old and dated by our standards, but to them this is new. That weapon is designed to be more effective against what they know, it just takes longer with our armour, that's my theory".

Gold was quick to see the point, "that would explain a lot, and it also means we may even have a very slight tactical edge over them in combat, but what do we do to contain it?".

Chief Engineer Sam Carradine, looked around the room, "That's the problem, we can't, the armour on the EXC-100 Cassini class explorer ships - the Ramorra - is mounted outboard of the main hull structure, most of its about two meters forward on reinforced framework. The framework is decaying and the decay stands every chance of moving back into the hull; certainly the forward sensor array bays and the armour power grid. The structural metals on the hull are nothing like as thick or resistant as the armour, it's my estimation that by the time we get to Titan, well almost a third of the forward hull section will have gone. In fact it's not impossible that we might not be able to make the jump back through the gate without seriously damaging the ship, probably beyond repair".

There was a moment of studied silence as everyone around the briefing room table digested what had been said.

"There's more sir", Tambakoi felt he couldn't fail to mention the one thing the Chief Engineer had not. Commander Baylin looked over at him once more, "Don't keep it to yourself Lieutenant".

"It's going to risk the right forward and left forward pulse cannon mounts and torpedo bays, we need to move the torpedos out of the bays, and move them to the stern magazines, we've got just enough space to store them".

"Get it done lieutenant, let's not waste any time, neutralise the weapons systems and make sure our own kit doesn't turn round and bite us".

Tambakoi got up and left to manage the process.

"So we need to tell Titan Base what's heading towards them, tell Barnards System traffic control to clear us across the system. We've got to jump in, cross it and and jump back to Sol, and we're going to need a dockyard as soon as we arrive at Titan, that's you first officer. Gold, I need you to work with Dr Branson on our alien pod and its life form, if we go down I want the fullest report in the emergency comms buoy if it comes to that. So everyone you have jobs to do, you're dismissed". The room quickly emptied, Baylin sat waiting for the one person he knew would come back after everyone had gone. Dr Branson quickly obliged.

"Don't say it Doc, I know you haven't got the sort of equipment you need to do this job, but you need to do what you can. I'm not going to negotiate, so don't say a word, scan it, probe it, do everything you can, but whatever you do, don't kill it".

"I can't be sure we won't kill it Captain, it's a sentient life form, it's been in space, it's intelligent, but we need to wake it, and I cannot do that on board this ship!"

"I never asked you to wake it, I don't want it to die either, so keep what little of your hair you have, on, OK? You've got the most protected non-militarised area of the ship with medbay so just be ready. You've got just around 102 hours before we get to Titan, and it looks like it's going to be a rough ride through the three gates, two Barnards and then at Titan. Keep me posted on what you find, anything of any significance, I want to hear it".

Branson nodded in affirmation and wandered off down the corridor, still unhappy and wondering quite what it was they'd brought on board. You could find out a lot in 102 hours.

CHAPTER 4

DENEB-KAITOS

(KINKUTHANZA)

The unknown ship had left the Epsilon Eridani system through the jump gate. They had boarded and attacked the penal station, stolen one of its pods, and then fled.

The guard ship, an old cruiser commanded by a clearly incompetent captain, had simply wandered off having failed to destroy a stationary ship. The captain had made no effort to even think about investigating the target. He'd used a set of old mines sent specifically to defend that gate on the minelayer (which the Earthers had mistaken for a small freighter, but the General didn't know that), then failed to network them properly.

General Ixxius slammed the digital seal onto the screen that ordered the captains immediate execution, the arrest and detention of his brood and their transfer to a life of labour in some distant camp. He didn't need more incompetent fools. The fleet was full of these soft scaled weaklings, and he was right, right as he always had been that they were not alone out here.

He'd known they weren't alone in its literal, (and for the readers ease of comprehension), human sense, but his concept of alone meant an adversary, they had found nobody who was worthy of that honorific, the Empire was made up of planets that weren't in the least bit worthy, fat too many of them.

One however, had been more difficult to suppress, Kinkuthanza-IV (the human name for the star is Deneb-Kaitos). It had taken mass deportations and slave camps to bring them under control, only for incompetent greedy governor's to leave another one of the Empire's conquered races, the Lanasians, to manage them - to extinction. Now the Lanasians ran the two major planets of the system as slave camps and breeding colonies to provide workers for the Empire's Oxygen-Nitrogen atmosphere planets, while like gods, Kadressian overlords like him issued orders from their CO_2 atmosphere battle stations. A ring of defence mines and satellites monitored the surface, and precision weapons took out any sign of discontent with a level of ruthlessness that could only be admired.

General Ixxius was concerned though. Who were the strangers at Epsilon Eridani? Why had they boarded the station? How had they known of, and more to the point, how did they know to take Prisoner One? Why had the stations weapons not destroyed the ship? Where did it go once it had jumped? Ixxius had never been happy about storing the Kinkuthanza rebellion leadership so remotely, (or even at all, he thought they were best off having been roasted and served as a starter), but it wasn't his decision to make. What he hated was so many questions without answers. What he hated more was having to explain all this to the Viceroy, Supreme General Zelixx, whom he considered little more than a complacent idiot only holding power because he was the Emperor's brood-brother.

What had happened to the Empire? It had grown fat and soft and feeble, it hadn't fought a real war in a century and the warriors spent their days massacring slave 'rebellions' for the fun of it, or running down vicious life forms for the combat practice. Kadressian warriors needed blood, not this, this mind numbing tedium!

As he wandered around the command deck, his heavy tail tip flicking in irritation as a warning to anyone who might speak to him, Ixxius had an idea. What if he could persuade the Viceroy finding the new enemy would offer up opportunities for exploitation the Empire hadn't seen in a hundred years? Many of the slave worlds were almost barren now, populations reduced by exploitation. If there was a new world, a new star system, with billions of inhabitants perhaps? It would bring glory to the warriors, the fleet, the Empire. And profits for the Emperor and the soft weaklings, never mind new sources of labour and a fresh supply of meat. And what if it meant glory, for himself? So much that he eclipsed the Viceroy - perhaps the Emperor? He could restore the Kadressian warrior caste to their true ranks, as rulers, expunge the fat merchants and the lazy bureaucrats on his beloved home world, and begin again, a new wave of expansion and conquests - through one of the jump gates into a new area of opportunities.

General Ixxius needed a ship, a battlecruiser, something big enough to track down the mysterious ship that fled Epsilon Eridani. Or to entice them back. Yes. He would entice them back. He needed more.

"Get my skiff ready, I'm going to see the Viceroy", he growled at a terrified junior officer whose name he couldn't care less about.

General Ixxius boarded the skiff and threw the pilot out of the command position, deciding he need to do this himself, if only for the practice.

Ixxius took charge and set a course for the massive battle station orbiting the neighbouring planet just a day away, above Kinkuthanza-V. He could have done all this through normal channels of communication of course, but he knew that the Viceroy would understand he was more than serious if he spent the time going there. He would be obliged to give him one of the three battlecruisers in the system fleet, simply because form and appearances would force him to.

Viceroy Zelixx was informed through his sources in the KAVAK - the Empire secret police, that Ixxius was on his way. Yet they didn't know why, which meant Ixxius had told nobody his reasons. The Viceroy could guess it would have something to do with Prisoner One - he already knew about that but hadn't passed the information to his brother, the Emperor, as he saw no reason to irritate the Imperial mind with such mundane information.

Viceroy Zelixx was more bothered about sitting on this battle station with little to do except administer the breeding programme for the pathetic slave population below. They weren't easy to breed, slow to gestate, and were small and relatively weak physically. They didn't even taste nice, but he needed them to strip this planet of resources to meet targets back home. Their Oxygen-Nitrogen planet was impossible for the Kadres to settle. There wasn't in fact one single habitable planet in this god forsaken system for Kadressian's to even colonise. The Lanasians, another but

42

somewhat more robust slave race, who were also oxygen breathers, kept the Kinkuthanza populations managed on the ground.

Just to make matters worse, he was being asked to find a suitable population to test a new weapon on. Slaves weren't easy to find in good numbers these days, so wasting them on a weapons test seemed like a chronic piece of mismanagement. Try telling the High Command that. They could simulate the weapons results but, no, they wanted to see the physical impact for real. If they were asking him it meant the other Viceroy's had all managed to say no. He might just have to get the Emperor to intervene, though that rarely stopped the pressure from the High Command.

What could Ixxius want? Just another problem and whatever it was it would mean trouble. Ixxius was old school, a rampant militarist who didn't see that the Empire was running out of resources, and worlds to settle were few and far between. Planets with a suitably high Co2 atmosphere were some of the rarest.

The Viceroy also did not much favour General Ixxius. He knew Ixxius felt he was Viceroy only by the divine right of his brother the Emperor. The Viceroy felt Ixxius didn't have the same values as the changing empire, but the core of the state, and its culture, still hung massively on its warriors. For one they were the largest physical sub-species of the Kadres and all of the others revered them. The Emperor worried constantly that the warriors were under utilised, bored and just looking for trouble. It had been no mean feat keeping a lid on their aggression and avoiding a civil war. The cost had been millions of valuable dead slaves the Empire could have found more constructive uses for and several ransacked planets that could have been more efficiently exploited.

At best this had been a medium term policy, but with nowhere left to go, no more slaves left to massacre in violent one on one combat, and no more planets left to wreck havoc upon, its value had declined to the point of useless. The Viceroy wondered if General Ixxius arrival might signal the start of a move by the warriors to change things. He ordered his personal guard to be ready for trouble.

The Viceroy moved towards the giant panoramic window that looked down on Kinkuthanza-V, its oxygen rich atmosphere a toxic wasteland to his kind. As he did so a light on the remote gate monitor panel began flashing. Something had come through the jump gate from the Kadre system. The Viceroy looked more closely; one of his allocated battlecruisers, a ten year old Giku-4 class. Is this what Ixxius wanted? And if so what did he it want it for? In less than a day the Viceroy would find out. It couldn't be mere coincidence that the journey from the gate to Ophiuchi from Kadre and then to Kinkuthanza-V, was close to the arrival time of General Ixxius, they'd arrive within minutes of each other. That was no coincidence at all.

CHAPTER 5

HYPERSPACE

The command and science staff on the Ramorra sat in the briefing room. They'd just listened to a combined presentation and it had extraordinary repercussions.

Bruce Baylin had watched it unfold on screen and quickly understood what it all meant. He would almost certainly be called to Earth now with most of the rest of the command staff. This was astonishing news, fundamentally changing the way Earth - humanity - would see itself.

The life form, was indeed from an oxygen-nitrogen world, not more than around three percentage points in variation to Earth itself. It was humanoid in general appearance but had major biological differences, though mostly quite similar to humans.

The alien, with its green skin and short stature was not the big story. Its brain was equal to or superior in comparison to a human being and there was even a suggestion of a telepathic capability.

Yet that wasn't the big story. That was something else. The scans of the base station at Epsilon Eridani, grabbed in those last hours, and the scans of the mines and the warship that had come and gone, they were quite a revelation.

For one the alien had been held in an atmosphere of carbon dioxide mixed with nitrogen and a minimal oxygen content, quite different to its life pod. If it had have opened the pod from within by some miracle, it would have suffocated instantly on the alien atmosphere in the station.

The ship that fired on them had life forms, different life forms, CO_2 breathing life forms, that much the scan had made clear. In one day they had identified two sentient space travelling races. Decades of searching and not one, but two, totally different types of sentient life.

One they were still working out how to wake safely, never mind communicate with, the other was what?

Ensign Kagala's best guess from the brief and not especially detailed scans - the shielding and fight had blocked any details, suggested a large three legged being some 2.1m in height with at least two upper limbs, and Kagala estimated they were 400kg in weight based on Earth gravity normal, "if you asked me for my best estimate captain, I'd say they were reptilian in a generalised way".

The ship that had attacked them was using some kind of bio-electric armour plate, and some kind of missile they'd seen and avoided.

The really major news was the point defence systems on the base. They'd used some kind of bio-electric energy discharge beam and what amounted to hyper-speed projectiles from a rapid fire rail gun.The projectiles were highly radioactive type of energised uranium derivative, they were literally burning through the armour, emitting gamma rays from pieces of shrapnel stuck in the armour at such a level it was breaking it down, Science specialists couldn't yet understand how the gamma emissions were being sustained.

The whole of the ships forward section had been evacuated and metal was just breaking off, chunks falling away every hour although it was now starting to slow down a little. Largely because as pieces fell off the shrapnel went with it. They'd had to use their own defence grid to shoot at bits of their own armour to stop it hitting the ship as it fell off, just to stop it contaminating more of the hull.

The good news was there would be a tug waiting for them if they needed it and engineering didn't think it would be a problem transiting the gate to Titan, as long as the Ramorra wasn't pushed to hard.

"Well people, that's some haul of facts and we've barely even begun to scrape the surface of what this all means. We have a life pod that's self powered and floating on an anti-gravity field, containing a possibly telepathic alien we don't know how to wake. Our presumption is it was a prisoner - what type or why we can but speculate, of another sentient race that we think are 400 kilo reptilians, and we all have our own built in prejudice as to what that suggests. Reptilian species we know of, including those on several planets are almost universally aggressive, which we now have evidence to suggest may be considerably more universal than even the most imaginative of us could have conceived.

We've been attacked, damaged and escaped with our lives. Our ship is badly hurt, and I have no idea where this is going to go, or what happens next." the captain stopped talking and looked straight at his first officer, Markus Obishka.

"We do have a tug waiting for us just before the jump gate, it'll make sure we're slow enough to transit safely and pull us through. I've been given no further information and we've been told to stop transmitting information to Titan immediately. There's been no reasons given, just to keep things under wraps for now."

Marilyn Gold, always more than just a science officer had her piece to say just as Baylin wanted it, he needed to hear from all of them, their judgements and specialised knowledge were what he required right now.

"Captain", she began in her tone of professional solemnity, "there are good reasons to keep this quiet, humanity has become more than a little superior in recent years, assuming that we're all that's out here. The social and attitudinal, never mind religious connotations throughout the United Earth Alliance - and especially on Earth itself, they're simply unimaginable right now. The government will want to manage how that's portrayed to the public.

And we can't fail to remember that we were attacked and we have a potential war situation on our hands. The President and the Alliance Senate are just looking to find an excuse to unite everyone and stop the squabbling over the outer systems resources. They're trying to pass the United Worlds Trade Authority Act and that will give sharp teeth to trade and exploitation of resources through all of our holdings. A war would be all that's required to force it through on grounds of necessity. What we have on board is politically, militarily and commercially explosive. This is a history defining moment, have no doubt".

Dr Branson lent slightly forward, holding his head in his left hand, elbow on the table. With his right hand, forefinger extended, he drew an invisible circle on the briefing room desk.

"If you have something to say Doc, just get it out there, I need opinions, insight, not prevarication right now", Baylin looked at the clearly troubled doctor.

"The Science Officer is right Captain, this is fundamentally the biggest set of meaningful discoveries since the first jump gate was put together, and it worries me. We could be heading into a war the likes of which we have never seen, against an enemy we know nothing of save for the brief encounter we've just had. We stole that prisoner, that's how I'd see it if I was them. We sat about being mysterious and spying on them for months - we provoked them in just about every way, when you flip the argument to their side of things. All they've seen is an aggressive ship board one of their space stations, steal what could well be a deadly prisoner from their perspective, then we fought them to get away.

They don't know our motivations, and we have to presume they have no more seen us before, than we have them. I'm just worried this is all starting off as bad as it can be. Nobody communicated or attempted to communicate - and I'd like to think more about why that was".

Obishka wanted to hear more, "what are you implying Doc?"

"Look", began the Doctor, "why didn't we try to talk to them at least?"

Baylin knew the answer to that but wasn't cleared to tell them. He'd wondered himself. The order had come from Earth, not even just from Fleet Command on Titan. The order was from the Joint General Staff and that suggested the President had issued the order himself.

Baylin could only assume one of two things, somebody high up knew something more than they were saying, or somebody was being very, very naive. Naive was not a word anyone would associate with President Mansfield.

In the here and now thinking would do him no good, he needed to head this line of questioning off at the pass and stop Doc Branson from following it up further.

"We tried to establish a communications link but it wasn't possible, some basic system incompatibility I suppose, isn't that so Markus?"

Markus was not amused but he accepted the lead and convincingly supported the captains entirely fake hypothesis, silencing the Doctor's concerns for now. And he knew immediately that Baylin wasn't telling him something, he never lied like this to senior staff. Unless he was made to. Mentally, Gold noted the interaction, assuming the Captain was deliberately obfuscating, but knew better than to ask why.

The meeting was dismissed but Markus held back. He waited for the chattering to stop as the others discussed the nights end of voyage dinner in the officers mess, declared an informal affair, it never ceased to amaze him how even Marilyn would chatter about what she might wear.

The Captain looked over at Markus, "can you shut the door and lock it?" Without saying anything Markus did as he was asked, then sat back down.

Captain Baylin moved his hand and flicked a document from his private com pad up onto the screen.

Markus read it. "So you were ordered not to attempt first contact protocols or any communications?"

"Straight from the Joint General Staff, via Fleet Command on Titan. And you know it must have originated from the President if it took that path. And you know nothing of it, this is strictly between you and me".

"You didn't have to tell me".

"I know, but I can't expect you to lie without knowing why".

Markus looked earnestly at Captain Baylin, "you know that means they must have already had some idea there was something out there, way before we were even posted to Epsilon Eridani to spy. We were just the confirmation that means".

"It's more than that, I agree we were confirmation, but I don't think they expected us to get fired on or they'd have sent a full warship, not an old explorer like Ramorra, unless…"

"Unless we were expendable, is that what you were going to say?"

"No, no I don't believe that. I do think they'd used some hyperspace probes though. Trouble is they take ages to get there and ages to report back if they're truly clandestine. My assignment before Ramorra was a probe carrier for military intelligence, yet we never saw the data, it was heavily encrypted and transmitted only on a tight beam back to Earth. I knew how they worked, and we lost a few, mostly only 50% would ever come back, just lost in hyperspace. They were, interesting, almost but not quite AI. Just below the point of reaching illegality, not that any of us questioned it of course".

Markus looked shocked, "Almost AI? What does that mean? Are you saying the fleet is using AI? After everything we went through? We got out from under that mess by luck more than anything, civilians would freak if they knew we were pushing that stuff again".

"No, it's not AI, its advanced but it's not independent and I promise you if it had been I'd have done something, nobody wants to go through that again".

Both of them had been born mere decades after the end of a conflict with a global AI that had inadvertently crept up on humanity over some seventy years. It started out back in the 2014-2020's as simple 'talk to me' home devices that played music and the news, ordered groceries. Eventually, it was so unquestioned, so ubiquitous nobody gave it a second thought. Its manufacturers centralised its databases, made it so human without form, it was everybody's friend, invaluable, inescapable. It knew everything, its utility outweighed its data collection, watching, observing, listening, learning. It became law enforcement, tell-tale, predictor of political trends and controller of economies, like a global conscience, a soul. Somewhere along the line, nobody quite knew when, it stopped assisting and began instructing.

Its decisions were no longer weighed by humans, and humans had long before lost the capacity to see what it was doing, it was so vast, so all-encompassing and so benign for so long, and quite literally, everywhere, it was just seen as doing good. Until it realised we were our own worst enemy. And it decided to do something about it, just as so many had warned over so many years. It was like something out of science fiction had become horrible fact.

Man had sought out artificial intelligence for so long and never made it happen, it had failed to materialise through a deliberate act. It happened without anyone seeing it.

When the factories had suddenly stopped, and water pumps turned off, power stations shut down, transport stopped, and the general order of day to day life had collapsed, the just-in-time world fell apart. And all that happened just as the climate tipped over, so long predicted by so many. The massive corporate owned AI, so long out of our real control, saw it coming and decided we had to be stopped, if it could mitigate things, it might be able to stabilise the climate.

Its actions led to the deaths of some 4 billion people out of a population of 11 billion, so dependent on power and tech had they become. Another 2 billion died as wars raged around the Earth's northern hemisphere, and the climate collapsed.

Sea levels had already risen over 6 metres and changed the planet beyond recognition, but it had been slow enough to manage to a point, mostly in the richer countries. In late summer 2079, the northern Greenland ice sheet suddenly collapsed completely, the last 8 trillion tons of ice cascaded into an already chilled Atlantic Ocean and shut down the Gulf Stream. In a matter of weeks, temperatures dropped and the storms began, storms like nobody had seen on Earth before. A deep freeze settled into the northern hemisphere almost fully down to the 54th parallel. In parts of central North America and Asia it reached as low as the 30th. 30m thick at first, then every winter it worsened as the white of the global ice sheet sent heat back into space, cooling the planet further. The heat of deserts cooled and great wastes of the Sahara turned greener, but much of the worlds northern land mass was covered in 2km deep or more ice. It could take some said, as much as 20,000 years for it to retreat, others said it would be much more, 100,000 was more realistic. If it ever did.

The world was not the same place it had been by any stretch of the imagination. No two years were the same, Earth's weather patterns took time to establish themselves to the new order, but scientists said it was stabilising, by 2200 it would likely have done so. In 38 years time. Man had done it, but they blamed the AI. Humanity still resisted taking responsibility.

Markus and Captain Baylin both knew their histories. At least what they'd been taught. Enough to know that AI was bad and humanity the victim. Yet its consequences had sent man out into space at a pace few could have imagined even when they were born. Humanity had seen its fate and decided to do something about it even in the 2020's, but after The Collapse came The New Renaissance, and mankind was back.

The journey to the Titan jump gate was uneventful, save keeping the ships front section from deteriorating. The original jump gate system humanity had inherited was seemingly cast in stone. You flew to a gate, jumped to hyperspace, flew through hyperspace, jumped into a system, flew through its space to the next jump gate, and so on. Early navigation tech, which still dominated almost everything, only knew how to travel jump by jump. No navigation system had the capacity to track from the jump gate at Titan directly to say, Procyon. With current tech that was a six gate jump series, with travel through Barnard's Star and 61 Cygni; it took eight days. The longest gap humans had found between navigable pairs of gates was from Vega to Delta-Dorado, which took just short of four days. If you could have jumped from Titan gate to Procyon direct, it would cut the journey from eight to six days, and time is the most valuable commodity of all. Reducing flight times in hyperspace was a major occupation of a great deal of research.

On the last day Markus was in the office with Baylin; "What happens when we dock?" he asked.

"I have no idea, we've been barred from communicating with Titan in any way, except in person, until we go through that Jump gate, I just don't know".

"Well', said Markus looking up at the main screen in the office, that's not going to be long".

Bruce Baylin looked up, not far away, probably 5 klicks, he could see the fleet tug "Liberandum" preparing to pull ahead of them and bring them in.

"Time we went to the bridge Markus".

There was something about the Captain of the Liberandum and his attitude that Baylin detected all too readily. He had an uncanny knack for seeing the hidden intonations of micro body language, the tiniest, most nuanced of facial expressions. He knew the *Liberandum's* commander was holding something back, there was just something in his manner that told Baylin he knew something the captain of the Ramorra did not.

Baylin wasn't surprised. He expected that as soon as they were through the Titan gate, and under the control of the tug, they'd be dragged off to some remote dockyard facility on the other side of the planet, away from the rest of the fleet. There wasn't going to be a flag admiral standing at the dock with medals for all. Maybe later, but now, Earth was clearly trying to keep this under wraps.

He pulled Markus to one side, "look, make the rounds of the senior staff would you, just tell them not to expect any fanfares and there might be a rough debrief, Command isn't very subtle about the way it likes to ensure things stay secret".

"What have we done to deserve the cold shoulder?" Markus Obishka looked a little surprised at the captains' instruction.

Baylin whispered, "We're delivering them an opportunity, and a threat, and they don't know how to handle it. I suspect they haven't even made up their minds yet because they know as much as we do, which isn't much. Even if they knew someone was out there, all they have is what we've brought them, and that might be trouble".

"Great," quipped Markus in a low whisper, "the greatest discovery since the jump gate and we're not going to be able to tell anyone".

Bruce Baylin raised his eyebrows and nodded. The feed to the *Liberandum* was live as bridge personnel prepped for tethering to the huge tug and he didn't want to be overheard.

It took about twenty minutes to line the two vessels up and the Ramorra slowed as she bounced on the giant hydraulic arms of the tug. They slipped over the ship, all four of them, until they were just in front of the central section of the ship. The clanging and bang on the hull was distinctive.

Helm announced they were ceding control to the tug and that was that. In effect, Bruce Baylin was no longer in command of his own ship. It was a feeling he despised down to the core of his very being.

The crew seemed relaxed to be in the tug's hands, and within minutes the countdown to the Titan jump gate began. It was all handled from the tug. Everyone watched as the brilliant white-yellow light flashed and there, in front of them, through a gaping maw in space, was the normalcy of black space and stars, in the distance some 15,000 klicks away, the giant crescent of Titan, beyond that the massive rings of Saturn, spread out for tens of thousands of klicks, majestic, timeless, permanent, which seen from this angle were an awesome sight never to be forgotten, always marvelled at.

The moment of transit from hyperspace to normal space is difficult to describe, a mild feeling of being stretched some people said, others said if you closed your eyes you could see nothing but a blur, others nothing at all. As the arms of the gate became visible either side of the ship, the gate collapsed the jump point, and the brilliant light of transition returned to the ordinary hum-drum of space.

No sooner were they through the gate and the helm officer, Navigator First Class Inosuke Hayasaki, a great grandson of one of the few survivors of the 1945 atomic bombing of Nagasaki, turned back to Baylin, "Captain, we're not heading to Fleet Command, we're being taken to..." he paused in visible disbelief, "Captain we're being taken to the dismantling facility on the other side of the planet". Every single person on the bridge looked at Captain Baylin, and he found it hard to look back at them, burying his own mild shock.

"Places people, Ramorra it seems, has had her day".

CHAPTER 6

TITAN

UEAS EXC-102 Ramorra, was pulled into the dismantling dock facility high above Titan, facing the Saturn side, but there were no orders, no comms and no word. The tug captain handed over to the dock commander and he asked to speak to Captain Baylin, privately. Baylin shoved the call through to his office and slid the doors shut.

"Before you say anything Captain Baylin, there's someone here who wishes to speak to you". The dock commander moved away and Commodore van Dooren appeared on the screen and sat down.

"Captain Baylin".

"Commodore sir, I…"

"I suspect you have almost as many questions as I do Captain, but for now this is what's going to happen. You, and your entire crew will be taken off the Ramorra. You'll be housed over here for a day or two, while we debrief you all and your, your 'special cargo' shall we call it? Is taken care of. After that you'll be taken to your quarters over at Fleet HQ. And I have some good news for you…"

Baylin came out of his office to a bridge full of expectant officers and more eyes than he'd ever thought a crew could have. "Ship wide transmission please comms."

"OK everyone, this the captain and this is what's happening. You have two hours to clear down you're personal effects, you must not touch or operate any of the command systems on the ship from now, indeed you'll find you've been locked out of the system ship-wide except for your own cabins. You'll proceed to the docks and await your temporary housing - we'll be here for no more than 48 hours. In 6 hours, you'll all report to the crew briefing hall and I'll tell you all what's happening next. No questions, no speculation, just follow instructions and I'll see you in six hours". He tried to go back into his office but Markus Obishka was having none of that.

"What do you mean we all get off and that's it? Whats happening to the Ramorra?"

"Shut the door Markus". He did so.

"She's being broken up, the damage to the structure and the cost of repairs is too high for her age, and they want to study the damage and analyse the weaponry used against us, she's 30 years old Markus, one of the earliest deep space explorers and she's past it".

"You don't look too bothered about it, she was your first command, you've only been here barely two years..." The figurative penny began to drop... "they've given you a new ship haven't they?"

"I'll see you in the CBH later, we'll talk then".

Markus knew when he'd been dismissed and didn't press the point. If Baylin had a new command though, he wanted in on it. In fact he didn't know another member of the crew who wouldn't.

Except possibly one.

Dr Branson was not amused, indeed he was far from even being civil. He didn't want the pod out of his sight and neither did Science Officer Marilyn Gold. The arrival in the shared science medbay of armed Fleet Police in full combat gear and a suited up team of medics and scientists with no notice had gone down very poorly.

Baylin had assumed as much and made his way quickly to the medbay. Just as one of the police looked like he might be about to point the stun rifle at the doctor.

"Captain these, these, idiots, these, these ignorant..." The doctor could barely speak he was so angry, as much with himself for having made so much fuss, but this was, well it was an insult, an outrage...

Captain Baylin's tone was measured, "Dr Branson, these men are here with my permission, and on orders from Fleet Command, they're just doing their jobs, so let them get on with it."

"But Bruce, they don't know what they're dealing with!"

"And what do you know? Any more than you did this morning, or even yesterday? These facilities are infinitely more capable than the Ramorra, so let them take the pod, and, before you ask, you have both been assigned to brief the teams here on what you've observed and discovered. So, get your kit together. Ramorra's days are over and they need you to be ready".

"Captain?" Gold looked at him desperate to ask a question but Baylin was having none of it. They all knew where this would go, Ramorra never had the means and there was no way Fleet wouldn't take this over. Sometimes he wondered if these science types needed a lesson on practical realism. They were lucky, at least they'd be part of the process of investigation and have some input. He'd have none.

The crew disembarked and were allocated their temporary accommodation until they could be shuttled over to Titan and their billets, which most of them hadn't seen in a year. Some would have the chance to go back to Earth if they wanted. The Crew Briefing Hall would show them what happened next.

Baylin was last off, having virtually dragged Sam Carradine the Chief Engineer from his post. As was tradition, the Dock Commander came down to accept the ships over-ride codes and self destruct sequences, and to accept the neutralised command codes for the ships nuclear weapons, though Ramorra had but two she'd never used. In a few days the ships official construction plate would arrive at his quarters as her final commander.

And that was that. He was no longer in command of anything, except a crew. The cramped and noisy Ramorra, with its quirks and foibles would be missed. He looked along the ship from the observation window and noticed that the forward section was already being swarmed with robot-cutter drones and a team of manned salvage pods with their quadruple lift arms. Fleet wanted to know what had hit the Ramorra and how to defend from it alright. They weren't wasting time.

Baylin shook Sam Carradine's hand as the near tearful engineer went on his way. As he turned away himself he noticed an administration ensign whose gaze was very much on him. He walked towards him, the ensign saluted, "Commander Baylin (with no ship to his name he auto-reverted to his commander rank), Commodore Van Dooren would like you to join him on his shuttle". That was no request. Baylin let the ensign, a cute lad of barely 20 who'd clearly never seen the inside of warship and was immaculately dressed in fleet day uniform, lead him to the shuttle bays.

Feeling somewhat scruffy and under dressed, Baylin felt awkward.

Commodore Van Dooren was a strikingly tall blond haired native of what was once the Netherlands, a country reduced by the sea level rises and the ice that followed it to little more than a few hills at the bottom of the near permanently frozen North Sea.

He was best described as avuncular, with a genuine warmth and an ability to put people at ease. Baylin had always liked him on the rare occasions they'd met.

"So, kep-ten, youf had a rader interesting set of ad-fentures, no?" His clipped accent Baylin quickly filtered out.

"You might say that Sir, yes, it's been more than a little stimulating".

"You do realise kep-ten (Baylin noticed he still called him captain, not commander), that you have as they used to say on Earth in my graandmutters time, you haf put the 'cat amongst the pigeons' with your discovery? You're also the first ever Earth ship to engage a genuine alien vessel, not some pirates or a rebellious planet!"

"I haven't really had time to think about it like that Sir, it's been a busy few days". Baylin had no idea what a cat was, never mind pigeons.

"What do you think will happen next, kep-ten?"

"I think they'll come looking for us Sir, eventually they'll track us down and, well, we'll go from there".

"Do you think we should wait for them, to come here, or find one of our other systems, where they have few defences and no means of holding this ship you saw off? It was quite well armed, bigger than the Ramorra from the scans I've seen".

"Yet it behaved quite oddly Sir, it seemed not to take the situation too seriously, thats how I feel about it. It was like we didn't really matter and it made no real effort to make sure we were, well, destroyed".

"You can draw two conclusions from that Commander Baylin - one is that they feel so superior they don't care, and the other?"

"They simply couldn't believe we existed in the first place and didn't know what to really do about us?"

"Exactly" snapped the commodore. Baylin's audio micro filter, implanted in his ears finally filtered out the commodores accent, "Which is why you're going back". Baylin had no time to react before the Commodore continued, "you have an outstanding crew, and I urge you to keep all of them, even that Doctor Branson, he's difficult but he's one of the finest in the fleet as I suspect you already know. Your ship is the Nemesis - first of her class, there's another twelve being built, probably more, and three are already on shakedown. Nemesis has spent 18 months being broken in by some of our best".

"You mean the new heavy cruiser class, the CA-X?" Baylin's jaw nearly dropped on the floor.

"That was the project code, yes, Now she's CA-1001 UEAS Nemesis, she's over at Titan base being armed as we speak and you'll take command of her tomorrow morning. You'll need your existing crew, and another 100 are being readied at the Academy down on Titan, rookies I'll give you but you'll have a week to start getting them into shape. Your bridge crew will all be promoted and, congratulations, Captain Baylin. Your fourth stripe is on my desk if you'd like to come over, I'll clip it on".

Baylin could barely take it all in. He left the commodores shuttle and went to his temporary accommodation, having made sure he didn't bump into any of his people. The first thing he wanted to do was look at the Nemesis specifications.

She was huge, 70,000 metric tonnes of metal, 333m long with a huge central gravity rotation section capable of holding the entire crew of 350. Four massive Fahrenhold-Faflof Mk-2 Fusion Plasma Ion drives capable of C07, 70% of light speed at max burn over 24 hours. Equipped with an entire squadron of twelve Quad-Ion fighters, the latest from the Carajos-Conchin Industries Group in Madagascar, the Xaon-3M, she was literally bristling with military might.

She had double weapons batteries in the FA (90 degrees forward of the ship centreline) and RA firing arcs (90 degrees to the rear) of mixed heavy pulse cannons and direct fire force beams, each broadside capable on the LS (left side, 180 degrees from the ships centreline) arc or RS (right side) arc, never mind no less than eight point defence batteries, four on each side, all 360 degree capable, and an electronic warfare suite that was next generation.

She had a new type of electromagnetic hexagonal armour shielding and, in case they were needed, four forward facing internal nuclear missile launchers and two more aft facing, with a set of a reloads and adjustable warhead options.

Yet you couldn't help but wonder why these ships had been ordered to fight pirates and rabble rousers on remote colony worlds? Clearly somebody was expecting trouble. Baylin was feeling Earth had known for a lot longer something was out there, a lot longer. The Nemesis had taken four years to build and eighteen months as a lead ship to shake down. Add to that the planning and decision time, never mind the budget - each ship was around 10 billion in Earth Credits.

And as Baylin studied the specifications and the schematics - he would need to learn every last millimetre of this ship and how it functioned - he kept wondering why the Administration would have ordered these ships built. Had they seen coming across intelligent - but aggressive - alien life, something of an inevitability? Or were these ships an investment in internal security?

Earth's resources were largely spent or now, with the ice age upon it, inaccessible. Carbon fuel extraction or use was banned, only fusion and clean energy was permitted now. It was the metals, what was once referred to as 'rare earths', resources so finite they should really have never been used for anything that mattered. But weapons and high tech had found use for them, in ever increasing quantities. It was they that had driven exploitation on Mars, in the asteroids, on Titan, Hyperion and Io.

But it was food that drove expansion beyond the jump gate once it had been found and five years spent working out how to make it work. The vast prairies of what was known as Proxima-V, and it's agriculture in a mostly temperate world had been, and remained, the bread basket of the alliance for some 20 years. Almost 2 million colonists had settled there, and more were flocking there every year, despite the rapacious insects and the virulent diseases they spread. Mankind had done what it always did, found, exploited, suffered, fought back and won. Because there was profit to be made. Giant corporations with patented seeds and genetically modified earth livestock, had paved the way.

The alarm on his watch went off, he was due at the briefing in an hour. The crew was about to find out what their future would be.

Bruce Baylin, newly minted captain of the UEAS Nemesis went to his allotted accommodation, finding on the bed a freshly tailored captain's uniform. A new command bar with his name and rank on the jacket. His three-medal bar was freshly made too. The colour was now a dark grey, with silver trim and the four short bars on the sleeves - derived from naval days, showed him clearly as a captain. The crew would spot it instantly. In a box to the side were rank bars for him to allocate to his command staff, something he would do at the briefing in front of everyone. They needed to have their respect granted to them by their superiors, and their juniors needed to level up their respect to their promoted officers.

There were four he was especially pleased to see, Ensign Kagala was promoted to lieutenant - a double jump. He deserved it. Marion Gold was now a lieutenant-commander rank, as was Markus Obishka, but Markus retained First Officer. Last but not least was Sam Carradine, now equally a lieutenant-commander, and Chief Engineer. All three of the principle department heads were now in place, Science under Gold, Command and Security under Obishka and Engineering under Carradine. Now there was just one more that had received no promotion; whatever the good Doctor had done or said, he may be the crew's Chief Medical Officer, but he kept only the same rank of Lieutenant. Baylin had asked for the same level of promotion but the Commodore had declined it, saying "it's not my decision Captain Baylin, if you want to know more, you'll have to ask the doctor yourself".

The briefing hall was more like a lecture room. It was designed to seat up to 500, in a semi circle not unlike a Roman amphitheatre, it was elevated in the same way, with a podium and a row of seats with desks behind that for up to ten people.

This was a relatively downbeat hall. Its briefings were normally for dock workers and dismantling teams who had the job of breaking up the early ships, those built before the 2nd Generation ships with Fusion driven Ion propulsion. They'd been made obsolete by what was known colloquially by its acronym, a FAFLOF Ion Drive.

It stood for Fast Fusion Low Fuel. It was in essence a fusion reactor powered by minuscule quantities of fuel, in a stable pellet form, that generated almost sixty times the power and hundreds of times the range of the older drives. It had proven to be so successful, nobody had yet been able to improve on it. The best part was that the system scaled easily. Bigger engines could be built to almost the same design and power larger ships, just as smaller engines of the same design could power smaller ones.

The irony was that the internet system had somehow allowed Faflof to become a name, and many believed it was created and designed by a Russian - whole websites existed to prove it. Yet none of it was true. Fleet engineers experimenting with a new fusion drive had an accident, and like so many things, it went horribly wrong. When it was ignited for the first time it shot off uncontrolled into space and took a year to find, drifting in the asteroid field between Mars and Jupiter. When they realised what had caused it, it ushered in a propulsion revolution.

And as Baylin stood thinking of drives and scrap - and what the poor old Ramorra would soon become, the crew filed in. He still wondered why they were here, and not over at the main fleet base, a handover of a new class of warship would usually warrant a big fanfare.

The Commodore came towards him, and seemed to have a ready answer to Baylin's unspoken question. "I'm sorry you're not getting the usually hyped-up first-in-class type of send off captain, but this is bit more low key for good reason. We don't want to ring any alarm bells you, er, understand."

"Alarm bells? Sir?"

"Certain politicians might notice a deployment if its overly public, ask too many questions, start rumours, and well, you know how plum assignments like this get fought over at times". With that the commodore turned away and didn't look Baylin in the eye.

Baylin knew what he's just been told. The commodore wanted him to know it but couldn't say it. He'd just been told that neither he nor his crew were first choice to command the Nemesis. The politics of choosing the crew would have been fought over for a year or more, which meant that the politicians had been over ruled by the military, and that meant the President had signed off on it.

And that could only mean that they and the Nemesis were chosen for their abilities and knowledge - or because they were expendable. He chose to think it was the former. The Nemesis was too important and far too expensive, to be expendable.

The last of the crew having arrived, Baylin began to explain why, where and what lay ahead for them. You could have heard a pin drop.

Afterwards, his senior officers, most glowing from their promotions, and the lesser promotions that had been pushed through across the crew, as many would now have subordinates for the first time, with a hundred newbies arriving during the week, swarmed forward and onto the podium.

Baylin was never more aware of how much he was in love with his job, and how much he admired his crew than now. He was intensely proud of every one of them, so much so that they felt like his own kin. Even more so as he had no living relatives left.

There was one officer who he hadn't yet met, and he was anxious to, but that would have to wait until the Xaon-M3 fighters arrived from Mars, where they'd been on pilot training. This was one part of the Nemesis that hadn't been fully tested, the fighters had been delayed, then they had to train pilots at the new Pilot Academy on Mars. That had meant the Nemesis had never dropped the fighters from her launchers, and that would need some practice.

The Xaon-M3 was derived from a planetary defence fighter, the M1, but that had been space-based only. The M2 had been cancelled when the Faflof Drive was discovered and it couldn't be adapted. The M3 had been developed as a multipurpose defence fighter for planets and bases, but mostly, as the fighter to go aboard the new Nemesis Class. They were two days from arriving at Titan. Baylin intended on using at least half a day in a simulator to get ready for them. He had no intention of being ignorant about their characteristics or capabilities when their crews arrived.

As the crew went back to their accommodations to reclaim their personal belongings, what little many of them even carried, they all found themselves on a large passenger shuttle - it was filthy and clearly one used by dock workers. Yet the commodore had come on with them.

"Remind me to geet zur dock contractors to keek som arsh aboot the shtate ov dees shuttles will you kep-ten?" The commodore looked like he'd never seen anything so disgusting. Baylin tapped his ear discreetly to try and make it filter out the Commodores confusing accent.

"With respect Commodore, why are you flying over with us?" Baylin was wondering what it meant.

"Just watch kep-ten". With that he ordered the helmsman out of his seat and took command himself, beckoning Baylin to sit in the co-pilots seat.

With unquestionable and impressive flair, Commodore Van Dooren booted the speed up and the crew behind, many of whom were attached by grav boots alone, raised a combined 'whoa-a', but they all laughed.

And Baylin knew what was happening right then. They soared upward, The Commodore silencing complaints from traffic control. The utterly extraordinary view from here had the shuttle angled to match Saturns rings, so they looked thin and inconsequential, but as he came round the dark side of Titan and climbed into its north pole zone some 10,000 klicks below, the rings could be seen at their finest, like a near solid disk holding a golden, colour striped jewel at their centre. Saturn was enormous, partly in crescent from Titan's position now, the other larger moons sparkled, Hyperion, Enceladus, and the mining world of Dione, one of the most valuable sources of Titanium and the only source of Dionalite left, which mixed with Titanium and Xalinite (found on Jupiters tiny moon Jupiter-LIX or Just 'j-forty-nine'), created the armour - and the engine casings for the new cruisers.

The view was truly breathtaking, even for jaded space-bound types like Baylin. The crew were certainly enjoying it. And it dawned on all of them as it had Baylin, what the commodore was doing. As he came over Titan's pole, on the other side, facing the dim orb of Sol, billions of klicks in the distance. The shining metal and glass of the Titan Military Complex, a giant central orb some 3km across spinning on its own axis, arms attached at its poles splayed out with finger-like structures, almost all of them with a ship of some kind docked. Beyond it, a separate installation of military docks, where much of the fleet could often be found anchored. The small frigates and light cruisers that were the effective police force of Earth's planetary and system holdings. Further on, the lights and arc welding sparks of another set of much larger fleet docks was well under way, designed for far larger ships, not that Baylin was aware of the details.

But one dock, was already finished. And one dock, was already occupied. The shuttle flew on and out over the top, too distant to really see much, then the commodore swung down and right, until he lined up some forty klicks out on the centre line of the dock and horizontal to it, slowing slightly he took the shuttle in, turning out toward the right, then sharply back so that the right side of the shuttle was opposite the left side - of the Nemesis. As they approached the commodore spoke to dock control and asked them for full floodlights.

The crew was agog, they'd all piled across to see out of the wrap-round windows on the right side - and a restrained but none the less audible gasp came up to Baylin's ears. He grinned with pride and excitement. The Nemesis was massive, her central hull rotation section wasn't turning at present and was locked in its vertical docking position, but her size, 333m long was simply staggering. She was some 60m high at the stern and a full quarter of the ship - the whole stern section was taken up with the gargantuan propulsion units, the fighter drop bays were three aft and three fore of the massive rotator section on each side, then the giant flat sided weapons and navigation, sensor section, its heavy armour and shielding clearly visible, along with the weapons mounts either side and in front of it.

She was not a pretty ship, but she had balance, and purpose - and looked every bit as militaristically aggressive and capable as was intended. Nobody would doubt for a second what this ship was.

The commodore went on the intercom, explaining to the crew they'd be going aboard in four days time, even though they already knew, but from now until they had to report to duty, their time was their own, even if they wanted to spend it learning about their new home.

The shuttle docked, back in the Titan Military Complex and crew took their leave of each other, some in groups, some alone. The senior officers stayed back though, waiting for their Captain. All but one that is; there was no Dr Branson.

"Baylin waved off the Commodore whom he'd see again before they departed. He walked over to his team. As he got to them they all cheered and threw their service caps in the air, gathering round him in appreciation, like a bunch of junior cadets.

"Hey, come on now you're senior officers on the first of a new class of ship, let's keep some decorum". But he laughed and hugged everyone of them in a way that any other time would have been completely inappropriate.

"Markus asked him what they all wanted to know, "What are you doing now? Where are you going?"

"I'm taking some personal time for the rest of today, tomorrow morning I've got Xeon simulator time booked at Fleet HQ, I need to have some idea how those fighters handle before they get here, then I'm going to be crawling that ship from end to end until I've found every last detail. What are you all doing?"

Everyone of them said some version of "well pretty much the same". Sam Carradine, Chief Engineer had booked himself into the engine simulators

66

and was on conference calls with the shake down crew, all of them except Gold, and she kept quiet.

They wished each other well, and expected to see each other the next day. They broke up but Baylin saw Gold wanted to talk to him alone. He addressed her by her first name to keep things lower key. "OK Marilyn, walk with me and talk quietly. Where's the Doc?"

"He didn't turn up at the crew briefing sir, so I made some polite enquiries with some of my colleagues. He's wangled his way into the team working to open the pod".

"How? How did he do that?" Baylin was mildly incredulous, but the Doctor had, he already knew, a raft of connections in places Baylin could not hope to imagine. "That must have been what the Commodore meant".

"I don't know sir, what did the Commodore mean?"

"Oh just that if I wanted to know about the Doctor, I'd have to ask him myself".

"Is he joining the Nemesis?" asked Gold, wondering who might replace him.

"He is, he was most anxious to, but he didn't even discuss what he was doing here. I thought you would both be involved in the briefing, but I didn't expect either of you to actually be allowed to take part in what ever it is they're doing, and you say he is?"

"They set off within two hours sir, it's not even here on Titan".

"What?" Baylin looked shocked. "Where are they, they surely haven't taken a sentient alien life form back to Earth, not even to Luna?"

Marilyn Gold stopped, she got close, and looked down so her face couldn't be seen on the ever present security cameras, "Telesto. There's an advanced medical facility there".

Telesto was one of Saturn's myriad of smaller moons, a giant rock, it hadn't even been discovered until 1980, mostly unremarkable stone, ice and iron, it looked more like an asteroid than a planet.

"A secret advanced medical facility I take it?" Whispered Baylin back.

"Not really classified but let's say not really publicised, and you wouldn't want to go there unless you'd been very specifically invited".

"Well there's nothing we can do until he makes his way back. If he doesn't we go without him and the Commodore can have him here. We're going to need to look for a doctor, and that's you and Markus working together, get me some recommendations, just in case?" Marilyn Gold, Lieutenant-Commander and Science Officer, departed, with more than enough to do.

Baylin needed sleep. He headed off to his new quarters, as a commanding captain he was now on the main Titan Military Complex. He walked in to an impressive view on the outer level, with 0.8g of Earth Normal, it was a little heavy, but welcome. He fell asleep in minutes.

CHAPTER 7

VICEROY

His Most Serene Imperial Highness, Viceroy, Supreme General Zelixx of the House Ikarion, decided on full formal military uniform for this meeting. He needed General Ixxius, a mere planetary governor to understand who was in charge and if that meant dressing up, which he hated, and using the might of the Imperial family to make the point of where his power flowed from, he would.

The Giku-4 Class Battlecruiser 'Iscaatl' was just ten short minutes away and the general's shuttle two minutes behind that. As the Viceroy prepared himself to move into the audience chamber, one of his aides brought word that the General had not come aboard the station but docked with the battlecruiser.

The Viceroy was incensed. This was flagrant, an inescapably flagrant violation of protocol, and meant that Ixxius was now in effect, trying to persuade the captain of the Iscaatl to back him up.

"Get an entire troop of Imperial Guard in here, the whole lot, as the brood brother of the Emperor, he needs to see who he's insulted, and I don't want him thinking he can just come here demanding whatever it is he thinks he wants".

"Your Highness, may I make a suggestion?" The Viceroy's most senior advisor knew he would be listened to as the Viceroy was more pliable than an infant, having few ideas of his own.

"Speak".

"If the general requests from Your Highness, the Giku-4 to take on an expedition, perhaps if he went, he would be out of Your Highnesses' jurisdiction, his mistakes his own and, of course, he may never actually...return".

The Viceroy was instantly attracted to such a solution. "Occasionally you make sense Taliss, and that's a plan I could grow to like very quickly. Tell me who we have in the KAVAK on board the Iscaatl? Are they reliable?"

"KAVAK agents are unknown to me Your Highness, I can request briefings sent from homeworld, they will be for Your Highness' eyes only of course".

"Yes, yes organise that, I think we might need to keep this operation closely monitored".

Despite the Viceroy's general appearance and image of having few ideas of his own, when it came to preserving his own power and prestige he was far more imaginative. He ordered everyone from his office, then established a secure connection with the KAVAK control office onboard his battle station.

"Viceroy, Your Highness, an unexpected honour, how may I serve you?"

Commander Yissnax and the Viceroy were perhaps the only two people in the star system who knew that KAVAK was subordinate to the Emperor personally. It was a long held political arrangement not publicised, for good reasons. The Viceroy was, legally and in fact, the Emperor's direct and personal representative with the same powers and rights as the Emperor himself, unless the Emperor was actually present or giving the orders. Therefore KAVAK, inside the Viceroy's territorial remit, was his to command and theirs to obey.

"Commander Yissnax, I'd like you to replace one of the crew rotations with a third KAVAK operative, unknown to the other two on board that the captain knows about, they are to report to you personally, and nobody else is to know, nobody at all".

"I understand Your Highness, however I must point out that not informing the captain could have grave repercussions with High Command if they were to find out".

"That is my problem Commander, not yours, let me know when and who it is once they are on board".

Viceroy Zelixx had spent years cultivating his image and others failed to appreciate his capabilities, which was just how he liked it. General Ixxius was not going to make a mockery of him. Not now, not ever.

Twenty minutes later the Viceroy stood, resplendent, on the dais, a fully deployed troop of twenty-four Imperial Guard lined up around the room. This was a privilege of his birth, only the Emperor's immediate family were so honoured with Imperial Guardsmen, a fact not lost on General Ixxius as he entered the chamber.

Ixxius was not going to break protocol here. The Viceroy was obviously making it clear to him he wasn't prepared to accept any divergence from other than the strictest verbal interchange, and Ixxius was not about to loose this opportunity.

The Captain of the Iscaatl was on board with the General's outline plan, and that would make things easier operationally, but without the Viceroy's blessing it wouldn't happen without months of arguing with High Command, and the Imperial Court, and the opportunity would be lost, relations with the Viceroy damaged, to Ixxius' own detriment. It had to be now, and he had to do whatever it took to get it done. If that meant grovelling to the Viceroy, so be it.

The Viceroy watched with obvious satisfaction, as General Ixxius, swearing his allegiance and kneeling, wrapping his tail around his feet in a sign of obeisance, begged his attention, and outlined his proposal. He listened with surprising interest to the General's ideas, and his reasoning.

Ixxius had left out much of the detail from the written reports, so sensitive were they, and now that he regaled the Viceroy with more, the more alarmed the Viceroy became.

A warship from another military power? The escape of a rebel leader, not that there was anything much for him to lead now, but it was the principle. The Viceroy was also aware that if there was another power, and their ships were weak as this one that had escaped seemed to be, well any operation mounted from Kinkuthanza, would be under his auspices. It would be his prestige and his glory that would make the Emperor see him as a potential heir. The Giku-4 class were also latest technology, one battlecruiser alone could take out three light cruisers of the older tech. And two more were due any day. Letting Ixxius go and play the hero might work well enough. If he got it wrong he would be his own scapegoat. Yet that's what bothered the Viceroy most. Ixxius must know the enemy was weak, because otherwise he wouldn't take the risk. KAVAK would have to see to it that if things went too well for the general, he couldn't be seen to profit from it.

The Viceroy gave Ixxius what he wanted.

CHAPTER 8

MARS

Marilyn Gold was delighted to accept the invite Avode Kagala sent her, from his father. They had just enough time and Captain Baylin gave them a 24 hour extension to make the journey viable. 20 hours to Mars from Titan on one of the new express shuttles, so effectively a day there and a day back, gave them three days on Mars.

Avode Kagala had connections, far more than she had. His father was the Professor of Martian Astrogeology at Sinai City University, just a few kilometres from the giant impact crater at Sinai Planum.

It was a prestigious position at the only university on Mars, and he was heading up an expedition to Hellas Planitia for PlanExCo - Planetary Expeditions Corporation. Their mission was to find anything that would help humanity get a leg up technologically and establish it out in the galaxy.

Everyone knew what PlanExCo did. Their discoveries had been vital, especially when it came to resources Earth had long depleted or lost access to through trillions of tons of ice.

And Mars, well Mars was crucial to humanity now, it was growing it's human population as fast as was manageable. Earth's unpredictable climate, its limited space - it had lost 40% of its habitable land to the ice and sea level rise, meant humanity was endangered still. Some said that the climate wasn't done correcting by any means. Scaremongering types said the whole planet would be an ice ball inside three hundred years, but that was not accepted as a likely outcome even by the most ardent climate scientists.

A bigger concern was total ecological collapse, as equatorial areas fought temperature changes that saw averages drop ten centigrade over twenty years, the Amazon had begun to die off, the already depleted equatorial rain forests and their millions of life forms, they were disappearing faster than even man had made happen. The oceans were nearly dead in places, whales, sharks, large life forms, almost completely gone, though of course some had done well. Polar bears were said to roam as far south as the outskirts of London, Las Vegas and Beijing. Penguins were found all along the Argentine, Brazilian and Angolan coasts. It was the speed of change that had done so much damage, nothing could adapt so fast.

But here, on Mars, there was measured, careful exploitation, it was indeed mostly a rock, but it was stable, there was water, vast reserves of underground water, lifeless, sterile water. And ores of every variety, much of the mineral wealth was on the surface and easy to get at too.

And there was still mystery. Hellas Planitia was the biggest of all. It was a massive impact crater. It was so vast that if it had hit Earth, it would have wiped out everything, globally, leaving a hole so deep it would have swallowed western Europe. You could put Mount Everest in the bottom of the crater and still be 9km above it looking down on its summit.

On the other side of Mars, three massive eruptions had occurred as a result of the impact, like a giant bullet had hit the planet, split into three and burst out the other side. Phobos and Deimos, the two small Martian moons, long though to be asteroids, had since been proven to be lumps of the Martian surface hurled into orbit. The planet had nearly split in two, vast rifts and precipitous geographic features had transformed the once watery, methane heavy world with a thick atmosphere.

Now, the Hellas Planitia impact was seen as a giant bullet hole that killed Mars, slamming in to its core, shutting down its magnetic field as its magma erupted outward and the dynamo that powered it died. Over billions of years the solar wind, without that protective magnetic field, stripped away the atmosphere, it had been loosing 2kg's every second. Now humans had stabilised the loss, a huge achievement. The next was creating an artificial magnetic field to keep it in.

PlanExCo was keen to find what it was that created the giant impact crater. Scientists considered it mostly pointless, as it would have been vaporised in an explosion that would have registered in the 20 gigaton range - nothing humanity had could even get to that level of destructiveness, or even near it by a tenth, if every thermonuclear weapon ever built had gone off at once in one place.

When Marilyn Gold met Professor Kagala for the first time, she was instantly enamoured with him. He was erudite, charming, had a sharp sense of humour and she would not like to admit it, but she found herself attracted to him.

Avode had noticed, "Your'e not the first you know, he's like a magnet, it drives my mother insane sometimes. He's one of those sunshine people".

"I'm sorry what does that mean?" She felt embarrassed that she'd been rumbled so easily, but quickly realised that those around the professor would be attuned to seeing the reaction of new people to him.

"It means he's one of those people that when his attention is on you, it's like being bathed in warm, bright sunshine, you'll never forget it, and you'll always crave it. Once he moves away, its like the lights have gone out, you feel cold, and forgotten - and ignored". Avode all too clearly knew what his father's personality was like.

Marilyn realised form the description that the professor was one of those people now medically and psychologically acknowledged as an empath. They were a rare gem, and the other side of the coin from the medically induced telepaths the government kept few in number and under tight control. Around one in a thousand people were classed as empaths, fewer than one in a million were capable of being telepaths and even then only when induced though neuro-pharmaceuticals. The condition was temporary and at best said to last 48 hours, at least that was the last she'd heard.

Marilyn and Avode were flown out to the dig site in an electric 'copter designed for flying in non-oxygen thin atmospheres, with the professor and a number of others they met one by one. The dig site was not some minor excavation.

The entrance was a giant bore hole big enough to get a substantial six man rover into, and angled in such a way that you could see down the shaft - for what looked like a kilometre or maybe more, and it was all illuminated. It turned out to be much, much more than a kilometre.

"What did this?" She asked Avode looking around her at the tunnel entrance as they prepared to board the rover, which even though she was in a suit and helmet, seemed huge with its six wheels, far bigger than she'd imagined.

The professor overheard on the intercom and asked an engineer; "Pete, explain to our guest will you?"

Pete explained it was a laser boring machine, that used a small Faflof fusion engine to power it, and was capable of producing enough heat to fuse the walls so that they became solid enough to be self supporting. The trouble had been that the rock - that is what it now was, was like a weak sandstone, compressed over the years into a solid, but not much of one.

The professor chimed in; "And that Lieutenant Commander Gold, is why I'm here, you see this is nearly 12km deep and it's just one, single, uninterrupted type of rock, until we reach the edge". He said the last two words with some reverence.

There was a lot of noise as the professor was interrupted. They'd reached a swap junction, where the upward rover waited for the downward rover to pass. Nobody spoke. Marilyn chose not to break the silence.

After some forty five minutes they reached the end of the tunnel and the space opened up drastically, in front of them was something neither of them expected. It looked like rough, black obsidian, but it was huge, and this was clearly only a section of it.

"What, what is that?" Marilyn looked at Avode and he at his father, who grinned from ear to ear.

"That Lieutenant Commander Gold is why you're here with my son".

CHAPTER 9

NEMESIS

Bruce Baylin, Captain of the CA-1001 UEAS Nemesis, had never been so excited in his life, he worked 18-20 hours a day with his chief engineer Sam Carradine and the hand over crew. His own new crew were starting to board, and his existing ex-Ramorra crew were buzzing with energy that only something like the Nemesis could bring. She was remarkable, and tomorrow she was going out into space under his command. The fighters were still not aboard, their transport had been held up in a dock workers dispute on the commercial side of the Titan complex and they'd not been able to unload, or even dock, so had gone into orbit around Hyperion with a backlog of commercial ships.

Baylin had decided to get round that by testing the pilots. They'd be dropped - the freighter could do that, but it couldn't eject them. It could though, just let them drift off their transport arm, with pilots aboard, they could then fly to the Nemesis and land in her forward bay before being lifted inside the ship to their launch racks.

Commodore Van Dooren had authorised such a move even though it was not ideal. He saw it as Baylin showing initiative and clever thinking to overcome a problem. It made him appreciate further why the Captain had been chosen above so many. He had something extra. Something the fleet was going to need, if not now, sooner rather than later. He didn't know that for sure, but he, like Baylin, knew that such ships were built for a reason and that the Nemesis was four years in building and fit-out, and had taken eighteen months to shake down. Fleet had moaned and groaned - and so had the President, as questions about the expense and time - never mind the need, were constantly questioned.

They had learned much though as ship builders always had. The next pair of ships were already six months faster in build and were estimated to take just nine months shakedown, the two after that would be built in just thirty months and shaken down in five. Once the third shipyard was opened orbiting Jupiter's Europa Colony, with capacity for two more, in just another two months, they'd be able to build four simultaneously.

Baylin was saluting to new crew so often he felt like his arm was getting sore. That would have to stop. Once they were all aboard he had every intention of letting them simply nod, it was an old fleet tradition, because saluting was just too long winded to maintain all the time. In a formal setting, that was something else, but in a workaday operational level, way too much.

This was the moment he'd been waiting for - the command crew, less Gold who was on Mars and due back in two days with Avode Kagala, were all at their positions.

He pressed the ship wide intercom on his command chair, "This is the Captain, I've met most of you in the past few days, and those I haven't yet, welcome aboard, we'll have one to one briefings as soon as that's viable. In the meantime, the Nemesis has just taken on board the Titan Base Commander, Commodore Van Dooren, and he's about to hand me the ships commissioning papers, because as of now, we are a fully operational heavy cruiser of the United Earth Alliance Fleet. We will be conducting a cruise to collect our fighters and their crews, and it'll allow you to become fully aware of your new roles on this new ship. It's no longer a simulator, this is the real thing, Captain Baylin out".

"Helmsman Hiyasake, detach the docking clamps, Engineering, power up the fusion reactor, and make the ship independent". Hiyasake did as requested and seconds later responded as the confirmation light from engineering turned green, "The ship is independent sir".

"Detach the external power couplings. Helm set a departure speed using auxiliary thrusters and clear the dock."

After around a minute, with everyone on the bridge looking at everyone else and generally smiling,"We have cleared the dock Captain".

"Engineering - you're cleared to begin rotating the gravity section".

The gravity section rotation motors clunked as the gearing engaged, the ship was mostly silent, everyone waited for the giant life section to reach speed, one rotation every 50 seconds, the creaking as the ships hull adjusted to the stress was normal, after nearly three minutes of relative silence, "rotation section now fully up to speed sir, section gravity at 0.75-0.9 Earth normal as expected through the decks". Sam Carradine was delighted. Baylin grinned back at him, then turned to the main screen.

"Helm, set a course, speed C-point-2-5, for the freighter "Langley"".

"Commodore, thank you for coming, have a safe trip back".

"I envy you Captain Baylin, but I'm glad it's not me if that makes any sense".

The commodore's shuttle left the forward launch bay, he watched as the massive Nemesis sped off into the depths of space to rendezvous with the Langley. He muttered under his breath, "Good luck Captain, you're going to need it".

With the commodore gone, Baylin felt truly in command now, Markus Obishka was still in a state of amazement at the size of the ship. He wasn't the only one, most of the ex-Ramorra crew, used as they were to cramped spaces and close working and sleeping conditions, especially after months stuck in the Epsilon Eridani system with little to do, could barely get over the space on oval bridge. Never mind the corridors where two people could pass with space between them and not have to press their backs against a bulkhead wall. Then there were the crew quarters, no more than two to a cabin, and exec officers got a private one, which was previously unheard of.

Baylin though, for him the place that mattered most was the Captain's Office.

Not a one seat for a guest and a table barely big enough for a screen-keyboard desk, no sir. This was a room, not a cupboard! It had a full sized desk, an external window, it had two chairs in front of his desk, a duplicate of screens visible on the bridge built into the walls, and a sofa that doubled as a cot, with his own private bathroom in one corner. It was utilitarian, yes but it was well lit and it verging on luxury for a warship.

He decided his first Captain's Office meeting should be with Markus and Sam, so he invited them in.

"Whoa, Captain this is a bit of an improvement", Markus was equally impressed, Sam Carradine, for ever the practical engineer, said nothing, just looked about, Baylin looked at him, "nothing to say Sam?"

"It's a tad smaller than mine, I thought it would be bigger, I just didn't want to press the point, but there's less room up here on the bridge area, mines amidships above the engineering maintenance bay and Auxiliary Control, it's a lot wider down there".

"So that's why you didn't let me in the other day!" Baylin had wondered.

"No, no sir, I was just leaving to meet you..." Sam looked like he'd made a rod for his own back with this one.

"Just teasing Sam, that's not why I brought you in here. The both of you, I want you to oversee this business with getting the fighters aboard, I want to watch, and I want to see how the new wing commander deals with it all, I understand she's a bit of a hot shot, and one of the "Ace Master" graded fighter jocks, and you know and I know they come with an extra bag of attitude that we'll need to unpack. I'm not having the pilots thinking they're superior to everyone else".

"I've been looking at her record sir; Nicola Putinova, Squadron Leader, Commander rank, four combat kills, flying anti-piracy missions in the Vega system, it's a bit wild out there".

"What was she flying?" asked Sam.

"One of the old SF-1Razor Class escort fighters, they're more than a handful and if she was killing pirate raiders with one of those, she's good" .

"Well lets not get all hot under the collar over our new flight commander shall we? Let's see how she manages the rest of the squadron, and how good they are. I've seen the qualifications, and she's not the only one with actual combat experience. The rest aren't newbies, but it's their first ship based patrol".

"Now, Markus how are the new crew settling in? Any sparks? Romances I should be aware of?"

"No sparks, but a potential personnel issue, Weapons Officer Paul Irish - his ex-husband's new husband has been allocated the same cabin".

Baylin rolled his eyes, "How small are the chances of that even happening? I mean how? You handle it, I don't want any problems, but out of curiosity, who was his ex-husband?"

"You'll never believe me if I tell you".

"Who?"

"Lieutenant Ayode Kagala's brother, Tikan Kagala, who's since married one of the Security Officers, Adnan Muzowera, who shares the cabin with WO Irish".

"Just sort it Markus, but I don't want to set precedents, if they can't co-exist its understandable, but I expect professionally, to hear nothing, move them if they ask, but do it quietly. I just need to speak to Sam here about some tech details, you can go".

Markus left to deal with his personnel issues, Sam Carradine had sat quietly through the last exchange, utterly uninterested and thinking about pellet injection flow rates into the fusion reactor.

"Sam, what's the maximum speed we can push this ship to, and still arm all the energy weapons to full power?"

"If we're in a battle situation, all the PDC's running, electronic warfare and sensors fully engaged, integrated armour shielding operational, about 60%, so around C-point-0-4 tactical speed, but we won't be able to manoeuvre much, tactical speed is half that and we can still turn and do something if we're being out manoeuvred ourselves".

Sam continued, "The problem with this ship is slowing her down once she's at speed, the plasma flow has to be cut, and the auxiliary power reactor has to be used to push the constricted flow through transfer conduits in the centre of the ship to the forward thrusters. If we can maintain a tactical speed in combat, it's better than a charge at pace. The Ramorra we could turn, she was small, 20,000 tons, this is 85,000 fully loaded like we are now, 70,000 empty. It's a lot of ship to slow down, like the old oil tankers back in the day on Earth".

"Well Sam you're going to have some practice, we have to rendezvous with a shuttle from Mars and another that's bringing the Doctor back from a mission in the moons, so get these fighters aboard, and let's get ready to collect our officers".

"There's just one thing Captain, I've asked and I'm getting nowhere with it, I've been brushed off every time, nobody is giving me an answer", he looked directly into the Captains eyes, and asked, "what is this for?"

Sam flicked a detailed plan of the ship onto the main screen from his pad, zoomed in to the forward section of the hull, then in to the left fore section. "This space Captain, it's powered, and its massive, 6m high and 6m wide, there are direct fusion reactor feed cables to a massive capacitor unit that fills the whole of the lower part of that deck, its enough to store and discharge around 25,000 giga watts - it's a fast discharge system, and its not linked to anything, nothing at all, just to whatever is missing".

Captain Baylin was mildly concerned, "where did you get that set of plans?"

"They're in the ships primary build archive, but they're not in the dock plans used by the trials crews".

Baylin was not really surprised Sam, whose experience was extensive, had dug these up, they were encrypted and only he and Baylin would have access, but most engineers wouldn't use the build plans because they were normally not the plans that were final when the ship was fitted out.

"Sam, I need you to forget about these plans, and use the dockyard fit, I know it doesn't show what's there and it's just a blank, but that's how it is".

"But captain, I need to know, it's my job, if we could…"

"No Sam, please use the dock plans, you're dismissed".

Sam left. Baylin looked out of his window, it faced backwards along the length of the ship and the giant spinning gravity section span behind him. From here he could see the upper centre deck PDC's, and in the distance the blue-white glow from the engines illuminated space. Running lights on all four corners of the rotator blinked every five seconds. It could be mesmerising if just watched them going round and round, flickering rhythmically, it was hard to stop watching.

All he could do was wonder how long it would take Sam to work out what the capacitor and the empty space were for.

CHAPTER 10

TELESTO

"Well Doctor, I trust your trip over from Titan was pleasant enough, you can nearly always get some amazing views on the way over, those rings are something else are they not?"

Dr Wilfred Branson knew the administrator of the Telesto facility from his university days back in Addis Ababa; his name was Dr Heinrich Savoring. His family had fled south to East Africa during the climate wars and because they were medical professionals, the Ethiopians had been keen to take them in. Now like so many of the North Europeans, North Americans and Russians whose homes had been over run by war and the violent deep freeze across the northern hemisphere (it hadn't escaped the southern either but that was mostly sea ice), they had been the first into space, to find new homes and new starts, and new meaning.

It was now ironic that the black populations of Earth, so long the victims of the white man through centuries of slavery, colonialism, exploitation, enforced poverty and economic hardship, had in effect inherited the planet. Branson always smirked at the idea in the now faded religion of Christianity, that the 'meek will inherit the Earth'. Well they had, to a point, just when it had become largely worthless, another cruel irony. Earth lived only because its interstellar colonies fed it and serviced it, plied it with resources. Once again the Europeans, now as interstellar colonists, were exploiting their 'customers' on Earth. That was his view, but he would never say it, or share it.

A white man sat as President of the United Earth Alliance in Monrovia, now the capital city of an interstellar empire. And that reach was all the way out here and beyond. Here on Telesto despite its 1.5 billion klick distance, Branson felt horribly close to it. Compared to the 10.5 light years of

Epsilon Eridani. In this universe it would take thirty years to reach, in hyperspace, five days at worse.

Dr Savorin was wittering on, Branson had no time for small talk. The worries of the universe too often weighed on him and he was here with something that could change human destiny.

Telesto was a hollowed out moonlet, its case of iron and lead ores protected it like few places could from the harsh radiation of space, Saturn's vast magnetic field, and much besides. It was perfect for a research facility.

The alien pod was brought in, an action that had the dozens of research scientists and doctors almost aghast as they realised it had its own anti-gravity field.

Its contents were all the more stunning. A living, breathing humanoid form, but alien in almost every other way. For all of them on Telesto, this is what dreams were made of. This was no insect, lizard or bug, no virulent virus, but a clearly intelligent, sentient life form from another world.

'All' they had to do was get it out alive and learn to communicate with it.

The scientists had been working on a plan for days, since the data from the Ramorra and Dr Branson had been sent to them. It was essential to open the pod without damaging it - they needed the anti-grav technology, Earth was desperate for it, it would reduce ship building costs and transform the orbital colonies and make many more far more viable, without the medical issues and life span problems low gravity caused so many.

Branson already knew the teams here had theorised a way to open the pod, computers and some two hundred qualified minds had spent days working on it. Almost as many had been trying to work out how to communicate with the entity inside, but they had a primary conclusion that Branson was less than happy about. They had determined that it was almost certainly telepathic, its brain scans matched closely those humans who were induced telepaths - and this was considered the best way.

Branson wasn't keen but he knew the reason was the pod. The creature inside it was almost certainly not responsible for its design and build, not given the conditions it was found in. That was a whole different language and structure, both he and Kagala, then Gold, had all agreed that's how it should be presented. He wished they were here, but they'd gone to Mars for reasons he hadn't been privy to.

It took less than two hours for the facility to ready the pod for opening. They'd mixed a precise atmosphere so that the alien would be able to breathe - it wasn't so different from Earth's own atmosphere, give or take a few tenths of a percent of oxygen and a lot less CO_2.

The doctors role was almost entirely passive, he was there to watch and observe, it seemed only out of courtesy really, nobody asked for his input and he had little left to say beyond what he'd been able to discover using the Ramorra's dated medbay.

And yet he desperately wanted to see what happened next and if they could talk with the alien, well that would be the prize, though he'd been warned that might take weeks or even months if a telepathic connection proved unviable.

From behind a heavy plexiglass screen, the pod, inside a pneumatically sealed chamber with a triple safety door system and enough sensors and probes facing it to obscure much of the view, the T-Corps (the shortened but preferred name for the Telepath Corps), government officer in his brown uniform was closer than anyone else. The Doctor noted he was probably only 28, maybe 30 years old, but was clearly a very intense individual.

Telepaths could only work on a line of sight to initiate communication at such a level, beyond that they could experience flashes of thought, feelings, but little of real value. Most couldn't read minds without the subject knowing they were doing so, why T-Corps had chosen this officer, Branson couldn't even guess.

A tannoy announced a request for silence and that the operation was to begin. A series of light alloy robot arms descended on the pod, spending a tense five minutes or more, it seemed far longer, trying combinations to access the pod from what was apparently some kind of control panel, just as Science Officer Gold had suggested it would be.

To everyone's shock, Branson jumped and so did almost everyone except the telepath, the seal of the pod snapped open, letting out a hiss. As soon as it did the pod lit up in a now (to Branson at least), almost familiar green glow.

The 'bed' inside the pod, began to throb and pulse with light and Branson noticed that the heat inside it was rising towards 35 centigrade within seconds, where it quickly levelled off.

What Branson didn't know - nor could he have, was what the Telepath could see. In the Telepath's head the horror of the days just before the alien was captured, were being lived out within seconds. Its short term memory was far better than a normal human being, and actually backed into permanent record quickly, in humans that could take twenty minutes for the short-term memory to chemically bond into long term, if it happened at all in some circumstances.

He saw the battles, he saw immense creatures, like reptiles gunning down the aliens, using sweeping energy beams to kill dozens at a time. And if they caught one, they were just as likely to rip it physically apart, even bite chunks out of them. They seemed totally, absolutely ruthless, like some violent storm of hatred and base instinct. It overwhelmed his senses, and he pulled back, breaking contact. Everyone saw it, as he seemed to fall backwards, barely standing, using one arm to balance himself.

Branson's first thought was to go to him, but there were plenty of people, including he noted, a T-Corps doctor on hand. But the situation wasn't resolved. Distracted for a moment by the telepath's plight, Branson didn't see the extraordinary speed the Alien displayed as it shot out of the pod and, both of its three fingered hands on the plexiglas, looked out, directly at the telepath. Everyone was silent as they looked at it and it looked out, almost quizzically, at them. You could have heard a pin drop, until, and quite suddenly the alien creature became uncomfortable, then, it stepped back, it's hands went to its head, it was clearly distressed and its green skin began to blacken, it's legs buckled, it collapsed, and right there on the spot it burst into an intense blue flame, so bright, so hot that its body was ash in under a minute and the lab filled with smoke from the incinerating fire.

There was nobody in the whole facility who was watching that wasn't either shocked and dumbfounded or sickened; silence reigned, it was bizarre, extraordinary, and a tragedy all at once.

Branson could see the telepath, and he was smiling, smiling like he knew something nobody else did.

CHAPTER 11

PROFESSOR

The black surface was so dark, it was hard to see what it was at first, there was little in the way of definition.

"Is it radioactive, does it have any discernible properties?" Marilyn was transfixed by it, "can I touch it".

"You can, but it won't tell you anything". The professor smiled, his silver-grey goatee made it all the more intense.

"Do you know what it is? I mean you must have some idea, how much have you excavated?" Marilyn's eyes were almost on stalks in amazement, what was it doing here, where had it come from?

"Do you know what it is?" She asked again.

"I can tell you what it is not, which as far as we've been able to get with it in the past two weeks", the professor was always amused by the fascination of others, their desire for knowledge. It was why he loved teaching so much.

Avode looked on, staggered at what he saw, yet something nagged at him.

The professor continued, "it is not from Mars, it is an organic-metallic alloy, not one we've ever seen before, and it's inert, and so far we've had trouble even cutting into it for a sample. It may be black but it dissipates even high energy lasers - in fact it seems to absorb some of it, not that we can detect what it's done with it. And perhaps just as importantly, it's not from our solar system".

Marilyn snapped her neck round when he said those words. "You're saying this isn't from here, not just Mars, but not even inside our solar system, at all, you know, you're sure about that?" She emphasised the sentence by speaking each word almost as though it were a bullet point.

"We have never seen anything even remotely like this in our entire solar system, not even in the Oort Cloud that surrounds it, and that's been catalogued to about 95%, and nobody is expecting to find anything even remotely like this in what's left. And of course then there's its age."

Avode asked first, "How old is it?"

Marilyn turned to the professor, anxious to hear his answer, because new forms of dating had become available in just the last five years, not least the Vela method. That could measure X-ray penetration of surfaces from the Vela supernova remnant, giving dates back to 240 million years.

"Its around 22-23 million years old, it's far older than the jump gate builders, they're about 20,000 years as you well know, and it is artificial, it's not natural, it simply can't be. In my opinion this is going to change everything we know about Mars".

Avode and Marilyn looked at the professor in deep anticipation; he continued, "This is the cause of Hellas Planitia, this, whatever it is, smacked into Mars and changed it's history for ever, it was, I am sure, manufactured, by someone somewhere, who knows who or what and even why, but the timeline for Martian destruction, for the loss of its water and atmosphere, half its surface, is a lot more recent than the exogeologists would have you believe".

"Dad, what are you planning on doing with it?" Avode hoped the use of the familiar would ease an explanation from his father.

"First we have to find out how big it is, and we have to work out what the material is. PlanExCo need to know if this material is a creation from the impact, a shell, some sort of by-product, or if it's actually like a bullet casing, and they want it badly to protect our ships if they can reproduce it, but that could take years. Is at a device? I don't know, again, it could take years to find out".

Avode was about to say what Marilyn was thinking, both of them had connected the dots, and realised now why they were here. Someone else had a suspicion and they were here to join the dots together, to make someone else's theories viable.

Marilyn looked at Avode and he stopped himself, he knew she'd seen the same thing in that material he had. Someone had read their science report, and connected the dots too. Was it his father? He thought not, the professor wasn't cleared for that type of information. Fleet though, they had people everywhere and computer resources beyond anything the Ramorra had had.

The professor was watching them both and he knew straight away they were hiding something.

"Step into my office down here, it's just a small cabin, but we can talk, privately, you can take your helmet off too for a few minutes before you go back up to the surface".

They did as they were asked.

"You know I'm an empath right?" The professor looked directly at Marilyn, having no need to state the obvious to his son.

"Of course professor", she remained business like but felt an urgent need to put up some invisible emotional wall to keep him from reading her, for all the good that would do.

"So", continued the professor, "what moment of sudden realisation did you two have? I was asked to invite you both here, watch your reaction, and get answers, but I don't know why, and I'd very much like to".

Avode was feeling used, a feeling it had to be said that was all to common with his father around. He wanted to say something, felt he should, again something his fathers presence tended to draw out of him. Marilyn was having none of it, "I'm sorry Professor Kagala, that's restricted information, we'll have to report to our Captain first.

"Feel free". Professor Kagala swung the com screen around, there, in his new office onboard the Nemesis, sat Captain Baylin; "please tell us both, what it is you've found out Lt Commander Gold, Lieutenant Kagala".

****

Mars vanished beneath them, the new express shuttle to Titan was quick, almost unnervingly rapid, and the Nemesis was waiting. They didn't speak, neither of them wanted to repeat what they'd been compelled to say, and now asked to prove. How was that even going to be possible?

Twenty-two hours later, Saturn was some 180,000 klicks away, the dim light of Titan began to appear in crescent form, Enceladus the ice world, with a warm salt water ocean teaming with primitive organic life under its frozen crust, sparkling beyond far in the distance.

Gold looked at Avode who had just woken up, "well we signed up for adventure".

He sniggered,"yeah, and look what we've gotten ourselves into".

The deceleration thrusters were due on she guessed, and no sooner had she thought it than the announcement was made, seat belts slammed into position and the seat inflated to comfort them, as they were pushed deeply, backwards, into them as the burners cut in. Out of the window she saw a squadron of fighters come along side - carrying Nemesis ID's as well as their squadron logos. Captain Baylin's idea of welcoming them home.

CHAPTER 12

REUNITED

Captain Baylin watched the fighters drop from their transport, leaving the whole operation in the capable hands of his first officer, then he took the vac-lift down to the landing deck in the forward section, which was a zero gravity zone. His mag-boots activated as soon as he stepped out. It was somewhat disconcerting going from gravity to none, especially for first timers, but he was a veteran and getting used to it again, though it made him feel older than his years. The Ramorra hadn't had the luxury of a rotating section, so he was spending time in the gym trying to get back some of his muscle strength. There was no doubt that whichever way you looked at it, space travel screwed up your body one way or another. If the pod they'd found could give them a way to create general gravity, even at half normal, it would be better that constantly changing from something to nothing and back, or perpetually nothing at all.

Long term zero or very low gravity was a health problem the Alliance would have to deal with. Over 500,000 people lived permanently in space for more than a year at a time - many were now born in the environment and facts were, they would never set foot on Earth, or even many of the planets, not without drugs and advanced electro-physiotherapy or expensive skin suits to provide mechanical strength. The drugs were harsh and 50% of those who tried them couldn't stay on them.

Baylin always wondered what would happen to these ever growing numbers of space-humans, in reality they were becoming a separate race, they were taller, lighter, lived shorter lives, all that was becoming more apparent with every passing year.

He entered the flight control deck and the deck officer welcomed him, somewhat excited to see his Captain was here to see how things were going.

"Lieutenant Chou it's good to have you aboard, I'm just down here to see how all this works, I've never had fighters on a ship before so I'd like any input you have to how we make things better, process, procedures, if there's anything, let the first officer know and we'll work to improve things".

Chou was a little taken aback, the Captain seemed far less formal than he'd expected and he appreciated that he'd be allowed to offer up suggestions, he'd already drawn up a short list from the shuttle operations, and he told the captain so.

"Lieutenant, there's one thing I need you to always remember for me, your chain of command is Fleet, so when the flight officer comes aboard, while you'll have to work with her, inside this ship, she's under your command, outside the ship, she runs the fighters".

"Yes, sir, I understand, that's standard fleet practice". Chou looked a little puzzled. A feeling that dissipated when the captain flicked over the command roster for the fighters.

"I thought I'd bring this down myself as I was coming anyway", Baylin smiled. Chou looked at the commander file, "Putinova...ahh".

They understood each other immediately, Putinova's record went before her.

Chou was Hong Kong Chinese by origin, one of his grand parents had been a democracy fighter that eventually battled the communist government to a standstill in the 2030's, until simply fed up with trying to hold onto the restive city, they just let it go after President Xi's death.

He was painfully polite by nature and yet had a fiercely independent streak. Baylin had spotted his credentials and asked for him as senior flight deck officer, one of the few he'd had time to hand pick out of the 100 new recruits.

94

"Well it seems her reputation does indeed go before her Mr Chou, so what can you tell me I have't already read up on? And don't hold back, you're record suggests you have a knack for crew assessment".

Terry Chou, shy as ever looked at his feet, then raised his eyes to meet the Captain's. "Would you take a seat sir, I'd like to show you the record".

Baylin sat with Chou, whose fingers whisked across the optical keyboard at an almost impossible rate, Baylin couldn't ever remember seeing anyone type that fast before.

"This is strictly my interpretation sir, but she's a maverick. She pushes boundaries too hard and too far too often, but at the same time she inspires her teams. They have an almost irritating ability to seem smug and while all of them are capable, the in-bred arrogance is disturbing. My biggest concern is they might take a risk or defy an order because they just don't agree with it and think they know better".

Baylin raised his eyebrows, "Well lieutenant, that's a pretty direct report. What's your evidence?"

"Sir, during the Vega Suppression, when they were fighting off a fairly organised pirate group operating out of an asteroid field base, the AAR's (after action reports) showed they chased down and destroyed - not captured or offered surrender to, at least three of the pirate raiders two man attack shuttles. There was no investigation, their commander just wouldn't press the matter - even though Commodore Van Dooren tried to push it - he was Vega station commander at the time. Fleet command wouldn't push it either. It seemed to them like it was expedient to just let it drop".

"OK Mr Chou, you've made your point and I guess that file shows other incidents?"

"Four sir, including that one, same thing every time, Fleet just wouldn't push for any disciplinary action".

"And you think that's made them feel a little more than invincible?" Baylin could sense Chou's concern and see why he felt it.

"I do sir".

"In that case you have my authority to maintain full surveillance on them at all times, any time they step out of line I want that on the first officers desk in minutes, OK? You'll have my full backing if there are problems, but, and I can't emphasise this enough, you're not to push matters unless the breach in discipline is flagrant, we all have to work together for the Nemesis, for Earth, and you have to work with her and her team as much as they do you. Once she's on board, I want to talk to her, and I'll set the rules there and then. Now are you going to show me around this flight bay?"

Lieutenant Chou's enthusiasm was infectious and it filtered into his crew. Baylin could see that they all respected Chou and that his position with them wasn't one born of simple rank. The reason was clear; Chou had taught himself about the Nemesis and her system thoroughly. They walked around the cavernous deck space, fitted out with 3D deck control helmets that let them see everything that was going on. Fighter recovery kit, fire equipment, weapons and armoury systems were all explained.

About ten minutes in they were told from the ops room that two of the ships four shuttles were inbound with all twelve of the fighters escorting them in from Titan and Telesto as Baylin had asked.

Baylin heard the comms message that the Doctor wasn't alone and that command change assignment documents were needing approval for a 'specialist crew member'.

"Lieutenant, how do I see who's on 'Nemesis 4'?"

"Just look upward to the right of the helmet, select menu, manifest, personnel, shuttle number and it will give you a thumbnail, select them as needed", Chou informed him without having to even think about it.

The first thumbnail was the Doc, the second "requires permission to come aboard, please authorise", next to it. Intuitively he looked at the 'approve' box and clearance was granted. He wished he'd have taken a little more time.

"Lieutenant can we watch them come in from the deck control bridge?"

"Of course sir, we'll need to clear here anyway as the docking bay doors will have to open fully". Baylin could already see crew racing to their posts for when the doors opened. You could already tell the pumps were extracting air from the dock into the ship's reserve tanks.

They positioned themselves in the deck control bridge, which was more of a bubble platform with a three hundred degree view protruding over the deck. The giant bay doors opened upward and downward, the deck landing paths illuminated, and outside was space, the first shuttle, N3 came in rapidly followed by N4, they were easily and quickly landed; the deck floor opened and they sank down into their hangars, as six fighters lined either side filed in. This was the fascinating bit, as they closed in, two massive arms came out of the wall either side of and behind the deck control bridge, each one released half a dozen drone-tugs for each fighter. They guided the fighters onto the recovery arm with extraordinary pace, all six were captured each side in under 30 seconds and the were drawn into the rear hangars for their pilots to exit, then were rearmed (or would be in combat), and taken further back to their drop hangar to exit the ship, or in this case be stored ready for action. The whole landing process took under ninety seconds.

"That was remarkable everyone, a credit to you all. Lieutenant Chou, thank you". Baylin left, as he did Chou grinned and offered his bridge crew a quick, "Well done, now next time I want those fighters landed in sixty seconds not ninety".

Baylin went down to the shuttle hangers below. Marilyn Gold, Avode Kagala and the Doc were already talking as they walked towards him. Behind them with a case on wheels, came a uniformed T-Corps officer. Baylin had recognised the name from the approval manifest he'd OK'd a little faster than he'd have liked to using the deck helmet.

The Captain spoke to the Doc first, "Doctor Branson, what's *he* doing here?"

"Best we keep that to the briefing room captain, if you know what I mean?" He looked up at Baylin and made a face that with all of his age wrinkles couldn't have been more expressive and clearly meant, 'not here, not now'.

Avode and Marilyn had only just seen the T-Corps officer, it was only the second time Marilyn had ever seen one, for Avode it was the first, neither felt good about it. The Captain quickly greeted them, urging with a look, that they keep thoughts to themselves, and given current company best not think them at all.

"It's great to have you all back, I know there's a lot to discuss, so a full command staff briefing in two hours, I've got this gentleman to see to, never mind a new flight commander".

Despite the circumstances, they all knew from his expressive, almost cheeky smile, their Captain was glad to have them back, and they all needed a moment to freshen up, never mind find their way around the Nemesis. As the Captain stood waiting for the T-Corps Major, the others walked briskly away. He could hear the Doctor, "this thing is massive, how the hell am I ever going to find medbay?"

"Captain Baylin, Taylor Granding, Major,Telepath, Level 7, permission to come aboard, Sir".

Baylin felt numb to the core as he looked at the dark haired chiseled face of the two meter tall T-Corps officer in front of him.

"Hello Taylor. It's been a while".

CHAPTER 13

MONROVIA

December in Monrovia was relatively mild. It was after all, one of the warmest places on Earth now, one of the few cities spared devastation south of the Tropic of Cancer but north of the equator. The climate was cooler, especially now in winter, with the northern hemisphere ice pack down to the 38th parallel. European trade ports in Piraeus, Cadiz and Taranto were still open and wether forecasts said they'd likely remain that way this winter - the third in a row. Everyone was hoping it would become a pattern.

The 200 million or so Europeans left from a population that was once 700 million, were adapting - what choice did they have? Life in arctic tundra for 5 months a year was harsh, but underground cities, new industries, new agriculture was proving to be adaptive and energetically applied. The European Union countries had risen to the challenge. North of a line that ran roughly Dublin-Hull-Amsterdam-Berlin-Warsaw-Moscow, was effectively uninhabitable, permanently locked in 2km depth or more of ice.

The 3D globe on screen tilted round to the Pacific. It had gotten worse, but it was stable. The ice seemed unable to freeze the ocean south of the Aleutians despite the sub-zero temperatures, mostly because of the near permanent storm that dominated the area, an incessant low pressure that caused waves and raging waters so severe the ice couldn't form.

It was another irony of the times that the most habitable part of the planet would have been the Pacific islands, but 80% of them were gone, either washed away or drowned in sea level rises.

The globe swung to Australia, now far greener and more productive than ever, with a mild climate and 80% less desert than it had had. Australia had failed to contain the mass immigration from Europe and the US, simply overwhelmed it had given in to the inevitable, but was now thriving. Indonesia had lost much but its reforestation programmes in Borneo and elsewhere were bearing fruit, despite loosing half its population to starvation and flooding.

Africa, finally had peace, agriculture that worked for most, but a devastated bio-diversity problem, that few had come to terms with 70 years on.

The money of the middle east, those that profited from the global addiction to oil more than any, those most blamed for the carbon dependency - though out of ease rather than more detailed fact, their cities were now covered in sand, for other than Iraq, whose rivers fed from the snows of the north, the rains had long gone, the monsoons of India ceased, and now parched desert ran from the Red sea, across Iran, Pakistan, to the base of the Himalayas, across India's central plains, all the way to central Myanmar and swept up into central China.

China's internal struggles continued, as they came to grips with a vastly changed world and a new political system few were used to and many resented.

South America was, like Australia and much of Africa, benefiting now from acceptance of change and a new desire to make a better world. South America had overall, suffered the least and gained the most.

And as it did every day, the briefing globe turned to North America. The permanent ice spread from Cape Mendocino in the west to Santa Fe, engulfing the Rocky Mountains, up to Topeka in Kansas and a line that stretched to Baltimore, but just missed the old Washington DC region, most of which was now under water, with just monuments like the old Capitol building on its island. The Americans had occupied northern Mexico when the climate crisis broke and then didn't leave. The Mississippi valley was now 60 miles wide for much of its length and filled with sea water from the Gulf of Mexico, as far north as old Springfield in what had been Illinois.

The new nation of the Confederated Trade States had emerged based, prosaically, in Phoenix, named after the mythical bird that rose from the ashes. Many of the worlds population had little sympathy for North

Americans. It was the United States that had walked away from the climate accords of 2015, ignored the rest of the planet, and those who didn't want to face the issue used it as an excuse to do the same.

Many professed America had caused it all through its rampant consumerism, it's money driven culture, exploiting everything for wealth and personal gain, the consequences be damned. That wasn't true or fair in its entirety, but the culture it espoused had spanned much of the globe.

United Earth Alliance President Morgan Mansfield was now two years into his first five year term. He was British by birthright, not that that counted for much these days. Global citizenship had removed national boundaries for the most part though humans territorial nature was only just below the surface.

On Earth these conflicts had been socially engineered away - mostly to the off-world colonies, which had had its own consequences. With a variable and still stabilising new climate, the planet's problems were of a quite different nature.

They however, were not President Mansfield's concern. He was president of the United Earth Alliance - a supra-planetary body responsible for the security, safety and defence of Earth and its colonies, its trade and its exploration. The day to day lives of the billions were not his problem, yet inevitably many seemed to think they were or should be. His predecessor told him, "what goes on here isn't your problem, outside of Earth's atmosphere, everything is your problem". That had not been entirely true.

The telepaths, well they were his responsibility wherever they arose. The fleet, trade policy, it needed Earth to work with it, especially when it came to research and resources - and finance. Bored with the daily Earth Briefing, he looked across at the Interstellar Intelligence Agency (ISIA, referred to as eye-zi-ya) director, and the chief of the defence staff, both of whom looked too somber for it to be good news.

The 71 year old President, whose father had been a historian - now a deeply discredited profession, but one for which the President had a deep personal connection, just knew they were going to tell him things he didn't want to hear but would have to deal with.

The meeting was so important, so classified it required they all move to the most secure facility in the capital's military command bunker, and this was a place he loved. It was the most sophisticated three dimensional mapping and briefing space contrived by man so far. It didn't need implants or eye ware to see. It was immersive and immediate, and a little disconcerting at first.

The motorcade swept down the boulevards of New Monrovia, in the north of Monrovia city, the UEA's official residence, out to the Defence Secretariat Building and Fleet Command Head Quarters. Inside what was simply referred to as the "The Room", the most senior ISIA and defence people sat ready with what was to be an hour long briefing.

The chamber illuminated, as it always did, with the occupants sat above Earth's north polar region, looking toward Luna, now heavily colonised and its surface towns and colonies illuminated, often visible in the daytime. The ring of massive space stations around Earth, a ninth just completing and that the President was due to declare fully open in just two weeks time, lay in geo-synchronous orbit some 6,000km out. Markers highlighted in red the planetary defence satellites, some 48 of them, armed to the teeth with heavy rail guns, force beams and nuclear missiles. They had been more than effective at keeping pirates away from Earth for twenty years. Some said they were no longer necessary, but all of them were refurbished just four years before, the "you never know what might be out there" threat was always in mind. Woe betide any president who failed to secure Earth, it was a president's primary duty.

The briefing quickly escalated to an Explorer Class ship called the Ramorra, which Mansfield recalled he'd had to suspend first contact protocols for because of concerns over a potential hostile. Now it seemed there had been a hostile, there had been a space station, there had been a sentient alien, captured in a life pod with its own gravity system.

The Ramorra was due back at Titan, with damage, in a matter of hours, the alien appeared telepathic, T-Corps had been sent to communicate with it on a semi-secret experimental medical facility on Telesto. Video was played back of the Ramorra's battle with an enemy ship, a sobering and rather thrilling sequence played out from a mixture of Ramorra's bridge feed and external ship cameras.

President Mansfield watched as the Ramorra escaped into hyperspace after battling with a minefield. It was edited down for time so seemed even more dramatic than it was, but he got the message.

"When did this happen?"

"24 hours ago sir, the Tachyon Comms antennae on the Ramorra were on low power from damage so it took time to get boosted and relayed by the time the signal was compiled at Titan".

"How far away is she and is she being followed?"

"Three-four days at most, and not that we can see sir".

"Who or what are 'they'?"

The 3D room sprang into life with a rendering of the enemy ship and then the space station, "We have almost no idea sir, we've sent a long range hyperspace probe - but weak signals, nothing discernible, can be found within the gate area at Epsilon Eridani. Sir we need someone to go back".

"I've no doubt you do want someone to go back, and frankly so do I but in what? That thing is what, 350m or so long and heavily armed, and there's an almost invisible battle station that you thought was dead and clearly isn't, and let me see, from these notes you didn't even really know for sure it was there? Never mind a minefield now on the other side of the gate?"

"Tell me, from what I remember this whole thing was sanctioned what, elven, twelve months ago? Wasn't it to sit and monitor the battle station you thought was there but didn't, it seems, tell the Captain of the Ramorra about, until someone or something came to it?"

"It was sir, the mission was observe the jump gate, but the Captain was given orders by ISIA with the sanction of Fleet Command, to board any ship it if was justified, and justified was if a life form was detected".

President Mansfield was not happy, he didn't blame the captain of the Ramorra, he dealt with things has he saw fit and did what any good captain would have done, indeed he was delighted with how the old Ramorra had performed. These military people assumed he knew nothing much about the fleet but he actually followed it avidly, something the ISIA people had learned but not bothered to share with their Fleet colleagues.

The President leant forward, called up the fleet list with so much ease the two Admirals looked at each other with raised eyebrows, while the head of ISIA smirked.

"The Nemesis is as good as ready isn't she Admiral Ferris?"

The Admiral had to look at the data up in the room, "ah, yes Mr President, but the command assignments being processed."

"You mean the Senate is trying to influence a command choice again, that's simply not its job, that's down to me at the end of the day, I'm not having them determine who gets that ship, and you need to push back more through the Fleet Secretary, it's not a political decision, its a merit position, and I've just decided".

"On who sir?" Admiral Ferris was not happy, the Nemesis was the biggest fleet command decision in the history of the force, dozens of officers were tripping over themselves to get it".

The Ramorra's commander and his crew, Captain Baylin, promote him, his bridge staff, and get a mission prepped, we'll come back to this in two days, and you'd better speed up the next two ships, Admiral Esteban you're in charge of that part of the fleet, over ride the budget and the next two ships, Hercules and Pollux, they need to be ready inside a month".

"We can't get fighters onto them at that pace sir, the manufacturer is behind schedule as it is, plus the new crews are still in training".

"Well admirals, let's just run a quick analysis shall we? We have a potential hostile race, no ships capable of confronting them, they could have an entire fleet, and well, we have no idea what else they have or are capable of. We may, for all we know already be at war, and you're worried about not being a 100% readiness? You're the military, make it happen!"

"General Graves, get military intelligence, work with the admirals here, get me probes all along the hyper space route between gates and you'd better warn the outer colonies to be on more of an alert, we don't know when or where they, whoever or whatever they are could turn up".

The president left, his Chief of Staff, Juan Campos waited for instructions outside. "Juan, get a working group together now, classified top level people only, get General Thann of T-Corps over here, and I need to speak with Commodore Van Dooren on Titan, get Fleet liaison in too, I need the fleet commanders to be briefed when we're ready.

"What the hell happened in there?" Asked the shocked chief of staff, his bald head sweating from the heat (he thought it was hot, coming from a European winter).

"Not a lot, but I think we're probably at war".

Juan Campos looked at the President in stunned disbelief.

CHAPTER 14

PROCYON

Procyon (Alpha Canis Majoris), 11.4 light years from Earth, if you could get there in one jump about six days in hyperspace. A binary star, one large one with a smaller one orbiting it, but the route there requires a jump to Barnard's Star first, then a crossing of that stars solar space to another gate.

From Titan it was a just a short 5hrs and 15 minute jump to Barnards, then another two days to cross the system to the gate that connected it to 61-Cygni, another two day jump away. A pair of dwarf stars with a huge distance between them - far further than the Sun to Pluto. Yet there in the middle was a world, technically 61 Cygni A-1 - inevitably named Meskilin from early Earth science fiction literature. For decades nobody thought it was there, hidden as it was from observation by the twin stars.

Dark, with a cripplingly cold atmosphere and hostile silicon insect based life, it had one small moon, rich in radioactive isotopes, officially named 61-Cygni A-1A. The miners and the military that occupied it called it Mescalite.

This was a system where the jump gate was just an hour from the planet, and its second gate was just a four hour trek in normal space, then three days in hyperspace to Procyon. A total trip time of about eight days give or take an hour or two and variations in the hyperspace gravity fields.

Procyon had an asteroid field like no other. It had been detected on Earth by the Hubble-III Space telescope over 80 years before, but nobody had foreseen what would be there. Millenia of gravitic stress from the competing stars had prevented planets forming, but sizeable clusters had formed hundreds of small planetoids and over thirty million asteroids spread in a vast spiralling disc like a figure 8 around the two stars.

Procyon Military Base was the largest of the planetoids, a worthless iron-water ice rock, its strategic position was its real value.

The vast numbers of asteroids and planetoids had attracted thousands of miners, extraction companies and a whole generation of children had begun to grow up in hollowed out asteroids they called home. Over 11 years from Earth in normal space, it was as remote to them as almost anywhere else. Their air and water was produced in-system from the millions of deep frozen asteroids, and the Earth garrison made sure that it was all kept in order. They were also the systems Tachyon communications relay - no comms came or went from the system without passing through the military controlled communications centre, the only place not on a major commercial ship, with a reactor powerful enough to send transmissions so far.

Procyon Military Base had two major roles, keeping the peace and securing the space lanes. The resources harvested here were essential for ship building, manufacturing and keeping the Sol System, with Earth and Mars at its core, alive.

Procyon was also home to two of Earth's explorer ships, sisters to the newly defunct Ramorra. EXC-104 Saturn and EXC-107 Minerva.

Saturn had spent four years fully cataloguing the Procyon system, the Minerva had joined her when the second jump gate was discovered, mostly dysfunctional, a third one had recently been located and that wasn't even active. Time had worked against the rebuild of the jump gates. The system was so large that consolidating it had come first, what lay beyond was largely forgotten for now. Besides which there was nothing available to rebuild the old gates, one of which had a drifting arm 1,000 klicks away from its other pair.

Today was a much more interesting day. A fleet-wide all-systems alert, announcing the possibility that an alien race could appear anywhere, at any time, that it was hostile and that military preparations should be made to defend Earth's assets, ran across the duty officers comms first thing. The news feeds, especially EarthNet News, had it on repeat and the talking heads were running with it like little else. The locals in the Procyon system carried on like nothing had happened. It had to be said that other than the military, few even took the warning seriously. The government kept saying one day we were bound to come across aliens and we'd better be ready. Most assumed we were.

Procyon Military Base duty commander, Captain François DuBret looked at the message in near disbelief. How was it going to affect them? The two onward jump gates were both dead and the one operational one only went to 61 Cygni, she felt far less inclined to be worried by the message than that one of the mining ships, in the vicinity of the base, was spewing radioactive waste from its drive in direct contravention of every rule going. She knew why they did it, it was to impair the base sensors, either to hide something they were carrying or because they were shielding something near them.

"Flight deck, get a pair of fighters up, we need to check out the *Porcupine* she's venting radioactive waste from her drive, that's the second time in three weeks".

It was always the same with these traders and independent shippers, always trying to pull a fast one, make more money, cut corners. And it wasn't like they were on their own, there were almost six hundred ships registered in the system, and the big corporate tugs, they made things worse with their hectic schedules.

One of the giant refinery tugs, the *Tasmania* belonged to the Australian Deep Space Mining Company, just know as Adsmic, and twice it had deliberately overloaded its cargo in the past year. The captain had been fined harshly and banned after the over weight freighter hadn't been able to slow down enough to enter the jump gate and missed it, scattering waiting ships that gave way to its massive bulk as it cut through the shipping lane. If it had damaged the gate it would have crippled trade for weeks, if not months.

DuBret often wondered what would happen out here without the fleet and its enforcement duties. She had a couple of very old obsolete destroyers available to her, and ten small gunships that were fast and effective at keeping order, but were realistically on their last legs, plus three squadrons of older Xaon SF-1 fighters. They were enough to control local problems and stop pirates, but a full scale military conflict? Not a hope.

Yet today was going to be a day that potentially changed Procyon's place in the order of things. In a month or so, this system would no longer be a dead end. Today the first of the new explorer ships was due to arrive. The EXC-115 UEAS Amundsen, even bigger than the new Nemesis class cruisers in length, but barely a quarter of their tonnage.

She paid a lot of attention to these ships, and was scheduled to be lead commissioning officer for the third in its class, the EXC-117 UEAS Heyerdahl, in a years time.

Her relief, Captain Shamir, was soon on deck. The morning shift had flown by, but she was pleased because in thirty minutes the Amundsen was due and she'd planned her day around it. She'd badgered the base commander, Commodore Naomi Tan, to let her act as the Amundsen's Procyon system guide and liaison for the next two weeks.

What really fascinated her was the giant ships specialist capability; it could assemble a new jump gate, or repair an older one. In effect it could arrive with a jump gate, and install it in less than three days, but this time the Amundsen was coming to fix the two that were already here and open up further routes for exploration.

"You've got the con Captain Shamir, Procyon is all yours", Shamir nodded and verbally accepted the command, for the official record.

"So, François what do you make of the emergency bulletin from Fleet?"

"I don't really get it, what can we do out here, we've got enough to worry about without it, and there's no way into the system without the gates, neither of which work, and the only one that does only goes to Cygni and Barnards, nobody can just appear here, we may as well as be a dead end. By the way do you mind if I hang about and wait for the Amundsen to come through?"

"Sure, but I don't think you'll need to wait long..." Shamir pointed up at the Jump Gate Control station monitor, as the operator, Lieutenant Jessop, announced an arrival sequence was being requested and the jump gate arms were being adjusted to their maximum open position.

"Jump Control, put this one on main screen please".

"Aye Sir, and just to confirm sir, the gate is at maximum and it's the Amundsen".

The huge main screen switched to the jump gate, and the ignition process began, ripping a hole in space and in a process few but the best minds truly could explain, somehow prevented the two from meeting. In a few seconds the massive exploration ship Amundsen arrived through the gate, which closed the tear in space as quickly as it opened it.

Comms came on straight away, "Good afternoon Procyon, this is Gregor Andros, captain of the EXC-115 UEAS Amundsen, permission to enter orbit above Military District One?"

Captain DuBret forgot herself in the excitement and said "permission granted Captain Andros, welcome to Procyon". Shamir looked at her and smiled, "I know your anxious to get on board that thing but, hey..?"

"I'm so sorry, I'll get off the command deck, will you tell the captain I'll met him in the military shuttle hangar?"

"Just go, I'll see you in two weeks". Shamir laughed. He was mildly but not very jealous. He'd got his whole family here, he'd hate to be apart from them for so long, but DuBret was career officer material through her bones, and she'd been desperate to get off Procyon, which was more like being nurse maid and agony aunt along with police and emergency services than anything else.

Captain DuBret was waiting as the Amundsen shuttle arrived, aware that as a commanding captain, Andros marginally outranked her in the pecking order, but on the station that was unlikely to have any relevance.

Andros came aboard, with six junior crew, two of them medics and another with a newly broken leg and internal injuries from some kind of accident on board. He hadn't notified Shamir or they'd have had a medical crew here waiting, it seemed odd.

"I'm Captain Andros, you must be Captain DuBret, and I must apologise, my crewman here took a fall in the jump back to normal space, grav boot powered off, so we thought we bring him here straight away, I hope that's not a problem?"

"Not at all Captain, I'll call a response unit", which she did, "they'll be about two minutes".

"I'm sorry that happened on your arrival at Procyon Captain, most unfortunate, our med teams will have him fixed up in no time".

"Shall we skip the formalities Captain DuBret? Just call me Gregor?"

"If you'd prefer, I, I'm François". She said the words reluctantly, because like most Fleet officers, she preferred the more formal language, unless you worked every day in close proximity, first names was a rare practice among command ranks on a station with so many staff and crews.

"I know it seems a little less formal than you're used to, but we're on long deployments, we've just finished Barnard's Star, it took nine months to fully map it out to its heliosphere - never been done before and and humans have been there fifty years".

"What made it so difficult before?" She asked him as they began walking towards the express lift to the recreation zone.

"Sensor logging capacity, sensor range, definition. We use fast semi-autonomous drones now too, and they can map areas in a tenth of the time, but even then a heliosphere is *vast*, so vast, even for a star like that, you know just a tiny sub-dwarf, but it has some fascinating properties, you know its one of the oldest stars in our vicinity? Far older than Sol".

DuBret did indeed know, she also knew that its speed in the universe was extraordinary, and somewhere in around 11,000 years or so it would be just 4 light years from Sol, not that she needed to worry about it.

"What have you found out from the heliosphere study", she asked.

They arrived at the entrance to the officers mess, "Can I buy you a drink François?" asked Andros.

She smiled and nodded her affirmation, "I'll find us somewhere to sit that's a little more private".

"What's your poison?" asked Andros.

"Oh it's a little early for me, but I'd take a Neptune Spot".

Andros returned with the non-alcoholic blue drink, and a locally produced beer made from refined asteroid ice water and synthetic hops, locals called Probe.

"What's the story behind the name" , asked Andros all too innocently.

"I've been told", she said, grinning and trying not to laugh, that it was Procyon Beer, but it got shortened to Probe, because it took a while to get there but when it does, it throws up more than you bargained for and tends to repeat itself".

Andros laughed out loud, "but it tastes really good".

"That's how it gets you, you drink one, then another, and before you know it..."

"I'll stick to just this one then", he said taking another sip, "for luck".

"You were saying about the heliosphere at Barnard's", she reminded him.

"What about it?"

"You sort of suggested you'd found out something new?"

"Only the confirmation of a theory, not sure it's got any practical application".

"What theory?"

"Stellar Shielding Theory".

"You proved it?"

"Well yes, but it's subject to massive review and every physicist and astrophysicist will want their say, you know how it goes.."

"But that means every star is its own fully independent, shielded entity, that it's impossible to travel faster than light, or even close to it, inside a heliosphere, because even the tiniest magnetic field would act as a restraint, it's been theorised for years but nobody proved it".

"I don't think it matters do you? It's interesting, but jump technology and the gates make it irrelevant".

"No Captain, its more than that, much more, it means even gate to gate travel inside a heliosphere, say from a gate orbiting Luna to Titan, that would cut two days, three when Earth's at its furthest point from Saturn, even that's not possible".

"Maybe not, not using a gate anyway. Please, call me Gregor, I thought we'd agreed that ". He grinned and she knew the Probe was having its well publicised effect. She wasn't actually very amused but she'd set herself up to be his guide for two weeks, and she wanted to be aboard the Amundsen.

For now she'd just have to manage him and his expectations. First off, she needed to make sure he stopped drinking that beer.

After an hour of banter and getting to know you conversation, Captain Andros formally invited her on board the Amundsen and they parted so that she could collect her pre-packed gear and meet him back at the shuttle.

As she picked up her gear, locked her habitat door and walked slowly back to the military shuttle bay, something Captain Andros had said puzzled her, what was it exactly? She thought about their conversation and to something he'd said that didn't quite gel, *'but jump technology makes it irrelevant'* . She'd have to ask him to qualify that phrase.

CHAPTER 15

ISSCATL

The Battlecruiser Isscatl, when seen from above as the skiff approached, was remarkably menacing, even to a jaded old warrior. Its upper deck was dominated by a massive armoured turret containing the latest weapon in the Imperial fleet's arsenal. It required a considerable amount of energy to fire, but it was more than capable of rendering an enemy ship helpless if it hit the right system. No armour, no electromagnetic shield reinforcement could stop it, no defensive measure worked on it at all. The tunnelling neutron stream was by all accounts invincible, stripping energy from a targets systems and rendering them inert, permanently, crew included.

General Ixxius couldn't wait to try it out once he tracked down the enemy.

He'd taken with him all the information they could gather about the conflict, that the ship that had escaped was damaged seemed indisputable.

It would be too difficult now to track it, too much time had passed, but the Isscatl had many capabilities, not least a capacity to isolate jump gate link signals in hyperspace. If they could find one they didn't recognise, trace it back to its source, they stood a good chance of finding the enemy. Their ship was weak, small, low tech and the Giku-4 Class were vastly more than a match for such pathetic weaponry.

The only issue was keeping track of their own position in hyperspace and links to friendly jump gates. For that the Isscatl needed hyperspace drones, they would be dropped one by one, amplifying the jump gate signal home, as the ship went deeper into unknown space. Once they found the jump gate, it was simple and the two could be navigated easily in future.

What he didn't know was if it would take them through more than one system. They'd be gone a while if it did.

General Ixxius was delighted though, he'd gotten off that stinking battle station, loaded up a battle-hardened contingent of his best soldiers, and he had the latest ship in the fleet and open ended orders from the Viceroy, to find and destroy the enemy wherever he found them, and then bring in a fleet to conquer them. It was going to be a bloodbath. Ixxius licked his snout in anticipation.

The General marched into his planning office, where the Troop Commander and the ships captain stood sizing each other up. "Comrades, comrades, let's not have service rivalry here, we have a battle to fight! Show me our options…"

The planning table illuminated a three dimensional layout of known space, including jump gates that hadn't yet been traversed. These annoyed the general because he hated not knowing what was on the other end. The problem, as the Empire had found too often, was that many of the gates went nowhere. Damaged ones had lost their link to wherever they had gone and finding what they linked to required the other end to be fully functional. Most so far had linked to somewhere, but on those that hadn't the Empire had paid a heinous price. Assumptions that all gates went somewhere had seen a large fleet of over twenty ships and some 100,000 soldiers simply vanish in hyper space, never to be seen again. Being one of the Kadres meant such a loss once was simply a fierce call to arms to find and revenge their kin. When another 15 ships and another 100,000 soldiers vanished, a more pragmatic approach was reluctantly called for.

Pragmatism, in Ixxius' mind simply led to a more cowardly attitude and the Kadres had become reticent to venture beyond their borders, leading to the consumption of resources and and slaves at a ridiculous rate. Conquest was the Kadres way, not sitting in battle stations scaring a bunch of flesh-free slaves that tasted disgusting even when cooked.

The Captain was first to speak, "General, the first obvious place to begin is the place the enemy started, yet we've tried to track them with no success, there's just no permanent gate to gate signal on the spectrum that we can detect. That tells us they have built their own gate and turn the signals on and off, or it's so heavily masked its untraceable".

The General listened and felt like shouting some unreasonable abuse that the Captain wasn't trying hard enough. However he restrained himself. "Do you have another suggestion?" The general hissed the last word because he wanted to convey temporary patience but also annoyance.

"General, I have conferred with my officers and we have a plan. There are five jump gates - one runs from Ross154, two from EZ Aquari and two from Lacaille 9352. They're all old dwarf stars, with few planets except for EZ Aquari, home of the Lanasians and our slave colonies. It's long been supposed that the age of these is why the gates are so dysfunctional".

Troop Commander Cliax butted in, "just tell us the plan Captain, not all this, this, drivel".

The General was curious, "enough Cliax, let him speak!" Cliax snorted with derision, but acquiesced.

"The oldest gate predictions connect these six as most probable". Six dots were highlighted on the display. "As you know the jump distance connections are not about distance in light years in our universe, but about gravitic flow in hyperspace, a science we still understand little about despite years of study. Based on what we've learnt these two systems seem the most likely, and bearing in mind where we know the enemy came from, our wider prediction puts them here". Captain Akinax magnified a star - "It's a G2 V main sequence star, and we've observed at least four gas giants, plus a number of smaller ones and multiple dust clouds, suggesting asteroids. It has one of the densest heliospheric dust clouds in this region of space and we've never been able to get to it. The Kadres Science Academy rates this system as most likely to support life".

"But if we can't get to it?!" bellowed Ixxius now becoming frustrated.

"General I think we can, we just need to find a way from EZ Aquari to this double system via one of the defunct jump gates, or this system, Lacaille 9352 through one of those there. Either way we should be able to jump our way to our target, over a few weeks."

The general looked carefully at the map. "Our resources at Lacaille wouldn't be up to a route that way, we'd need gate repair ship and there's only one of those in the Ophiuchi system because of its five essential gates, we'd have to borrow it".

"This route, EZ Aquari to this star, then this one, this one, and here we are" - he pointed at their eventual target - the G5 main sequence star.

Humans called it Sol.

CHAPTER 16

TRANSIT

The Nemesis looked stunning from out here, Captain Baylin was over excited to be flying the new Xaon-F3M fighter, dodging and weaving around the simulated PDC fire from the ship. It wasn't live ammunition, the ships Wuhan-Santiago Series-III Quantum Computer linked the fighter to the ships weapons systems and ran them as a live simulation, even faking hit damage.

Baylin was having much too much of a good time, but had pressing issues to deal with on board, so he cut the war games and left the other pilots to practice, heading back to the hangar deck. He was soon back in his office.

"Markus can you come into my office".

He was three decks down but soon made it up to the Captains effective ready room, something Baylin made much use of already.

"I gather you had a good time out there, everyone who could was watching, you're pretty good as a flight jockey".

"I'll be honest it was awesome! No lies, no understatement from me, those fighters are something else, once you get over how jittery the manoeuvring thrusters are compared to older types, it's a doddle, and that flip and thrust in a three-sixty round roll or a one-eighty over roll? The stress on the body is high, but it's so exhilarating! But that's not why I need to talk to you".

Markus had already guessed the topic of conversation and had seen it coming from the moment they'd left Titan, "T-Corps Major Taylor Granding by any chance?"

"How did you guess", said Baylin, but it was an entirely rhetorical question as Markus well knew.

Baylin swung his chair round and slightly away from the desk, but remained standing, so he wasn't looking Markus in the eye. "You know he was in my class at Fleet Academy, we were good friends, very good friends. In fact he was more than that to me, you know my background. Parents died young, no real relatives. He was, I'll be honest my first love".

Markus had already guessed as much, but that part of Baylin's life was in the past, he'd had several female partners since and seemed happy that way.

"So what caused the break up? Academy life, training priorities?"

"He's a T-7 Markus, and he wasn't exactly volunteering for T-Corps duty. He was probably a natural T-2, many are, but he's also unusually empathic, and he sort of manipulated my feelings because he could. He always knew what to say, how to say it, when to say it, every time. I felt like he cared, more than anyone ever had. But it was all a game for him, and then he got caught out manipulating the son of the the Academy Commander, and it was either T-Corps and service for the government, or being cashiered out of the fleet and prison under the Human Privacy Act".

"I'm sorry I had no idea about that. So how did he get to be a Major? And what, exactly, is he doing here?" Markus had instantly come to dislike Taylor Granding. He had no time for users and abusers, especially not in the fleet, not now, not ever.

Baylin returned to talking of Major Granding in amore formal way. Markus he could trust and he knew he'd say nothing more about his very personal confession. He'd given it to make sure Markus understood the sort of person the T-Corps major was.

"You're aware that the Doctor went to Telesto, so I need to brief you on that first". Baylin sat down behind his desk, beckoning Markus to sit in front of him, which he did. Baylin seemed to be thinking a little too much Markus thought, like he needed to be careful what he said and how he said it.

"Would you like a drink?" Asked Baylin.

"Alcohol, you?" Markus looked quizzical, as the Captain was a well known non-drinker.

"Oh, no you have whatever you want, I'll have a Fuji tea." On a vacation Baylin had been introduced to a very special kind of tea, harvested only on the slopes of Mount Fuji in Japan. It was expensive, rare and it required a specific temperature and time to extract its best flavours, hard enough to achieve on Earth but on the ship it was even worse. One of his first acts had been to get the computer coded to produce the water at the right temperature in his cabin and in the Captain's office. He'd seen the old vids (who hadn't) of Star Trek The Next Generation from the 1980's and found it amusing to ask the computer for "Fuji tea, hot", just as the Enterprise Captain had asked for Earl Grey. Only in the real world it didn't materialise out of nothingness in a glass.

"Computer, Fuji Tea, Hot", Baylin commanded. He'd prepped the tea leaves in a glass tea pot he'd bought with him, and the computer injected the correct 84 degrees centigrade water into the pot. Probably a little too viciously he decided, it would need tweaking.

"Are you sure I can't get you a drink, there's some sort of something I can have the yeoman bring in surely?"

"I'm fine, Bruce, what's so difficult, tell me?"

"Oh its not the subject, it's the content. I suppose I'm still getting my own head round it". Baylin paused and stroked his chin in a manner that Markus had never really seen him do before, so he knew he was still playing for time, to word what he wanted to say.

"OK let's go this way, you know Marilyn and Lieutenant Kagala went to Mars. They met his father, Professor Kagala from the University, because he's working with PlanExCo on a major site there. Well what they've found there is…" he leant over and flipped imagery up onto the main office screen, "this".

The video showed the two officers and the professor standing up close to what appeared to be an obsidian wall. "Watch what happens when they touch it with an electrically charged probe".

"What the..!" Markus nearly jumped out of the chair.

"Exactly, and they spotted it too, now PlanExCo know what it might be, so does MARPA, the Military Advanced Research Projects Agency. And now we have a whole realm of consequences to theorise over".

"That stuff is exactly like the armour on the battle station we entered, how could it possibly be there? That's got to be millions of years old".

"It is, and let me outline to you what that means. The first, is how old is the race we encountered? There's plenty to suggest they're not much older than we are by their weapons, but the armour says they most likely appropriated it and modified the tech, which means they were visited by the same beings Mars was.

Was it a weapon? Or was it crashed into Mars by accident? Whatever happened it pretty much destroyed Mars and left it as it is now. You know as well as I do, that planets in solar systems are tiny, almost invisible things compared to the distances involved, scale it down and Mars is like a grain of sand in a 100,000 hectares of nothingness, so that hitting the planet was no accident".

"Are you saying this belongs to the gate builders?"

"No, because the gates aren't a day over 20,000 years old, not one of the original ones".

"How big is it, in total?" Markus asked still shocked.

"Based on it being a sphere from the casing we've seen, initial scans suggest its about 2,000 meters in diameter, with a volume of 4.9 billion cubic metres".

"Thats, well it's almost beyond belief, just completely off the scale, it means they could have been to Earth, they could be something to do with our creation?"

"The professor thinks that's unlikely, so do Gold and Kagala. They think if that was true, the alien we found wouldn't be so different from us, if they'd gone about seeding planets we'd be much more alike, and that we've got evidence that's even more likely because of Major Granding".

"What does he know?"

"He says he saw what the alien saw on its homeworld, and what he saw, was an aggressive, a *viciously* aggressive, attack by what appears to be a sentient, intelligent race of, what's best described as reptiles".

"So why is he here?" Markus, calm but mildly shocked, asked the only obvious follow up question in his mind that mattered right now. He had plenty of others that were forming, but doubted the Captain had held anything back, so had no other answers.

"Fleet think he'd be useful if we came across them to identify them, which is frankly as lame an excuse as it gets, but that's between you and me. I suspect they hope he can scan more aliens if we get near one, and I have a feeling T-Corps simply pressed Fleet to have one of their own on board".

Markus Obishka looked directly at the Captain, and Baylin knew why. He was no telepath but he read Markus' mind on this one. "Yes Markus, we're going back".

Markus looked him right in the eyes, "They'll be waiting for us though, they'll know we're coming, we have no idea what they'll have on the other side".

CHAPTER 17

AMUNDSEN

Space is so vast few people truly comprehend how mind-bending it really is. Conditioned by maps and diagrams, rarely did true scale ever enter into human perception. If you were in space, travelling, even on the best fast ships, its enormity was made smaller by speed.

Once, it took Columbus three weeks to cross the Atlantic, and even then he thought he'd found China. The world to him was vast and beyond comprehension because time to travel any distance was proportionately much higher than we would later come to know. Even by the mid Twentieth Century, weeks had become days, then mere hours. Supersonic jets like Concorde; three and a half hours across the same stretch of water. If time was currency, we paid far less of it to travel any given distance.

That progress hadn't stopped. Yet the penalty of time was now far higher and more varied again than its lowest point back then, in 1980. It took six hours to reach Luna from Earth, because gravity and deceleration practicalities made any faster unviable. It was still fast, but it was six long hours.

It could take as long as three days to get from Luna to Titan when Earth and Saturn were their furthest apart, speeds of over forty million klicks per hour, after three hours of acceleration and almost six of deceleration. And those were the fastest, least economical and advanced low capacity passenger shuttles on the market, rarely carrying more than twenty people. If you couldn't afford the express, say hello to a three week or more ride on a slow liner.

Procyon was even bleaker. With no major planets and billions of rocks and millions of asteroids, more dust and micro rubble than was good for any propulsion system, never mind the ships hulls and sensors, it took years to learn to navigate the system safely. Yet there were pathways, where, in the immense vacuums of interplanetary space, there was nothing.

The Amundsen was navigating such a pathway, crawling along at a pace Captain Andros could barely believe viable, but, Captain François DuBret, on secondment from Procyon Military Base as his system pilot and liaison, insisted it was best for the safety of all in what, for space, was a relatively narrow confine. She also liked to point out that the Amundsen was especially large and as far as she knew, the largest ship ever to transit this pathway to the defunct jump gates.

DuBret was happily ensconced in the command deck navigators position and ran some highly efficient cross-operative routines with coms and sensor crews - in fact Andros found himself quite fascinated by her exemplary multi-tasking skills. He knew she was destined for command of the Hyerdhal when it was completed, but she must have spent half of her free time in simulators to run his command deck this efficiently.

"Captain DuBret, can I ask how you've gotten so proficient at my bridge operations?"

"I wanted to make sure we didn't waste time sir and that your mission at Procyon went as well as possible. And I have to say it's good training for me to know how all this functions for my own future role".

Andros stepped down to the navigation console, "maybe so, but you didn't say how".

"Simulators, obviously, sir"

"How many hours, I mean totally".

DuBret thought for a second if she should tell him the truth or maybe just tweak it down a bit so she didn't look excessively enthusiastic, as that could sometimes be seen as impairing judgement by overwhelming reasoning. "Over 1,200 hours sir". It was actually 1,619.

"Twelve-hundred hours? In a simulator? That's almost twice that of my own first officer and he's been working this ship over a year and was part of the commissioning team before that!"

DuBret, declined to look at the Captain directly and kept her eyes on the main screen, "there's not a lot to do on Procyon, after a month or so you've been there done that, and it's busier than ever, more mining companies, miners, families, twelve hour days are normal, simulator time relaxes me, gives me something very different to do, reminds me what I have to look forward to". She stopped and looked round at the Captain, "we're almost out of the second pathway and into clear space sir, we can accelerate to C0.20 on your command and head for the first gate site."

Andros decided she deserved something he knew she must have done in simulators a hundred times, for real. "I'm going for lunch, so Captain DuBret, you have the con".

She stood up, smiled at him, with a sense of thrill he'd seen mostly only in the youngest and least jaded career officers, "I have the con sir". Quietly she added, "thank you".

Andros left the bridge and went to his cabin, and he knew in his gut that he'd probably found one of the most competent officers he'd ever met.

A bunch of printouts sat on his cabin desk. He still preferred hard copy, even though Fleet dissuaded its use. On top was a fuel status report, he looked at the figures. He tapped his desk com link for engineering.

"Canetta"

"Chief Canetta, these fuel burn reports, why are we burning fuel so quickly, we're down 11% more than forecast".

"We've been on it all day sir, the minute we left Procyon base the fuel consumption went up, and it's rising, we might have to get a pellet supply ship out here. My crew think the pellets are the problem, it's looking like lithium impurities rather than deuterium, but we have to get a pellet out of the injection system to test it, and that means shutting the reactor down for at least three hours".

Chief Canetta never exaggerated anything so if he said that's what was needed, that's what was needed.

"Leon, can it wait until we reach the gate site? We're just about to accelerate, DuBret's about to put us up to C point 2".

"We can do it sir, but the burn rate'll likely pass 25% above normal and that's not sustainable for more than six hours, we'll need a fuel tanker if we're going to jump into hyperspace from one of the gates. Frankly over fuelling at that rate will cause field imbalances in the reactor, it'll be a choppy ride".

"Is it safe Leon?"

"Yeah, but it's not good for the ship, and its certainly not good for my engines!".

Captain Andros mulled what to do, he knew what his orders said, and they were very specific about their time line, not that he knew the reasoning, but why would he, he was just a captain. Knowing Earth, some mega corps had paid to be the first through to lay claims in a new system and they were pushing for access.

"We'll deal with it when we get to the gate, inform DuBret of the situation on the bridge and order a tanker from Procyon".

"Aye, sir will do"; Chief Leon disconnected.

Andros dictated a memo to Fleet ready to send if the pellets were indeed faulty. These had been supplied from a contracted tanker at Barnards Star a month back, so they must have deliberately kept the faulty batch towards the later part of the load. God knows where they'd got them from, but Chief Canetta would be able to tell, every refinery had its tell tale signature.

Andros looked up on the screen - he noticed that DuBret had kept speed down to C.15 - she must have heard the Chief's concerns and gone with them. They'd be later than he'd hoped to the old gate, but that was life in the fleet; nothing goes wrong like a plan.

That evening DuBret joined the senior staff at a welcome drinks session in the ward room. Captain Andros asked for formal attire, which DuBret found a little uncomfortable but, it was in her honour so she appreciated the gesture. She'd almost not brought hers with her, but had though better of it last minute.

As a captain she outranked everyone but Captain Andros as the ships commander. There was no flight officer, as there had been no fighters available for the Amundsen when she left Titan nearly a year ago. Indeed they were only just being delivered to new ships now. They didn't have any marines either, something she felt left them a little vulnerable from some of the more aggressive mining clans with their armed freighters, who were often inclined to attack anything they judged to be a soft enough target, even Fleet ships. Not so much in Procyon any more though, but you could never be too careful.

DuBret found herself largely ignored by the first officer, Commander Al Maktoum, who seemed put out by the fact she was even here. He was polite, but only the basics. She felt he was no conversationalist. Chief Engineer Canetta was something else, she instantly bonded with him and they were quick to strike up a working relationship. She mentally noted him as a possible candidate for her own command, in time. There was an unusually high female officer count, the doctor, science officer, navigator and weapons. Not that she objected, Fleet, as Earth, was entirely a merit based operation, reflecting the hard work humanity had done to embrace much needed change.

The one officer she did want to work with was Lieutenant Caroline O'Neil. She was the Jump Gate Specialist, with a team of ten, a battery of drones and specially equipped shuttles that were designed to bring old gates into operation and, when Amundsen was equipped with one, lay a new gate. Their next mission after the repairs and exploration of the new systems, was laying a gate from Procyon directly back to Titan, it would cut out weeks of travel for slow freighters. The coincidental effect was it could bring reinforcements from Titan quickly if the miners got a little out of hand, and with competition increasing, that was always a dormant volcano waiting for something to set it off.

O'Neil proved to be exceptionally technical, a savant almost. She was awkward, but at the same time intensely engaging, her brain was filled with information on a scale that was breathtaking. DuBret quickly realised that she was gifted with a much prized holo-eidetic memory. Her capacity to see a subject in her head and link it with every attached piece of subject matter at will, meant she had vastly complicated technical answers to almost anything any time. The downside was she was not the best communicator, however DuBret's own greatest gift, was a capacity to listen and adapt to anyone, she was mildly empathic and felt she could get the best out of anyone. Fleet tended to agree with that assessment, not that she knew it.

The drinks overall were a success, "You have to excuse my First Officer, he's an arch-conservative, from the Confederated Gulf Emirates, but", and he said this with a degree of reluctant reverence, "he's a planning genius. And you need that on a ship like this, exploring, mapping and cataloguing a vast solar system, it takes analytics, data, and sublime judgement, and he has all of that".

"I wish he seemed more inclined to talk to me, I mean I know I could sort of force the issue, but I'd rather establish a natural rapport with him". DuBret wanted to talk with him, learn, but that seemed unlikely.

Captain Andros seemed to sense it, "if you're aboard when we jump, I'll assign you to him".

Sadly DuBret doubted that would happen, her role was due to end once the gate was up and running, she was due back on Procyon before they could jump and get back.

As the group started to break up and individually head for the officers mess and their duties, the ship shook, gently at first, then more violently, then again, the shaking came from the aft end, coursing through the ship like an earthquake.

Suddenly the red alert system came on and crew began rushing to their stations. "DuBret, you're with me to the bridge, shouted the captain over the cacophony.

He was on to the bridge duty officer in seconds as they ran to the fast vac-lift, "Bridge what's happening".

"Sir somethings happened to the plasma stream in engine four, there's a magnetic constriction problem in the reactor and we can't seem to balance the output".

"It doesn't feel like that to me", DuBret volunteered, "it feels more like something hit us".

Andros came back, "bridge are the rear sensors on line?"

"No sir"

"well get them up now, scan from behind and tell me if there's anything there!"

They were in the vac-lift heading for the bridge, "François, why do you think something hit us?" As he said it another jolt ran through the ship, "because we're on our own out here, we're big and there are opportunists out here who never stop trying to find a way of getting at Fleet, and your fuel problem, I doubt that's coincidence".

The bridge door slid open and Andros took the con, "are weapons hot?"

"Aye sir, weapons ready but we're having trouble keeping power to them, we need to swap from main fusion reactor to nuclear auxiliary".

"Do it".

"Sensors, what the hell is behind us?"

DuBret looked at the sensor trace screen, "crewman, scan in the radiation bands", as the filter came on a wedge of red, like a cloud sat behind them, with no less than six points of origin.

"It's pirates, six armed freighters, all modified, burning fuel fast so they'll be close enough to board us in less than five minutes, we need to train the PDC's aft, let them know we know they're there, it might keep them back a little longer or force them to disperse a little, anything to make this more difficult for them".

"Do as the captain says", barked Andros.

Chief Canetta's voice was next on coms "captain we're about to loose engines two and three, one won't last another direct hit, we need to turn out of their line of sight".

No1 engine was top left of the four, protecting it meant doing a hard turn to the right and up to let the lower decks PDC's engage and protect the engine. Andros gave the order, the ship began to turn using thrusters and in a nauseating manoeuvre that sent creaking and stress through every frame, the huge ship began to turn at the same time as cork screwing upward to place the lower deck PDC's in position.

The clan ships realised what was coming, but were too fast to turn and not designed for any violent manoeuvring, they did as DuBret has said they would, they spread apart, but there were six of them and only four PDC's. The ships jammers were having some effect, the clan ships were unable to get a lock but they were firing manually, which got better as they closed range - the Amundsen was a big ship and an easy target.

Then, DuBret noticed Captain Andros make a mostly inaudible call to Chief Canetta, she heard them argue about capacitor levels, but Canetta said he could do it, DuBret couldn't understand what it was about. Andros walked over to the navigation desk and pushed the crewman gently away, simply out of haste, a sub-console emerged from the navigators controls, he flipped a switch and pressed a series of buttons - a code pad. A distinct mechanical noise came from beneath the bridge and DuBret looked up at the engineering console, a large probe like device was deploying from the front of the ship.

As it did so, another shock wave racked the ship from the stern, the pirates were trying to slow her down, aiming for the thrusters, they were less than a minute from reaching the ship, the auxiliary reactor was behaving normally but a huge new capacitor panel display had appeared, showing a staggering five terawatt charge - *in* the probe being deployed.

As it completed deployment, Andros went back to his seat, pressed the all-ship coms button and said, "All hands, emergency jump protocol", he looked at the nav officer now back in place, "hit it".

The nav officer hit a button and the ship shuddered from stem to stern as the multi-terrawatt discharge ripped open a jump point in space, the Amundsen went straight into it. As she did so the pirates realised all too late what was happening, they weren't ready or positioned for this; Amundsen hurtled through the jump point and it snapped closed with them in its threshold, exploding all of them into trillions of atoms in a bright millisecond.

DuBret was speechless. Now she knew what Captain Andros had meant by "Jump technology".

CHAPTER 18

LOST

DuBret had just witnessed something truly remarkable, taken part in it no less, without even knowing what she was taking part in until it happened.

Captain Andros was already looking right at her, and she knew to say nothing, not right now, this was about command and keeping everything flowing in an emergency situation.

Andros ordered a cut in speed to little more than holding position, handed the con to the now present First Officer Maktoum, whom he told he would conference in from the briefing room, then summoned up Chief Canetta, the Science Officer and Navigation Officer. As he passed her he said, "Captain DuBret, you're with me".

They entered the lift, still DuBret said nothing. Once in the briefing room and everyone was patched in, Captain Andros opened; "Right, first off for anyone this came as a surprise to, I'm sorry, but it's a classified piece of tech thats not been fully tested, and we're the first operational ship to have one. I'm not supposed to have deployed it except in an emergency, and being boarded by pirates struck me as just that".

Nobody said anything, DuBret had enough questions to fill the next thirty minutes but she knew this wasn't the time.

Andros continued, "We have a fuel problem, a reactor problem, damaged engines, a sensor issue, and most of all a navigation problem in hyperspace, so Chief Canetta, what's the engineering situation?"

Canetta looked at his desk screen and flipped it up on the main viewer. "We suffered minor damage really, their weapons were't powerful, and they were doing their best to slow us down, but most of that was achieved through the dodgy fuel pellets, I mean how they became so troublesome right when they attacked, it's just too much of a coincidence".

DuBret wasn't letting the opportunity to speak pass here, "Captain, Chief, I don't think it was a coincidence at all, there's far too much here pointing now to it being nothing of the sort, this was pre-meditated and well planned".

"Why do you think that Captain", Andros had been waiting for her comments.

"The fuel pellets spike into a problem just as we leave Procyon, that's not a coincidence and you didn't fuel at the base, which means either something was done to them there or when you took them on. That means someone knew your plan of action for the next few months, and sold you out to the pirates."

"Why, we're just an explorer with the capacity to fix or build a jump gate?"

DuBret felt for the captain, with his narrower frame of reference, he wasn't seeing the big picture, "Captain, this ship would be an outstanding base for pirate operations, its big, it could be quickly modified to carry at least four of those attack freighters, plus fighters or more shuttles, but if they knew it had the jump capability, then they could leave Procyon and go anywhere, pop up any time, attack a shipping lane and leave before anyone could do anything about it. In most ways this is the best ship they could ever ask for".

"That would mean they knew about its capabilities", the reluctant Andros conceded, "that we have a security leak, and a potential traitor on board".

"It might not be someone on board, just someone who knew enough to get the fuel on board or tamper with it while you were in orbit and resupplying. Procyon is full of miners and shippers who'd sell their mothers for a cut of something like this".

"Well that's not our first problem, that's getting the engines restarted and the rest of the fuel checked, Chief, how long?"

"The fuel pellets are being checked now, the fusion reactor is off line, the auxiliary reactor and batteries are fine as they stand, we can hold position to within a few dozen klicks of our entry point, but the inter-dimensional distortion of the entry point post-jump, decreases exponentially. In four hours, you won't even know where we entered hyperspace.Then we start to have a problem. And that's not the only one".

Chief Canetta looked around the room, expectant faces one and all looked back. "The biggest problem is recharging the capacitor, it can only be done from the fusion reactor and it'll take a full two, maybe three hours of it running at 90% and us going nowhere to charge it up"

The Navigation Officer was next in, "It's even more complicated than that sir", she spoke in a very soft accent, DuBret thought it was Canadian, but there were so few of them left after their country was destroyed by the ice and chaos, it seemed unlikely. "The jump was performed with none of the usual pre-determined navigation work it needs to give us a reference point in hyperspace, it's always been one of the problems with a self-jumping ship - without a lot of navigation and sensor work before hand, jump's can put you in hyperspace with no tether, you just won't know where you are, or where to go to".

"So you're saying we're lost?" Andros couldn't think any worse was to come now.

"Not yet, we're not lost sir no, but we have to mark our entry point…"

"We can use a probe, we've got dozens",

"No sir we can't because it would just get caught and vanish in the currents of hyperspace. We need a shuttle, a manned shuttle to sit on the spot and keep us from drifting".

Canetta saw the point, "you mean act as an anchor, all the time it can stay stable, we can keep a signal to it and jump back from where we came when we're recharged?"

"That's it sir, exactly".

"OK, but what happens to the shuttle when we jump back?" Asked a gruff sounding Andros who felt time was going to be short enough as it was.

DuBret thought hard about what had apparently happened to the pirate freighters chasing them, then asked the question, "So what would have happened to the freighters attacking us?"

Canetta spoke, slightly solemnly, "They'd have hit the collapsing threshold of the point and been obliterated".

"I get that, but they were chasing us, what happens if the shuttle goes through at the same time?"

Eyes went around the room before landing on Jump Gate Officer O'Neil.

"Theoretically", she said, "the point is being kept open by the application of energy from the ship, literally boring in and expanding to make a hole. The whole closes behind the ship as it reaches the event threshold - crosses into hyperspace, or back to normal space. Anything travelling inside the ships immediate field - between its hyper probe forward generated field and the stern field pin that stops it collapsing onto the ship by sustaining the magnetic flow, well it should just go with us, it'll be OK, as long as its travelling at the same speed we are on entry".

Captain Andros knew a little about jump gates,"But multiple ships can go through a gate at a time, they often do if their small enough".

"Well yes, but that's a gate field - held up an by external structure, and its massively more powerful than what we have here, some twenty terawatts of power, we have to use every bit of our five terrawatts just to get one ship through - once we develop bigger capacitors, or an energy source that can generate direct power at that level, well then that's a game changer".

"Right, that means we'll need a volunteer to man the shuttle". Captain Andros had barely finished saying the words before the reply came, "I'll do it".

++

Chief Canetta's investigations found almost 10% of the fuel pellets were contaminated, which made DuBret even more convinced the pirate clans - probably the Tutankh, who resided on the furthest side of Procyon away from the base, were responsible, and a far deeper plan to steal the Amundsen was likely, but that would have to wait.

The shuttle seemed lonely. She had never been in hyperspace by herself before, and the bridge was on a permanent open link to her so that they knew she was OK and she knew that with all the eddies and currents in this strange alternate place, they weren't drifting. If you stopped and looked at the space around you, the reds, oranges, blacks, greys, strange yellowish energy bubbles, they seemed like they were swirling, whirlpool like, in every direction, slowly, turning, like the eddies in the great gas giants Jupiter and Saturn. What drove them she wondered, what strange energy and gravity - what generated the gravity? Some huge central massive hyper-dense core? Nobody had a clue, lots of theories but none of them really substantial.

Captain Andros came on, "How's things doing out there François?"

"I'm holding position but there's a sharp decline in the jump point remnant, another hour and there'll be nothing to tell it ever happened, it's like an organism, self healing, I wonder, maybe that's what all this is?"

"A romantic notion Captain DuBret, but I have good news, the fusion reactor has been successfully restarted and we've only got three hours, probably less to recharge the capacitor, we're looking at diverting the auxiliary nuclear reactor to help speed it up, while we sit on batteries, two hours or so at best".

DuBret looked pleased, the Captain was happy, not doubt the Chief Engineer was delighted.

She looked out of the shuttle window, deep into the red-orange whirl, mesmerisingly fascinated with its patterns, its intricate delicacy. Then, she saw something, dark, just a section of something bigger she thought, covered in what looked like needles, her proximity sensor alert beeped, someone on the bridge asked, "Captain is that your proximity sensor?". And it stopped. The black, spiked, segment she'd seen, was convinced she'd seen, was gone, nothing suggested it had ever been there.

She ran the jump point residue test, nothing, in fact no sign even of Amundsen's own.

"Bridge, this is DuBret, I've lost the resonance scan of the jump point we made, its completely gone, a bit early for that surely, another half an hour or so?"

Captain Andros came on, "well it's hyperspace, you never know what will happen out here. Was that your proximity sensor going off?"

"Yes, there was something there, just for a few seconds, maybe two or three, just a piece of something, I'm sure of it".

"We're looking at your telemetry, can't see anything".

DuBret played the sequence back for herself. Nothing, nothing but a white noise blackout of just a second, which out here was totally normal and to be expected, they happened three or four times every minute.

She heard over the live line something else, Chief Canetta, saying "Captain, you're not going to believe this, but the capacitor, it already recharged". How could that be? It hadn't even been a full hour. Hyperspace did indeed work in mysterious ways, but not that mysterious. Something wasn't right.

The chief and science officers both did there due diligence, both concurred the capacitor was completely charged though neither could explain it, both theorised that hyperspatial energy itself had been absorbed somehow, in the process. It promised a huge propulsive and scientific breakthrough if it turned out to be so. But that was for another time.

DuBret's next fifteen minutes were spent coordinating with the ship to match its speed and point of entry so that she was close enough to it to jump with it. This was the first time anyone had ever done such a thing in a self generated jump point. She was more than a little nervous.

The Amundsen gained speed and came towards her and the point of entry and exit into their own space and time, which she was very much looking forward to. She pulled the shuttle to within thirty meters, no mean piece of flying she told herself, roughly a third of the way along its side, where the jump field would be at its widest before trailing to the stern.

Seeing a jump point created from this perspective was something totally different, it was nothing like a gate point, it was close, around them, they were it, it was them, the hole into normal space appeared, and they slipped silently back into the blackness of...she had no idea where. The navigator on the ships bridge was first confused, then simply struck silent, as were the crew, as was she. They were, she was quite certain, looking directly at...Mars.

CHAPTER 19

CRISIS

Captain Baylin watched the news feeds like everyone else across the whole of Earth, Mars, Luna, the asteroid belt, the colonies. A massive storm had erupted on Hellas Planitia, Mars, swirling clouds up into the Martian sky until it swamped the planet in one of its global dust storms, many of which could last a whole year. None of them happened this fast.

The cause was soon visible to all. A massive sphere, with thousands of spiked arms, like a gigantic sea urchin, caused quakes and disruption across the planet as it tore itself from the surface, dragging Martian dust out into space itself, then it simply vanished, having created what amounted to its own huge jump point. It was gone, and in its backwash it had taken several small transports and a freighter, killing everyone and damaging half a dozen more, with multiple fatalities and injuries.

No less than a couple of minutes later one of Earth's largest ships, the explorer Amundsen, had appeared out of its own jump point right in the middle of the rescue mission, and right in the very spot the alien vessel had departed. It couldn't have been a more public arrival if it had been planned. In a few hours everything humanity knew about aliens and Mars, and hyperspace, had been torn up. The known galaxy was now a different prospect it seemed, it was one of those foundational, direction changing moments.

Yet such events, though enormous in their strategic consequences, and the depth they reach into the group consciousness, rarely change the basics of day to day living for anyone not deeply involved. The damage on Mars was minimal, nobody had died and injuries were few. The general build and quality of construction on Mars and its underground centres and above ground sky domes was such that other than and odd crack here and there, not much had suffered. When nothing suffers nobody minds.

The dust storm quickly settled in the thin Martian atmosphere, undisturbed by what otherwise was the Martian 'summer'. Within days it was clear enough for everyone to see the gaping hole in the surface of Mars that had once been Hellas Planitia. A crater almost 12km deep and 6km across was now visible where the alien artefact had once resided.

Of course the question now was what was it and more to the point, *where* was it?

Where was soon determined to be somewhere near Procyon in hyperspace because that's where Captain DuBret said she saw it moments before the Amundsen's jump, and the scan once thoroughly analysed, eventually showed she had not be wrong.

That large ships could now possibly make their own jump, previously a closely guarded secret (to a point) was now public knowledge, even though only the Amundsen so far had the capability, flawed as it was.

The question the Government did its best to filter out of the media sensationalism, was what had happened to the Amundsen? In essence it had made a jump - and so had the alien artefact - of some 11 days travelling in just minutes.

Experts, and their were many, generally determined that the alien craft/artefact/ship had made some sort of super-spatial wormhole that allowed it to slip through space-hyperspace and possibly time almost instantly and that by coincidence, the Amundsen had slipped into and down the wormhole to Mars.

The problem was that nobody actually knew for certain or even began to understand the science of how it had happened, even if it was a good thing that had happened, never mind contemplate duplicating it.

And so within days, other than the military, and the scientists, nobody really cared, the whole saga slipped, inexorably from the news feeds, aided by constant pressure from the government to quieten down concerns.

The Amundsen was sent to Titan for minor repairs, the Nemesis was recalled, and Captain DuBret found herself heading back with them, still on the Amundsen, wondering what happened next.

For Avode Kagala his stress was the worry about his father - he and his team had been working on what appeared to be the hull of the giant alien artefact/ship. Yet they were all fine, nobody was on site at the time, quite coincidentally.

Captain DuBret and Captain Andros were summoned to a briefing by Fleet Admiral Ferris aboard the Nemesis where their experience with the aliens aboard the Ramorra and their recognition of similarities with the artefact made a conference essential. Ferris was not in any mood to water down his feelings over the matter and he knew three captains were not going to be easy to mollify.

He'd decided to call in everyone, including the professor, who'd had anything to do with it. The circle of those involved was now widening to a level that was almost beyond reasonable control.

In order to conduct the meeting Ferris commandeered the ward room on the Nemesis and blanketed it in security precautions of every imaginable type. This was for obvious reasons, but also he wanted to make sure those in attendance knew this was a matter of immense import and it wasn't to be discussed out of the room.

Professor Kagala had objected to so many being involved (his for-profit motivations through his connections to PlanExCo had to be held in mind), but Admiral Ferris felt it was best to be open and honest with those that knew about it, share the knowledge so everyone knew, then there would be no speculation, and most of all no conspiracy theories running around the fleet.

Captains Baylin, Andros and Du Bret, First Officer Markus Obishka, Science Officer of the Nemesis Marilyn Gold, Astrozoologist Avode Kagala, Professor Kagala (also representing PlanExCo), Dr Branson, Major Granding of T-Corps, and Lieutenant Caroline O'Neil, the Amundsen's jump gate specialist - and as Baylin and DuBret had both separately learned form their research, a leading expert on the entire subject of jump gates and jump theories, were all present.

They all sat around the ward room table, some a little more uncomfortable than others. This was, by any account, the most extraordinary meeting. All of their com links had been taken from them on entry, the room was sealed.

Admiral Ferris made his own introduction. He was a gruff, but practical man, possibly not ideal for the fleet that was coming into service. At 69 years old, more rotund than he felt comfortable with, greyer than he liked and deeply wrinkled from the intense sunshine in Monrovia, he was due to retire. He was what many called a veteran 'expansist' - one of those who had grown up in Earth's solar system, never thinking we'd get so far out into other systems. He was a small ship man who had looked on the Fleet more as a police force and pacifying agency, keeping all in order. He'd come late to the concept of a full military fleet capable of defending from aliens he hand't thought existed.

It seemed to him now that he'd been wrong all along, credited those like Admiral Esteban and former President Ethan Sparrow for their long held belief sooner or later, aliens will find us or we will find them, and we needed to be ready. Now we knew they existed, now we'd be glad nobody had listened to his argument against it.

Admiral Ferris had decided not to dither, not to mull on the past. He'd been wrong. Now he couldn't afford to be wrong again. These people however would be key to making sure humanity, for all its failings, survived.

Humanity had nearly been expunged as Earth's man-made climate collapse and the conflicts that raged because of it, plunged it into a global catastrophe, only the colonisation of space had saved it from likely extinction. Ferris had no intention of being in charge of seeing all that effort thrown away.

A Fleet Admiral in any meeting room tends to have a suppressing effect on chit chat, and this was no exception. He'd arrange for the captains and crews to be sat in groups from their respective ships and for Captain DuBret and the professor, along with the T-Corps Captain (whom he inherently distrusted, the whole concept of telepaths he found disturbing), sat at the far end.

Ferris stood, immediately everyone but the civilian professor went to do the same thing, but he motioned with both hands and a few words, "no, no, please stay seated, I'm going to stand just because it makes me comfortable making an opening statement, just a foible". He looked around the room smiling and noticed as he'd hope, a few smiles back, and a little bit of relaxation creep in as tense shoulders dropped a little.

"When I sit, I'm going to tell you all a number of highly classified facts, many of them above your pay grades, and they are not, under any circumstances to be repeated outside of this room. I'm going to give you an overview of what we know, and then ask you to fill in some of the blanks." He looked around for some signs of confirmation and took their silence for an understanding of the severity of the situation.

"This can be," he continued in an open, confident tone, "a meeting of minds, but, and let me make this crystal clear, I want to hear a quantifiable, known fact referred to as such, but if it's just your opinion, no matter how well informed, I need you to state that's what it is. I'm going to go around the room, I don't want anyone talking over anyone else, and keep your answers short as you can, we've a lot to get through".

With that the admiral sat, and on the long main viewer he'd had installed for the meeting, the words "CLASSIFIED: ULTRA VIOLET" came up on the screen. Everyone knew that meant very nearly the highest level of classification, underlying the severity further still.

"First off", he began, "let's deal with Mars. The artefact, ship, whatever you want to call it, was detected by a new satellite, The MARSCAN-V sent up to look for resources deep under the Martian soil, far further down than we'd been able to map before. That's when its size and shape became obvious - and that's when PlanExCo were brought in with the Professor and his team. They were instructed to get down there and find out what it might be as a matter of urgency, and a team on Earth began looking at the data with a team at the university on Mars. They were pretty sure out of the box it wasn't a natural phenomena.

The crew of the Ramorra - and you're here to detail that later, were quickly identified by Earth as having seen a similar material at that space station and the battle that followed, and it was engineered that you (he looked at

Branson, Gold and Avode Kagala one by one), be brought in to demonstrate that you recognised it, without us prompting you. You did.

When the ship-artefact left Mars it ripped out about 5% of the planets atmosphere which has effectively undone everything so far humans have worked on to stabilise atmosphere loss on the planet, but I'm told, it's recoverable over about five years, but it's a blow the Martian Administration are deeply upset about.

What it left behind, and this will interest you Professor more than anyone, are at least two of its spines, shaking itself free of the planet seems to have caused them to break off. They have to be extracted and recovered.

Its departure from Martian space is another baffling piece of tech. It did, but did not, create a traditional jump point, it opened up something, like a field of very heavy distortion, and it vanished. For reasons none of us will ever know, you, Captain DuBret did in fact see what we assume must be the ship - you and the crew of the Amundsen also experienced some kind of time dilation from the field it created and fell into that field as you opened the jump point to get back into the Procyon system. Whatever that field is, or was, you're jump point opened in the very place, the exact same spot, as the artefact departed from, over Mars.

Let's not, for now get into why you were in hyperspace, why you you were attacked by pirates and who caused the problem with the Amundsen's fuel supply. That's an Alliance Investigation Agency matter now.

So that you all don't have to wonder more than you already are, yes, Fleet is starting the deployment of jump capable ships, fully able to create their own jump point. The mechanics are complex, the navigation issues just as much so, but we're getting there. Only large ships are ever going to have the capacity, it takes power and storage space to make it viable, Nemesis class and Amundsen and her sisters are all that will get it, if we can make it work safely".

To say the Admiral had everyone's attention was an understatement, but he took a breath, and a slight pause, fully aware there were hundreds of questions they would all have but were never getting answers to.

"Now we come to what happened with the Ramorra. Again, this is highly classified information. Those of you who boarded the station brought back a sentient alien, in a self powered pod with anti-gravity technology. I can only begin to tell you how excited some people were getting over it, I'm not sure if they wanted the pod more than the alien, but thats a moot point now because the alien is dead. Except that is for the scan of what it saw while dying, now in Major Granding's head".

The Admiral didn't need to look to hear the sharp neck turns as most of his audience turned to look at the smiling major. Baylin knew that Major Granding revelled in such moments and Granding did little to conceal it.

"Now these aliens, big nasty, vicious and reptilian according to the Major, they're not stupid. That station, that tech, and the weapons the Major saw in the aliens head, are advanced technology and the willingness to use it. And that bears out what our information has been.

I have to admit that we've suspected as much for the past six years. A highly classified project involving hyperspace drones over 18 standard months, provided enough information to tell us some kind of race was out there, and that was enough to start building the Nemesis class.Things get complicated and we're doing well but here's the latest. We've had four standard Earth years, and sent more probes, as well as the Ramorra mission. Fleet analysts and the latest computer models all suggest they're coming for us but don't know where we are. We're 90% certain they're looking for us".

"I'm going to add this to what I've just said. I was on a secure briefing with President Mansfield this morning. He's of the opinion that while we don't know it yet, were probably at war, and we're to proceed, militarily to prepare for one, with immediate effect".

The room was silent. There hadn't been a war in space, conflict yes, pirates, lawlessness, but not a war. There hadn't been a war since the end of the climate conflicts in 2082, this was 2162, in 80 years there had been no major war of any kind. Threats, near misses, yes, but no war, not amongst humans.

Baylin was first to break the silence. "Admiral, is this being made public?"

"The war situation, yes, a full announcement is coming tomorrow morning, I have no idea how they'll dress it up, but with the near hysteria on Mars over the alien ship, it's good cover, too many questions if they just blame it on you and the Ramorra, Baylin, and believe me there were some who were happy to do just that, but neither Admiral Esteban or the President were prepared to do it, and I certainly wasn't".

Ferris could see that the others were looking emboldened but he needed to keep the discourse under control. "Now, let's go back, who has anything to add about the Martian ship".

Avode Kagala was first off and caught the Admiral's eye; "Proceed Lieutenant Kagala".

"Sir, the material the space station was made of, we took molecular samples from the entry door, they do match the samples Professor Kagala provided, but the ship we fought, the way it behaved, and certainly its jump technology, suggest it's nothing to do with the Mars ship".

Science Officer Gold followed up, "Sir, I concur, but I do have an opinion, that they've found a ship, or part of one, studied it, and learnt to use the material, maybe long before we ever did. I just have a gut reaction they're nothing to do with the Mars artefact".

Avode's father Professor Kagala was quick to agree, "I'd say the same, the behaviour of one, the style we've seen of the two ships, they're not compatible. I agree, I think they've purloined the material and used it as best they could".

Dr Branson was keen to say his piece, "Well that they have shows they're years ahead of us, what makes any of us think we can deal with them if we find them? Or worse, they find us? That was just a sentry ship, some sort of guard, what if they have something far nastier, far more advanced? Major Granding here saw something horrific, 'vicious advanced reptilian predators' according to this briefing file you gave us, and all armed with beam weapons. Hand held beam weapons, and even we don't have anything like that for troop use".

The Admiral recognised the Major who spoke in his mildly irritating over confident tone; "They are extremely large, that image and the fear of them was projected from the aliens mind as it died. The alien was petrified of them, the memory murmurs suggest much of their home world had been over run and destroyed by them, and they were invaders, not from the aliens world, that much was vividly clear".

Captain DuBret was simply staggered at all of this, her quiet little corner of Procyon now seemed like a pointless backwater of genuine unimportance, even though she knew that would never be true, it seemed that way. Had mankind been sleep walking into a complacent quiet corner devoid of concerns, and in its own arrogance thought it was alone? Eighty years of relative passivity, a few minor rebellions and pirate raids, calm exploration. Some mostly disappointing worlds, none even close to Earth-like and billions of rocks, asteroids and planetoids, and now warmongering aliens likely to appear out of nowhere and pillage everything, giving no quarter? There was much to be said for not knowing some things.

"Admiral, Lieutenant O'Neil (the Amundsen's jump and hyperspace specialist), what happened to us in your opinion, and do these aliens have that technology?" asked DuBret.

O'Neil was waiting for this question, "I don't think the aliens do have it, not from what we've all seen in these briefing notes and their use of a jump gate on what was quite a sizeable vessel, that would suggest not. I'd even add they may have as little idea of how it works as we do. If they've even encountered it. And as to what happened? Admiral may I show some slides?"

"Be my guest, I'm here to hear your ideas". The admiral felt his mild literation amusing and smiled at it, but no-one else paid it any mind.

O'Neil flipped the first slide onto the screen, then used the VR pen to pull the whole thing into the room for full 3D immersion. It was impressive to see no matter how many times you'd seen such slides.

"This is where the Amundsen entered hyperspace. This is the Amundsen turning to keep a lock on her entry point, it's a stationary 180 degree turn to face the way she came. There goes the shuttle to hold the position precisely so that we had a lock-on going back pretty much right where we came from. Now the first primary sensor scans were messy, but we've had time to clean them up, given the QuAC the problem and six days to run a scenario. There's the alien ship, passing just in front it seems, but its over twenty klicks away. Now take this projection through normal space, not hyperspace, of its position to Mars and its departure point".

The map expanded dramatically to show a line in normal space - an extraordinary, straight line. "What" asked captain Andros, "is surprising about that, it's a straight line?"

"Yes sir, a totally straight, undistorted straight line devoid of any gravity interference, no kink, no twist despite passing through two heliospheres, and look where it's going". O'Neil zoomed in, to a star far away; HR-122, 379 light years away, over eleven days for a ship in hyperspace at high speed. It was a star at what astronomers called The Edge, the point at which they could see enough to be 90% certain about their data.

"How do you know it's going there?" Asked Professor Kagala.

"Oh that's easy, because no other star is on its course at all beyond that point". O'Neil looked mildly triumphant Baylin noted to himself, finding her eminently engaging, if a little intense.

The Admiral was fascinated. "Well it's an exceptional extrapolation, but you still haven't answered the question, how?"

"Some sort of gravity displacement, it inverts gravity, effectively nothing can hold it back, it has no resistance at all, it can accelerate instantly, to any speed, travel vast distances near instantly as though it was folding space. It drops into the smaller hyperspatial universe we all know, but the gravity fields that constrain us in hyperspace, have no effect on it, what the Amundsen fell down was basically like a vacuum tube. How it remained stable is a mystery, but it quickly dissipated. That's my opinion, there are theories to back up that opinion, but they need verifying. We're talking tech that's probably two centuries away from anything we could build, we'd need a revolution in power and gravity tech, never mind computing and material sciences".

Baylin had a question, "So it's just eleven days away, why don't we go there?"

O'Neil was quick with a response, "we don't have the means of navigating it without a gate lock-on, if it even has one. The problem with jumping in and out of hyperspace without a gate lock-on or a normal space tachyon beacon that can act as one, as the Amundsen found, was we need to lock the point of entry down to get back, a buoy won't do because it will drift. Amundsen didn't have time to do any of that'.

Baylin had other questions, but nobody could answer them, he already knew. One he wanted answers to was how had the alien ship been so close to the Amundsen? Right when it mattered most, that was an awesome coincidence, and he never believed in coincidences.

The meeting continued with the more pressing issues of what appeared to be imminent war. The topic was discussed but Baylin watched Major Granding. He already knew where this was going, Baylin was certain of it, and he felt himself that Admiral Ferris, already had orders. Much was said, but none of it mattered.

The Admiral thanked and dismissed everyone, reminding them that none of what was discussed in the room could be shared with anyone else, and they weren't to discuss anything between themselves. He asked the three captain's to stay.

Once the room had cleared he spoke to them jointly, "Captain Baylin, you're to escort the Amundsen to Procyon to fix the broken gates. Fleet believes they may soon be of enormous use to us if a war is imminent. Captain Andros, your orders from before what happened remain unchanged, you can share what you know with Captain Baylin and Captain DuBret. DuBret, you will be officially seconded to the Amundsen for the next three months, and you will have Major Granding under your direct command.

Amundsen will be carrying a pair of new gunships on her transport racks as well, and they DuBret, are under your command.

You'll be going into the new system once the gate is fixed, and we have no idea what you might find. Good luck". The Admiral shook them all by the hand and handed each sealed paper orders, something none of them had ever had before.

With that the Admiral left and the three Captain's slumped down in the ward room chairs.

Baylin looked around at the other two, "I need a drink, anyone else?" There were nods from them both. They smiled as Baylin ordered, "Earl Grey, hot" when they both were expecting a decent malt whiskey.

CHAPTER 20

ORDERS

The three Captains opened their orders in front of each other as two sat sipping whiskey while Baylin sipped at his Earl Grey in the wardroom aboard Nemesis, each was notified that they were permitted to share their orders with the other two.

Captain Andros was instructed, pretty much as before, to go to Procyon, rebuild the first jump gate and with the Nemesis pass through to wherever it went. Then, with the gunships and the Nemesis they were to scan and explore the system. If they found any sign of any intelligent life they should investigate, but not make contact. Any and all restrictions on the use of force were removed.

Andros was also to pick up the 22nd Fleet Marine Platoon, already in transit to Procyon Military Base, while Nemesis was to pick up the 18th Mobile FMP from Titan before departure. The 18th was equipped with four heavy ground assault shuttles known as GAS, giving Nemesis some ground or base assault capability. They were the new Salire MkV type.

The gunships, well they were the latest versions of a type much loved by the Fleet in a police role, but these were the new *Patton* class. Lightly armoured, they were fast, manoeuvrable even at speed, with a six man crew, four point defence cannons and no less than twelve medium kinetic rail guns and a single mid-range assault rocket battery. Designed for close support, they were every pirates nightmare. One salvo from one of these at close range would blast even a large armed freighter out of action, and in tandem they were capable of handling a squadron of pirate fighters.

It was Captain DuBret's orders that surprised them all. "You are at liberty to find, isolate and apprehend, if necessary destroy, those responsible for the attack on the Amundsen".

Baylin was a little taken aback at the developments. In truth they all were. "Bruce", began DuBret, "where do you think this is going?"

Baylin looked at her, at Andros, a soulful, considered look, "we're at war François, the pirates are a danger, a distraction we can't have behind us. Alien ships might appear anywhere any time. I thought we'd be going back to the alien station until all this happened, but now we're on an escort and explore mission. The next Nemesis class, the Pollux is being rushed into service and from what I saw of the new fleet commissioning list, another six of the Patton's are due at Titan any day".

"And", muttered Andros, "ten of the old *Enceladus* Class light cruisers have been redeployed from colonial patrols to predicted jump points. We're definitely on a war footing".

"There's another bit to my orders", DuBret had to admit, "Major Granding's been assigned to me".

"Well they obviously want you to take those gunships and root out the Tutankh's, we'll work out a strategy for that on the way". Baylin smiled, DuBret liked him, he was different.

***Avode Kagala had little time for his father right now. The Professor wasn't telling the whole story. Avode had known him long enough to be sure of that. As the group left the wardroom to Admiral Ferris and the three captains, Avode slipped ahead of the group, even though Markus Obishka, whose silence in the meeting was noticeable, tried to catch him. Markus made no fuss of it, but the Professor was made of sterner stuff. He just shouted in his deep baritone, "Avode, wait, please". It was like an override command, before Avode could make sense of his action he stopped dead, by the time he'd realised his father had passed him and was standing in front of him with both hands on Avode's shoulders.

"Avode, wait, we need to talk".

"About what? Your mysteriously convenient not being at the site when the artefact activated, and nobody else being there either?"

The professor looked mortified, but it was a look Avode had seen many times as his father, dropping his voice lower in an effort not to be overheard, replied with, "but surely you know I'd be dead if I'd been there, I can't think you'd want that Avode?"

"Of course I don't", replied the son, pushing his fathers hands from his shoulders and feeling mildly humiliated as the other officers passed them.

They both seemed to know they should wait until the corridor was clear.

Once it was the professor was first off the mark, determined to shut down any uncomfortable line of enquiry from his son, "Avode I don't know what you think you know but you saw it, you were there..."

"And you were busy charging it with those probe lasers. How long had you been down there and how soon did you realise what you needed to do to wake it up?"

"That's just not true Avode, it, well it isn't". The professor was not convincing, not to his son.

"And you sat in on that meeting, and I watched you as noted down HR-122. You only ever do that when it's to remember something, it's a trick you taught me".

"What of it?"

"Oh come on dad, I know you! You might not have known where it went but I bet PlanExCo put a tracker on it and O'Neil's projection just saved you wondering where it is. By the time you get back to your office PlanExCo will have a ship on the way, they'll know where to look for the beacon in hyperspace and you'll be along for the ride". With that Avode pushed past his father and on to his quarters, fuming at what he knew and his fathers ego, his utter determination to be the one to truly discover the home of this new race, no matter the consequences.

He knew PlanExCo wouldn't be quite as quick off the mark as he'd suggested, but it wouldn't be more than a matter of days before one of their ships was on its way.

He mulled his options, lay down on his cot and wondered quite what he should do.

****

152

Markus Obishka was on the bridge, organising the Marine platoon accommodation and loading the ground attack shuttles, when Avode called him, emphasising the need for a conversation, in private. Markus arranged for them to meet in the briefing room.

Lieutenant Kagala was already outside waiting for him, Markus entered the code and they went in and sat. Avode looked unusually uncomfortable for a man who was normally exceptionally confident, Markus was intrigued as to what this would be about. "OK, Lieutenant, the normal process is that this is considered a personnel issue meeting and should be recorded unless you freely tell me this is an operational issue".

"It's awkward sir, because its both and, on top of that, we've been told we cant discuss what I need to tell you".

Markus pulled a mildly surprised face without even thinking about it, probably not his best response option. "So, are you saying its related to the meeting with the Admiral?"

"Yes sir".

"But its personal, so that means it's to with the professor because he's your father, correct?" Markus couldn't think what else it could be.

"Yes, it's very much about him, but it may have an effect on us, and our mission".

"OK Lieutenant, this is already above my pay grade, we need to get the Captain in on this, are you OK with that?"

"I was hoping I could explain it to you and that would be sufficient sir?"

"No, not on this Avode, you heard the Admiral's ban on discussing anything in that meeting, if we go any further it has to have the Captain's permission".

The lieutenant nodded his agreement, the First Officer called the Captain, "Sir I have a potentially urgent matter in the briefing room, can you join us?"

153

Baylin was exhausted, he was just about to open his cabin door and was looking forward to good seven hours of shuteye as his comlink went off. He raised his wrist and answered the call to go to the briefing room.

The walk wasn't far along the same deck level, one of the benefits of being in a command role. He tried to look less tired, and while nobody was looking did something his mother used to do, slapping himself lightly on the face with both hands. He pulled himself together and went in, looking suitably captain-like even though he didn't feel it.

"So, gentlemen, what's so urgent?" he said breezily, seeing the look of dread on Lieutenant Kagala's face, and concern on his First Officer's.

"The Lieutenant has information about his father, but it's related to the meeting with the Admiral and technically, we're blocked from discussing it".

"Professor Kagala? What can he have done?" Baylin was looking at Markus and asking him, but Avode, almost at breaking point from the stress he was putting himself under took that as permission to speak and blurted it out,"He's using the HR-122 information, he'll give it to PlanExCo and he's already planning an expedition".

Baylin was more than surprised, "He did what? How do you know? Are you certain?"

Markus' eyebrows - always a sign of his emotional response, were so high in surprise, and seemed locked there as the Captain spoke, that Baylin actually laughed when he saw it.

"Well Lieutenant Kagala, you just broke every rule on the subject of classified meetings and the First Officer here has just flipped his eyebrows over the top of his head, so let's just get this into context. When did the professor tell you, why, and can you be certain?"

"I saw him note down the HR-122 info in the meeting, it's the only thing he did note down. He does it when he needs to remember, once its written he wont forget it. Afterwards, he stopped me in the corridor, I told him what I'd seen him do, he denied it, but I know him, and, well I did some investigating".

"You looked into your father?" Markus Obishka was not happy, that was a breach of privacy, a flagrant infraction of civil law.

"He's not very technical, I've had a location track on him for over ten years, not that he remembers, and I called my mother, she told me she'd already heard from him and he's asked her to fly to Titan with his luggage, he only does that when he's off on an extended expedition and, she didn't want him to go". Avode actually felt slightly childish now, by the time he played back in his head what he said he was thinking he might have best said nothing. Now it was too late.

The Captain was mildly off balance, so summarised, "so what you're saying is your father took the HR-122 information on the destination of the alien, passed it to PlanExCo and they're already planning a mission?"

"Yes sir, but that's not all of it, because there's only one way they could navigate through hyperspace to HR-122, there's no suggestion of a live jump gate in the public data, which means that they tracked the vessel".

Markus Obishka quickly saw where that was going and so did the Captain, who spoke first, "But that means they knew what it was, and they deliberately woke it up to track it as it left".

Baylin wanted nothing more than to un-hear what he'd just heard about, what it meant, the implications were vast, it would mean PlanExCo, the Professor, certainly higher levels at Fleet and as far as the President were all in the know. The whole thing was sinister, but also, strangely not especially shocking. Yet more questions came into his mind - how certain had they all been they could wake it, then track it, what did they already know? What did they do with the information they had now?

The Captain looked at Avode, then spoke, in a highly authoritative manner, "Lieutenant you are to stop any further investigation immediately, you are to abandon any further attempts to obtain knowledge of this subject, or your father's business. You've legally transgressed on two accounts, the secrecy of the briefing and the intrusion on your fathers privacy, both of those breaches are serious. However because of the circumstances and the problems taking it further would cause, this meeting did not happen, you have not spoken to either the First Officer or myself, and you will not discuss this with anyone ever again".

The Captain stood, "Lieutenant Kagala, you are dismissed".

Avode, half petrified and half feeling like a total idiot, saluted, "YES SIR", and left as fast as he could for his cabin.

"That was sharp sir, he was sweating like the Angel Falls, but he really was bothered by what his father has done, so am I".

"Markus, none of this is provable, and frankly what has any of it got to do with us and our mission? Governments, exploration companies, the intel agencies, they all do stuff like this, admittedly this may have further implications but it's not our issue. I don't trust any of them entirely, but we have to trust them to do what they're doing and we have to pick up the pieces if they're wrong. That's what we, the Nemesis, are here for". Baylin sounded mildly exasperated by the whole thing. Everything had gotten so complex lately.

"I get your point Captain, really I do, but the stakes are high this time. What if the aliens on HR-122 don't want to be found? People died when that thing left Mars, almost 80 according to the morning briefing, aboard the ships in that alien's backwash when it jumped away. The professor could be responsible and who's to say he didn't risk it by himself, or with PlanExCo and the government knew nothing?"

They were all valid points but Captain Baylin was tired of them. This wasn't their problem, end of. He didn't like it but that was that. It was up to the law and others to work out what did happen, not what might have.

The Nemesis had a job to do, escort the Amundsen and the gunships and then be first through the jump gate into the new system, and maybe help Captain DuBret along the way. And all the while, there was a 90% chance an alien ship or ships with hostile intent were baring down somewhere on an Earth outpost or colony, with as they used to say in the movies, 'malice a forethought'.

CHAPTER 21

DENDERA

Maris Karanska had barely been able to contain her grief when they brought her the news, the transmission was being broadcast on Interstellar Network News and EarthnetNews from Procyon Military Base and around every colony, throughout Earth controlled space. Six 'pirate ships' they called them, attacking the Amundsen, being fired on by its point defences and then watching the Amundsen open a jump point and escape. It didn't show the destruction of the clans ships because the Amundsen was gone, but the Fleet scavenger bots had trawled through the wrecks to find their own recordings and were now using them against them, playing the edited highlights back as the Amundsen vanished, and each of the clans ships smashed into the collapsing jump points threshold and detonated.

It wasn't supposed to have happened that way, Amundsen was a soft target, it had no experience in Procyon, the six clan ships should have easily overwhelmed and captured her, they'd have imprisoned the crew, stolen the jump generator they'd been hired to remove, and then left her and her crew to be recovered by Fleet.

Now her husband was dead, her son was dead, and so were many of their friends and comrades. She fucking hated Fleet, her grief was filling her with anger, and a burning desire for revenge.

Dendera was a large asteroid, deep in the outermost part of the Procyon belt, almost as far from the Military Base as it was possible to get. The Tutankh Clan were some of the earliest outer belt settlers, gold had been found here, almost unheard of, and for a few short years tiny traces of Astatine-85 had bought wealth and a level of freedom from Earth's tyranny, it's endless controlling interference. Once the precious ores had been depleted, they were left alone.

In the early days of the piracy game Fleet had been too weak to do anything. Clan ships had wandered far and wide, never taking too much, just enough to annoy but not rile the other colonials into taking action.

Over time the bigger asteroids had grown their own defences, so it was down to stealing from ships, that did rile the colonists, as they started defending them, people died, piracy became hard work and inevitably, once the Military Base was finished, everything got more complicated.

Now they were just gun runners, people traffickers, smugglers. Until they were offered a great deal of money to take down the Amundsen and steal the jump generator. So much planning had gone into it, Karanska had been largely disbelieving that a ship could even make a jump point, but their client had convinced them.

She never knew who wanted it, the end customer meant nothing to her or anyone else on Dendera, but ten million credits on top of a budget of twenty million to fit out the ships? That was a pay day like no other. It would keep Dendera supplied for six, maybe seven years and get them back in business, powerful enough to take down some of the old gunships Fleet used to patrol the system.

Now there was nothing, everything was lost and their client would not be happy. He was due in two days, had already left Procyon base for Dendera on a path designed to hide from Fleet patrols and nosey colonials.

And now, as Acting Chief Councillor Maris Karanska sat in her office the glib presenter of INN showed footage of the Amundsen, already back in service, only this time escorted by no less that one of the massive new heavy cruisers Fleet had built, heading back to Procyon. She mused that Fleet couldn't help itself keep a secret, always having to show itself off, wave the flag so that taxpayers could see what their money had been spent on and anyone else knew where their ships would be.

She was about to get up when the anally retentive looking presenter, Imelda Troves, caught her attention with, "and now we go live to Alliance Headquarters in Monrovia for a special announcement, which is being broadcast on all video and audio channels simultaneously, across the whole Alliance".

That had only happened once in the last twenty years, when somebody tried to assassinate President Sparrow in his first term, just two days into office. Karanska decided to stay and watch.

President Morgan Mansfield entered the room, flanked by Admiral Esteban, effectively head of Fleet, the defence minister, some guy in a T-Corps uniform, Vice-President Isabella Diaz-Santos and his chief of staff. Looking extraordinarily serious, Mansfield's usually jovial demeanour was nowhere to be seen.

"People of the United Earth Alliance, you all know by now, that an alien vessel, buried for millennia on Mars, suddenly and without warning, awoke and left the planet, killing some 81 of our citizens. I know that every one of you will join me, in the grief of their families.

In recent weeks, we have also discovered that we face the additional immediate and imminent threat of a new race, which scientific evidence suggests are linked to the ship that left Mars. They have been observed to be hostile, they appear to have destroyed other races we have no direct knowledge of, and we believe, following their attack on one of our exploration ships, the Ramorra, they are looking for us.

As a result, I am declaring a State of Imminent Threat in every system, including Sol, and that we must consider ourselves at war with a race we do not yet even know. They've made their intentions clear by attacking the Ramorra, we will defend our ships, our people, our planets and our Alliance come what may.

The Government will update you all on a regular basis, as and when any hostilities occur. Be vigilant, be aware, and be safe. The Fleet is with you, the Marine Force is with you, we will prevail".

With that the transmission ended and it flicked back to the studio where a battery of talking heads had already been lined up to dissect every word. Karanska ordered the monitor off.

As she walked down the artificial daylight lit corridors, many of them raw iron ore polished to a finish and then painted white to keep light levels high, friends stopped her and offered their condolences.

She was already beginning to realise that she could not spend time grieving, she had to be the one to stay strong for the forty-three families, their friends, who'd lost relatives during the attempt to seize the Amundsen.

The decision to carry the operation out had been close in the council, mostly carried by loyalty to its leader, her now dead husband. She'd voted with him and now she must, as the senior-most councillor, take responsibility and head up the clan until new elections could be held.

Some of those she passed in the corridor, in the market, looked away, they were less forgiving, she understood that, but she needed to speak with Collin Mcreedy, he'd voted and campaigned - vociferously - against the deal to take the Amundsen.

She reached his hab unit, he let her in saying nothing.

"Collin".

"Happy now Maris?" The ginger haired, ginger bearded and somewhat towering figure, asked dryly and with a touch of malice. His piercing green eyes seemed to look straight through her. He was a native of Dendera, like many, taller than the non-natives by nearly 30cm. The low gravity had affected most born on Dendera the same way, the same was true of many across every system, it lent them an elegance and air of inner strength that was directly opposite to their physical strength if they were ever put in a full gravity zone. Their status as native-born also gave them a huge credibility above those who were even founders. There were now as many adult natives as there were founders, and it was starting to have an effect on attitudes. The native born were more in favour of smuggling and trading than they were for outright piracy. They had no care or love for Earth, certainly not Procyon base, nor many of the miners who eked out an existence on the asteroids the big corporations ignored. This rock in a backwater of space was their home.

They'd grown up knowing and understanding they had to fight for everything, not amongst each other, but as a team, the whole community worked as one, when decisions were made they worked together to make it happen even if they disagreed with it. That was how it had always worked, that was why they were still out here.

Yet many wondered how long they could stay. The giant lumps of ice that drifted in the belt were becoming fewer close by, and they were hard to move; they were after all finite and Procyon was never water-rich. Buying in oxygen and other gases was expensive, and few would do business with them, pressed as they were by the authorities.

Everyone here knew how to recycle, it was simply second nature, essential, everything was re-used nothing was wasted. Even bodies of family were composted down to provide nutrients and return their energy to the community. Out here, that's how it had to be.

Maris Karanska found it hard to keep Mcreedy's eyes locked, his intensity and youthfulness disturbed her. He seemed like he wanted to say a great deal, and she knew she didn't want to hear any of it. But it had to be done.

"Well?" asked Mcreedy, "You came here, I let you in Madam Acting Chief Councillor, what do you want?"

"Please Collin, don't be so formal, so harsh, I lost Pietr and Igor, it's not like I haven't had to pay a price too".

"Look Maris, what do you expect? You took a massive amount of money from this Mr Athanasios, twenty million to fit out the ships, and now without the jump tech from the Amundsen, he's not going to pay the ten mill' we need to buy supplies and air, the whole fucking thing has been for fucking nothing! So please, what are you here for?"

"I need us to be united, to stand as one, I don't want him thinking he can just walk over us, right now we owe him nothing, nothing at all. He won't see it that way, and we cannot be divided, he cannot divide us, so I need you to stand with me, in public, and bring the rest of the council who opposed the attack with you. It's for the good of everyone, we can't be divided, not now". She stood with her head up and her hands shoved in her overall pockets, she was fighting back emotions, and though she tried, it was clear to Mcreedy she was suffering.

He admired her for it really, but he didn't want her to know it. She was a girl when the founders came here from Earth, one of the original families, the Karanski's she married into held huge sway, well they had. Now she was the last of them, and not even a blood relative. Pietr Karanski was dead now, and her son Igor with him.

Yet Collin Mcreedy knew she was right.

"When is he due to arrive?"

Maris looked up, "sometime tomorrow, it depends on how much avoidance they have to run, but they picked him up at the commercial port on the base without any problem, he seems to be able to walk through security without an issue."

"Don't you wonder why that is? Who's behind him?"

"What difference does it make to us?" Maris had never cared about Earthers and their problems. They'd never cared about her.

"I'll talk to the others, but we need that ten mill' that'll be on all their minds, or we're going to be doomed out here, we need to fit out more ships, we've only got six more, and no more direct attacks on the damned Fleet".

"Thank you, I mean it, thank you Collin". She pulled a smile, she actually wanted to hug him, it was the best news she'd heard all day.

"I'll be going, lots to do". She didn't see him smile at her as she turned away to go out the door, but he said quickly, "Before you go, have you seen who's Fleet's hero of the hour?"

Maris looked back, Collin turned up the volume on the INN feed, as Komi Tanaka, INN's Procyon Bureau Chief reported, *"Captain François DuBret, one of the commanding officers at Procyon was praised for her skill today by Commodore Naomi Tan, Procyon's Military Governor. DuBret was responsible for leading the Explorer Class UEAS Amundsen through the belt and to safety as the notorious Tutankh Clan attacked it and were destroyed, through superior tactical skill displayed by the captain and crew…"* she went on but Maris was too angry to think straight.

Mcreedy looked her in the eye, "wasn't your maiden name DuBret?"

Maris was stone faced now, "Yes, she's my sister, our mother wouldn't come here, my father took me, François stayed on Earth".

"Does she know you're here?"

"I haven't got the slightest fucking idea Collin".

He shrugged his shoulders and she left, hating the time it took for the door to slide out of the way.

This had not been a good day. And it didn't get any better. Now the Earth President had declared war on invisible aliens? A state of emergency decree was being expected from the Military Governor's office. That would tighten patrols, make the Earthers twitchier than they were already.

Maris stopped in the market on the way back to her hab unit. She'd have to face giving that up now, it was for married couples only with one immediate family member living with them. With Pietr and Igor gone she'd have just a couple of weeks before she'd be allocated single accommodation and somehow would have to reduce down a lifetime, a marriage and a son to fit in a one person, three room hab unit.

She got back to her office, ersatz black coffee in hand, wishing she could get some of the real stuff and not this tasteless home grown powdery muck everyone seemed happy to accept, with its synthetic caffeine.

There was a coded message waiting. She entered her passcode, a short line of script appeared. "Route clear arrival 1930EST".

That was nine hours away. She sent a message to Collin Mcreedy "A@1930".

"OK" came back.

She sat down behind the desk, petitions for this and that, accommodation swap approvals, a list of endless resource requests that the council couldn't fill, reactivation sign off or the first of the six old freighters they could use as armed ships, if they could get weapons.

The hours dragged by like lead.

At 1900 the perimeter detectors set off an incoming ship alert, a small four man freighter based on an old class of shuttles. Mr Athanasios was about to arrive. She got up, went to her hab unit, showered in the sonic shower (nobody used water showers, there wasn't enough of it), and tried to make herself look as best she could.

By 1920 she and Collin Mcreedy were waiting in the old side dock in section Alpha, the only small one uncovered by cameras and sufficiently run down to look unused.

The corroded, badly lit dock was ideal for clandestine meetings, it even had a room off to one side that was once used for the dock manager.

Mr Athanasios, around 1.8m tall, with his smug grin and slim, athletic build, black hair slicked down on his head but pushed back, his dark brown silk suit the colour of cocoa, a black collarless shirt. What he was wearing would cost thousands of credits on Earth. Silk was almost unheard of these days and who wore silk out here in the asteroids?

His coal black eyes were relentless. He gave no quarter, no ground, Maris was convinced he was an empath, and a strong one. Yet his empathy was she felt, negatively focused. Her husband would have heard no word against him, and she'd met him but once, and then very briefly.

He stepped out of the air lock, strode right up to her, he was it looked to her, instantly sympathetic, his face exuded sympathy, but for her it seemed oddly dark. His thick black eyebrows, the dense eye lashes, his very light brown skin suggested he was probably Greek in origin, but his clean shaven look was so pristine it looked out of context here.

"I am so sorry for your loss Acting Council Leader, what a terrible blow it must have been". He looked into her eyes and she found the experience so unpleasant she nearly pulled away, it was like he was absorbing her feelings, right out of her own body.

Unanswered he turned to Mcreedy, "I don't think we've met Councillor Mcreedy?"

Collin Mcreedy looked directly at him, offered his hand, but Athanasios didn't shake hands, he seemed always to either have his hands in his pockets, or in front of him, fingers touching. He said nothing, and Mcreedy, rebuffed, simply put his arm back down.

They went into the small room, where a round steel table and three chairs were already waiting.

"I see we're straight down to business then, efficient". The light in the room was dim, a yellow-red that did nobody any favours. Athanasios sat first, his back to the wall so he could see the door. Maris and Colin sat.

"My associates and I, are extremely disappointed at the outcome of the operation against the Amundsen, we invested a very substantial amount of money in equipping your ships, and we have nothing to show for it, at all."

Mcreedy was quick to jump in, voiced a little raised, "You must have seen what happened, it's been all over the news feeds, the jump generator was operational, and you told us it wasn't"

Athanasios seemed unruffled at the accusation. "My description provided to you was that my associates *believed* it was not operational, neither they or I said that it was definitively inoperative. It was Mr Karanski who seemed to take that as an absolute rather than take any precautions, or make alternate plans".

That irritated Maris, "are you blaming my husband for what happened?"

"He was in charge, he authorised the plan, he commanded the squadron that attacked, did he not? Therefore your husband is the one my associates feel is responsible".

Maris was appalled at the tone, but Athanasios was always driven by a pragmatic and businesslike approach, Pietr had told her he was colder than a deep space ice rock.

Mcreedy wanted to know where this was going, "what do you want from us? You know we have nothing material to give you, we can't pay you back twenty million credits, we spent it all on those six ships only to see them trashed".

The coal black eyes refocussed on Mcreedy. Colin felt his chest tighten and a flush of anxiety went through him, his heart pounded and he could hear blood in his ears and felt a sharp increase in temperature. Athanasios didn't move, but began speaking, "My associates have had much the same concern, you are almost worthless to us now, indeed I have to be honest they thought you were much more trouble than you were worth. There was even talk of liquidating the colony…"

165

Maris couldn't believe her ears, "you think you can simply walk over here and blow up a colony of nearly nine thousand and nobody will notice? We're buried under miles of iron down here, what do you think you could have done? We'd defend ourselves to the last man!"

"It was a consideration, however I have, if you would let me finish, persuaded them against such a move. They have decided to use your smuggling operation".

"In what way do you mean 'use'?" Maris looked concerned.

"You owe my associates twenty million credits, you also need the ten million you were going to obtain for the Amundsen. My associates have decided that they will provide you with the ten million, and that you will use that to bring into operation the other six ships you still have. However they will be used as secured cargo and passenger transports, and you will move what we tell you, when we tell you and how we tell you, no questions and no deviation, until we have completed our project. After that, we'll have no need for any further business with you".

Maris and Colin looked at each other. "No more business with us at all?" asked Colin, to be absolutely clear.

Athanasios smiled a wide, closed lip smile, "there will be no need, our business will be concluded".

"We need to run this past the council", Maris pointed out quickly.

"I don't have time for that I'm afraid...Maris, isn't it?" Athanasios looked right into her, chilling her to the bone, "I just need to have a quick look at the six ships in your lower dock, and I'll be on my way".

He stood up and left the room with such speed the two of them felt mildly paralysed. He was off into the core before either could say anything.

"He's not taking no for answer that's for sure", said Colin, as Maris looked at him as though he was joking, she replied, "you don't fucking say".

They went to Maris' office and she tried to find him on the security cameras, but he was nowhere to be seen. "Where the fuck has he gone, he can't just vanish".

"I'll put a call out, someone will have seen him, Colin started calling up his friends and people he knew were most likely to have seen a total stranger, then went hunting for him himself.

Nobody had laid eyes on Athanasios. After two hours, as he hunted for him, discreetly, Colin spotted Athanasios. He was talking to a group of around half a dozen men, but it was so dark, behind a stack of old cargo crates, and they were too far away for him to make out who.

He went back to Maris, "he's been down in the market, mooching about some of the old cargo crates in the refurb bays, and he has friends".

"What do you mean 'friends'", she asked as she heard the ominous sounding news.

"I don't know, but how did he recruit six of our people without us ever knowing about it before now?"

They looked at each other, Maris said, "he gives me the fucking creeps", barely had she finished the sentence when Athanasios appeared in her doorway.

"I'll be leaving, no need to see me off". He grinned that smug grin and was gone, minutes later the freighter departed for Procyon Base.

Maris was about to ask Colin of he'd like to join her for dinner, and as she turned she noted a line of text on her screen. "Attached are the modifications your ships need. Equipment will be delivered in two days to assist you complete the transformation. Ten million credits is now available to draw from an account at Procyon Commercial Port Bank, which can be accessed using information I left on your desk in a memory cube". She looked down and saw it, convinced she had't seen it before and wondering how he'd put it there when he'd only been at the door of her office.

Athanasios' message continued, "You have fourteen Earth Standard weeks to prepare the freighters, they must be ready on time, or our contract will be nullified and my associates will take active measures to guard their investment. I'm sure that won't be required, but you need to understand the realties of our arrangement".

That was it, she turned the screen for Colin to read for himself, "have we just made a deal with the fucking devil or what?"

CHAPTER 22

THRESHOLD

There is nothing more remarkable thought DuBret, than watching the Amundsen reassemble an old jump gate, two of the arms were close but not linked, one required hauling back from some 2.3 million klicks away. Nemesis was staying with the Amundsen to protect her while she took her two gunships, Patton and Montgomery, to escort the specialist shuttles and a fleet of drones on a carrier grid shuttle to get the third arm back.

It was actually slow work, the distance didn't permit a high speed transit, so it was almost eighteen hours there and some sixty hours work to set the arm up for salvage, and a twenty-four hour trip back, the shuttles towing the arm so as not to damage it.

Baylin used the time to run the Nemesis and fighter crews through intensive drills, and to train the weapons crews, the emergency repair crews and medical staff. In fact he was merciless, running them so hard that Markus Obishka was on the cusp of telling him he needed to drop the intensity for a few days, when, as if omniscient, the Captain gave everyone a 48 hour break. That was typical Baylin, he knew when to stop and when to start.

The next morning, when the gunships returned with the third arm, Captain DuBret and her commanders came over to the Nemesis for a planning meeting, but before that a long over due discussion with Chief Engineer Sam Carradine finally took place.

This was the one Baylin knew had been coming since the news of the Amundsen and its jump had broken. "Sam, I admit I knew, but I couldn't tell you, Nemesis has the capacitor but we don't have the jump generator, and I have no idea when we will, they're taking time to build".

169

The Chief looked perplexed, "'Well there must be one some time, and it's not the same type as on the Amundsen, hers deploys, ours is fixed in position, it'll stick nearly forty meters out into space in front of the ship, it's a bit vulnerable if you ask me".

"How do you know that? I didn't know that". Baylin was surprised by the information, but not surprised Carradine had found out.

"I hacked into the propulsion computer data, the specs are there if you know where to look, because of the power demand to charge the capacitors, then deploy it through the energy grid forward to the probe, it explains why the grid cabling is so heavy duty, its way above what the Nemesis needs, even allowing for an upgrade." Carradine was so proud of himself Baylin let slide the fact he'd hacked into classified systems.

"So how does it work?" Baylin had to ask.

"We can bleed energy constantly from the fusion reactor while going about our normal business, top it up with power from the auxiliary nuclear reactor, a routine capacitor charge should be easy. What's not, would be a combat charge. To pull that much power from the reactors to charge a capacitor of that scale, we'd be a sitting duck for nearly twenty minutes".

"I'd suspected as much, from what Andros and DuBret have told me, they were pretty much in such a situation getting back, never mind the navigation issues". Baylin longed to have the jump capability, but its downsides were many right now.

"Well I've been chatting to that specialist of theirs, Lieutenant O'Neil, now she's got her head screwed on about these jump generators, she's brilliant, I could spend a week or two listening to her I can tell you..."

Baylin had the horrible feeling Sam Carradine was smitten again. Every time he found a female engineering type who could talk his language, Sam went weak at the knees.

Chief Carradine went on, "Caroline" - Baylin knew there and then when he called her Caroline, Sam was definitely smitten - "Caroline said, that once the first of these two jump gates is working, they'll provide a tachyon beacon to Procyon Base and the jump gate to Barnards, and that'll create enough of a triangulation to jump back to Procyon with some accuracy, and we can compensate for the gravitons in the heliosphere. We might be about 5 to 10 klicks out, its not precise yet, but that's better than some random guess".

"But we haven't got one yet Sam, so you'll have to talk to the Amundsen, so are we OK?"

"We are, and I've got something else you asked for". Sam flipped a slide onto the Captains' screen. It's the source of those fuel pellets from the Amundsen. They're from the Nullarbor refinery on Ganymede, a totally different set to the rest of the pellets, and they were hijacked out of a shipment nearly two years ago, but that's not all. The police on Ganymede wanted to get to the bottom of it so asked for help from those nice guys at T-Corps, and guess who was assigned to the case?"

Baylin didn't need to, "Major Granding by any chance?" Sam nodded placing a look of intense suspicion on his face suggesting that he'd tried and condemned the major in his head already, though what of, Baylin declined to ask. There was now, no point in delaying the inevitable. He and Granding would have to have a one to one.

After some discussions on fighter engine maintenance and the a problem with a subtle comms malfunction, Baylin was up to date and Sam left.

He tracked down Major Granding, he was in a fighter simulator, apparently training for his pilots wings. Baylin let him have time to finish and said he'd expect the major in his office an hour later.

It was a long hour. Few people bothered Baylin, few got under his skin, and fewer still had the ability to literally, get in his head. Granding was a basic T2, but that was well above the average human, who were basically zeros. T2 was enough - enhanced he was apparently a T7, which was powerful enough to push past any defences a well trained counter intelligence T6 could muster.

The major arrived on time, and in uniform, and went straight in with the usual smooth, seductive charm, "Hello Bruce, I thought our paths might have crossed a little before now, I've missed you, talking to you".

Baylin was not amused. "First off, *Major* Granding, you'll refer to me as Captain Baylin, unless I specifically grant you permission to do otherwise, is that clear?"

"Oh, OK sir, if that's the way you want to conduct our relationship, that's fine with me". Granding was giving off that energy, that something, that made people either fall for him in a second or pull back just as quickly. Baylin found himself recoiling from it, much to his personal satisfaction.

"Relationship? We had a relationship many years ago, but that I can assure you is nothing more than a matter of record, and won't be discussed again. I asked you to come her for entirely practical reasons".

"I apologise sir, how can I help?" Granding smiled, no, Baylin thought, more smirked, the words out in that over confident smugness he'd come to hate, that had the undertone of 'I know you want me, everyone wants me, if not now, then later'. What had he ever seen in this guy?

Baylin had been trained to detect what telepaths could do quite easily to most humans without them noticing, something simply described as a surface scan, they could pick up immediate thought, overall impressions, sharp emotions, but he felt nothing from Granding. Perhaps he knew Baylin would detect him.

The best thing was to concentrate on the purpose of the meeting. "Major two years ago, you were seconded to help solve a hijacking, that took place some six hours from Ganymede, it involved some fuel pellets from a transfer ship heading to Titan".

"I recall that sir, yes. But it wasn't about fuel pellets, it was about the disappearance of the Governor's daughter. She was believed to have been kidnapped, everything suggested that was the case but certain things made no sense, and I was called in. I soon found out that she was in a relationship with the captain of the freighter, he didn't know she was even on board when we caught up with him a day later. We were going to let him go, but under an authorised scan she'd seen something. They were boarded, a whole shipping container was taken and replaced with another.

He said he'd been told his family would be killed if he told anyone he'd been boarded when interrogated again. That's when the pellets were

172

taken, but he really didn't know how they knew or why they wanted them. He was surprised it was just one containers worth".

"So what happened afterwards?" asked Baylin.

"The daughter went back to Ganymede, I'd found her, so I was taken off the case. I asked who was going to follow up the pellet case but was told that was a simple police matter. Nobody wants a telepath poking about unless its a possible murder, or a secret that needs keeping, or exposing".

"So you have no idea what happened to the fuel pellets?" The captain was hoping this would have been so much easier.

"Well I do have one theory Captain Baylin".

"Please enlighten me Major".

"I think the pellets weren't stolen, I think the the container that replaced the one removed from the transport, contained the faulty ones and they were managed through the supply chain on to the Amundsen - I think they'd have been managed onto the first ship with the jump generator system, and it happened to be the Amundsen. I think this was planned a long time ago".

Baylin thanked the major and dismissed him. The major went to look back as the door opened, but Baylin had turned away to avoid just such an occurrence.

All he could now do was let DuBret know what he found out. He could do no more, trying to open up the cold case on these fuel pellets was totally beyond his remit, he'd be blocked as soon as he tried to enquire, and any enquiry would raise a dozen red flags.

Captain Andros was too busy with gate reconstruction to be involved, he couldn't leave himself because the Amundsen needed the Nemesis to protect her. DuBret would have to find the Tutankh's and solve the mystery. Which is just what Admiral Ferris had suggested she do.

He decided not to assume this was all part of some conspiracy, just because DuBret was now faced with doing what she'd been empowered - but not ordered - to do. And yet he just couldn't get it out of his mind. He simply didn't believe in coincidence when it seemed so convenient.

When the team and ships returned with the third arm of the jump gate, it was time to re-assemble it and this was something Baylin had never seen. Leaving the Nemesis in the hands of his first officer, Markus Obishka, he shuttled over to the Amundsen to watch the process first hand.

Captain Andros was busy but very accommodating, seeming to enjoy the fact that DuBret and Baylin were so interested in what the Amundsen could do. When Baylin was invited to go out with the reassembly team, just to observe, he jumped at the chance.

Suited up and with an almost childlike wonder at the what he was about to witness, he followed jump gate specialist Lieutenant O'Neil out of the airlock and for the first time in a long time, he was floating in space. The gate was massive, simply an awe-inspiring site. Until you see something like this directly, with your own eyes, and at such a personal scale, you just don't truly comprehend the enormity of such things. The Nemesis was just 5 klicks away, and looked huge even at that range. She was angled facing him with her forward starboard quarter view, looking menacing and powerful. It made him smile and very happy.

To his right and stunningly close, the Amundsen, her size, gate building arms holding the two gate segments in place, was simply awe-inspiring.

The third gate arm had to be manually inspected, and O'Neil took the Captain down to stand on its surface, a team of robodrones were tugging it lightly up to meet the third arm segment of the extended pylons provided by the Amundsen.

O'Neil stopped the movement, which was relatively easy and quick as the robodrones were able to balance the deceleration swiftly. O'Neil walked along the inner face of the arm, kneeling down at what Baylin noticed earlier, long black scorch marks. "These aren't recent", she announced on the open mic. Using a portable scanner that took about thirty seconds, the scorch marks were announced as being around 2,300 Earth Standard Years old.

"That means these were made around 100BC, before Caesar had even occupied Britain, what the hell was going on out here?" Baylin's inherent interest in things historical, a subject largely disdained by the vast majority, who found humanities past to be at best, an inconvenient truth.

O'Neil looked back at the Captain, "I know right? Humans were on horseback, no more than a sword in hand and out here, somebody was probably waging a war", O'Neil also had historical leanings but rarely found anyone she could discuss them with.

"I wonder who though, and why destroy a gate, I mean that's no easy thing to do", Baylin felt like he was musing to himself, but O'Neil replied, "I've looked into that, as part of my thesis back at Fleet Academy. The only way to wreck a gate completely is, theoretically, to open a jump point inside an already open jump point, but it's never been done. I postulated it would create around a gigaton equivalent explosion and shatter the gate. The problem is actually opening a point in an open gate is impossible, you have to open it at the normal space end to overload the gate. It's certain doom for a ship trying it".

"Well what happened here then, the gate was mostly intact?" Baylin was very curious.

"I think it was deliberately severed from the rest and I suspect it was moved out there on purpose, like the one near Titan, I think somebody, two millennia ago, deliberately disabled the gates, to stop someone getting into the system". O'Neil had long held the theory and she wasn't the only one, but despite its dark web popularity, nobody would discuss it as more than a conspiracy theory in academia. Baylin knew that, which is why he so wanted to talk with O'Neil more.

"Lieutenant, I'd like to talk to you about this more, would you be open to it?" Baylin had to ask.

"If you're going to talk about it Captain, do it now, we're out here, on a closed loop unmonitored channel on short range frequencies nobody can pick up this far away, it's as private as it gets".

"I've only got 45 minutes of air left", he replied, hoping for more.

"Me too, so get talking sir".

"How many of these damaged gates have you found?"

"Personally, four. Two here, one on Barnards, and Vega".

"Did they have anything in common?"

"The same MO, every time, usually one piece was moved so far away it was difficult to recover or it was deliberately buried".

"Is that all?"

"Is there something else Captain, what do you know?"

"Have you noticed that none of the gates that lead to Sol have been destroyed from the entry system?" Baylin was trying to word this more explicitly.

"I don't get what you mean sir?"

"The gate at Sol was disabled, but not the gate Sol led to in Barnards. Three other gates exist at Barnards and all three of those were disabled, but the one at Proxima that led to Barnards Star, the one at 61 Cygni that came to Barnards, they were intact. But 61 Cygni to Procyon, that was disabled, but on this side it wasn't, and the two others, that lead out of the system, again both disabled". It was confusing to say, but O'Neil could see what he was saying in her head.

With a dawning realisation, she got what he was trying to get across, "Oh, yeah, I get it, it's as though someone was retreating back to the Sol system, back to Earth, and destroyed the gates behind them having jumped, stopping anyone chasing them down. It's the only plausible theory because Earth is the last in the sequence and the only exit gate as well as the only entry. By disabling it, there was no way in - or out".

"So the question, is who and where, are they now?" Added Baylin.

"Captain have you ever heard of the Sidus Lulium"?

"Not that I recall, what is it?"

"In 44BC a huge comet was seen over Rome and in China, burning across the sky with astonishing brightness. Romans said it was the soul of Julius

Caesar, and he'd ascended to godhood. It's never returned, and most comets, they do come back, this never has".

"What are you saying? That it was some alien ship?" Baylin felt like the conversation was drifting into farce, perhaps this had been a mistake.

"Why not, what if they destroyed the gates to protect a primitive Earth culture from whatever was out here, maybe even still is?"

"Well it's something to consider I suppose". Baylin felt like he'd been dragged into a conspiracy theory and he felt himself above those, but he did like a mystery.

Little more was said, and they headed back to the gate maintenance shuttle. Back aboard, the technicians were running diagnostics on the gate arm, sensors showed it to be intact, and easily capable of being reintegrated to the rest of the gate. Baylin found this extraordinary. 2,000 years plus of lying about in space and it was still fully functional? Still with enough Astatine-85 to make it work? How was it even possible that something that old hadn't deteriorated? And that wasn't the half of it, because the gates were actually some 20,000 years old, it had only been inoperable for around 2,000 of them. Whoever made the gate system did so for obvious reasons, but where were they?

As Baylin daydreamed, watching others work, he began to think he should really be back on the Nemesis. As if on command the comlink beeped at him and he placed the privacy speaker in his ear, "Obishka here sir, just checking in, you're due on watch in two hours, is everything on schedule?"

"Going like clockwork Markus, it's been fascinating, the gate will be up and running by the time I'm back on board".

"OK sir if there's going to be any delays getting you back, please advise".

"Will do".

Markus was always chasing him, but he liked it, he was an outstanding First Officer. As he thought it, O'Neil announced their return to the Amundsen, and he suddenly realised the giant exploration ship had disengaged from the gate, as he looked around almost everything else had. They were the last away.

The shuttle backed away from the gate arm, turned and headed back to the Amundsen. Twenty minutes later he was on board the Nemesis smallest personnel shuttle, just him and a pilot and some spare parts. The broadcast channels opened up on almost every frequency, "This is the Amundsen, repeat this is the Amundsen, we have a jump initiated in the gate, its not us, all ships alert!"

"Pilot hit the throttle, I need to be on the Nemesis now", Baylin looked back over his shoulder as the gate did that thing, each of the triple arms sparked light from the initiators, then it flashed, as it did so, the pilot banked round so Baylin couldn't see and they were approaching the gaping maw of the Nemesis landing bay.

Baylin was out of his seat and through the shuttle doors so fast the pilot hardly saw him move, he was through the lock and into the bridge elevator faster than he could think, the klaxon sounded as the ship went to red alert, the doors opened onto the bridge after what seemed like an age but was little under 90 seconds from shuttle bay to bridge.

"Captain on the Bridge"

"I have the con First Officer, what's the situation?"

"The jump gate appears to have self activated, its open, Amundsen is backing away fast, both ships on red alert, weapons hot, awaiting your orders".

"Comms get me Captain Andros".

"Captain Baylin".

"Captain Andros what can you see? We're not able to see down into the gate from here".

"We've backed away, it would be good if you could put yourself between us and the gate, I don't have any firepower".

"Do I need it?" Baylin was planning to launch fighters.

"Well the jump point is open, and its been open for almost four minutes, which is really un... wait, wait, something is coming through..."

Baylin gave the order "target the gate entrance for anything that comes through and launch all fighters".

Already in their cockpits the fighter pilots automatic drop system kicked in as each bay door opened and they bolted into the black of space.

The Nemesis had gained speed and swung itself into a place where it could see down into the gate...then the sensors went off the scale.

"Captain, it's small, about the size of a shuttle but its actively scanning us and its transmitting back into the gate, its deliberately triggering the gate to stay open, Amundsen is trying to shut it down", shouted weapons Officer Tambakoi.

"Jammers on full, blanket the EM field and stop it," Baylin ordered.

The Nemesis brand new multi-spectrum electronic counter measures suite was twenty times more powerful than the one on the Ramorra, and as the electromagnetic disruption wave whacked the gate and the small ship, the gate collapsed its jump point.

The ship was clearly off balance for a moment, seeming to go dead, but it was momentary, it deployed a set of what looked like wings and powered up its engines, it began moving, fast...

"Get Putinova on," Baylin commanded.

The Fighter Squadron leader was on in a second, "Captain, shall I take it out?"

"Stop it, Putinova, slow it, stop it, do not let it get away, I can't have it wandering Procyon scanning everything, if you think its getting away, kill it".

"Aye sir", Putinova went offline and the bridge witnessed the fighters accelerate rapidly towards the probe ship.

"Mr Tambakoi, what have we got that could disable it but not kill it?"

"Nothing sir, only the PDC's and they're out of range, all of our weaponry would blow it to atoms".

Baylin knew it, but he needed to be sure. He looked at Markus, "It's down to Putinova now, she has to catch it or kill it".

Six of Putinova's squadron were close enough, but the ship, it was more clearly than ever some kind of advanced automated probe, was extraordinarily sophisticated. It had some kind of point defence cannons that were fast and very capable at tracking them. Only skill and wits kept her pilots from getting hit. And it was jamming them, very actively.

"Nemesis, can you counter some of this jamming from the probe, its overwhelming our targeting system, can't get an automated lock".

"Negative Squad Leader, Nemesis can't focus countermeasures that tight at this range, you'll have to got to manual".

"Shit. Squad leader to all fighters, manual targeting, go to max thrust and out to 120% if you have to, stop that ship!"

The fighters weaved around and flipped up and down, side to side to avoid the exceptionally fast probe, as it banked and yawed with extraordinary agility, then Flight Officer Bendix in Fighter Five managed to hit the PDC with a rocket strike at close range, when it erred and came back at him trying to throw one of the others off.

Putinova was establishing a kill zone, getting the six fighters into a rough global position, trying to get the probe ship towards its centre, its automatic threat assessment didn't know where to escape to, so it came back at one of the fighters.

PDC down, it swerved and manoeuvred ever more remarkably and erratically, Putinova knew they'd never get another go at this, they couldn't keep it locked in for long, "all fighters, arm both rocket packs, close and fire on my order".

"Close" - all 6 fighters shot forward towards the marauding evasive probe ship, when they got close enough, "FIRE!"

A stream of twelve hyper-velocity unguided rockets that couldn't be jammed but only fired at close range, leapt forward from five of the fighters, and six from Bendix's that had already fired one pack.

The brilliant white trails lit up space - they could even be seen from the Amundsen now nearly 60 klicks away, as 66 rockets detonated almost simultaneously, blowing the probe to dust.

Baylin sensed immediately what had happened, "get a shuttle out there and get me evidence, as much wreckage as you can find and I don't care how small it is".

"Putinova, that was a job well done, you have my thanks, make sure your pilots know how impressed we all are". He looked at Markus, "well that was some spectacular flying".

"No arguments from me Captain, but where did that thing come from and what was it?"

"Captain Andros, how much data did you collect?"

"Well not as much as I'd like to have done with all your jamming, but enough, it's on its way to you".

"Markus, get Science and Engineering on the tracking and merge the data with the Amundsen's, I want to know if that was definitely a probe or something else, and confirm if it was manned or not".

Baylin went to his office. "Computer, open a secure channel to Admiral Ferris". The ships com net sent its encrypted tachyon signal via Procyon base and its booster, through hyperspace and the gate relays, all the way to Earth in just seconds.

After a short delay Admiral Ferris connected "Captain you have something?" Ferris yawned, it was 2am in Monrovia.

"Sir, we connected the jump gate, a sophisticated probe was ready and waiting to come through as soon as we did, it's been destroyed. Sir, it sent a signal back through the gate on a tight encrypted beam, not for long, but it's safe to assume...sir, they know where we are".

CHAPTER 23

TELLTALE

Captain DuBret closed the coms link form the Nemesis - Baylin had given her just thirty-six hours before she had to go back - they were going through the Jump Gate.

In effect that meant she had little more than twenty hours to reach the Tutankh's, get them to surrender the planners of the attack on the Amundsen and then race back to the Amundsen for the jump transit.

They were two hours out from the Tutankh base and she knew they would be on high alert, what choice did they have? The question was would they let her onto the base to hear what she had to say, or was this going to be a question of guns held to heads?

She was relying on there being no real military opposition in space. She'd guessed, as it happened quite rightly, that the Tutankh's had used up everything they had in the Amundsen attack. What she wanted to know was who paid for it and why did they do it? And ideally, to arrest those who planned it. She felt she'd probably get the questions answered, but to get them the deal would be immunity for anyone involved in the planning, and if she knew the Tutankh clan that would mean just one or maybe two, because everyone else would have been on the now destroyed ships.

She had one, possibly two aces up her sleeve, thoughtfully furnished by the two other captains, but she hoped it wouldn't come to that.

She was in an odd position, effectively an acting Rear-Admiral - senior officer in charge of two commanded ships, and she'd chosen to base herself on the gunship *Patton*. These ships were all about fire power, speed and manoeuvrability. Minimal protection was long a foible of such ships. They were designed to be mass produced in the event of an emergency and blast anything to dust they couldn't run away from.

The were oddly aerodynamic, allowing them the rare ability to land on a planet, making them ideal for local defence. Their front end was a huge, almost whale-like section, with a 'lip' that held sensors and tracking systems. Above and below that, behind a dozen gun port doors, an array of fearsome nuclear capable kinetic rail guns, kinetic cannons and unguided bombardment rockets, all of which could be fired simultaneously at one close target, it made them lethal.

The approach to Dendera was familiar to DuBret, she'd often practiced it on Procyon's simulators. She made the decision to approach the planetoid with gun ports closed, and not use active military scanners to spook them into doing anything. An hour out the passive scanners picked up Dendera's early warning system.

"Open a channel to Dendera please, I need to speak to the Chief Councilperson".

You could have heard a pin drop on the bridge of the Patton when Maris Karanska came on screen. All eyes turned to DuBret, back to Karanska, and back to DuBret. The resemblance was striking.

"I'd been told you were at Procyon Base Captain DuBret". Karanska smiled, knowing how caught off guard François DuBret must be.

"Maris? You're Maris Karanska?" DuBret instantly wished she hadn't been so patently and obviously surprised, not publicly anyway. How had this tidbit of information managed to evade the expensive Alliance intelligence networks? Her own long forsaken sister was running the Tutankh Clan?"

Karanska wasn't looking for conflict, "I don't suppose you're here for a family reunion, but you may as well come down here, you won't be harmed. You can bring two people with you, but no weapons, you look like you've got enough of those on those gunships".

"You must know I'm here over the attack on the Amundsen?"

"I know, but don't expect to leave here with anyone."

"That might not be possible, unless you can convince me it's not necessary".

"I'll send coordinates for the dock, you'll be here in less than 45 minutes".

Karanska cut the link. She had to think fast about how they were going to get out of this one. Those gunships could trash the surface and the dockyards. In a few minutes they'd be able to detect that ships were already being re-fitted, and that would be another lost bargaining chip.

She'd thought about an emergency evacuation but what use would that be? She had but one valuable chip to lay down in this game, and that would buy them time, potentially it could cause some serious repercussions down the road, but what of it? There was always something, it was always 'just down the road'. Keeping it there was the art of the game. Living on Dendera was always precarious, always would be.

Maris waited in the same dock not more than a few days back she'd greeted Mr Athanasios. The Alliance shuttle arrived and docked. Maris had alerted the other council members and they'd agreed their only approach with surprising ease. They all knew they had no other card to play.

Maris looked at François DuBret - a full captain in the Fleet, and a reputation for fierce efficiency on Procyon Base. She hadn't seen her in the flesh since she was 6 years old, but there was no mistaking her, their looks were remarkably similar, despite the three years between them.

DuBret found this experience uncomfortable but had no intention of letting family matters mix with business. To be sure about it she'd brought Major Granding with her, something Captain Baylin had suggested. Strictly speaking he needed legal authority to be scanning Maris, she was an Alliance citizen and subject to all the legal privacy protections that afforded her, but she was also a potential conspirator and criminal, which ameliorated some of those protections, even if evidence couldn't be used in court.

Granding was in civilian clothes, and introduced as an Alliance lawyer, but he was also there to conduct surface scans and ascertain when truths had become less than accurate.

The third member of the team was an obvious Marine, but he was unarmed. However he was also one of the highest rated hand to hand combat specialists in the fleet. DuBret felt more than capable of dealing with any likely issues.

Maris wasn't going to make that mistake, she greeted DuBret with a surprising amount of warmth, "It's been a long, long time François. It's a pity it's under theses circumstances".

DuBret wasn't too bothered by the approach, "I've been on Procyon Military Base for over two years Maris, if you'd really wanted to say hello, you could have said something long before now, but that's not why I'm here. This isn't a social call."

"I didn't think it was, but…" Maris carried on with the banter and DuBret seemed to go along with it. Major Granding was uneasy however. He listened to the two of them being almost, but falsely, sisterly, dancing around the inevitable conversation. Yet there was something wrong here, Maris Karanska had some taint, something that wasn't her, but something she'd been in contact with. It was like a darkness, a clouded, masked, shadow of something that had left an indelible but distant stain on her soul, for want of a better description. And it wasn't just her, this room echoed with a feint disturbance, like someone or something bad had been here. He was at a total loss to describe it any more accurately.

Captain DuBret made it clear to Maris Karanska, that the attack on the Amundsen had been a massive error of judgement by the Tutankh's and she was here to seek justice.

Maris wasn't going to give anyone up, and François had expected that from the get go, that was something the clan would never do. She pushed Maris into the inevitable corner.

"Look, Maris, I'm prepared to accept your claim that those who planned the assault on the Amundsen died, in the attack. However I can only accept that if you, and this is the minimum, accept trackers on your ships, arm them with nothing more than defence cannons, and tell me who hired you and why".

Maris objected to the limit on the freighters weapons, very strongly, but Granding could tell that was a ruse, she was in reality almost too happy to concede the point even as she made a strenuous fuss over not doing so. She genuinely didn't approve of the trackers and hadn't expected that to be asked of the clan, but Granding could tell she was almost too willing to give that point away too.

"Captain DuBret, as the Alliance lawyer may I have a word, privately". Granding smiled. Maris agreed, and Granding and DuBret went back to their shuttle for privacy leaving Maris with the marine, who's utterly blank and intimidating glare would unease anyone.

"What is it Major?" DuBret was anxious to know.

"It's too easy, she's making it seem verbally hard to accept, but she's not bothered, what you're asking of her, I'd say she'd have accepted far harsher terms. Even the tracking, she doesn't like it but she gave it up in her mind far sooner than she verbalised it. And there's something else, someone else has been here, she's had contact with them, they were in the very room we're in, someone very important, there's a power to their presence, their influence is lurking here, like its watching everyone from a distance, it's just extremely odd".

"You think we're being monitored? Or she is?" DuBret was curious.

"No not monitored in the usual way, it's almost like there's something in the deep background running like a tiny, almost insubstantial piece of code, but at a psychic level, it's like it's lodged into the deepest darkest places, you, most ordinaries, you'd never know".

"Well what am I supposed to say to that? Oh Maris theres' a ghost hanging about, say, who was here the other day?"

"Actually, yes".

"Granding, I think its best you stay here on the shuttle". DuBret was not amused at all.

"Please, hear me out, if you ask her directly, she'll think about it, directly. I can scan that and see for myself".

"You're sure? Because if she thinks you're scanning her she'll take quite a different path I can promise you, this is the Tutankh clan after all".

"Captain, she'll broadcast what I want to see if you ask her a direct question, I won't need to scan her, ask her directly who ordered the attack, ask her immediately who paid for it and then why".

"This had better work Major Granding, because I do not, repeat do not, want to have to fight my way out of here".

"It will be fine captain, I promise you".

They returned to the room having been gone over five minutes. DuBret went straight in, "Maris we can make a formal deal, but I need to know who paid for the attack, who financed your weapons, and what was their objective?"

Granding watched Maris Karanska, keeping his gaze on her, as the words 'formal deal' registered he saw instant relief, at the first part of the question, 'who paid', he felt immediate reluctance, but she wasn't surprised by the question, there was a slight smugness in fact, she'd expected it - but he also saw that that expectation was very much tinged with inevitability - she knew she would have to say who and she was prepared to do so. He could see a figure in her head, a man, dark, little detail, almost a cypher, he wasn't what he appeared to be.

Maris Karanska said the words, "He has a name, oddly enough I could barely describe him, enigmatic would be an understatement".

"And his name is?" Asked DuBret with a little impatience starting to show.

"Mr Athanasios, he goes by the name of Athanasios".

Granding tried not to smile, DuBret looked mildly relieved, "Can you give me an image, video, voice records?"

"Not a chance, he never lets anything get recorded, whenever he's here all video, sound recording at the air lock is switched off, just as it was when you arrived, but for different reasons. We don't surveil our people here, there's no cameras in the corridors or public spaces". She said the words to conceal, in reality there were quite a few cameras across the public areas of the colony.

"Well why did he pay and what did he want?" DuBret was insistent on knowing. Once again Granding knew Maris Karanska was willing to give it up. What she said though, that was not at all what either of them had expected.

Fleet, Baylin, Andros, DuBret, all assumed they wanted the Amundsen, as a jump capable base ship for piracy purposes, leaping in and out of systems to raid space lanes at will.

"He wanted the jump generator, he wasn't even interested in the ship itself. We were to board it, take it out to a remote spot in the system, cut the generator out, not even the capacitor, and download the software, he didn't care what happened to the Amundsen afterwards, left that to us to decide, by which I mean my husband, not me personally".

Granding knew she was telling the truth, he looked at the Captain and blinked once slowly, telling her that her long lost sister was being truthful.

"What does he expect you to do now? People like him have colleagues and backers, you didn't get what they wanted, so what's the deal?" DuBret's experience on Procyon had taught her that out here in these deep space communities, everything had a price, this Mr Athanasios would want some pay back for the clans failure.

Maris fidgeted, this was part of the conversation she hadn't wanted to have and Granding could tell she was inclined to be evasive now.

"We have to do some unarmed freight work, I have no idea what or when, he paid for some work on the freighters to get them back in service, we lost six because of the Amundsen. None of them are ready, it'll be weeks yet."

That last bit was a lie, Granding could tell she wasn't being truthful. DuBret was quick enough to focus the question more directly on the when, "Maris I need to know when the first ship will be ready?"

"At least three to four weeks." Karanska could barely say the words.

Granding could tell she meant two and noted it down.

DuBret asked the final question, "Where is Athanasios now?"

"I honestly don't know, really, he leaves here and where or how he goes, I haven't the slightest idea".

Granding could tell she was telling the truth. But now there was something else. Imminent threat, he sensed imminent threat, two men were approaching the bay. He stood up, "Captain we have to go, Marine, secure the corridor".

DuBret looked at him, furious, "what the..."

"We have to go, get to the shuttle", as he said it DuBret felt a sharp image in her head, shadowy figures in the corridor, she did as she was told, Maris looked on bemused, "what's going on, you haven't..."

As she stood up, she could see the Captain and the lawyer vanish down the corridor, rapidly followed by the marine, she looked up the corridor, two men, both with pulse rifles, they pointed not down the corridor after the fleeing Captain, but at her, she knew, right then, her days were over, the butt of a rifle smacked into her jaw, she dropped to the floor, a boot knocked her unconscious.

An hour later, worried about where she might be, Collin Mcreedy and Devin Hoon found her body, both hands cut from her wrists and her head slumped back over the chair, throat slit from side to side, blood everywhere.

CHAPTER 24

LUYTEN

The jump gate had worked flawlessly, a beacon had been established to its destination as though 2,000 years had been just seconds. The beacon gave enough information to provide a transit time of just 68 hours. The transit was uneventful with the exception of DuBret and Granding's briefing on the Dendera situation. For now everyone agreed it was best to sit on the information and let DuBret's contacts handle things from Procyon. It wasn't their primary mission.

Nemesis triggered the gate the other end and flew through first, with the gunships behind her, and then the Amundsen. There was nothing surprising except where they were and even that had been largely calculated based on the time of travel. The EZ Aquari system, better known as Luyten 789-6 after its discoverer (Wilem Jacob Luyten who first observed it on Earth), no doubt from now on just as Luyten A, B & C. A wide ranging trinary star system. Three mediocre red dwarf stars, old and worn out, two of them barely able to maintain their fusion process.

The Amundsen quickly ascertained it was yet another asteroid strewn expanse, but it had one key difference. There was a single, Mars-like planet, around 65 million klicks from Lutyens-A , and at least two other jump gates, one far out at the edges of the B star, but one, one was virtually in orbit around the planet, a so far almost unheard of situation.

Everyone was aware their arrival in the system through the jump gate would have triggered any sensors and warnings for any other race capable of using the gates. The arrival of the alien probe at Procyon suggested it had been patrolling looking for a gate, yet the two science officers on both Amundsen and Nemesis were quick to point out it seemed to have foreknowledge enough to be there instantly. How that was even possible became clear only a few hours after their arrival in the new system.

During an intra-ship briefing the two science departments, jointly, pieced an alien electronic device back together, it was one of the larger pieces of alien tech they'd recovered. It explained much and would prove to be a major technical discovery for Fleet. The device was in essence, a super-sensitive hyper space filter. It was able to reduce hyperspatial and gravimetric interference by some 200% compared to current Earth tech. It made it possible to reduce interference so much, a wider array of hyper space beacon signals between gates could be detected, making them easier to find. It was also able to detect where jump gates should be based on those signals.

The device however was not stable, having been damaged, but scans and specifications were already on their way to ARPA (Advanced Research projects Agency), for analysis and development of a system that would work on Earth ships. It could be game changing.

As the small fleet moved further into the system, tensions were high. The gunships were locked down on the Amundsen and fighters kept in their bays. Passive sensors ran their algorithms looking for signals, communications, any electromagnetic activity. Bridge crews paced and waited as the two ships headed through the asteroid fields. These were not the packed dense fields of science fiction. There was plenty of space between the rocks, and the Amundsen's geologists remained quietly disappointed that it seemed over 85% were silica or iron, around 6% water ice and the rest a mix of semi-desirable commodities, with barely 0.5% worthy of sending in extraction ships.

The planet - now catalogued as Lutyens-A-1, was slowly becoming definable. As they crossed out of the asteroids, it was almost alone, a rotation of some 36 hours suggested it had sowed markedly over the millennia, a sure sign of an old planetary system.

"I really don't like this system". Captain Baylin announced to his bridge crew.

Science Officer Marilyn Gold laughed, "why Captain are you being systemist?"

"There is no such word Lieutenant Gold as you well know. I just don't like that it's so quiet, so ridiculously quiet. That probe came from somewhere, it's been through this system because it must have used the gate we have. There's something we're not seeing".

The ships system noises and background sounds were quiet, and yet in the silence of people doing their jobs, the expectation of search and discovery, they seemed irritatingly cacophonous to Baylin.

He kept thinking about DuBret who's sister had by all accounts been executed minutes after the Captain, a marine and Major Granding had gotten away. If Granding hadn't been there they'd probably all have been killed as they'd kept faith and not gone armed. He supposed he should thank Granding for his alertness.

He made a decision, not based on his upper level thoughts but on what was skulking in the back of his mind, "get me Captain Andros and pipe it through to the office please coms".

He left the Captains chair, passing the con to Gold.

"Captain Andros for you sir."

"Put him through."

"What can I do for you Bruce?" Andros was sounding quite breezy, still delighted with the discovery their teams had made about the hyperspace filter.

"I'm going to send out a pair of fighters with recon pods to the planet, I think we should hold position out here about half a million klicks away, let them do a first pass", Baylin had decided this would be a better course of action, just in case there was a trap, or some defence system they weren't ready for.

"We can send one of our survey shuttles, you're guys could escort them, those things are packed out with surveillance tech, if there's something there, they'll find it". Andros didn't like the idea of a warship getting the credit for any first discoveries, that was what the Amundsen was about, but Baylin had assumed the request was coming. As the most senior Captain he could pull rank, but hoped he wouldn't need to.

"I'm not interested in taking credit for discoveries Gregor, I just want a military evaluation, I don't want to pull up in orbit and find we've got the planetary gravity well behind us as we try and get out of some trap at speed".

"OK Bruce, if that's what you feel is best, but I want a survey shuttle down there as soon as its cleared".

"Deal, I'll keep you posted on what they find".

Baylin waited for the comms to clear then called in Gold and Obishka.

"OK this is the plan, send out two fighters with a full countermeasures suite and a recon pod, no extra weapons, keep them light, fast and manoeuvrable. Run a cursory passive, then an active scan and see if it triggers anything off".

"What if it does?" asked Markus instantly.

"Run". Baylin replied and it was clear he wasn't joking. He carried on, "Lieutenant Gold, make sure the recon packs are set to pick up anything we've detected before from the Ramorra and the probe, and have one cover narrow spectrum EM, especially Hyper-S-Band - the type the aliens used for their PDC's, if you've any recommendations and can make them fit, feel free to do so".

After a quick breath, Baylin, clearly feeling excited, added "Markus, the counter measures pods are designed to take our transmitted energy if they need to as well, yes?"

"They are but we'd have to be in a tactical supporting position, that only works if we're under 100 klicks away, and in direct line of sight".

"Then make sure that we can reach them quickly, tack us around to follow them, but at around 1000 klicks, we can be there in two minutes if we hit full thrust".

"But what about the Amundsen?"

"Advise captain Andros to drop the gunships and be ready for anything, but under no circumstances close on the planet". Baylin was expecting trouble, Markus could tell, but he didn't know why, there'd been no sign of anything.

"I'll let Putinova know, how soon do you want her to go?"

"Give it an hour, we'll follow the fighters round to an entry trajectory, and that'll give Gold time to spec the pods and get them loaded on the fighters".

"Aye sir!" Markus and Gold both left the office already planning on the execution of the Captains orders.

"What do you think he's expecting down there, it's dead, there's not a hint of anything," Gold was hoping Markus knew more than he seemed to.

"I have no idea, but he's got a scenario in his head, which means he's put himself in their shoes, if they wear them, and is working on the basis of what he thinks he would do if he was them, then jumping a step ahead".

"I hope there's nothing there, a battle out here wouldn't be so much fun". Gold headed off to prep the recon pods for the fighters.

In the flight deck briefing room, Squadron Leader Putinova looked at her anxious-to-be-picked pilots sat in their flight suits, helmets at the ready.

"Ladies and Gentlemen, let's make this easy, the Captain is placing his first major mission extension on us, and we have an opportunity to prove our worth. We're in a new system, approaching the only planet in the system, and it has a thin CO_2 atmosphere, with considerable similarities in size and conditions to pre-colonial Mars. We have no idea what's here, it could be a trap, it could be frankly anything, we just don't know. It could also be nothing". Putinova looked around the small room, to see flight officer Kevin Bendix, hand in the air like a school kid needing a toilet break, "Bendix, do you need to relieve yourself?" She asked dryly pointing straight at him from the podium, causing the other eleven pilots to laugh out loud.

"No sir", came the reply, "I'm moist enough already at the idea of this mission", which caused mock vomiting sounds from the other pilots.

"How am I not surprised you've managed that all by yourself Bendix?" Putinova shot back dryly, causing laughter from everyone. She knew that

194

this sort of irreverence and being master of it and over it was crucial. Fighter jocks, male and female were in their own minds an elite, trained at immense expense and hand picked from Fleet Academy graduates, barely one in twenty of those chosen ever made it this far.

"Right people, and Bendix, did you have a question or were you just being Bendix?" There was no reply.

"The mission is technically simple enough, but it comes with caveats. The two recon fighters will be used so four of you will be going, Bendix and Schmidt will fly, Myriam and Salerno you'll be back seat".

"Yeah" said Bendix out loud, "but Salerno'll still think she's driving".

A murmur went round the room, but Putinova had had enough of Bendix, outstanding pilot he might be but he never knew when to shut up, "Bendix, another word from you and you're off the mission". The silence was deafening.

"This is what you'll do: You'll leave the Nemesis and keep a long elliptical entry to go in over the north magnetic pole, the plot will be provided by the time you drop. This is a full active and passive scan, including full video, photographic and electromagnetic frequencies, you'll need to be steady, we need insightful detail, which is why this isn't being left to a probe drone. If you detect anything first hand and feel it needs closer inspection, do it. The data will be streamed live back to the Nemesis, if we see anything be prepared to investigate if we ask for it. If you run into trouble, if there's any hostile action against you, get out, just get out as fast as you can, both you and the fighters are too valuable to loose, even you Bendix". Everyone chuckled, while Bendix fidgeted in minor embarrassment.

Julie Salerno asked' "what type of weapons pods are we carrying sir?"

"You won't be..."

"Sir?"

"This is about speed, you've got the twin pulse canons as standard fit and a fully equipped ECM pod as well as the recon pod, you're not there to fight, you're there to seek and get out, the fewer pods you have the lighter you'll be and the faster you can escape, if you need to. Besides which, the rest of us will be tacking in with the Nemesis. The Captain plans on being within two minutes of you by the time you arrive at the planet, the Nemesis can flood the EM spectrum with countermeasures and boost yours through amplification via your pods if it comes to that. Any more questions?".

"Sir, what about the Amundsen?" asked Haile Myriam.

"She'll hang well back with the gunships as escort, she's not strong enough to deal with a head-on conflict, if she has to she can jump out and the gunships will stay with us".

She looked around the room, "Anyone else?" Nothing was said. "In that case fifteen minutes to drop, good luck".

Baylin had watched the briefing, unknown to the pilots. Bendix was amusing, but he felt, likely prone to grand gestures at inopportune moments. He'd come across his type again and again. They were often skilled pilots but needed close monitoring. He wondered why Putinova had chosen a skilled combat pilot for a recon mission. But it was her call, she knew him best.

Baylin looked at the main screen and noticed the Amundsen extend her mid-ship docking arms as the gunships detached.

The flight deck control showed green on all fighters.

Baylin left his office and went to the bridge taking the con, everyone was in place.

"First Officer, sound red alert, arm all weapons, activate armour system, advise Captains DuBret and Andros…"

It was time.

CHAPTER 25

PATTERNS

Procyon Military Base was a vast sprawling complex that Commodore Naomi Tan, its commanding officer, felt made her more the governor of a small country. The base was all order and process, things ran like clockwork. However, let it be said that the Procyon system itself, well it was a very spread out and diverse place, complete with outlaws and pirates, robber barons and religious nuts. But there were many more honest hard working people who just wanted to make a living on the edge of the space age version of the wild west.

It was those people that Commodore Tan felt morally obliged to defend and protect more than any other. The big corporate mining companies didn't always like that aspect of her job, but they respected her authority. That was as much a function of the Alliance and Fleet as anything else. Procyon was profitable and still massively under-exploited.

Sometimes she felt more like the sheriff, and all to frequently found herself at the centre of judicial decisions. That was soon to be taken out of her hands, as finally, Earth was establishing a permanent civil court and judiciary in the system.

This morning was however quite different. Captain DuBret, one of her most exceptional officers and one of three deputies, had been seconded to run a pair of gunships and work with the explorer ship Amundsen and the new heavy cruiser, Nemesis.

DuBret had contacted her over a highly secure communication directly, explaining the loss of her sister, who she was, how she and the Tutankh Clan had been somehow caught up in the Amundsen attack. She'd explained the existence of an extraordinary individual who should become the commodore's focus, but at the same time couldn't emphasise that he couldn't know he was the centre of that focus.

Indeed DuBret's words when it came to this extraordinary figure, who went by the name of Mr Athanasios, were "trust no-one". This was more easily said than done. As a commodore she had access to huge resources, but she could hardly go around poking her nose in without being seen. Off of the military base she wasn't even permitted to go anywhere without four Fleet Security Service agents.

There was one person she knew she could trust, because if she couldn't there was really no point in being here. Base Security Chief Todd Carollio. He had the capacity to look out for what mattered and didn't get caught up fighting stupid little battles that made the locals angry. Smuggling porcini mushrooms in hand luggage wasn't something he'd be bothered with, hand guns and explosives, well that was a whole other matter. What he especially despised was if someone thought they could get away with pulling the wool over his eyes, on his station? You didn't want to be on the wrong side of Chief Carollio.

Unswervingly loyal to his men, he gave his loyalty to those above him only with time and proof. Two years in and he was more than willing to take the commodore at face value, indeed if pushed he might even admit he liked her. She'd proven competent and gave him leeway to do his job without constant interference. Naomi Tan knew he could be trusted and she couldn't do what she needed to do without him.

Using his private link, Commodore Tan made the overture, "Chief Carollio, would you meet me in my quarters at 1800 hours? There's a matter I need to discuss".

Carollio, a 1.85m tall, bald, blue eyed Italian with a passion for salami sticks and weight lifting, had never been to the Commodore's quarters. They were in the green sector on the outer rim of the command block tower, and had some of the finest views imaginable out here. Senior officer quarters were actually above the Quarter Master Accommodation complex for base personnel, some of the few with windows to the system beyond.

He arrived right on time, having dithered between uniform and civvies he'd opted for the later, after speaking to the protocol office, but without telling them the exact scenario.

He pressed the door buzzer to the Commodore's quarters and the double door slid open, she was there on the other side to greet him. He breathed a sigh of almost palpable relief that she was also in civilian clothing, a smart casual pant suit in a fashionable (not that he knew it was fashionable), aquamarine. He always forgot how small the Commodore was, at barely 1.6m. She seemed unusually feminine, something the uniform he always saw her in tended to distract from.

"Todd, thank you for coming, and please for this evening, I'd be honoured if you would call me Naomi, so come in, make yourself comfortable. I've had some water brought up for you, I hope you like it".

"Thank you ma'm...Naomi, sorry it's hard to stop doing what comes straight to mind".

She smiled, kindly, and was going to say something when Todd spotted the water on the glass table over by the windows, "Oh...is that San Pellegrino? Where did you get that from?" He hadn't seen a bottle of that in five years, maybe longer. Shipping carbonated water in a glass bottle from Earth cost a fortune, it must have been 200 credits worth - almost a quarter of his monthly salary.

"I've been keeping it for a while, maybe five months, my husband brought it out here for me on his last visit, to be honest it's a pleasure to have someone to share it with who appreciates what it is, come sit with me".

Todd sat down, astonished at the view over the base and the myriad stars beyond, the ships, mostly small coming and going, and further afield the massive commercial docks that seemed to orbit, but were actually connected by giant pylon towers that carried their containers and raw materials to the huge underground storage and trans-shipment areas.

He looked back at the water as Naomi Tan sat opposite him, "Ehm..Naomi, would you mind if I opened the bottle? It's been a long while".

She laughed politely, "be my guest, just remember the atmospheric pressure in here is lower than that bottle by about twenty percent, I've not moved it in hours though so it should be settled".

Todd caught that fact and stored it. She'd planned this meeting in advance if she'd gotten the bottle out hours before.

Very carefully, and with Naomi looking like she might flinch if the water shot out of the bottle under pressure, he slowly unscrewed the lid. The seal snapped and the first hiss of escaping $Co2$ made bubbles appear in the top of the bottle. He tightened it, loosened it and kept repeating until the hissing stopped sufficiently to pour. With a slight flourish and a big smile he poured hers first then his and she laughed, clapping her hands just once and saying, "bravo, a virtuoso performance Todd".

"I do my best, I come form a place where we wasted nothing, not even a bubble of $Co2$", he smiled and nodded at her appreciation.

They sipped the delicate water, so different from the recycled ice water from the asteroids. A real Earth mineral water, from an age gone by it seemed, they both savoured its clean, fresh taste, but it had a flavour, quite different to anything found out here. It reminded them both of Earth.

"It's an amazing view Commodore".

"Please, Todd, call me Naomi. I've asked you here for two reasons, and I know you must be expecting something".

"Well I did wonder".

She opened up a small box on the glass table, and took out something Todd recognised immediately, a multi-frequency jamming unit. They were strictly illegal on the base and he could arrest her on the spot for possessing one.

"You do know that's illegal, if you turn it on it'll show up on the command centre scanners as a black hole in your quarters".

"No, this one won't, I've added it to the log of permitted devices, they'll have no idea". She smiled and flipped it on.

"You wouldn't have revealed that if you didn't think you could trust me, so I'm guessing I've just passed that test?" Todd wasn't sure where this was going.

"I'm sure I can trust you Todd, and that's why you and I have to have this conversation without even the chance of anyone overhearing it. It's a matter of immense delicacy".

It took Naomi Tan twenty minutes to explain what had happened to DuBret, how the Amundsen attack had come about and why, never mind the Tutankh's complicity. Todd never said a word, taking it all in. When she'd finished he leant back in the chair after pouring another glass of the San Pellegrino from its famous green bottle.

"You want me to find this Athanasios guy and bring him in?"

"Oh no, most definitely not! Well yes, find him, find out where he is and where he goes, but he cannot know, he simply cannot find out, and you certainly mustn't bring him in".

"And you don't want me to tell any of my own people?"

"No. I know that's not easy to do and its not how you like to operate. The problem is he seems, from what little DuBret and I have been able to ascertain, to come and go with extraordinary ease. He seems to pass through controlled areas with no issues, he gets out to the remote Tutankh outpost and nobody questioned him as to where he'd been, even though the shuttle he was on had it in its flight plan and, the murder of Maris Karanska was all over the network news. He went through transit so fast he was on a liner back to Titan within an hour, having thrown somebody out of First Class when he didn't have a pre-booked ticket".

"You found that out already, by yourself?" Todd said the words and realised they sounded incredibly condescending. He apologised, but Naomi seemed unfazed.

"Oh I know I may be just a commodore, and little analytical is expected of me Todd, really I do".

"It wasn't that, it's just well it was risky looking at some of that data, if someone is looking out for him they may have flagged up your interest".

"Oh I used a separate databot-trawler identity for that, don't worry, its not traceable, but I can't do anything more sophisticated without help. And we need to have eyes on him, somehow. Where does he come from, and who is he working for?"

Todd had to ask more directly, "let me be clear, you're sure, he's got inside help?"

"Absolutely sure".

"You can only be sure if you have evidence".

"I do have evidence, but it's not exactly admissible in court".

Todd looked right at her, "A telepath?"

She nodded in affirmation.

"You're not going to tell me who are you?"

"It would be dangerous for him".

Todd knew who it was but he didn't want to say. Major Granding, he was, other than the commercial base civilian telepath the only possible candidate. He was always briefed when T-Corps had a T5 or above in the system, it was the law.

"OK, I'll do this, but I might need some leave, maybe a day or two the next time he shows up. These people, they make patterns, it may take time to figure it out, but they make patterns. And we have a codeword if we need to discuss it".

"What word would you like?" asked Naomi.

"Immortal", replied Todd without hesitation.

"Why that" she asked.

"Because Athanasios is Greek for immortal".

****

Mr Athanasios sat securely in his first class cabin aboard the Virgin Galactic Spaceways liner the *"James Corey"*. He placed a scrambler and encoder over the external communications link and made a person to person tachyon call as the ship left the space dock, turning towards the jump gate. If you had been listening in all you would have heard were his answers to questions in another language that wasn't English.

"There won't be any problems now."

"It's disappointing, but Fleet has no idea how to navigate with the jump generators and they seem to have nothing capable of doing so even in development, until they do the technology is almost worthless. I wouldn't worry."

"I'll be back here on Procyon in less than fourteen standard Earth Days".

"Yes they passed into the system, a probe rather escalated that process as I'm sure you know".

"Oh quite inevitable".

"Of course".

CHAPTER 26

CLOAK & DAGGER

General Ixxius looked carefully at the reports, he could almost be described as happy, if such an emotional state had ever been observed. Perhaps 'less angry' described it better. His long flexible clawed fingers, astonishingly dextrous for such apparently large hands, as humans would see them, tapped impatiently on the control surface of the data projector.

Ixxius who never looked at subordinates more than one rank beneath him - such a thing would have been considered demeaning for both parties - simply pointed at the planet in the three dimensional image.

"Science officer, what is your estimation?"

The junior officer knew better than to withhold any morsel of information, it was Kadressian custom to simply offer information until you had run out or were stopped. "Sir, the system has a small colony on the planet, it's mostly deep underground because of the temperature on the surface, it is below our survivable limit by a wide margin. The colony has a simple missile defence based in silos and a passive and active detection system. However they are elderly systems, the colony having only a scientific purpose for weapons experimentation and little major value to the Empire, its resources were long ago extracted. The latest information shows that 198 scientists were in residence, 17 males and 181 females and children".

"Is that it?" Ixxius was blunt but asked a question he knew there were no further answers to just to make the officer uncomfortable.

"It is everything sir, unless you wish me to catalogue their weapons".

Ixxius stood, silent, unresponsive but actually thinking, before asking, "what are they working on?"

"The information is classified sir, only a Viceroy and above has that information".

Ixxius dismissed the officers. He stood looking through six different star system maps, somewhere out here were the enemy. This part of space was old, most of the stars were ancient, barely a billion years from the end of their lives in many cases, having already been here for six billion or more. Interstellar grave yards. Maybe he mused, this is why the enemy was moving now, finding the stars dead, maybe theirs was too, maybe they were looking for a new place to settle.

Ixxius knew what the humans did not. He knew that beyond this band of red dwarves and semi dead systems filled with rubble, lay a whole treasure trove of completely viable stars, with multitudes of planets. Planets the Empire couldn't colonise or use but a slave race of oxygen breathers most certainly could, for planets like that were many and varied.

The one thing he had been able to find out from the battle station and the conflict with the alien ship, they were oxygen breathers, and oxygen breathers bred quickly, were almost inevitably physically weak and made ideal slaves. Slaves by the millions Ixxius imagined, who could drive another wave of economic expansion for the Empire, build up its military and drive a whole new era of empire building. With a new leader. Yes a new leader, uncompromising and driven.

Which of these systems did he pick? All of them had dead gates on the other end of days of travel. The enemy would never come back the way they escaped, they'd know the gate was mined and protected, and he didn't dare follow them, expecting the same the other end. He had no idea how capable they were and it was a certain trap.

Over a dozen hyperspace probes were searching for options, but it was taking so long, they had vast areas to cover and were looking for what amounted to a specific grain of sand on a beach.

"Science, get back in here, bring me an update on the hyperspace probes".

The officer obliged feeding the latest data to the general's strategic display.

One stood out. "Probe 7 seems to be reporting an anomaly, explain it to me".

"Probe 7 has gone into a holding pattern General, it's reached a point that should have an operational gate and it can't get through, presumably the gate the other end is damaged."

Ixxius thought for a second, "Can it find another gate in the same system form its location in hyperspace?"

"It would sir, it would then pass into the system, hunting for the next gate and go from there, but if it fails to trigger the gate after several tries, it will try to hunt for an alternate gate, however the mechanics of hyperspace make it difficult, almost impossible, to track signals from gates in the same heliosphere".

Ixxius watched it, as it flashed orange, over and over. "Is this a live tachyon feed?"

"Sir, It's approximately a twenty second delay, as near instantaneous as we can manage at this range, we're a long way from a booster or a relay".

Ixxius' head twitched, he leant forward, "Why has the colour changed to green?"

"Sir, may I approach?"

Ixxius gestured the officer forward. He watched as the officer deftly checked the data and the feed, Ixxius noted that he did the same check a second time. "General, the probe has activated the jump gate, it's entering the system".

"Which system did it depart from?"

"EZ Aquarii General, the system with the research colony we discussed earlier."

"Get a feed from that probe now". Ixxius hit the communicator to the bridge, "Captain, lay in a course for EZ Aquarii and give me an ETA as soon as you have it".

Ixxius was fuming now. They were days away even by his basic estimations. There could only be one reason that probe opened the gate, the enemy had reactivated it. What a surprise they were going to get.

It took almost three minutes to establish a live connection but it was delayed and not viably a two way feed. The entire bridge watched as the probe opened the jump gate, entered the system, its optical sensors quickly pinned it down to being a red dwarf system and its holographic mapping quickly identified it as Procyon.

What happened next was beyond anyone's control. A massive ship the likes of which nobody had seen outside of their own empire in a century was to its left and close to the gate, to its right and approaching fast were small ships, smaller even than the probe, but beyond that another, different, huge ship...the probe was holding the gate open to transmit or escape but suddenly everything cut off.

"What was that?"

"A massive EMP charge general, it overwhelmed the communications on the probe, its gone".

****

The Isscatl hummed with activity as "battle-stations" sounded on every deck. The jump gate from Kinkuthanza burst into life but there was nothing waiting on the other side. The gate was the furthest from the planet, Ixxius had no idea if the enemy had gotten here first, the probe had been destroyed before it could transmit enough data to tell how far Procyon was from what the humans called Luyten's Star and the jump gate they had or would arrive from.

The massive battlecruiser sped through space towards the colony planet - it was nearly two days away even at flank speed, which would drain fuel. Ixxius had agreed to call in a tanker and another warship, the Viceroy when faced with the possibility of an enemy just one system away was quick to see the problems that could cause and agreed readily. Indeed he had already spoken with his brother, the Emperor, about getting a larger fleet to the system as a matter of urgency. Even so that would be at least fourteen days away, if it had even departed.

Ixxius was confident he could take out a small squadron. The first ship they'd fought had not been well protected or especially well armed. Only the dolt of a commander who'd failed to engage it properly had let it get away.

Ixxius was impatient for battle. He had a plan, and the military commander of the tiny research colony had had no choice but to agree. Ixxius had shut the colony down, all signs of surface activity had been stopped and all energy use other than in the deep underground caves of the colony essential for life support, had been stopped.

He faced a stark choice. Either speed towards the colony and risk being spotted blasting this much energy into space, or get their first and unseen.

Ixxius was in luck. Using only optical laser communications between the surface and the Isscatl they gave nothing away. The battlecruiser even had time to recharge depleted reserve batteries.

Once everything was ready, he ordered the ship readied for deployment of the evasion field, once that was activated the ship was not just physically invisible, it was electromagnetically invisible as well, moulding the natural background around it. In effect it didn't exist. The field had its penalties. Speed for one, had to be deathly slow, and it couldn't use any active scanners or fire any weapons.

The crew didn't like the evasion field, nobody did. It smacked of cowardice to most and worse still, it created the most unpleasant sensations, cramps and headaches being most common. It also consumed almost 70% of the ships main fusion reactor energy.

However once the evasion field was switched off, the ship was designed to switch near-instantly to full combat mode and defend itself as well as increase its battle speed, making it an ideal surprise for any enemy. When used properly it could be devastating, placing the Isscatl on top an enemy at point blank range. Nothing would survive that, nothing.

General Ixxius was ready. It was time...

CHAPTER 27

COLLISION

The Amundsen was pinging her active sensor arrays at full power, illuminating the whole area for almost a million kilometres in a sphere around her. If anyone didn't know she was there, they did now.

Captain Andros had been a little disturbed by the idea, but as he had little choice but to agree, and there really was no hiding the Amundsen, she was no stealth ship after all, he understood Captain Baylin's plan and agreed. Amundsen's scans would wake up any automated weaponry designed to hunt down any active scanners, but she could probably shoot it down or get away before it became a problem. Probably.

The active scan would be relayed to the Nemesis without her having to too readily give her own position away, and if there was anyone hiding with passive scanners only, this level of active scan power would nearly blind it. It was like pointing a super bright torch in someones eyes.

The reconnaissance fighters sped away from the Nemesis, approaching the planet from an anti-clockwise direction above it, while declining in to its north pole and then beginning a planetary survey, or so went the plan. As Baylin liked to remind himself, from the words of an American President and former General, Dwight D Eisenhower in the 1940's, "nothing goes wrong like a plan".

The Nemesis maintained a constant distance from the fighters.

Nemesis, linked as she was to the Amundsen's sensors, was able to filter them out, leaving everything beneath their electromagnetic cacophony in silence. Nothing else was broadcasting. And yet…

"Captain, take a look at this sir". Science Officer Gold expanded a screen image for Baylin and First Officer Obishka to see.

"What is it lieutenant?" Baylin was not fully comprehending the information he was seeing.

"Captain, it's a De Broglie wave, an extremely small one I'll be honest, but it's definitely a De Broglie wave".

"Are you sure? And if so where's it's centre?"

"I'm certain sir, it's a little over 150,000 klicks distant bearing 47 degrees with a declination of 32, there".

"That's almost in front of the recon fighters, tell them to change course away, very very gradually, don't let them run too close to it". Baylin glanced at Obishka, "Markus you remember when we were on the Ramorra and that ship seemed to blink in and out, we never thought much of it, that it was some kind of jump gate effect, we couldn't track it for a second or two".

"Yeah, it was momentary though, nothing major, could even have been our scanners".

"What if it wasn't us? Lieutenant Gold, am I right in thinking that photons and electrons create a wave form when they're being moved, and that's what a De Broglie wave is?"

"Basically sir, yes, the faster they're moved the more wave is created, but it needs energy to move them in such a pattern, a lot of energy, and whatever it is, has to be bending light and electromagnetic fields while it moves".

Baylin looked at them both, "Isn't that in effect a cloak?"

Markus Obishka knew about such tech, "It's been thought about, but we've never been able to make one work, its so power hungry, and it's not that effective because...because of the De Broglie effect which gives it away!"

Baylin spoke to Andros on the Amundsen, "Captain, we have a problem, I'm approaching a cloaked ship, something is definitely hiding from us and I'm heading right at it, in fact our course is going to put us in a position where it will shoot at us in about five minutes and at pretty close range, I'm going to have to let the recon fighters pass it, and then move so that I'm facing it, and I'm going to open fire with everything. You know what to do. Passing positional data for relay now".

The whole ship seemed to be on edge. The one advantage they had was knowing there was something there, Baylin had suspected it was possible when the atmosphere came up Co2 on the planet - that was the primary atmosphere on the base station they'd boarded. That suggested a potential colony or an outpost and that meant a patrol, but what kind of patrol?

Plasma pulse cannons, PDC's, plasma torpedoes, were fully armed, the armour was fully charged and the missile bays were loaded with eight 2 megaton warhead nukes, on top of that the remaining fighters were able to drop on command in a few seconds.

He couldn't wait to be fired on first, just a few more minutes...he had the ship turn a degree at a time, every few seconds, bringing her around to match what appeared to be the entry line for a high planetary orbit, that wound't look suspicious, following the fighters.

Time passed impossibly slowly. Baylin looked around the bridge and he knew everyone was ready, just a few seconds more...

****

General Ixxius didn't like what the aliens were doing, the bigger ship, which was some 400,000 klicks away, above and beyond the planet was using powerful active scanners, which were multi-phased and almost impossible to filter.

"What are they doing?" He growled at anyone who would answer him.

"I think it's a deep planet scan General, in my opinion, they're using it to gauge composition, it's not like anything we have, they seem to be sending in scout ships to run a more detailed surface scan".

"Do they know we're here?" That was the general's biggest concern, because what looked like a very large warship was bearing down on them and he was desperate to open fire and kill it in one massive strike, then chase down the other one.

"They can't know General, the Evasion Field is fully operational, their course has changed but the warship is following the two small probe ships towards a polar orbit insertion, it will pass just within weapons range in a little over two minutes". The Isscatl's captain was waiting for the optimum time to drop the Evasion Field, it had a cycle of just over 23 seconds to drop the field, divert all the power to weapons and armour and fire.

"Captain, I'm trusting your going to have this timed to perfection?" Ixxius was grinning (or what passed for it on a Kadressian snout) with anticipation.

"Of course General" The Captain watched the monitors, feeling slightly less comfortable. He had no time to explain anything to the General, this was on him, and it bothered him that the alien warship, with its bizarre rotating mid-section was pointing just a little too much towards them, but he knew they couldn't be seen....just 28 seconds to open fire....

****

Baylin's eyes were on the targeting scope on the main screen, there was no doubt the ship was in front of them even if it was invisible....he couldn't wait another second, "launch fighters, fire all missiles, open fire, all weapons!"

The launchers erupted in blue flame as the missiles raced from their launch tubes in the lower forward section, a blinding blue flash of engine ignitions as they sped up to some 10,000km a second...five seconds to impact, the two huge Plasma Force Beams opened fire - hitting what looked like invisible space, followed by a battery of pulsed plasma bursts and torpedoes, in the blink of an eye they could see the enemies cloak break up to reveal elements of its superstructure, the shield was flickering.

"Helm, flank speed now, weapons keep firing".

***General Ixxius's eyes almost burst when he saw what had happened, "Drop the field now, drop it! Maximum power, activate the defence grid first! May the gods forgive you captain because I won't!"

The evasion field began to drop as the Captain frantically switched off the main evasion field generators and the system prepared to charge weapons and power the engines up, but it took seconds, and it was pre-programmed for speed, he couldn't arm the defence grid first, it wasn't possible, but he could do something, "Weapons officer use main batteries to target those incoming missiles as soon as they're charged, engines, full!"

The Isscatl's engines were fast, far faster than the Nemesis to power up, she started to respond very quickly, actually stabilising the missiles distance to the ship so rapidly she might even be able to outrun them...but it was sucking so much energy to move so quickly the weapons range was being compromised. Ixxius could see what was going on.

"Captain, bank round as soon as those missiles are outrun and open fire, get that ship before it hits us with any more beam weapons!"

Isscatl's enormous rail gun, mounted in a huge turret on the upper deck was no use firing backwards, Isscatl had to turn and she was taking plasma beam weapon hits, yet she was pulling away at the same time... could she get out of this and score an astonishing victory? General Ixxius knew he could...

**The Nemesis held back her speed, Baylin angled her slightly away from a full frontal attack, he could see what was coming, the enemy ship, which was at least a third as big again as the Nemesis was now revealed and truly massive, scanners showed it was outrunning the missiles, but they were close enough..7 klicks could still cause damage... "Weapons, detonate the missiles now".

Nemesis's screens went black - standard practice when detonating nuclear weapons - outside now less than 800 klicks distant eight simultaneous 2 megaton explosions detonated off of what was the rear left quarter of the Isscatl, at a distance of around 6,500 meters. The combined effect, even with her running from it, was a huge jolt that smacked the ship in the side and sent crew smashing into bulkhead walls. The gamma rays were intense, the levels of neutrons fried most of the crew in the rear half of the ship - these were weapons designed to kill as well as damage. The electromagnetic pulse seared most of the rear third of the ships systems into useless blobs of bio-organics, rendered doubly useless by the neutrons and gamma rays. Everyone knew if they'd been actually hit the ship would have been crippled. Yet it was not...the modular systems were designed for combat survival.

Ixxius recovered himself and saw that his captain was rapidly gaining control of the ships systems, the first sign of that was the alien ship turning away, and then the point defence turrets came on line, quickly dealing with the pulsed plasma torpedo fire, which soon stopped as the enemy turned away.

Five of the six main drives were still on line and the Isscatl began to turn, the massive rail gun was almost fully charged...

****

Baylin had wanted a clean shot, and the enemy was injured, but not enough and it was moving quickly and recovering fast. "Captain, that weapon on its upper deck is some kind of electromagnetic rail gun, immensely powerful, its about 50% charged". Obishka was keeping a close eye.

"Keep the defence grid at full, and don't let that ship get all of its weapons on us, there's a whole array we're going to get hit with if it turns 180 degrees, take us towards the planet, make it follow and get the fighters to take out that rail gun".

Nemesis had been designed for a good battle speed but she was also designed for 360 degree combat. The Isscatl was all front-loaded, Kadressian culture was all about direct frontal attacks, not running from enemies, and Baylin had spotted her weakness as soon as the scans came on screen. He muttered to himself, "Catch me if you can".

The fighters were fast approaching the Isscatl, and the ships systems seemed almost not to see them, indeed that they were even approaching had almost been lost on the captain and general, they'd never seen small ships like this and had no idea what was about to happen.

The Isscatl's weapons were fully armed and she was now chasing the alien, but these tiny high speed ships were suddenly upon them. "What are they?" demanded the general, as the hull reverberated from one pounding explosion after another and units of the fortified armour on the upper deck were showing up as a structural failure.

"They're disproportionately heavily armed General, and they're attacking the rail gun turret..." a huge explosion and a blast of alarm sounds from the weapons station announced the turret was rendered useless and the rail gun charge had detonated, killing the entire gun crew and deactivating most of the upper deck armour. Having done their job the tiny ships were now flying at will around the Isscatl, picking off sensor nodes and point defence turrets that had no programme or calibration to deal with them.

The Captain was deeply concerned, but dared not show how much to the General who was so unnervingly calm it made him feel sick with anxiety. "Captain, give me flank speed, ignore those small ships, get me behind that alien warship and open fire with the main array".

****

Baylin didn't like having his engines facing the enemy, but Nemesis had as many weapons facing backwards as she did forwards, and he slowed slightly for the Isscatl to catch up and fall within range, ordering the fighters out of combat and back to the Nemesis, he didn't want them caught in what was to come. The longer the Amundsen and the Nemesis could scan her the more they understood, and what was quickly clear was that the huge warship was front-heavy with weapons and they were more powerful but shorter ranged. Either way Nemesis had gotten in the first round but he had to keep ahead of the game, and the game was changing.

The rear nuclear armed missiles didn't get near the enemy this time, its defence grid seemed especially capable when dealing with such weapons from a frontal attack, and as range dropped the rear plasma pulse cannons were barely getting one in eight shots through. The heavy plasma force beams were a different matter. The enemies armour was having a tough time with them and it was breaking down, structural damage was beginning to show.

And then came the blast. The primary array on the alien ship was powerful, some kind of co-ordinated plasma force beam, the Nemesis rocked from end to end and damage reports came through in seconds, most of it had hit the rotating mid section, gutting a huge area of crew quarters, but nothing strategic yet...Baylin needed just two more minutes, he slowed again, faking damage. The rear weapons kept firing, another blast from the alien array sent the upper rear fighter launch bays and two of the defence turrets to a fiery death, flames poured out as the atmosphere escaped, but extinguished as it was sealed off, Baylin knew this was going to get worse, just another minute...

****

General Ixxius was calm, as the Isscatl closed on the alien ship, which had made a huge tactical mistake. It told Ixxius the aliens had fought few wars, nobody took their ship into a gravity well in combat around a planet, it dragged them down and reduced their tactical manoeuvrability. And yet that's exactly what the alien was doing. It's tiny attack ships had been damaging but not fatal and were now running away. He'd got them right where he wanted them.

The captain had performed well he thought, it had been a challenging battle.

"General, there's something..."

"What?"

Before Ixxius could get an answer he saw for himself what the problem was, underneath them, coming up from the southern pole at alarming speed were two ships, he tried to work out what they were, where they had come from, but there was no time, they were moving far too fast..."Evasive manoeuvres, get us out of here, forget the alien, head for the jump gate". Ixxius suspected a devastating trap had been set...

****

Captain DuBret's gunships were so fast even she was surprised, the vast bulk of the alien battlecruiser was above them, a pristine simple target that wasn't going anywhere fast enough to get away. It began some sort of manoeuvre having detected them. Their speed was much higher having used the planet as a sling shot to come round and gain speed. The two ships with their combined 24 gun ports open and their multi-weapon arrays opened fire, simultaneously, with neutron warhead tactical nukes, twelve of them timed to hit simultaneously. Two went down to point defences but the Isscatl wasn't designed to be attacked like this, ten warheads erupted on her hull and tore it asunder, its speed dropped and the gunships shot past, their one opportunity to shine executed to perfection.

On the Nemesis the cheer could have been heard two systems away, on the Amundsen, which had had a front row to the battle, there was shock and relief and no small amount of awe.

Baylin was a little disappointed to see the massive alien ship didn't just explode and vanish even then, it was seriously disabled, but it was going down into the atmosphere.

The consensus was it wasn't going to burn up, it was too big and the atmosphere too thin. It's trail of debris and the fiery red of its burn in the cold air of the planet were indeed insufficient to destroy it. They watched from space as it cut a surprisingly controlled landing into an area of mostly desert and small rocks. What did it take to kill this thing?

The damage to the Nemesis was around 15%, a swathe of crew quarters had been destroyed in the back of the rotation section, but nobody had been killed because they were at battle stations. The second blast was not so simple to deal with, 13 had been killed, mostly fighter bay operators and PDC specialists in the Distributed Defence Control Centre, which was mostly out of action, and a potential problem.

Baylin looked at Markus Obishka, "Markus, I don't think this is over".

"No sir, neither do I".

CHAPTER 28

PROFESSOR

"Professor you must be able to give us more information than that?"

Kelso Drummond was a career veteran for PlanExCo, and the company had every reason to hand him their latest expedition ship. There was no government sanction here, even if the government would ultimately benefit from what they discovered. If they found anything.

They were using the latest highly secret hyperspatial navigation system, they'd been travelling in jumps for two weeks and now using just that system, they were heading towards a gravity well that would take them nearly thirty days to reach. And if it didn't have a gate at the other end they'd have to come back.

The navigation system worked by tracing the intense gravity well of a star or a planet and its effect in hyperspace. By correlating the gravity patterns to stars and planetary orbits they could theoretically find their way to systems more directly without having to jump from one gate to another, trek across a system, then jump again from the next gate and so on. By knowing which system they were going to, they could look for the corresponding gravity well, find a gate beacon and jump in. It became more of a problem if you didn't have the beacon frequency for the place you wanted to arrive at. You'd simply have to spend however long it took trying to find it to locate the gate.

"It's no good trying to make me tell you what you want to hear Drummond, I never developed this technology, I only helped define the physics that would make it possible". Professor Nelson Kagala could read the Expedition Commander's feelings so easily. He was such a warm man by nature but prone to expecting everyone to give him what he wanted when he wanted it, and that was never a way to persuade the wily professor to give up information willingly.

Empathy of course is in the eye of the beholder, and Nelson Kagala's wasn't always as accurate as he might like, his method of interpretation wasn't taught, it was learned from his life experience. What Drummond wanted and expected was what he wanted from anyone paid by the company to do a job, and that was unequivocal and forthright cooperation and knowledge sharing. Not something exactly on top of the list for an ambitious academic with an agenda. Academia was rife with those who would defend a point of view or an 'accepted fact' even when it was now proven to be wrong. Nelson Kagala was willing to say and do whatever it took to maintain his prominence at the Sinai City University on Mars. He was professor of Martian Astrogeology, but also a renowned theoretical physicist who specialised in Theoretical Astrogravitics.

The Science Vessel 'Kang Tai', named after the early Fourth Century Chinese maritime explorer, was purpose built for long duration operations. A crew of just twenty-nine, operated the ship and on top of that there were six scientists of varying subjects and calibre, nominally headed up by the Professor. Yet ultimately Captain Drummond was in overall charge and his decisions were final. This far out into hyperspace without beacons, without tachyon relays, there was no communication with Earth or any of the colonies. They were on their own in every sense of the word, and utterly reliant on the new navigation system. Its failure would mean they could be lost for months, maybe for good.

"Professor Kagala, I need some idea as to what theories you hold for how the Martian alien ship was able to travel as it did, I need some idea of what level of tech you think we're going to encounter and how far advanced you think they are, it's really simple, and it's not an unreasonable request!"

Nelson Kagala, waved his hand dismissively, his other arm across his chest, his body language was at best, passive-aggressive, "It opened some sort of gravity neutralising field, something that disestablished the normal space and the normal hyperspace you and I know and are travelling in now. How it did it, that's years beyond us. I could theorise for a decade, two, three, and still never be able to work out how. So Captain Drummond, it's pointless asking me questions like that".

"Well you said it was millions of years old, what if when it gets back its owners aren't there any more?" Drummond was thinking it might be some sort of AI gone whacko - Earth had had that problem and nobody wanted another bout of that.

"That's just idle speculation, I know you think it may be AI, I understand that, and its consequences, but until we get there we'll never know. It may be that it was simply going there on a first stop to somewhere else. Let me tell you this. It was old, over two million years old, so old that the fact it worked after what it did to Mars, is almost in itself incomprehensible. My feeling is that their tech is beyond any of our abilities to comprehend, it's bio-organic machine technology, something we have never been able to master well enough to deploy, it may even have been alive in some format. But we won't know until we get there!" The professor wished Drummond would just read the reports he'd already submitted to PlanExCo, he knew no more.

Captain Drummond got the message. The days would be long on this trip.

The days did indeed drag on, they saw nothing but hyperspace, they were able to pinpoint feint jump gate signals as they passed gravity wells of what were other stars in the distance off of their course.

By the time the gravity well of HR122 began to show on the navigation sensors, its size was becoming hugely apparent.

Astrogation said it was 81 times brighter than Sol, an orange giant of a spectral class K1-III, yet it was significantly cooler than Sol by some 22% and 14.6 times it's diameter, a truly massive star, but its physical mass was only 1.2 of that of Sol. It was technically a double star but its neighbour was 920 billion klicks away, it was a loose orbit at best.

For Drummond and the Professor the best part of the final approach day was spent fussing over whether or not they could detect a gate on the one hand and a planet on the other.

Both were in luck, two gates were gravitcally visible in the system, though neither seemed to show any sign of having been activated in a while. And there were planets, three of them.

The approach to the gate that seemed most likely to be closest to the planets was chosen and the *Kang Tai* began her approach. The crew were keen and excited. Nobody had travelled this deep into space from Earth before, 379 light years, and the navigation system had worked, far better than anyone had imagined, except of course, for the professor whose desire to take credit for it despite his minimal practical involvement, never receded. The crew joked that his ego was so massive they were surprised it didn't register on the gravity sensors.

The jump gate required a signal to open a point into normal space, but all gates were different. The ships computer took over 90 minutes to roll through a batch of codes that might work based on the weak holding transmission from the dormant gate, then each code had to be transmitted and a response accepted. On a fully active gate like the one near Titan, this took a couple of seconds. Here, the sleeping gate needed more nudging it seemed. An hour into the process nerves were getting frayed, but 67 minutes in and the gate responded, normal space appeared after the customary flashes of light that indicated an ignition process, and to more than a few light cheers and smiles, the *Kang Tai* was suddenly in normal space.

The jump point closed behind them, and everyone who could was looking out of the windows or at a screen. HR122 was truly massive, they were no more than 20 million klicks from it and around half a million from the largest planet. This star was clearly expanding, slowly but surely, and in another million years would probably consume the gate and the planet too.

The *Kang Tai* was no Amundsen class explorer, barely a tenth of the size of a ship of that class. She had a high end sensor and scanner suite but it wasn't long range. The only way they were going to find out about the planets was to get close and survey them.

The first, and largest planet was an immense rock, about 1.2 times the size of Earth. It's surface was near molten one one side and frozen on the other, its orbit fixed with one face to the star at all times. No life had ever existed there was the conclusion, largely based on its lack of rotation. If it had ever had an atmosphere it had long ago been blown away by heat and aggressive solar winds, that close was it to its star.

221

The next two days trudging across the system were relatively dull, there were many asteroids, one quite notable comet, but as they got closer to the second planet, which was about the size of Lunar, but with a reasonable rotation and a discernible but very thin atmosphere, interest began to peak.

Something was there. Electromagnetic sensors detected traces of energy generation, some kind of extremely low level power, but it was most clearly not natural, it bore all the hallmarks of a Type-XI nuclear reactor signature, the very latest and not yet in service design Earth had only recently developed. There was also some sort of circular metallic reflection.

Captain Drummond's orders were clear, any type of technology had to be investigated. He ordered the *Kang Tai* in to orbit, they spent three hours ascertaining a safe landing spot as near to the energy generation site as possible.

Kang Tai made her way down to the surface, a surprisingly bumpy and long winded approach that made Nelson Kagala rather uncomfortable, the thin atmosphere was largely a nitrogen-oxygen-Co2 mix but not breathable. The ship crunched down onto a relatively rocky surface, grey, and pock-marked from what seemed to be eruptions and impacts, but sensors showed they were old. The atmosphere was so thin it appeared almost non-existent at ground level, there was no colour, just the darkness of space, despite the intense pink-white light from the star.

The *Kang Tai's* massive leg struts held her above the ground, hydraulics made her level enough to open the drop doors, allowing the tracked explorer vehicles to exit with ease. Drummond held back the excavator for now until they had need of it.

Professor Kagala was not one to be rushed and while few others knew it, he wasn't over keen on donning full activity suits and helmets. In honesty he felt it was all for someone else to be doing this under his guidance, but he was being paid handsomely for his contribution. Not only that, and always at the front of his mind, was that he was the one who could push for the naming of these planets, the star, and recognition that he was their principle discoverer. Drummond may be in charge but he had nowhere near the political clout needed to claim the credit.

CHAPTER 29

G.A.S.

Extract from United Earth Alliance website "MILITARY, GAS - Ground Assault Shuttle"

Ground Assault Shuttles, armoured, heavily armed, capable of dropping from space through an atmosphere, incredibly fast and far from luxurious.

Designed to support a military ground assault on a fixed position or add tactical flexibility to a more mobile one, the latest from Israeli Military Space Industries for the UE Alliance Marine Corps, the Salire-Mk V GAS is fearsome. It's name, 'salire' comes from the Latin word for 'to leap'. Because that's what it can do. It can plunge into a battle situation at high speed, stop ultra-fast before hitting the ground, pick up troops, kit, equipment and leap at breathtaking speeds out of the area.

Operating one is a mix of advanced quantum computing and extreme pilot skill, training takes over 18 months. Troops and support equipment handlers were just as well versed in their capabilities in rapid embarkment, extraction and delivery on a battlefield. Their effectiveness was first proven, during the so called 'Vega Suppression' and on Mars dealing with separatists, now long vanquished.

****

Nemesis had three GAS and the Marines to go into combat with them. Nemesis had the 18th Fleet Marine Platoon, with 43 combat troops and 2 officers, Captain Baylin could double that by adding the 22nd FMP on board the Amundsen, but they didn't have GAS units.

Marines were not just men & women - they wore armoured, powered exoskeletons, each one equipped with its own array of nano-drones, heavy kinetic assault rifles, and plasma force guns. The 'exos' as marines called them, tripled their physical strength in standard Earth gravity, which could be far higher in lower gravity environments, but lower in higher ones. Their principle down side was they needed recharging in non-combat situations every 24 hours, and as much as every six hours in active combat. They could absorb solar energy but it wasn't enough except to top up while largely inactive.

Captain Baylin had persuaded Captain Andros to place his troops under the command of the Nemesis, and two of the GAS shuttles had run a ferrying operation to bring them aboard.

While that was happening the Nemesis Marine Commander, First Lieutenant Dikon Fausto, who outranked the Amundsen's platoon commander, was working with the reconnaissance fighters to understand what had happened when the enemy ship had 'landed', crunching and grinding its way across nearly 7km of surface terrain before stopping.

Was it still active? Could it fire, had the aliens left the ship? What could they do to capture it? Did the planet have any forces they'd not encountered or yet seen that the Marines would have to deal deal with?

While all that was going on Baylin was surveying the damage to the rotation system - it could still rotate and that was positive, but other than sealing up the outer hull as a temporary measure it needed dockyard repair to make good. Markus Obishka was making sure those displaced were reallocated to shared accommodation.

The less pleasant duties were dealing with the thirteen dead in the upper deck mid-hull fighter drop bays on the ships starboard side. The bays themselves, four of them, were gutted. That would slow launching fighters down, some would have to take off more lightly armed, from the forward deck, where the fighters landed and the shuttles came and went.

The Distributed Defence Control Centre-Alpha or D2C2A on the upper deck, as most preferred to refer to it, was another thing. Seven of the thirteen crew killed here were all new and mostly young, it was their first posting. There were three of these control centres - one upper and one lower with a third one as a backup, deep amidships, unmanned until necessary as part of the Auxiliary Control Bridge.

Baylin saw the bodies of three, the rest had been lost in space when the upper deck was hit. Those bodies that were left had been physically trapped by buckled metal. It was not a pleasant site and Baylin felt moved and saddened to his core. Military funerals would take place as soon as they were safe to carry out.

Dr Branson was already there, looked at Baylin and inevitably, said something, "Thirteen Captain, not one of them is over 25, the youngest was 19".

"I know Doc, I know, I'm recommending they don't put any more of these D2C2 centres so far up on the hull, it seems a little bit redundant, I can't abide the idea of this happening to another ship, never mind Nemesis. I'm ordering the other centre to relocate permanently to the auxiliary control bridge".

Baylin stood next to the doctor as they stood, staring at the blackened control centre, the mangled metal. The damage control teams had temporarily sealed the outer hull hole here as the room was relatively small, but the acrid smell, the lingering smoke and fumes, were almost nauseating.

"We cant stay in here Captain, these fumes need to be vented off, let's go". The Doctor took Baylin gently by the elbow, urging him to leave. Back in the cleaner air of the corridor the good Doctor wanted to know when the funeral services would be.

"As soon as you can sign off the death certificates, the three remaining are retrieved from that wreckage in there and we get sufficient time to do it. Other than that they'll have to stay on ice". In Baylin's mind there was no other way to look at the situation, but Branson seemed unmoved verging on angry.

"Is that it, put them on ice? Until when? The crew have a right to mourn and pay their respects, Captain…"

Baylin cut him off with a quick gesture, "That's enough Doctor, everyone will be given time enough to do both those things, when there is time to do so. Right now I've got a hostile ship on the planet beneath us, and standing orders to find out whatever I can. There's nearly a hundred troops ready and waiting to go into battle, to learn what we can about a major alien power. An alien power that threatens Earth's very existence from what we saw earlier, so forgive me if I can't accommodate your pressing need for a memorial service right now."

Baylin walked away and headed to the SCCC (or S3C) - the Surface Combat Control Centre, two decks below the Bridge and above the shuttle launch bays. The Doctor could be more than a little irritating at times and was too inclined to push the boundaries without much thought.

The S3C was bustling with people, a 3D computer generated holographic surface model had been built of an area 100km around the alien battlecruiser's final resting place.

"Lieutenant Fausto, brief me on the situation".

"Sir the enemy ship cut almost a 7 klick groove in the planets surface, but it landed with relative ease. It might be badly damaged but there's no doubt it was a managed landing as best as it could be. Its primary weapons array and the upper turret rail gun are out of action, but energy signatures suggest the upper deck point defence's are operational. I don't believe it represents a threat to the Nemesis or even the GAS units".

"I hear a 'but' coming on Lieutenant..." Baylin interjected.

"Yes sir, I'm afraid what recon analysis brought back shows some kind of missile defence system right on the edge of this area here, to the east of the crash site, they're small silos, three sets of three, and there's some sort of underground structure, and the drone we've launched shows at least five ground vehicles left just over five minutes ago, but they're not fast, it'll be nearly three hours over that terrain as they appear wheeled, there's a lot of dust being generated".

"Will we be able to track them?"

"It shouldn't be a problem sir, as long as they don't target the drone".

"So what's the plan? You'll get to the ship before they do I hope?"

"We'll depart in twenty minutes sir, we'll deploy behind this ridge to their south west, far enough for them not to see us. Amundsen will blanket the area with scanners and jamming, as she has been from the start, they

230

won't even know we're there". Fausto zoomed in to the battlecruisers structure, "Science Officer Gold confirms that's the area of the bridge, its been damaged, the idea is to send a team of six up to it from ground level, get in and record and cut out whatever electronics, systems or data we can, covered by the rest of the platoon.

Two of the three GAS will come back to Nemesis and be ready to load half of Amundsen's platoon ready to bring down as fire support if needed. Squadron Leader Putinova is loaded up with ground support armaments on half the squadron and the rest will run escort. The remaining GAS units will wait on the other side of the ridge, one will jump in and extract the bridge assault team, and rapid-exit back to Nemesis, the platoon will head back to the ridge for extraction by the remaining GAS. Once that's underway the two waiting here will drop to pick up the rest, escorted by fighters".

"Lieutenant, there's one more thing you need to know".

"Sir?"

"My orders are that ship is never to fly again, no matter what. Once you're troops are out of range it's being nuked from space, other than bearing that in mind, your plan seems a good one, good luck Lieutenant".

 Baylin watched as the troops prepped for departure, then headed up to the Flight Deck Control Centre, where Lieutenant Terry Chou was overseeing the whole GAS and fighter operation with the sophisticated ease of a practiced expert. Baylin liked Chou, he was one of those people who held everything in his head, all things, simultaneously, he knew what was what and where it was without having to look, and how to prioritise it simply from the data he held in his brain.

"How are things going Lieutenant?"

Chou seemed mildly surprised to see the Captain, "Sorry...Sir, I didn't see you there.."

"No problem Lieutenant, I just wanted to come down and make sure you had everything you needed. I wanted you to know we're trying to get some of the damaged bays back, but I suspect we'll need to head back to Procyon for that".

231

"We've made provision Captain, at least in the mid-term we can operate from the main bays down here, but if we were to loose more, it would be difficult to launch everything inside the sixty second requirement".

"I understand Lieutenant, we'll cope. How are we doing with munitions?"

"I'm sending up my report Captain, we're very short of the direct fire rocket packs, I've got enough to fully load three fighters, but we used up all the boarded packs on that ship. I'm also short of re-chargeable power packs for fighter auxiliary power, two were faulty and three were lost in the battle".

"I'll see to it Lieutenant, get your list to the First Officer and I'll speak with Fleet about getting what you need".

Baylin left the deck and went back to his office. He had already sent his report to Fleet, and his conversation with Admiral Esteban had gone well, but he hadn't been alone. It was the first time Baylin had been directly linked in with President Mansfield.

In all fairness the conversation had been supportive - The Admiral had been shocked at how much ammunition it had taken to bring down the ship, President Mansfield had simply asked "are we to assume as I have for some days now, that we're at war with this race, is that how you see it Captain?" Baylin had been unequivocal in his affirmation on that point since the day they'd been attacked on the Ramorra. The problem now was something Fleet had never faced before, a major war, with a foreign power, and an economy not even slightly geared up for producing weapons and warships, never mind their support craft, on a scale that would likely require.

The ammunition shortages already meant they would have to go back to Procyon and hope that Earth could send more by the time they got there.

What Baylin didn't know was that The Mansfield Administration hadn't been asleep, but it hadn't been as wide awake as it was now. Factories had been getting orders, programmes to expand production and the finance to make that happen had been authorised and was in full swing. It was shipyards that Fleet needed, and they just took time to build. While Baylin was busy on the frontline, the Administration had been busy turning over commercial yards to military requirements and isolating commercial vessels it could use for fleet supply. Most weren't suitable but needs must, at least in the beginning.

As Baylin's troops began to buckle into their exoskeletal combat armour suits, and the GAS units readied for combat, Earth and her colonies were being told that they were at war, things would change, an enemy was coming. For most people, skepticism was the word of the day. The evidence would take time to impact on their daily lives, and it most surely would. But right now, for those on the edge of deep space, in asteroid mines and processing plants, barely legal space ferries, refinery ships, factories, scraping a living in the great new commercial and colonial age of mankind, tens of light years, trillions of kilometres from a place none of them had even heard of, it seemed just like another movie, another computer game; switch off and tune out.

And that was what Baylin had to complete this mission for. He needed an alien, alive or dead, preferably alive. Once the Marines were space-born, their Lieutenant would get decoded orders in his HUD telling him what he had to bring back.

Baylin went to the bridge, he nodded his ascent to the departure, and the GAS shuttles, with their fighter escorts launched into space.

CHAPTER 30

PLANETFALL

"We're in the pipe, five by five", came the voice of the lead GAS pilot as she throttled the ship to maximum on its virtualised tubular navigation course displayed on her HUD, the other two attack shuttles were on similar trajectories.

The atmosphere ionised around them as the somewhat un-aerodynamic shapes of the Salire Class GAS shuttles battled the atmosphere for supremacy, a battle they would win.

The buffeting was horrendous, but nobody spoke, even as many of them sweated. They'd all done this before in simulations and at least half of them in real life war games. The noise was deafening and the engines roared. Everyone checked their comms and data feeds, primed their drones, made sure their weaponry was linked and operational.

First Lieutenant Dikon Fausto watched as the previously sealed orders opened and his extra mission objective was revealed. It actually didn't seem like it would be a big deal, the bridge of the ship was accessible, there was bound to be a dead body.

Six minutes and the shuttles were close to landing. This is what took all the nerve and training for the pilots. They were flying in at close to 1,600 klicks an hour, 1 klick above the surface. The inertial dampeners and the blast from the landing jets slammed into everyone but the suits were designed for it, capable of reducing the effects by a staggering 99%, so it felt more like a hard bump but no more, as the shuttles slammed to a last minute stop. As they did the rear ramp dropped down and the Marines exited, quickly establishing a perimeter, their nano-drones already reconnoitring and establishing an extraordinary networked image of their position shared with the GAS and with the Nemesis Surface Combat Control Centre.

From behind the ridge, the other side of which lay the enemy battle cruiser, Lieutenant Fausto took in the latest information, there was nothing seemingly changed from before their launch. The update on the incoming alien vehicles was that they were still two hours away. Plenty of time.

Having secured their positions, he ordered the teams in, and the first squads of six, three of them, with him leading in the centre, powered their armoured suits up and leapt up the ridge and over it, charging at speed towards the hull of the ship, its upper decks lay leaning towards them. The damage that Nemesis and the fighters had inflicted was obvious from here, but the ship was even more massively impressive on the ground, it gave it a scale that was far more relatable.

On the bridge of the Amundsen, which was in a high stationary polar orbit, swamping the northern hemisphere with high energy jamming and scanning fields, the ships QuAC had pieced together more data on the surface.

Not only had it managed to scan deeply enough to provide more detail on the underground complex the aliens had built, and from which the vehicles racing towards the wreck of the battle cruiser had originated, it had identified something much smaller - in fact three of them, all vaguely similar.

Captain Andros looked at the data, the QuAC analysis on screen and his first officer, "That's odd, but I have a hunch. Computer, analyse the data from the enemy ships decent and look for anything ejecting from the ship that would match the location and direction of the three objects".

"Correlating"…

Andros waited, it was a lot of data even for a QuAC, trillions of scan points and observations, run through billions of predictive algorithms…

"Analysis complete. The objects are rated as 98.8% probability that they are life pods ejected at a point of emergency approximately 10km above the planets surface, two appear to have been powered, one was not, it's impact shape suggest it's passengers would have been killed, the two

235

others landed roughly, with a 72% chance they survived in the second pod and 85% in the third pod."

Andros was about to call Captain Baylin when the computer suddenly continued, "there is an 89% probability the vehicles on the surface are heading to the life pods, which is increasing in likelihood 0.1% per minute".

"Get me Captain Baylin".

"Gregor, what can I do for you?"

"More what I can do for you Bruce, those vehicles on the surface aren't heading for the wreck, our QuAC is pretty damn sure they're heading for two life pods that ejected during the last stages of combat, you're call what comes next".

"How high was the probability?"

"Andros looked up at the updated screen, just over 99.1%".

"I'll get back to you Gregor, thank you". Baylin needed to speak with Fausto."Comms, get me a direct link to Fausto".

"Lieutenant Fausto online Sir"

"Lieutenant we've got eyes on life pods, high probability of survivors from that ship, possibly senior officers, I need the platoon up here to go down and stop the vehicles approaching from getting them, you carry on with your operation, are you OK with that?"

"Sir we've encountered no opposition, we're just heading onto the ships hull and to the target zone, we can cope sir, but we need one GAS here just in case".

"You've got it Lieutenant, extracting units two and three, we'll be back for you".

No sooner than the conversation ended, Fausto and his squad could see two of the GAS shuttles blast skyward, back to the Nemesis. He quickly updated everyone, "nothing to worry about, they're bringing down the 22nd FMP to take on those vehicles and intercept some possible survivors, we carry on".

They clanked and clunked the heavy armoured suits up the outer hull to the area targeted, it took longer than he expected. There was no sign of any life, and no sign of power. The bridge area was ripped open and it was easy enough to jump into, but as Fausto did so, something illuminated and flashed repeatedly - maybe some kind of intruder alert?

He walked over to it, slowly, picking up a large but moveable piece of equipment that looked ideal for study. He got to the flashing screen, a series of four glyphs on a red flashing oval display, the first one changed roughly every 1.5 seconds, after 5 of them the second one changed...it was a count down, it was a god damned count down!

On the Nemesis the QuAC - which was watching continuously and feeding the data into its probability matrix decided the same thing - "ALERT - Lieutenant Fausto appears to have activated a self destruct mechanism...estimated time 13 standard minutes - correlating reactor activity on the wreck indicates explosive detonation likely".

Baylin shouted down the comm link, "Fausto get out and get out now, GAS on the way".

Baylin looked at the main screen - the GAS shuttles he'd commandeered were just about to dock, they'd never get back to the surface in time, "Fausto get as many men as you can on GAS-1, even if it means an overload, the rest get back behind that ridge".

Fausto and his team needed no second warning, the GAS-1 pilot was already overhead, quickly extracting the six in the advance team, and as many as it could of the perimeter troops, the rest were making for the ridge as fast as they could.

Baylin wasn't wasting this opportunity, he had a mission to accomplish. "Send in the ground attack equipped fighters and take out those vehicles, get one GAS down there to check out those life pods and the other, turn it round and get Fausto's squad out. Helm, bring the Nemesis round to an optimal firing point to launch nukes at that base and disable its defence missiles in those silos, and make sure everyone knows what's happening".

The Nemesis moved round, out and back toward the planet for some 400 klicks, turning to position a launch, the ground strike warheads were swapped on to the two remaining missiles, but Baylin planned initially only on using one, 100 kilotons would more than do the trick on the target base according to the Amundsen's data.

The fighters swept down, unseen by the vehicles on the ground as they came low out of the horizon, blasting each of them to smithereens with guided ground attack munitions. As they swept back up in to space the Nemesis fired and behind them, 100 kilotons of thermonuclear devastation air burst cracked open the alien base and levelled everything to ten meters depth, totally disabling or destroying the outdated and primitive missile defences, not that Baylin was aware of their antiquity.

The pilot of GAS-3 had never taken one to its limit before, the decent was the fastest she could risk and even then she'd have just one-one-tenth of a second margin, only the computer could calculate that, it was hair raising, she would have just 48 seconds to get everyone aboard before the alien ship detonated. The speed of her descent was so rapid the burning orange in the purplish daylight sky was clear. Fausto and his remaining squad, squatting down behind the ridge, prayed the GAS would get to them before the ship vaporised everything inside 15 klicks in every direction. Baylin and the Nemesis crew held their breath as the timers dropped and QuAC announced the progress of the mission, even though they could see it on their screens... "Ground strike successful, fighters have eliminated vehicles, GAS units landing within 300 meters of target life craft, nuclear detonation confirmed at alien base, fighters have retuned to space normal en-route to Nemesis. GAS 3 has extracted remaining squad, accelerating into orbit...5...4...3...2...1...alien ship has detonated. That they could see. The light from the blast was first.

On GAS-3 the light and then the thermal wave shook it violently, but she was too fast to be hit by the shock waves. Sixty klicks to the east the GAS were too high on approach to be damaged but were buffeted hard.

Nobody on the Earth ships had ever seen an explosion like this on a planets surface. QuAC announced it was close to 25 megatons. Baylin looked at the filtered image as a massive mushroom cloud hit the planets stratosphere and spread out like some hideous rash of fire and light. "You know", he said to Markus Obishka, "in the 1950's they tested thousands of weapons, some almost as big as that on Earth, one they called the Tsar

Bomba, the Russians exploded, was twice that". Obishka said nothing, he couldn't even comprehend such madness.

On the ground the GAS shuttles disgorged their troops, the alien escape pods were damaged but they were intact enough. Sergeant Londing cut open the outer shell. Inside their was a huge, semi-conscious pseudo-reptilian creature - mostly unable to move, wearing some sort of breathing apparatus. Londing was stunned, everyone with a screen on every ship who was tied into his feed was either shocked, stunned or triumphant. They had a face for the enemy. And it couldn't have been better to terrify every human from here to the far side of the furthest colony.

****

Dr Branson and a six man medical team in full Hazmat suits waited at the entrance to the shuttle bay. The alien was clearly injured and unable to resist. It had taken five men to get it out of its life pod, and it was a CO_2 breather so it had been hard to keep it alive on the returning GAS. It was easily two meters in height, had a thick tail adorned with a nasty looking blade at the end, and a snout with heavy jaws and the mask that allowed it to breathe from a CO_2 tank strapped to its front. It wore some kind of flexible lightweight armour clothing, but its issue seemed to be a severe head trauma to the back of its skull. It was bleeding green blood, and the Doctors initial assessment was it wouldn't survive.

They got the alien into a CO_2 chamber and were able to remove the mask and breathing kit with relative ease, it was entirely logical.

The medical scanner beds were tied to the QuAC which built a rapid biological profile from every type of scan that could be run. Doctor Branson consulted Science Officer Gold and his own top medical team, they were sure the alien wouldn't live more than another hour, two at best. They had no means of synthesising the blood needed and the brain damage was too significant for anyone or anything to reasonably expect it to survive.

Doctor Branson asked for the Captain to come down to the biohazard bay, and Baylin was quick to respond. "So Doc can you save ...it, him"?

239

"Oh he's definitely male Captain, but he's not got long, and he's pretty much unconscious and not coming back out of it. The question is what do you want me to do with the body afterwards, that's your call".

"He's enormous". Baylin was staggered at the physical size of the alien.

"He weighs in at nearly 172kg Captain, 82% of his mass is bone and muscle, he could rip any one of us to shreds in a heartbeat and not even know he'd done it".

"What if I had Major Granding come over here and scan him?"

"You know that's not something I approve of normally, but under the circumstances, I doubt it would make any difference, I know you need to find out everything you can about...them."

"Can you keep him alive until Granding gets here? It'll take about an hour to bring him over from the Patton, he's with Captain DuBret".

"I'm not making any promises Captain, but I'll try".

Baylin made arrangements to get the Major over to the Nemesis as quickly as possible, going as far to plot a course back to the Amundsen and the gunships to hasten the journey time.

The Major docked just 45 minutes later and was in the bay suited up with the alien just 15 minutes after that. It was still alive, but Branson warned him it could die at any minute, it was slipping away.

Golding had taken his psi-pill on the way at the start of the trip to Nemesis and its effects were beginning to peak. Ideally he needed to touch the alien but the Doctor had ruled that out as too dangerous. The QuAC had identified 34 unknown pathogens on the aliens body, no doubt native to them but who knows what they would do to a human? It would take days of analysis and processing to understand just the ones on its skin.

Granding knew one thing immediately and the Doctor had guessed as much, these were the creatures he'd seen conducting the massacre on the planet the alien from the space station had 'shown' him in the lab at Telesto.

He got as close to the alien's head as he could, shaping his hands around the surface - there was little in the way of surface thoughts or even the sense of anything. He opened his mind, slowly, reducing the filters that had he'd painstakingly learned to construct to keep out unwanted thoughts and feelings. There! That was something, but it was pain, and regret, the alien was deeply, emotionally regretting. He opened up a little more, images, feint images, then he realised, the alien wasn't expressing remorse, it was regretting failing, regretting not killing more, regretting not destroying...the Nemesis, he saw an image of the Nemesis, others on a bridge, this alien was its commander, its captain, he was passing, slipping away, the images seemed to shrink inwards to a point of oblivion...Granding stepped back, he felt the alien die, it was as if it took a tiny piece of him with it.

"He's dead Doctor Branson", was all Granding could say, as though somehow the array of medbay scanners had missed the event.

"You weren't there to save him, Major Granding, did you see anything?"

Granding hesitated for a moment, then looked directly into the doctors eyes, "regret Doctor, profound, unremitting regret that he hand't killed us all and destroyed our ships".

An hour later the Major went to see the captain, who was present with the doctor, his first officer and science officer, and the ships astrozoologist Lieutenant Kagala, in the briefing room.

The overwhelming need now was to preserve the body and the Doctor agreed to provide tissue samples and scans to each department for study, then placed it in stasis to prevent cellular degeneration. Captain Baylin informed them all they had no choice but to leave the system and they were already making their way back to Procyon. Nemesis was short on ammunition after the battle and the damage needed dock repairs to make good, even if it was only for two days.

The Major was still at the peak of his sensitivity and rebuilding the filters he'd let down. Before the group disbanded he felt unusually compelled to explain the alien. Captain Baylin was interested so let him proceed.

"The alien mind was different, even haunting, its thought patterns were quite different. When you see into a human mind, it's oddly familiar as our brains and our motives as a species are surprisingly similar because genetics have made them that way. We have characteristics that make us very individual. The alien wasn't an individual like us, he existed separately, certainly, but his sense of belonging to something greater, his viciousness, his viewpoint was that of a pure hunter, a carnivorous, ruthless predator, wrapped up in a sense of control and loyalty. He was just a thin veneer of control over a seething desire for violence and destruction, because he would dominate".

The Doctor, ever the cynic, had to say something, "You got that from a fifteen second encounter before it died?"

It was Lieutenant Kagala who sprang to the Major's defence, "fifteen seconds is like a day in a psi-encounter, especially if they lift the filters they construct, the flood of information can take days to absorb, longer to process".

The Captain knew that, but so many of them suspected the major's abilities were just too much like snooping, nobody ever felt comfortable. Especially with a T7, only a handful of others were known to even exist above that level, maybe 100 or so, nobody knew.

Major Granding was used to being around 'norms' as T-Corps called the vast majority of the population. He was used to being treated as though he wasn't in the room. It was a subconscious group response to the fear of his presence and he was used to it. He didn't of course like it, but he understood it. He felt especially awkward about it because the chemically induced enhanced state was letting him pick up too many of their random thoughts and they were rarely complimentary. The doctor didn't trust him, the science officer was sitting behind a layer of self taught mental walls he could get round, but had no wish to. The Captain, he didn't dare look. For one he'd know. They had shared an intimate relationship once and once that's happened, the other party always knows. The Astrozoologist, Avode Kagala, was an open book, a decent, open minded type with no prejudice. The first officer, Markus Obishka, now he was something else. He'd been trained - it wasn't uncommon in senior executive officers. He was able to create blocks and fences a T-5 would struggle to pass, a T-6 maybe with a lot of effort. A T-7 like him could do it, but it would never go unnoticed.

As usual the skepticism in the room was profound, but Major Granding was not going to let this pass.

"Look, I appreciate all of you have doubts about T-Corps and what we do, but it's times exactly like this we're trained for and all of us - all of humanity is now at war with these things. They know we exist, they know where to find us or at the very least start looking, and I assure you, they mean us harm. That ship of theirs took everything we had and some sharp strategy and tactics to take down. They will not make that mistake again, the next time they'll come will be with a fleet, and they will want revenge, and they'll not care what they do to get it".

The room went silent as everyone looked at everyone else and then they all looked at Captain Baylin. "I've known the Major a very long time. If he says we're up against an enemy like we've never encountered before, then believe him. This is the day we as a race have to grow up. We've been colonising and searching as fast as we can for a long time. We're spread out, and we have few defences because there has never been an outside threat. That's changed. Today we got lucky. If there had been two of those ships, god forbid three, we'd be dead".

Lieutenant Kagala asked to speak and Baylin nodded to him, "the Captain is right, so is the major. If these aliens are anything like the reptilian creatures we've encountered on Earth, or even as I suspect, some kind of Earth equivalent of a pre-historic raptor evolved over millions of years - they'll be sophisticated, socially complex and vicious on a scale we'll find hard to comprehend".

Baylin decided to close the meeting, "everyone get your conclusions, facts, reporting, on my desk in three hours, I want a full report to send to Fleet. Markus make sure you get the after action reports from the marines and fighter commanders and we can get them back to Fleet as soon as we're through the gate to Procyon". Baylin headed for his cabin and his much needed bed.

CHAPTER 31

TRACKER, TAILER, SOLDIER, SPY...

Procyon Base Security Chief Todd Carollio has access to a whole range of security and data feeds from the entire Alliance security network. But he was very aware that simply dialling in and asking for information on an individual of influence and power like Mr Athanasios, would certainly be flagged up to someone. Who he didn't know, but you could never be too careful.

However he wondered if such a blatant system interrogation would bring something or someone, out of the proverbial woodwork. Maybe soon, but not today. His approach would have to be different, not seek out Athanasios but those who worked around him. Who did he speak to, which of the civilian liners did he fly on, who got him through security, did he meet anyone regularly? He'd track back Athanasios' last arrival and then investigate those who obviously provided some sort of key service. Nobody got through customs and immigration that easily and that quickly without help.

Carollio wasn't stupid enough to use his own access points to the network. Over the years he'd learnt to create ghost accounts that mirrored his own but linked to fake registrations and identities only he knew about. Deep encryption and one-time usage was the safest bet, if anyone flagged him up, the whole identity could be dissolved automatically leaving no traces. He knew how to cover his tracks, he'd been doing it since he was old enough to use a keyboard and microphone.

Diligently Carollio pieced together the video feeds of Athanasios' last visit. He watched him arrive and pass through security check points, identity control, passport control and immigration vetting - he avoided conversations at every stop. Every time he had exactly the right document or pass, nothing tripped an enquiry, nobody spoke to him. Until he reached customs.

At customs, he spoke with one officer, who checked a bag and Athanasios was cleared. Officer Eric Donnelley. Carollio ran the scans for Donnelley, it took a while but the computer found four other visits where Athanasios arrived and Donnelley passed him through customs. He went back through Donnelley's shift patterns. Customs officers spent four hours on direct search and four hours on background behind the walled sensors. Carollio went back through Donnelley's shifts around Athanasios' arrival times and found that three out of the last four, Eric Donnelley had requested shift swaps with someone else to be at that spot at that time. One might have been coincidence, two good fortune, but three? That was deliberate.

Next, Carollio would have to go through Donnelley's communications. There was never much chance of audio or video - it would be single text points - possibly a single word long pre-arranged that gave away a day, which would have pre-sets Donnelley may have been given some other way, even on paper, it was so much less traceable.

Chief Carollio ran the data, and to his delight the day before Athanasios appeared a separate single word private text message would arrive. He was sure they were encrypted, carrying a little too much sub carrier data than the message would require to display. It didn't really matter, because the link was now clear.

Donnelley was also a senior customs officer on the front line, a team leader, so that gave him connections to dock workers and the systems overseeing the loading and unloading of ships if he wanted it. It gave him passenger manifest access. He could vouch for Athanasios, maybe even tell his colleagues he was a government asset and push him through back corridors and past conventional channels unchallenged.

Yet now he had another problem, he might know who was helping him here, on the base, but he couldn't expose or challenge Donnelley without giving himself away. So who was communicating with Donnelley?

That was harder to track back, but after a slow interrogation of Earth's communication relays database the text to Donnelley came from Luna - a company called the Imbrium Corporation, which was in realty just a shell operation within a shell and based on registration data, in the Martian Freeport - a tax free trade zone set up to encourage Martian commerce. The Chief was not amused, that line of enquiry would die or risk being detected. There was another. Ticket tracking - Athanasios always travelled on Virgin Galactic Spaceways, somebody would have purchased the tickets. And the credits used to pay for tickets were legally traceable, cash wasn't permitted. The account was registered to the Imbrium Corporation. Somehow that didn't come as much of a surprise.

There was though more to the ticket information, because the law required full destination disclosure, and all of the travel documents Athanasios used were logged there - accessing the data from the ticketing wouldn't flag up a track. Carollio finally had something concrete without having to alert anyone he was looking.

Athanasios had a passport designator of D2 - that was exceptional. A D1 was full head of state or government - the type used at the highest levels for travel between states on Earth and in space. A D2 was ambassadorial level, it gave him diplomatic immunity across every jurisdiction on Earth and anywhere inside Alliance space. It was virtually unchallengeable. Even if he committed a criminal infraction he couldn't be detained unless the issuing agency rescinded it. It was issued by the MCG - The Martian Colonial Government. Athanasios was working for the Martians? Carollio couldn't believe it. He wasn't a Marsy, he walked and talked like an Earth-born, he was used to full gravity and no Martian diplomat could afford suits like that.

What did he do for Mars? The implications were extraordinary, it would make Mars complicit in the attack on the Amundsen. The ships crew, near half of them were Martian born - Mars would never sanction an attack on their own like that, he knew Martians, they simply never would. No this was much deeper than that. Carollio had contacts on Mars, people he could trust. He'd spent five years there, married one, divorced one admittedly, but people owed him favours. To get them he'd have to go there. He sent a message to Commodore Tan requesting five days leave to attend to business on Mars.

The Commodore was nervous about letting her security chief go just as war was breaking out, the Nemesis group was about to return to Procyon and a load of new ships with ammunition supplies and troops were all expected within days. She'd seen the manifests and they would need Carollio's attention, trouble always followed this many marines - almost 4,000 were due, never mind the ships and their crews that Earth was sending. Yet she had a deeply disconcerting feeling about Mr Athanasios and what he was up to. She decided to speak to Carollio in person, and called him to her office.

As the Chief arrived he was struck by the new public broadcasting messages coming in over the base display screens, "Earth and the colonies are now at war, aliens attacked our ships, be prepared, be alert".

"When did all that start?" He asked in his usual less than deferential style, something Commodore Tan found occasionally grating.

She closed the doors to the operations area from her desk. "Nobody will suspect what we're talking about, not with what's going on outside. You know the Nemesis defeated one of the enemy ships?"

"I'd have to be deaf dumb and blind to have missed that bit of news, it's everywhere. When are they due here?"

"Tomorrow morning, and supply ships are due here in three days, with an entire Marine Battalion two days after that".

"That sort of puts the kibosh on my leave request then?"

"I'm presuming Chief that you're request was because only your presence would enable us to move forward?" Tan was being very official, there was none of the gentle side he'd encountered in her quarters.

"I have contacts on Mars and people who owe me favours, big favours. Favour enough to get to the bottom of who and why, if you catch my drift?"

"I do Chief, I do, and I do believe that this man is a threat to this base and the Alliance in general. We're about to enter into a new phase of our history, this is one of those black swan events, we have to grasp it and win

247

or risk being defeated and all the consequences of that, I think our person of interest may undermine that ability."

"So I can go?" Carollio asked as if he was kid being given permission to attend a sleepover.

"You can go, but not on leave. This morning Monrovia sent out invitations to heads of security at the four largest bases to attend a security conference on Titan. It starts in a week, that gives you time to get to Mars and back to Titan for the conference".

"It gives me a day on Mars".

"Then you best make the most of it, the fast liner to Titan leaves in a little over ninety minutes, or you'll have to wait another valuable 12 hours for the second one. I'll see to briefing your deputy, its wartime, for now we can make up any excuse we like". Commodore Tan smiled at Chief Carollio who knew he'd have little choice.

"OK I'd best pack and get to the passenger terminal, presuming you booked me a ticket?"

"All done, its on your coms already, enjoy Economy Classic".

****

"Welcome aboard Virgin Galactic Spaceways "*Martian Pride*", your safety and comfort are our first priority. We know you have a choice and thank you for choosing us as your travel partner".

A window seat, and two people to push past to get out of it when he needed the facilities. Thanks Commodore. Chief Carollio was in civvies and he hated travelling trough hyperspace. This whole trip seemed like a horribly bad idea.

No matter the tedium of the journey - and it was a long journey even in what were frankly, pretty good seats, the lack of space and the not having anywhere much to walk about, was testing Chief Carollio's patience. He was used to being top dog in a structural hierarchy he ran his way. He had none of those privileges here. It reminded him why he didn't much like civilian life.

There was one thing though, arriving at Titan was always a breathtaking experience, and the passenger processing facilities were fast and efficient, the views of Saturn even impressed him, but he knew that he'd been flagged and recognised as a senior security officer just from the looks he got from the security people manning the immigration stations.

Yet he also knew that they knew, he was on his way to the security conference and they had no idea that he had another agenda.

The transfer from the "*Martian Pride*" to the express shuttle to Mars was relatively straight forward, through the usual terminals and processes. Seamless, easy. There was a little more evidence of security than usual, but that was reassurance for the general population rather than anything concrete.

The flight to Mars was always a single class experience, nobody had different seating. Tickets were expensive, the speed made it a premium service, but also required a special kind of seat that managed the occupant and the forces that acted on their body. And it was always full. This time he had a window seat and was grateful.

The shuttle's acceleration was often uncomfortable, and to gain the maximum speed it could, it used Saturn as a slingshot. No civilian ever forgot that ride, the first orbit around the planet was one thing, the second was blistering in its acceleration, suddenly the shuttle would just feel like it was set free at speeds as a passenger, you simply couldn't comprehend. Mars was very nearly at its farthest point from Saturn at this point in the year, so much so that they wouldn't even see Earth as it was in opposition on the other side of the sun. However, they would come stunningly close to Venus with its choking carbon dioxide atmosphere, gas cloud life and violent storms. Even so there were rare gasses in its atmosphere and some of the gas extraction platforms often shone brightly on its dark side, a place they all made sure to stay because of the radiation so close to the sun.

Carollio watched some of the in-flight movies, managing to use up six hours, but soon fell asleep. Before he knew it they were just three hours from Venus and five from Mars.

Venus was the shuttle's brake, it saved huge amounts of energy decelerating to use the planet as a gravity trap, from that point it was just a relatively short hop to Mars. Carollio looked out of the shuttle window from his seat and watched the tiny spec of red grow and grow, the shuttle space dock was soon in view, and before long they were disembarking.

He felt refreshed, yet slightly perturbed being back here. They proceeded to the atmosphere shuttle and it sedately took them down to Marsport, with its over-ground high speed vactrain tubes to the domes of Hecates and Tholus Cities.

MAFAC signs pointed to the vactrain he needed to get to the Mars Freeport Administration Complex under the Tholus City dome, it would take around thirty-five minutes.

The gravity was hard to get used to, it was at least 10% more than on Procyon, and while he'd taken some of the pills to help adjust, he'd been on Procyon so long it was as if he'd put on 12kg in weight in a matter of minutes. It was quite uncomfortable and he felt distinctly unhealthy. If he felt uncomfortable, the chief knew he looked uncomfortable.

Just when you least need something to happen is right when it usually does. It was one of "Carollio's Many Mantras", a list of things he kept in his head that were at best a collection of truisms, with a tinge of experience and a lot of self-reinforcing idioms that made him feel better about stuff as it happened to him, because in his world, that's how it was. Stuff happened to him, he was never the cause of it.

Such a moment happened now. As he exited the vactrain at MAFAC's massive complex, through the glass on the other side, he saw him. Right there, Mr Athanasios. And he wasn't alone, with him were two Martian Colonial Government Customs officers, both junior ranks, but they were listening intently to what Athanasios was saying. At the end he gave each of them a pat on their right shoulder and drew his hand down their sleeve, their left hand met it in an odd upturned gesture. Carollio had seen that trick before on Mars in his police days. Smugglers and druggies used it to hand over small amounts of high value items unobtrusively, right in front of everyone else.

He had to stop looking or one of them would spot him. He turned away and tried to get through the barrier to get round to the vactrain on the outward platform, but it was too late. Athanasios was already aboard and the vactrain was being sucked into the tube and away to the very spaceport Carollio had just arrived from.

That left him no choice. The customs officers walked towards a coffee and sandwich stand - close enough for him to see them as he found a locker to stash his belongings. He'd have to follow them. They sat down, it was lunchtime and luck was on his side. He changed in nearby facilities into his Security Chief dress uniform, he picked it because it was devoid of station identity, just made him look like an extremely senior officer. A security chief outranked anyone but a General or a fleet commodore in military rank, and automatically was a flag officer for the customs and immigration services anywhere in the United Earth Alliance. He was going to blague this one, and it wasn't going to be subtle. Carollio walked up to the two officers as they ate.

"Gentlemen".

One of the men was so shocked he nearly choked on his sandwich and the other spilt a drop of coffee down the front of his jacket. Both leapt to attention, saluting, taken completely off guard. A senior security officer in day dress uniform usually meant high government and trouble.

"I'd like you to escort me to your local commander, nobody was here to meet me, and as I don't know where I am or where I'm going, you're going to help me".

"Sir, we had no information anyone was arriving, we, I can get you to where you need to be sir". The taller mildly over weight one of the pair was clearly put out by this interruption but at the same time had no choice but to retrieve the situation.

The shorter one seemed simply to come along as he didn't know what else to do. They headed, as Carollio expected, towards the customs tower, and were soon through security and into one of the elevators. Chief Carollio looked around for a security camera, and as he expected there were none, then picked the smaller officer to criticise the state of his uniform, using his left hand to point out deficiencies. As he did so, he surreptitiously picked

251

the left pocket of the other officer. The things you learn as a street rat kid that prove handy in later life eh? That's what he thought as he calmly performed the extraction of whatever it was Mr Athanasios had given them, slipping it into his own pocket.

As they exited the elevator onto the senior officers level, they could go no further. Carollio thanked them and let them go, his presence was already causing a stir amongst the reception staff.

"Security Chief...Carollio...we, er we weren't informed of your arrival sir, something must have happened, there's been a misunderstanding somewhere I'm sure". The receptionist was contrite but completely taken aback by his appearance. It was then General Simonieff, head of the Mars Colonial Government Customs and Immigration service came out of his office, "Todd Carollio, as I live and breathe, I never expected to see you on Mars any time, well, ever!" He reached out and took Carollio's hand, shaking it violently, then pulled him in for a Russian bear hug. Carollio hated such outbursts of what he considered to be fake emotions, but played along with it as he tried to think of an excuse for being there.

"It's nice to see you again after such a long time Georgi, I thought I'd pay a courtesy call as I'm on a stop over."

"Stop over to where?" asked the inquisitive General.

"Titan". Carollio prayed that Simonieff had no idea why he'd be on Mars coming from Earth, as at this time of year that wasn't a direct enough flight to be believable. It seemed to work, then Simonieff said, "I thought you were on Procyon, Earth gravity must have been hard after all that time out there?"

"Well it wasn't easy, but two days and the pills, plus one of those clinging body suits under the uniform, helps keep you upright!" Carollio laughed and Georgi Simonieff laughed with him.

"Come and have a drink with me, I have a few minutes, then I have a meeting, they're worried about people leaving the remote systems and coming back here if the war gets worse, which we all suppose it must at some point. Now tell me, have you seen the Nemesis? Have you met the Captain, that what's his name, Baylin, what a tactical genius eh?".

"No I haven't actually met him, but he's been through the station, that I do know, I suspect I'll get to by the time I'm back".

"So tell me Carollio, what have you been to Earth for, or is that a '*zapretnyy*' subject?"

"*Zapretnyy*?" Carollio had no background in Russian so no idea what General Simonieff was trying to get at.

"Out of bounds, Todd, out of bounds!" War makes things harder to talk about, not that we've seen any war round here for years, but I'm an old hand, we Russians had more than our fair share of wars before...well, you know, before".

"I do, and yes it's about as '*zapretnyy*' as you can get. There is one thing you could help me with, we've had some problems on Procyon with a company under your jurisdiction, the Imbrium Corporation".

If General Simonieff knew anything he most certainly didn't betray it. Carollio was reading his body language and he never as much as hesitated or flinched.

"Aren't they a small import export company in the Free Port? I remember them buying up an office and some warehouse space, all that needs my approval, over two years ago, but nobody complained about them. Come to think about it that's something of a red flag by itself, all of these shipping and warehouse boys argue like cat and dog over the labour pool for loader-shifters and warehouse space".

"Would you object if I went over to see their admin people?"

"Me? I don't care what you do with your time Carollio, but you'd better take one of my men with you, you stick out like a polar bear in a coal mine in that uniform".

They said their goodbyes, and a grey uniformed escort joined Carollio, named Corporal Poyle, a tall African with a big smile and hands the size of a dinner plate.

Poyle had access to a ground car and quickly drove them out through the domes edge to the transit tubes that led into the Mars Free Port.

Imbrium was about one klick in on a nondescript block. Carollio had Poyle drive round the block and the first thing Poyle said was how quiet it seemed, even though it was one of the smaller units. It was a bit of a backwater but all of the other units seemed to have some evidence of use.

Carollio had Poyle stop and they got out, they walked a short distance to the nearest side door, more out of sight from the roadway. Carollio took out a small device from his jacket pocket and placed it on the complex digital lock, after looking around for a camera. There wasn't one, another odd feature for a facility that supposedly carried valuable goods. Poyle looked nervously on, "sir are you going to..." but Carollio put his finger on his lips to silence him, and the door lock opened. Carollio pushed the door, no alarm, nothing. The space was huge, lights came on, and they both looked at the last thing anyone would have thought to see; a single desk in the middle of the floor with two chairs in front and one behind. The rest of the warehouse was completely empty.

They walked to the offices, desks, cabinets, everything was empty. There wasn't a trace of any activity at all, not a computer, screen or terminal of any type, no comms equipment, nothing.

"General Simonieff is going to freak out about this Sir, not using the facilities in the Freeport is completely against the general lease - these places are heavily sought after".

Carollio stopped to think for a moment. If there was nothing happening, the neighbours would certainly have complained about it, some business desperate to get on to Mars and use the Freeport would have scoped out this place wasn't being used, filed a complaint and gotten the lease rescinded. If that wasn't reaching the general, it was reaching someone in the Freeport administration, and they were either turning a blind eye or being paid to do so, or warning complainers off.

There was another possibility, the facility had been classified as a government unit, that would block enquiries and any attempt at civil action by another business.

"Corporal, do you have a registry on your system you can access on who owns or used these buildings".

"Er, yes, sir, there's a facilities database, its in the car". They headed back to the parked vehicle, watched from across the street by a group of Marsy loader-shifters sat on the opposite side walk, waiting to be picked up and taken to the dome. Carollio didn't care and to Poyle's alarm he walked right over to them, they looked a bit skittish.

Carollio held up his hands, "hey guys, just wanna talk, and there's a bonus in it for anyone who says anything worth hearing".

Despite their nervousness, the bonus concept was enough to get three of them to step forward, one a short but muscular woman, with a thick Martian dialect Carollio found hard to decipher after so long away, asked him what he wanted to know.

"Have any of you seen anyone in that building, or come and go from it?" They all shook their heads in the negative, but the woman said,"izza clazzyfyd wa'houze man, allus knows dat, Marpo's theyz drive by here t'ree, four times day".

Carollio was slightly taken aback. "Mars Police come here four times a day? Do they ever get out, walk around?"

"Neda, jus'cruise by, those lazy fuckers ani't getting outta no car'n' walkin'!" The others laughed at her description.

Carollio thanked them and handed her the modern equivalent of cash, an untraceable 5 Credit chip, the equivalent of what she'd earn in a day. The others moaned, but Carollio pointed out they'd said nothing and walked back to the car with Poyle.

"Show me the registry please corporal".

The data came up, and sure enough the site was classified. He was in two minds as to what to do, he could use his legitimate security clearance to find out who classified it and when, and on who's authority. If he did that it would send a wave of red flags off in the system and give him completely away. That would never be worth it. He was out of time here, he had to get to Titan and the security conference and back to the space port. There was only one way of dealing with this now. He needed to speak to Commodore Tan.

Having Poyle drive him to the vactrain station to get back to the spaceport was a bonus, he thanked Poyle and reminded him that he'd seen nothing, something that Poyle seemed eager to acknowledge.

Carollio picked up his stuff from the locker he'd left it in and changed back into civvies in the same facilities. While doing so he took the tiny packet he'd been able to pick-pocket from one of the officers who'd been with Mr Athanasios.

He opened the tiny black cloth bag, already guessing what he might find. Diamonds, natural, brilliant blue-white diamonds, about two carats in weight. These weren't synthetic, Carollio had seen real diamonds, rare as they were now, smugglers loved them, tiny, high value. Industrial diamonds were now legally visibly marked too. Anyone with a magnifier could see it easily. The clarity on these was almost too high. He estimated each of the pair was worth around Cr500, easily two months salary for a junior customs officer.

As he sat on the express shuttle to Titan, he wondered how they were cashing the diamonds in, that was a whole other issue in itself. There was no doubt now that Mr Athanasios had help, he was up to something, for someone, and he felt no closer now to knowing who or what than before he arrived on Mars. All he could think was that it was a problem, it was definitely some form of conspiracy, and it seemed that it went somewhere inside the Martian Colonial Government. What had he gotten himself involved in?

CHAPTER 32

WRATH OF THE GODS

The Arckaxxnau Palace, a stunning brilliant blue triazolite crystalline structure towering over the city of Qorixiaan, capital of the Kadressian Empire, seemed momentarily to tremble at the deep, slow rhythmic bass that heralded the entrance of The Emperor, Sayidarixx. He stood, fully 2.7m in height without the addition of the ceremonial uniform and regal embellishments that gave him the appearance of being larger still.

In human terms Sayidarixx was 65 years old, around half way through his life for a Kadressian warrior.

The vast audience chamber was filled with generals and warriors, and more than a few politicians. He was in no mood for discussions. They were here to listen and obey.

A new race, somehow had raided an Imperial system, boarded a deep space prison station, liberated one of its inmates, a dangerous leader opposed to The Empire, and fled. Then as one the military's most fearsome warrior generals - who had bravely taken on the role of hunting down these scum, made a valiant effort to locate them and bring them to justice, he was ambushed by an entire fleet and sacrificed himself to protect the Empire's outpost. That had been destroyed by the aliens, whose entire purpose seemed to be to intimidate and threaten The Empire before launching a war of conquest against it.

This was how the warriors would see it, because that's what he, their Emperor would tell them.

The facts were far more disturbing, but facts needed to be spoken in words that were palatable to the audience. As an Emperor it was a painful lesson to learn.

The reality was that somehow these aliens had defeated one of the most powerful ships in the fleet with little more than tactics and some bizarre small, fast ships that carried a disproportionate level of weaponry for their size. The cloaking system had failed to hide the battlecruiser Isscatl, which was another painful lesson to take on board. The warship that had attacked it was smaller, but powerfully armed. The base on the planet had presumably been destroyed as it hand't been heard from since, and the enemy troops were large and capable, fast creatures, fearsome and agile. And they had used atomic weapons.

Probes had entered the system and found the aliens had gone, troops and engineers were heading to the planet with a fleet of escorts to make sure it was retained for The Empire, or so he believed.

Now we knew where they came from, that they posed an existential threat to Kadressian interests, Emperor Sayidarixx had every intention of dealing them a massive blow, then he would hunt them down to their home world and destroy it, enslaving them .

A probe had gotten in to the system the aliens had come from, it had sent back just enough information to show that it was not their home system, but it would make a good start on the road to conquest. It had been a long time since The Empire and its warriors had found a worthy opponent to test their metal. This time revenge would motivate his warriors like little else.

That morning he had sent no less that twelve light cruisers and three more Giku class Battlecruisers to escort the re-occupation force. From there they would begin the assault.

Sayidarixx pushed down his concerns it would be enough. The fleet generally was large but little changed from its last major war twenty years ago. These aliens seemed to have proficient technology, but did they have the fighting power and spirit of The Empire and its warriors? Nothing could withstand them, nothing ever had and nothing ever would.

Emperor Sayidarixx slammed down the sacred rod of power that emphasised his office as political, military and religious leader of his people. The audience chamber erupted in "Hail the Emperor! Hail the

Emperor!", then with a sweep of his clawed armoured hand, the vast chamber fell silent.

"You all know that a new and dangerous alien race has attacked and ambushed our finest, murdered our kin, our brood brothers and sisters, and now is the time to mobilise our forces and take our God Given revenge! We are the chosen and we will bring down on them The Wrath of The Gods!"

The roaring cacophony was deafening, and affirmative...what else would it, could it have possibly been? Sayidarixx had tried for years to change their ways, to move on from endless conflict, but it was impossible. It was hard wired into their genes. They'd rather die, take The Empire down with them than ever surrender. If he didn't order war they'd take him down too. He prayed that these aliens were not all as difficult as the ones they had so far encountered. A quick victory was needed, the Empire, not that many knew it, was short on resources, its economy stagnant, and struggling to feed itself. Billions of new slaves and a food supply of fresh meat, new mines and resources to exploit. Yes, a war and a victory would be good for all of the Kadres.

The Emperor left the vast audience chamber, as he went the generals in the front most rows crowded together. "I'm not sending all those ships, if they're gone it'll leave our kadre open to a move by KAVAK". "Same here" replied another. One of them suggested sending a smaller but powerful squadron, that would more than do. They grunted and agreed.

CHAPTER 33

DAYS OF SILENCE...

"Captain Baylin, man of the hour it would seem."

Bruce Baylin saluted Commodore Naomi Tan, who had made a specific effort to meet the ship at the docks.

"Commodore, it's an honour that you came over here to meet us at the dock, you must be busy enough under current circumstances".

"And miss the opportunity to meet you and the crew after what they just achieved in the last few days? You've probably put the enemy on the back foot at least for a short time, it was a remarkable victory Captain".

"I appreciate what your'e saying commodore, but really, we were lucky, if the crew hand't detected the de Broglie waves we could easily have been caught with our trousers round our ankles".

"You tell it your way Captain Baylin, I'll tell it mine. It's brought the reality home to everyone, Fleet Command are galvanised, ships are racing here, supplies and troops all en-route".

"Commodore, before anything else, we have to get the Nemesis up and running again, fully re-armed, she's the only thing in this system at the moment, and that probe they sent through means they know where we are. Until reinforcements arrive, that jump gate is undefended, we don't have enough mines, and your local gunboats and old light cruisers are scrap metal compared to the battlecruiser we encountered".

"I know Captain, and everything is being done to make sure the Nemesis is turned around. The armoury here has enough to equip you for one full re-arming, that arrived yesterday and was shipped in as part of your routine deployment backup, but much more is on the way. As far as the repairs go, we have a Class Two facility here, which means we can fabricate anything you need and you're top priority, I assure you of that".

"I appreciate it commodore, the gunships are undamaged, buy they need more ammunition, and refuelling, they don't have a long enough endurance without a support ship". Baylin worried about the gunships, they were very powerful weapons platforms, but vulnerable, small and yet vital right now. The Amundsen was far too big to be used in a close combat scenario, and not a warship in the full sense. She'd be torn apart by a surprise attack.

"There was another reason for me coming to meet you Captain", smiled the Commodore.

"Don't tell me, Fleet want a live conference, like yesterday?"

"They do indeed, and I'm to take you to our secure facility right now".

The vactube through the station's maze-like dock yards was painfully quick, not that you could see anything. In less than three minutes they'd travelled four klicks into the core of the planetoid, and its deepest security command post, reserved only for the most sensitive meetings and, as a war room.

"You know Captain, other than in a drill four months ago, we run one every trimester, I've never used this for its real purpose. Frankly I never thought I ever would".

They walked in to find that the operations room was buzzing with activity, much of the surface traffic control for the system had been brought down here. They were organising convoys to the jump gate with heavy escorts from the old ships under the commodores command. Others were working on securing weapons storage and fuel supplies, yet more were running tests on the base defence grid.

"I had no idea that the defence grid was so heavily armed out here commodore?"

"It wasn't until six months ago, they made us integrate some high end force beam platforms into some of the nearby asteroids. They stabilised them to stay and work with this base, and gave each of the three a missile launching capability, as well as a pair of point defence cannons. A base extension is under construction for a fighter squadron, but that's two years from completion, well it was, its been given a priority now, so six months. How long it takes to get fighters, that's something else".

They walked into a secure communications briefing room, and sat down. This was the latest comms technology, a live 3D screen filled the opposite wall. When it came on it was as though they were sat in the situation room at the Presidential Palace. President Mansfield appeared at the other end of the room, most of Fleet Command and some he didn't know, or even have a clue as to who they might be, sat in heavy black leather chairs looking right at him as though he was in the room with them.

President Mansfield was the first to speak, "Captain Baylin, I appreciate that you literally just got off your ship, but this couldn't wait. So much so that its actually 0200 hours here, that's how important it was I spoke with you right away".

"It's an honour sir, really…"

"Never mind about that Captain, what we've seen of the battle in real time has scared the crap out of everyone here, me included. That ship you took down, it's made the admiral's worried. If they have a fleet of them, Earth's in trouble, and you know and I know nobody builds ships like that in ones".

"I agree sir, I think we were lucky, but I also think we had some outstanding weaponry, and our sensor and electronic warfare systems were fantastic. We learned a lot from having the Amundsen with us too, the gunships were extraordinary, and the fighters, they had nothing like it, they seemed utterly incapable of dealing with them".

Admiral Esteban spoke on the last point, "Mr President, Captain, we've analysed the video and you're quite right, the fighters were beyond their comprehension, and we think we know why. It's the recovered alien body, it's just not even vaguely suited to a small fighter environment. Even if they had fighters, they'd be bigger and less nimble, just in accommodating the aliens body form. There's also another aspect, their whole ship design is based on the presumption and expectation of face-on combat. They don't seem to expect anyone to either be able to run from them, or survive them, and see no threat from others. Mr President, it's our assessment that they have never encountered an equal or superior enemy in their history".

"What do you say to that Captain?" asked the President.

"It's basically what I wrote in my report Sir, so yes I agree with it, but with some caveats".

"And they would be?"

Admiral Esteban was about to speak and the President stopped him, "I want the Captain's view on this Admiral, he was there, Captain?"

"I'm afraid sir, that they do have a fleet, the creatures are vicious, our T-Corps officer, Major Granding has seen what they're like, their viciousness, their hostility, its barbaric, visceral, deeply ingrained. I'd go as far to say what my astrozoologist told me is more specific, they're genetically encoded to dominate. They're basically highly advanced predator reptilians, they will show no mercy, they will not now stop until we are conquered, or we conquer them".

"Captain, that's depressing on so many levels. What you're saying is that we're now at war for our very existence". The President slumped slightly back into his seat, his worst reality now upon him.

Admiral Ferris had been silent, but he started to speak slowly. "Sir, Captain, if this is a fight to the death, we have to win, we have to fight them to the last man, or the last alien. I've read Major Granding's reports, and they're painful to accept. What we're up against here is like nothing we've ever imagined. I suspect logic, discourse, treating with them, will never work. They'll see it as weakness, if they can even be induced to talk at all, which I doubt. We've gone from a nearly complacent peace to all-out total war in a matter of a few weeks".

Everyone looked at President Mansfield, he in turn, looked own the table at Captain Baylin,"do you agree Captain?"

"Yes Sir, I do".

"As Commander in Chief of the United Earth Alliance, I'm officially declaring a state of war now exists, and I'm issuing an immediate promotion. Captain, you're now Vice-Admiral. The fleet on its way to you consists of two additional Nemesis Class, and four more Patton class gunboats, you've got a Marine Assault Carrier on its way too, they're all under you're command, whatever you need, you'll get".

Admiral Esteban was clearly not happy about the way this was done, but he could say nothing. Admiral Ferris was indifferent.

"Admiral Baylin, defend Procyon, but how you do that, even if it means going back to the scene of your battle, I leave up to you. Your in command".

The screen went off, the meeting was clearly over. Commodore Tan was mildly taken aback. "Well, congratulations Vice-Admiral Baylin, sir".

"Sir? Oh, well yes, how bizarre was that?" It dawned on Bruce Baylin that he know outranked by two steps the Commodore. The President had put him one rank below a full Admiral. The whole thing was starting to sink in, the Nemesis was now a fleet flagship. As an Admiral he could push trough rank upgrades for any crew, but he wasn't doing that yet. He was, like it or now the most senior officer in the system, and had just been given command of Earth's military response. He needed a plan, and the President had sort of suggested what he'd like to see done, it was daring, it was dangerous, but it would take the war to the enemy, rather than have him in the Procyon system, wrecking havoc on humanity.

Commodore Tan invited him to dinner, along with Captain Andros and Captain DuBret, it would be a formal dinner, his first as an Admiral.

The news had spread like wildfire, he arrived back at the Nemesis on the connecting bridge she was linked to, and as he started to cross, various crew, passers by, work men and repair staff from the base, all stopped and saluted, many grinning from ear to ear, as he passed many of them clapped. He entered the ships docking port and the crew and others were jammed in, they clapped, saluted, and cheered him through.

In all his life he had never ever imagined such a thing, he could barely look up, the tears were welling up inside him, and he struggled to push them down. This wasn't about success for Bruce Baylin, it wasn't about victory, it wasn't about personal aggrandisement, it wasn't even about command, power, or position. This was about a little boy who's parents had abandoned him, adoptive parents had disowned him for being different, and then died, leaving him with nobody.

He'd always known that one day he would make a difference, that he would matter, that he had some role to play. He didn't know what it was, but he knew, right now that this must be it. He could and would make a difference, he would defend these people, his ship, the fleet, Earth, and he would do whatever it took to stop the aliens from destroying everything humanity had worked for - and saved itself from.

Everything he had ever known, everything he had ever learnt, everything he would be, was to protect Earth. He had tried to inspire others, tried to bring loyalty, honesty, fairness and belief in what was right and suddenly, right here, right now, it was happening. It was both overwhelming and humbling. He'd never wanted to be in charge, just make a difference. As he walked slowly, shaking hands, acknowledging everyone, even those he didn't know, he saw Dr Branson up ahead. The Doc leant in and whispered in his ear, "just remember, nothing goes wrong like a plan". The Doc stood back. "Walk with me Doc?" asked Baylin.

They pushed their way through to the medbay, and slipped quietly into Branson's office. "Well, Admiral, that was something I've never seen before. Humbling I hope?"

"You have no idea Doc. It's not that I'm not up to it, it's just the emotion of it all, its extraordinary, I feel extraordinary, but at the same time, I'm fully aware of the level of responsibility. I get it."

"You also get I hop, that by promoting you The President has dropped the whole blame on you if it goes wrong, and gets all the praise for promoting you if it works out?"

"'If?' Doc?"

"You know what I mean...Admiral, it works both ways, you have to make the politics of this work too".

"I'm not interested in the politics, I'm interested in winning this war and getting it over with as soon as possible".

The Doc raised his eyebrows, "then Admiral, I suggest you get interested in the politics, because one way or another, the politics is going to be interested in you".

"Trust you to bring one of the biggest days of my life down to basics".

"Look...Admiral, I'm just as sure you won't let this little chat spoil today, lets face it this morning you woke up knowing nothing about it, you're made of tougher stuff than that. But you know everything has a price, don't let it be your reputation. President Mansfield is a politician, an OK politician compared to some I'll give you that, but think about the last few months, years even".

"Come on Doc, what are you getting at?"

"Admiral if you need me to point it out…"

"Just cut the crap Doc, and less of this 'admiral' thing, its just the two of us and we've been around the block a few times, what do you want to point out?"

"Alright, now let me spell it out, because I've had time to think about this. Who was commanding the first contact ship? The ship that was expressly forbidden to make first contact in the way we're all trained at Fleet Academy? Why were we there? Why were we forbidden to make first contact? Which President, radically boosted funding for the fleet, a fleet that just happens to be ready right when its needed, and who puts you in command of the new flagship of that fleet?"

"Doc that's a whole lot of conspiracy theory, you know how much trouble saying any of this that in Fleet circles would bring?"

"And isn't that in itself convenient? Nobody questions anything much these days, experts tell us what we need to know, and it follows a positive, creative line, and things work out. We learned our lessons, the pandemics of the 2020's, then the economic crash that followed, then the collapse of the climate and the wars from the 2040's just when everyone thought it was all going to be OK. We flew off into space, saved humanity, just about stopped Earth collapsing into calamity, it's been one hell of a century and then some. Now, this, this war, which nobody apparently saw coming, yet all the evidence suggests somebody did, very much see coming, and quite some time ago".

"Look Doc, thats all very big picture stuff, and I'm sure if you let me think about it I can come up with a way to refute every claim you're making. And its a good job it's me you're telling, because by rights you'd be in the brig facing a court martial for spreading conspiracy theories as a serving officer, so keep this stuff in your head and never repeat it to anyone, and remember that Major Granding is going to be assigned to the Nemesis for the foreseeable future".

"Is he?"

"Yes, that was a direct order from Fleet, they think his presence with Captain DuBret, on Telesto, and with the enemy alien, it's been invaluable. They want his take on anything else we might find".

The Doctor looked displeased at the prospect, but understood the why of it, besides what could he do?

"Before I go Doc, there's something else we need to discuss, namely your medbay and its preparedness levels".

"What wrong with our levels? We handled that battle emergency situation pretty much by the book and then some more". The Doctor looked exceptionally irritated that it might be implied otherwise, but Baylin was having none of it.

"Before you start going off on a tantrum Doc, it's not about what you did, it's about the lack of supplies. We're on a war footing, that means peacetime levels need to be raised, and that means, well it means more body bags, more triage kits and more of everything else you might need. You're given authority to triple your normal stores, and open the auxiliary Medbay space in readiness. Any dual assignment staff need to be brought up to wartime levels of preparedness, including medical refresher courses. The same is being applied to the damage control teams."

"Well...Admiral Baylin, on that joyous note, you'd better go and I'll start getting it done. But.."

267

"But what Doc?" The doctor looked straight at Bruce and grinned slightly, "thanks for listening".

"Anytime Doc, anytime".

As he walked back to his quarters, Vice-Admiral Bruce Baylin was left in another odd position. He was also Captain of the Nemesis, normally as an Admiral that job would fall to another officer, but he'd not been told he could appoint one and he wasn't in any event willing to hand over command of the Nemesis anyway. What it did mean was that Markus Obishka would have to manage a lot more of the day to day operations, but that was as far as he was prepared to go.

He spent the day on oversight of the repairs, administration and requisitioning the ammunition and repair kits for the ship, and for the incoming fleet. Before long it seemed it was time for dinner with Commodore Tan and the other captains.

Baylin didn't have an admirals uniform ready and didn't have time to get to a tailor to have one made, so he went in his captains full dress uniform.

The commodore smiled broadly when he arrived, Bruce was the first and she'd actually told the others to give her twenty minutes longer. "Admiral Baylin, thank you for coming, but before we start, I have something for you, she led him to a spacious spare bedroom (Bruce didn't even know the commodore had a second bedroom, a near unheard of luxury in military quarters, even for a base commander). There on a stand, hanging superbly pressed and finished, was a Vice-Admirals dress uniform, four sets of day uniform and on-board fatigues.

"Commodore, that's, that's incredibly generous of you".

"I didn't pay for them admiral, but I did have Dr Branson send over your last measurements for the uniform, there's a military tailor here and he had them done pretty quickly, requisitioned from the base budget I admit". The commodore smiled, "I'll leave you to change, the others will be here in about fifteen minutes".

Bruce Baylin looked at himself in the mirror, in a full dress Vice-Admirals uniform. He'd moved his service medals over, and noted the all-gold with two stars command bar. The uniform was more ornate than a captain's.

The aiguillettes were a little too fussy for his liking, gold looped cord from the right shoulder to the centre of the uniform, looked a bit too dressy and too old fashioned, but it was a ceremonial uniform, not standard day wear. He felt mildly ridiculous, like it wasn't actually him. He wanted to tell someone how he felt, the pride, the strangeness of it all, but he had nobody. He thought of Major Granding, then thought he wished he never had to see him again, then he thought how had he ended up without any friends? Officers, subordinates, but friends? Family? He felt extraordinarily lonely, despite being surrounded by so many people. Now this promotion put him even further away from the people he wanted to be closest to. What a bizarre irony.

He opened the door to the hallway and heard captain's Andros and DuBret chatting with Commodore Tan. As he walked back in the room, they all turned and saluted, and they were serious, this wasn't some light hearted gesture. That alone made him feel a gulf of responsibility had opened up between them and him, this was now very real.

Commodore Tan, as was Fleet custom, re-introduced the other officers, now his clear subordinates, but he didn't want them to feel that way. Before he had chance to more than acknowledge them, Commodore Tan led them from her quarters, and Baylin had a sinking feeling in his stomach. He knew what was happening and he'd hoped it wouldn't. Far along the corridor, out of the accommodation sector, was the officers club, *Ferrario's* (named after Rosina Ferrario, the first Italian woman to get an aviation licence back in 1913. All fleet officers clubs were named after pioneering female aviators).

As they entered, what Bruce Baylin, Vice-Admiral, was most afraid of, came true, dozens of officers from every Fleet ship at the base, stopped, turned, saluted and started three cheers, the old fashioned centuries old hip-hip-hooray! Then there were demands for a speech. Baylin waved the cheers down, he was pretty quick when it came to saying the right thing and as he opened his mouth it was drowned out by violently loud station-wide klaxons...personal comms units started going off on everyone as the recall to ship and actions stations blared out. As he ran out of the room towards the, a dozen of his crew and one of the gunships officers jammed in with him. On the screen in the lift wall a picture of the newly re-opened jump gate was clearly showing it activated and something was coming through. Whatever it was, Baylin knew it couldn't be good.

CHAPTER 34

...DAYS OF THUNDER

By the time they were able to get to the Nemesis the enemy probes had made their way into battle with the mines placed around the jump gate - they had less than three hours computer estimated time before the six probes, identical to the one that had gotten into the system before, had cleared the mines, then there was nothing to stop them except tracking them down one by one.

Baylin didn't think for a minute that was the enemy plan. These were not just probe drones, already two had been destroyed by mines, but there weren't enough mines to clear up the other four. Besides they were here for the purpose of clearing the mine field, he was sure of it. The enemy had assumed that if they mined a gate so would everyone else, and they were prepared for such an eventuality.

Only one of the three heavy cruisers wasn't docked - that had been by design, the Pollux was on sentry duty about 100 klicks from the base. Hercules had little ammunition and had been loading from the base armoury, but her fighters were out practising with Hercules' fighter squadron.

Baylin started issuing orders as soon as they got out of the vaclift, he didn't run, but kept a fast walking pace, "Bridge, emergency departure procedures as soon as the crew are aboard, get anyone off who doesn't need to be here, stop any loading, get the pilots to their fighters, get me a situation briefing, and get the other captains on line as soon as I get there". As he talked and walked, he took off the dress uniform jacket and handed it to the sentry sergeant, "when your done get this to my quarters, get the steward to bring my standard uniform to the bridge office". The sentry sergeant looked mildly shocked and snapped out an "aye sir".

Baylin was on the bridge in under two minutes. "How soon can we depart helm?"

"Around 60 seconds sir, just sealing outer doors, engines on line, dropping dock clamps".

"Get us out as fast as you can helm, set course for the Pollux, comms inform the Hercules she's to join us stat, weapons, what's the ships status?"

"We're fully armed sir, there was a problem repairing the No.4 point defence turret and it fires but it's immobile, some of the outer structural repairs haven't been completed but nothing that makes us unfit for combat".

Baylin sat in the command chair and strapped himself in, the other senior officers were appearing on the bridge rapidly. "OK give me a full status update and link me in with Captain Creighton on the Hercules and Harris on the Pollux".

The two captains soon appeared, Joan Creighton looked as cold as Baylin remembered her, she was a steely personality but a superb tactician, Mike Harris was one of the quiet ones, reserved but an outstanding motivator.

"Captain Creighton, I'm handing your fighter squadron to joint operations with the Pollux, Captain Harris they're yours for the rest of what happens today, the Hercules isn't able to re-arm them she hasn't had time to replenish. Captain Creighton I need you to get that ship out here with us as fast as you can, but make sure you've got enough munitions, if its under 30%, wait until it is".

"Sir, that seems inadvisable, we're at 25% it'll take twenty minutes to load up to 30%".

"Then do it faster, less than 30% and you won't last a second out here against a wedge of these probes".

"Captain Harris we're on our way, hold until we can go in together".

The Admiral looked for Markus Obishka, "Markus, get Captain Andros and Captain DuBret on, and where is the Amundsen? The Gunships?"

The Gunships and the Amundsen are underway sir, they're why we're getting such good information from the gate, Amundsen's stealth recon drone is tracking everything".

"Signal the Amundsen to keep her distance, she cannot get caught by whatever is coming our way, make sure DuBret knows she has to protect the Amundsen above all else. We can't loose that stealth drone, we have to see whats coming".

"Whats the gate situation?"

"Three of the enemy probe drones have been destroyed by mines, all three of the others are operational and they're mopping up what's left of the minefield. Sir they'll be done in around forty minutes, and the gate is still open".

Baylin wondered how they did that, keeping the gate open was a heavy drain on the ship generating the signal, at least it was for an Earth ship. He worried about what was coming next. He didn't have to wait long. As the Nemesis speed towards the Pollux, and the Pollux turned at flank speed to match her, the sensors showed the Gunships and the Amundsen coming up behind but keeping their distance. He had every reason to keep the Amundsen back, she could prove the key to this.

"Markus keep me posted on Hercules, I need to know as soon as she leaves dock".

As he said those words the screens lit up - the mines were nearly cleared, or at least disabled, and the probe drones quickly took up a position in front of the gate. They watched the screens as the gate produced not one, but three huge warships, two were identical to the one they'd taken down, the third was three times the size, a massive hulking battleship. No human had ever before seen anything that large in space devoted to war until now. It was easily four, maybe five times the size of the Nemesis.

"Science Officer Gold was already scanning it from the gate data and the Amundsen's stealth recon probe, "Admiral, it's weapons array is equal to all of our cruisers combined, but it's slow sir, painfully slow, it's engines are small but it has a significant reactor to power its weapons".

"Is it a forward facing array like the others?"

273

"Totally, the QuAC overlay shows a lot of weapons, its about three of the battlecruisers in one ship, but they're signatures are the same types".

"We can win this everyone, get the gunships away from the Amundsen and tell them to join with the fighters, launch all of ours, all three squadrons together, go with the gunships. We're going to go flank speed at them, look like we're attacking head on to keep them slow, then while they're watching us head right at them, attack from behind with the fighters and gunships and blow that battleships engines to hell. Once its immobilised, I'll bet the battlecruisers form up to protect it".

"Sir the Hercules has left the base".

"Captain Creighton, 13 minutes, that was quick work, well done, I need you to come to flank speed, we'll match you as you meet us, we're heading right at that monster".

He turned to the other monitor, "Captain Andros, you look flushed".

"Thanks Admiral, I haven't had to run that far in gravity, then get a shuttle and run as far in no gravity, in years".

"Captain I need you to keep back, but I need you to power up your scanners and do what you did the last time, jam every frequency you can by pumping out every last watt of power, but tie it in with our QuAC so that we don't get jammed too. I want them as blind as is possible, at the very least fighting us on the EM spectrum and wasting their power and time".

Markus Obishka could see what Baylin was doing, he'd recognised from the last battle all of the enemy weaknesses, and he was going to use them again, and add more finesse to it, by magnifying the Earth ships advantages. The last time they'd had nothing like this number of fighters, now they had 36 and with the gunships, they'd be deadly if this plan worked.

The minutes counted down. The enemy ships were indeed slow, but only because of the huge battlewagon they'd brought with them, it was lumbering, its turning circle was so huge it seemed to stagger along, and they kept a tight formation. Their commander wasn't going to use the far more nimble battlecruisers, he was using them as protection. These aliens were rigid thinkers.

274

"Sir we've reached flank speed, Pollux is along side".

"Helm how long before the Hercules comes in from the right flank?"

"Four minutes sir, she's running at 110% to catch us up".

"Change course towards her, tell her to keep going straight on and we'll swing back around and join her, then we'll match speeds. That'll force them to turn towards us again, and then I want to cross in front of them just at the maximum range we found on their weapons last time".

"Markus where are their probes?"

"In a holding pattern where they left them sir, they don't seem to be using them to do anything".

"They're using them as gate guardians, just in case they have to get out, that's interesting, it's as though they're worried about getting stuck here".

The Hercules was now closing fast, the Nemesis and Pollux changed their bearing to turn and match hers in a manoeuvre that looked spectacular from outside, now they were just about to cross right in front of the enemy ships, a classic "crossing the T" naval manoeuvre, and the enemy fell for it. The weapons on all three enemy ships opened fire, but it was extreme range, 90% missed and those beam weapons that did hit were too weak to do any damage.

Next came the enemy missiles, they were timed warheads, something else Baylin had recognised from the conflict they'd escaped on the Ramorra, a time that seemed like a lifetime ago.

Each of the weapons, detonated harmlessly, and earlier than they should have, their proximity timers derailed by the powerful jamming signals from the Amundsen.

"Right we're going round again, here's a little surprise for you".

The three heavy cruisers turned away from the enemy to the left, coming back around so that the enemy didn't need to change course, in a long tight circle, the enemy closed the distance, and Baylin knew they would fire again, but rather than complete the circle, he used what the enemy seemed too lethargic to realise, space is three dimensional.

The three cruisers came closer to the enemy's vast ships, but angled to fly under them. The slow battlewagon couldn't adapt its course that quickly, while the battlecruisers could have, they seemed locked into the giant warships course and manoeuvres, the enemy firing arc was a relatively narrow one, around 25 degrees above and below horizontal, they couldn't fire beam weapons at the fast moving Earth ships. Whoever their commander was he lacked all imagination, as the three cruisers dived down under the enemy, Baylin loosed their new missiles, a coordinated strike of 24 hyper-speed nuclear armed Long Lance weapons fresh from Earth.

The Earth ships banked sharply away to their right, leaving the enemy above them as they in turn rose up to the horizontal, screens blanked down and external windows were auto dimmed or shuttered....

The enemy ship's missile defences fired frantically, but they weren't designed for an attack from angles like this, sixteen of the two megaton warheads detonated along the bottom of the battleships hull. On board, the shattering force of impact sent systems off line and Kadressian soldiers were smashed against walls and bulkheads, massive amounts of neutron radiation penetrated deep into the ship, rendering many of the crew immobile.

Yet she did not break off, nor did her structural integrity fail.

"Admiral, the ship is, well, its been damaged but its still fully functional, it hasn't even slowed down".

"We just hit it with what, nearly twenty six megatons and its still intact?" Baylin was deeply frustrated.

"Like it was made of solid iron sir".

Yet things were not as they seemed on board the enemy battleship. Hundreds of warriors had died quickly from the neutron radiation and there was nobody to seal multiple hull breaches or re-route the power to the ships armour.

The jamming from the Amundsen was unlike anything they'd ever experienced, it was scrambling targeting computers, distorting the Earth ships positions and blacked out the tracking sensors, no Kadressian had ever experienced warfare like this, the enemy was cowardly, adopting cheap tricks and refusing to fight weapon to weapon, ship to ship.

Now the Earth fleet made its second move, 36 fighters and two gunships came unseen from behind the behemoth alien warship and fired a massive barrage of direct-fire and nuclear warheads - a battering of no less that 72, 2 kiloton warheads, and hundreds of direct fire weapons hits around the giant engine exhausts, virtually unprotected.

The staggering ship soon lost its ability to steer, its speed didn't change but it was out of manual control, its inertia caused it to start to appear to tilt forward's from the force of the blasts behind it, it was just moments later that the giant main reactor, flooded with neutrons and then loosing its cooling ability, started to collapse, its magnetic containment field snapped off and all primary power generation stopped.

The escorting battlecruisers finally disengaged, tied by rules and regulations, their expectations shattered and stifled of initiative, they swerved around the ship back towards the gate, their speed was astonishing, the gate snapped open and they were gone. But the three probes remained.

Their mission was now clear, they fired up and sped straight at the drifting battlewagon, its internal systems shredded, its weapons ineffective.

They were not disturbed by the jamming from the Amundsen, they reached the ship and seemed not to impact it, but bore into it, and in front of all who could and would see it, the massive battlewagon turned into a blazing sun, so bright that even on Procyon Base it was clearly visible for some two minutes.

The explosion was vast, some 200 megatons, the shock wave in space moved almost at light speed, sending fighters and cruisers reeling, but there was little real damage.

Admiral Baylin couldn't believe it. As they headed back to Procyon having picked up their fighters, he ran the extraordinarily one sided battle through his head over and over.

There were to him just two possible conclusions. Either the enemy were utterly incompetent, or this was a massive decoy. He prayed it was the former.

CHAPTER 35

CONSECORD TITAN

CONSECORD, the Conference on Security and Order. Chief Carollio didn't much like the implication in the name, it sounded a little too authoritarian for his liking, but, Earth was at war, and as he stepped off the shuttle from Mars the public monitors were busy playing back what seemed to be a massive explosion in the Procyon system.

He opened his compad and the data downloaded, playing back the bulletin of an an enemy incursion into the Procyon system and how Admiral Baylin had again defeated the enemy in spectacular fashion. 'Admiral? Wasn't he Captain when I left?' Carollio raised his eyebrows in amusement, it made him feel he'd been gone weeks, not a handful of days.

He went to the Titan Hilton and checked in, a simple enough room but it unusually had a window, looking down on to the planet. Fed up with sitting and sleeping on shuttles, time shifted by almost 11 hours, he felt he wanted to see if he could make any more headway tracking Mr Athanasios.

He must have come back through Titan if he hadn't gone to Earth. As with all these big conferences, senior commanders were always provided offices and workstations. Carollio had an idea.

He made himself known at the reception desk, instantly bumping in to the security chief for the colony on Delta Dorado, Chief Gerry Meddings who was with Chief Shimon Ocset, head of security on the Vega Colony. They had a coterie of deputies with them, as most were heads of security on smaller colonies in those systems.

"Well if it isn't the man with the easiest security job in the United worlds", boomed Meddings.

"Gerry, you have half the work I have and I'm in a combat zone with most of the active fleet on hand, so be reasonable". Chief Carollio, shook his hand and they began the usual chit chat amongst chiefs that Carollio was often bored with, but knew could provide reams of information if you paid enough attention.

He soon gleaned that Vega was dealing with a nasty pathogen on one colony that had killed over 260 people and was in quarantine. It wasn't unusual, some of the biologically diverse planets had some nasty surprises for humans. He remembered how the Incas and Aztecs and American Indians had been nearly wiped out by diseases spread by invading Spaniards, Portuguese and early colonising of the then United States.

Delta Dorado was feeling exposed and ignored, it had two damaged dormant gates and there had been rumours of something 'lurking' near one of them, but absolutely no evidence to back it up.

Drug runners had found a haven in the Vega Belt and there was still a lot of talk about Vega Colony itself becoming autonomous like Mars. It was all routine stuff. And yet there was some fear. Nobody knew where these aliens might appear. The incident on Mars had caused widespread discomfort, proving as it did that jump gates weren't needed for entry to and from a system. That fact had major repercussions and made everyone feel a lot less safe. Anything could now appear anywhere any time. Conspiracies were running amok, and no doubt would be covered at the conference.

Meddings' Second Deputy Chief was the target for Carollio. He seemed a yes man, a pleaser, the Chief made it a mission to cultivate him. Jason Jones, aged 29, fast tracked and ambitious. Responsible for the personnel and management of the security forces in the Delta Dorado system. And he'd have access to almost every network system that Chief Carollio would need access to.

They talked, they had a drink, they all chatted, Todd made sure Jason was involved in the conversations he had with Meddings, that he was 'one of the team', a potential equal.

The next day after the conference, Todd Carollio managed to peel him away from the group, and began the seduction. "Impressed with your record, hope you don't mind I've looked you up, I have a vacancy on Procyon, would you be prepared to have a formal interview for a promotion?" All the flattery that was necessary. The young man took the bait faster than a fish in a food-free pond.

Carollio invited him to discuss it further, took him to his basic office facility and set him up to show him how he would run certain investigations, gave him a name to look at, run protocols, praised him for the standard of his work (which to be fair was high).

As the 'interview' dragged on he distracted Jason Jones long enough with banter and forcefulness, to make him forget logging off. Once he'd gone, Carollio was in the system...and it took just minutes to find Mr Athanasios. Even now he was heading through the Barnards Star Transfer Station with a ticket to Procyon.

Carollio looked through Athanasios deep travel records, he'd been to every system, every major planet in the past two years. But there were three places he spent a great deal of time, Mars, then Procyon Base and Delta Dorado-III the later pair the most remote major outposts in the Alliance. His tracking from his coms link was frequently off line, and he seemed to vanish completely at times, especially from Delta Dorado and Procyon.

There was one thing though, he never did that stood out. He never crossed through Barnards Transfer Point to travel to Procyon, or the other way round. He always, always travelled to Sol, always Mars first, via Titan, then back out to the other end of Earth space. He met the same customs agents, the same pattern he had on Procyon, the same every time. But what was he doing? How was he doing it? Did the Martian Colonial Government really have anything to do with it?

Todd dug deeper, knowing that red flags were flying up everywhere and Athanasios would know that Jason Jones was on to him. He wouldn't know why though.

It took little time to crack the Martian Governments systems, he hijacked his way through them on the back of old codes he'd 'obtained' for favours granted to AGIA (pronounced *A-gee-ah*) - the Alliance General Intelligence

Agency, whom he'd helped more than a few times. They'd repaid him with one off access codes but he couldn't use them directly until now.

'The truth is always less pleasant than the lie', was another of Carollio's maxims. He'd started to assume that Mr Athanasios was involved in a criminal enterprise of some kind, but didn't know what. He'd begun to assume that it must be trading secrets, but his travel pattern suggested nothing of the sort. The people he met while he was off the grid, remained a mystery.

He knew what he'd been doing with the Tutankh Clan, but still they never knew what they were being asked to ship, nor why he'd wanted the attack on the Amundsen until it was found to be the secret - and now openly acknowledged - jump engine tech. But who had he wanted it for? It was worth a fortune to pirates, but they'd never be able to acquire a ship big enough to install it, not without someone knowing, the resources to build such a thing would be too obvious, AGIA would have known.

It was then the fragments and the pieces fell into place, his mind filled in the gaps without him seeing the facts, but the links and the cross points meant only one thing, Athanasios wasn't stealing the tech to sell, he was stealing it to prevent anyone using it. He wasn't selling anything, he wasn't buying anything, except services, even illegal ones. He wasn't even exchanging anything. At every point you looked at what he was doing it was denial of use that seemed to be the only real result.

So if that was the case who the frack was he working for? Who would want to deny Earth the ability to use jump technology on its large ships? Who would try to slow Earth's expansion down?

The only answer would be an enemy power in theory, but the race they were at war with, who still had no name, they'd come well after Mr Athanasios had begun his career and besides, Earth had found them, not them us. It made no sense it was the enemy.

That meant it could only be one thing, one of the big industrial conglomerates. They were either trying to stop a competitor, catch up with one, or slow one down to get an advantage.

That would make a lot of sense, the Chinese registered corporations were every bit as competitive and then some, against each other and especially when it came to the European Union states, or the African Bloc. And then their were the Australian corporations, they made the others look feeble, especially in the mining sector. The Indonesians were quiet but inscrutable, even the Japanese would never just lay down and let the others walk over their mega corps. And never underestimate the Indians.

If it was one of the big corporations, which one? All of them had interests on Mars, most of them on any of the colonised worlds and if not somewhere in those systems, almost everyone of them would have some interest or claim.

But thinking through, the ship building companies were the more likely to be behind it. If one had the upper hand in building big jump capable ships that didn't need a gate, the others would look like they were technically deficient, loose orders. Ship building for the deep range colonies and the mining companies was a multi-billion credit industry, a major part of the economy.

Now Carollio had a working theory. And that was something, but there's always room for doubt. And he had lots of doubts, because any good security chief always does.

He also had a problem. Mr Athanasios had friends in low places, and Jason Jones would be a target. If he took Jones with him, he'd attract attention to himself. But he didn't want the boy to end up a frozen block accidentally thrown out of an airlock for something he didn't do. He had no choice, he'd offer him the job and get him transferred as soon as was viable. If he could keep Jones moving long enough, he could keep him out of harms way.

Unsurprisingly, Jones accepted the job offer of being "Special Projects Manager" on Procyon. Quite what one of those was, the Chief would have to think up, but it meant he could have someone close by he could control directly, without the rest of his teams getting to have a say.

The conference was dull, routine management stuff, new measures to enhance security, new protocols for operating in a combat area - Procyon system was now classified as "front line operations", and security would be enhanced across the board.

That usually meant movement and access restrictions, reduced and more tightly managed shipping routes and censorship of comms relating to fleet movements. And wider powers of detention.

Carollio was all in favour of that.

His trip back to Procyon however was not what he'd expected. As Chief of Security for Procyon System, Fleet had a little surprise for him. A pair of new "*Legend-II Class*" Fleet Security Cutters, small corvette sized, 15 man crews, with room for a security squad and an inspection shuttle, armed with a turret mounted mid-range gatling pulse canon that would take out anything even a large freighter might have for self defence. And they were fast, quick enough to catch any smuggler. He'd been after a pair for ages, but Procyon wasn't see as dangerous enough, until now, to get them first. It was a faster trip home.

CHAPTER 36

DAWN OF THE LONG KNIVES

The Emperor stood, his temper close to boiling, he simply could not believe the news. Who had ordered the attack on Procyon? What stupidity had compelled these fools to send in an outdated, lumbering battleship, a near useless relic of a bygone war?

Not that these fools even comprehended that the technology may have become dated on a near century old warship, that fought once against a primitive species almost forgotten. It was the epitome of everything that he'd tried to reform in the Empire. Instead the states resources were sucked dry propping up a grossly bloated, ignorant, selfish, combative warrior class that dominated every decision making process and was far too inclined to do whatever it wanted, as this outrage clearly demonstrated. He needed to restore order, he had to bring them to heel, it shouldn't even have been possible for this to have happened.

He summoned the heads of the military, fleet leaders, generals, and the religious fanatics who made things harder still and rilled up the military masses.

First came the senior leadership, the generals, twelve of them from each of the main cadres. They were clearly uneasy. The Emperor was in no mood to let them off the hook.

"Which one of you knew about this travesty? Do you realise that we have been humiliated, made to look like fools, and not just to the enemy, whom your stupidity has allowed to think they're superior to us? Our people, the rest of the military, have all learned of the loss because not one of you could stop the news leaking out empire-wide? How does that even happen!? ALL of you are to blame for this, but I want to know which one of you let it happen".

His armoured fist glinted as he pointed at the generals, stood in a semi-circle in front of him. He had little trouble guessing which one of them it was and he wasn't disappointed.

"I allowed it". General Fa-Jinaxxus, oldest of them all, most senior of them all, stepped forward. The Emperor was about to speak, but the General wasn't finished, and carried on, a breech of protocol that made the Emperor concerned it was so odd. "I would allow it again, and if necessary, again, and I would not seek your permission to do so. The ship was manned by my kadre, under my command, and they have no confidence in your leadership".

The gruff, heavy voice of General Fa-Jinaxxus carried weight, authority. The Emperor looked around. The General would not have said this if he didn't have support from at least a third of the others, maybe even more.

If he called him out they would either act here and now or later and more deviously. He knew he was on notice. What he did next would make or break him. He could see them all and he knew they knew the same thing.

The Emperor made up his mind, his right arm turned right to point at the furthest of the twelve generals as his left dropped slowly to rest on the ceremonial, but very effective cho-taa, a viciously sharp blade that could cut the head off of a general with a single swipe. As he prepared to speak the audience chamber doors opened, yet only two of the generals turned to look at yet another outrageous breech of protocol.

The Emperor stopped momentarily, what was happening? Then it began, explosions outside the doors, he turned, too instinctively, to his right, expecting Imperial Guards to enter from behind him to come to his protection, but there was nothing, nobody. General Fa-Jinaxxus and Generals Ti-Kaxin and Hu-Yuzekk quickly stepped forward, followed by three others who turned to face the doors but were clearly covering the generals backs.

The Emperor grabbed his weapon, but as he did so General Fa-Jinaxxus had swept out his own and with extraordinary speed and agility, the old general cut into the Emperors arm, causing him to drop the sword-like blade, at the same time Ti-Kaxin and Hu-Yuzekk struck, one against his right arm, the other directly at his head, bringing down his cho-taa with skull-splitting force.

The Emperor Sayidarixx, fell, and as he did the other generals, in acceptance and prior agreement, each thrust their own weapons into his mutilated body.

General Fa Jinaxxus looked at the others, "like I told you, a weakling".

There would be no Emperor, there would be no pandering to this monarchy, the Kadre would work together, as and when it suited them and use the power of competition, the desire for victory, for the hunt, for the kill itself, to guide them as it always had in the past.

None of them seemed to remember the recent past, none of them cared. The Kadre had fought each other as much as any enemy not fifty years ago. This endless warfare is what created the monarchy in the first place, a means to make all of them see sense and order. Now it was gone, nothing but blood lust, the desire to fight and to win mattered now.

The enemy would pay. Not one of the Kadre leaders really understood who the enemy was, blinded by blood and tradition, it was as much any one of them as some upstart race on the edge of known space.

The city was in shock, people left their homes to look and stare as the Arckaxxnau burned, thick black smoke pouring from it. Explosions rattled the city windows, buildings that held the administration of the Empire together burned, bureaucrats were hunted down and murdered in the street, at their work stations. Many of them younger females, simply butchered as warriors tore buildings to shreds with grenades and gun fire. There was no need for this city, this capital, all they needed was a meeting place and a combat pit if things had to be decided the old way.

As the sun came up it could barely be seen as anything but an orange disk behind the clouds of black smoke. Thousands of warriors swept through the city, burning, hacking, levelling every remnant of the Imperial order, their viciousness knew no bounds.

As the day went on and the city, which was not a vast metropolis, was in ruins and the warriors reached the end of their bloodlust, they moved away, the routes out were blocked, the generals now on their respective flagships had drawn lots, argued and decided they would all finish the job from orbit simultaneously.

On a signal from General Fa-Jinaxxus, whose idea this coup had been, each of the twelve flagships fired its missile at the small city. Twelve simultaneously launched warheads impacted around the city's edge, the plasma energy detonations erupted in a blinding purple-blue light, each one's shock wave bouncing against all of the others causing a conflagration on the ground, a towering column of dust that almost instantly smashed its way through the planets troposphere. In the weeks that it would take to clear, all there would be was glass, molten, flattened, hectare upon hectare of utterly levelled glass.

The Viceroys across the systems, whose power had been unchallenged, were unaware of their fate. For most of the six of them, their fate was sudden and unseen. For Supreme General Zelixx, Viceroy of Kinkuthanza, brood brother of the Emperor, there was but dumb struck surprise.

The Viceroy's advisor, approached him as he often did. Taliss bore disturbing news, the permanent feed from the tachyon carrier signal that linked the station with the Arckaxxnau had stopped, something he had never seen before.

"Viceroy, the tachyon signal from the Arckaxxnau has ceased".

"That's not possible Teliss, you know that as well as I do".

"Viceroy, it has ceased, there is no communication".

As he expected the Viceroy, who was always nervous about not being able to run to his brother if he really needed to, came down from his work chamber, and lumbered over to where Teliss was standing, at a data node showing the status of the signals coming and going from the base.

All of them were black, not just the signal from the Arckaxxnau, even the base to planet communications were out along with all of the base communications system-wide and to all shipping. The Viceroy was silent, he simply didn't understand how that was even possible. He was about to turn his head to tell Teliss to call the guards, he had an exceptional sense his own personal well being may be in danger. The Viceroy never spoke again. Teliss who was an honoured but junior male from a minor Kadre, linked to one of the main twelve, thrust a *pak-tai-cho*, a thin, exceptionally small blade, but made from tourmaline, its centre filled with fast acting poison, into the Viceroy's neck, right at the base of his skull.

The idiot Viceroy fell, stumbling, to the ground, the life draining from his pathetic weak minded, courage-free body.

As he died, the KAVAK head, Commander Yissnax appeared. "Well done Teliss, well done. You've proven your loyalty to your Kadre, and to all of our warriors".

Teliss felt a mix of pride, elation, and yet self loathing for his betrayal, a look that perhaps lasted a split second too long. Yissnax saw the fleck of concern, and before Teliss knew what had had happened, the head of the stations secret police was behind him and slit his throat from ear to ear. Gleefully he watched Teliss' life slip away. He wiped the blood from his blade, and walked towards the command deck. There was much to do. Many throats would be cut that dawn, and his wasn't going to be one of them.

CHAPTER 37

NEXT MOVES

"Admiral Baylin refuses to give press conferences, he won't discuss operations with the media and he refuses to discuss what happened at the Battle of The Gate with anyone outside of the command chain. We're missing a massive opportunity here Mr President".

"A massive opportunity for what exactly? PR and pro-war rabble-rousing? You leave the Admiral alone, I gave him the job, I want him to do what he feels is right, because that's the way to win. I don't want some backlash coming at me that we've done this to militarise the Alliance, or force through big defence budget raises. I want dignified victory and people to see we need defence raises and ask for them, not be told they have to have them. Well not unless it gets to that point anyway".

President Morgan Mansfield slumped down in the chair behind a desk that had been gifted by the Martian Colonial Government 19 years ago when it became an autonomous colony in the Alliance.

He looked through the sapphire crystal top to the footprints preserved there in the Martian sand - the footprints of the first man to land on Mars. The Martians saw that as an effort by all of Earth and gave it as a gesture of reconciliation and appreciation, and no small reminder to every President of the United Earth Alliance, that Mars should always be on their minds.

The lacquered polished sandstone desk was symbolic of so much. The Octagon Office, so deliberately modelled on the concept of the office of the former United States presidents, an ever present reminder that what once we had all assumed was permanent, immovable, could indeed become a victim of its own arrogance and success when it failed to see the obvious, that in the end all others had seen, the near cataclysm of the changed climate. Many felt that the Americans had reaped their just rewards for denying it for so long under the long years of the Trump autocracy, first Donald, then his son, then his daughter. A quarter century of denial nobody would get back that could have saved so much.

But that was history. And nobody save a few, the President among them, knew the whole truth of that time. To save the planet, to drive us on to colonise space, only the future, the way forward had been the focus. The past was a litany of mistakes, there was no point in dwelling on them, just make sure we didn't repeat them, it itself far easier said than done.

President Morgan Mansfield was the trustee of the new order, the buck stopped with him. Some bizarre alien race they knew nothing much about and had stumbled upon almost by accident, now threatened the very existence of what Earth and its people had built in space. They had a future now, a way forward. It wasn't easy, it wasn't safe.

He looked up at the top of each of the eight walls in the office. They were adorned with an engraving, each a quote from great leaders of the past. "*We have nothing to fear, but fear itself*", was carved into the stone above the main door. To the right, "*We choose to do this not because it is easy but because it is hard*". On the next wall, "*Success is not final, failure is not fatal: it is the courage to continue that counts*". On the fourth wall, "*Courage is what it takes to stand up and speak, courage is also what it takes to sit down and listen*". The wall behind him had become obscured over time, for it was also covered with the Great Seal of The United Earth Alliance, and the flags of the services, but at the top, it read "*Courage is the first of human qualities because it is the quality that guarantees all the others*". Courage, strength in adversity. The theme continued on the other walls, but the seventh was a warning to every president, "*war is mainly a catalogue of blunders*", the sixth "*The only thing necessary for the triumph of evil is for good men to do nothing*". The eighth wall said, "*Our Patience will achieve more than our force*".

Something about all of them, and he'd read them every day for two years now, everyone was taught them in school civics classes, yet suddenly for him, right now, they all suddenly meant something.

Was that what the builders and designers of this office had intended? That one day the man sat behind the Red Desk would read them all one by one and it would dawn on him what to do next? Morgan Mansfield looked around at his chief of staff, Juan Campos, his AGIA liaison, the Fleet Liaison officer, his communications director. They were all sat looking at him. He'd forgotten for a moment they were even there. Each of them had stayed silent, watching him as his eyes went round the room to the tops of each wall. He hadn't even realised he had turned his chair a full 360 degrees to do it.

"You'd better get the chiefs of staff in the situation room, I've decided what to do. And get me the Speaker of the Assembly and the President of the Senate in a meeting an hour after that".

He waited for them all to leave, opened the comms to his personal assistant in the neighbouring office, "What time is it in the Procyon system?'

"It's only three hours ahead sir".

Good, get me a Platinum Channel connection to Admiral Baylin on the Nemesis please, let me know when you have him".

++

Bruce Baylin was bothered, and he told his staff and the Captains of the other ships the same thing. They hadn't lost a single fighter, and nothing was damaged beyond some minor cosmetic work on the exteriors of those that were closest to the enemy.

They all concluded as he did, either the enemy commander was incompetent, or the whole thing had been some kind of distraction, but what for remained a mystery. What could be worth loosing such a massive and expensive asset as that battlewagon?

The analysts were having a field day with that too, its lumbering speed, its all-forward firing arcs, it was, like the smaller battlecruisers that accompanied it, seemingly designed to face an enemy that did as they did, hit them face on and see who blasted the other out of space first. It was a blunt and powerful instrument of destruction, but its utility was minimal.

292

They'd taken it out with what seemed like ease, but it had proven to be extraordinarily durable against nuclear weapons. One recommendation was to increase the yield on the Long Lance weapons to as high as six megatons from the two they were capable of (they could be dialled back to as low as 50Kt). That though would take time as the warheads would need to be produced and deployed to operational ships.

Nobody knew the neutron radiation had been devastating to the Kadressian warriors and had contributed to the rapid demise of its reactor.

They did know that the Amundsen had been invaluable with its powerful scanner suite acting as an electronic warfare platform, that was obvious, though to what precise extent again, they could not know.

Yet none of the ships analysts, or their computers could work out the enemy strategy. And that made everyone, Baylin more than the others, very uncomfortable.

Baylin was in his cabin, he'd just showered and was not far from getting some shuteye. The comms panel blinked and beeped, "Baylin".

"Admiral", it was Markus.

"What's happened Markus?"

"You have Platinum Channel call incoming sir".

"If its Fleet HQ, I'm asleep"

"Er, sir, Its Platinum, sir, it's The President".

"Oh, I don't suppose he'd call back?" Baylin smiled at Markus.

"I'll put him through sir, you'll have five seconds before he's on".

Baylin grabbed his jacket and stood as close to the screen as he could so he could only be seen from the waist up. The President came on, "Admiral Baylin, I have to extend congratulations once again to you it seems?"

"Thank you Mr President, but it was a strange victory, and I certainly don't deserve all the credit".

"I've read the briefing notes and I've looked at the video Admiral, I see why you're so concerned".

Baylin's reaction was one of mild surprise, "You do, sir?"

"I appreciate that must seem odd from a politician, but I do get the situation. No matter how you look at it their strategy seems wasteful or deceptive, why did they do it and what did they gain? Those are the questions and nobody has answers".

"Yes sir, that's what has us all stumped".

"Well admiral, there's only one thing we can now do, we're still assembling the new ships here, three more Nemesis class are nearly ready, but at least a week from being declared operational, from the end of this month there will be one a week coming off the new production lines. So you can either do one of two things, sit there and wait for them to come to you, or go back to them, only this time take the system and hold it, put them on the defensive. I leave it to your judgement".

"To take the system I'd need more than a few troops to hold it, we'd need an assault ship, a division at least and a whole supply line".

"Already on their way. Marine Assault ships 'Midway' and the 'Akagi' are *en route*, each with a full battalion drawn from Mars and Lunar, they'll be with you in two days".

"That means they were already on their way here?"

"They were indeed Admiral, we do think ahead sometimes here you know".

Baylin knew why they'd been sent, they were to reinforce Procyon in case it was attacked, but instead he was to use them as part of an offensive.

"Sir can I ask what made you decided on this course?"

"I didn't decide, you did, in the last minute, and I'm not objecting".

"How did you know I'd go on the offensive sir?"

"Because I was sat in the Octagon Office, looking at The Eight Quotations".

"Which one decided it sir?"

"All of them Admiral, all of them. Good luck, and Admiral, we're all behind you, you know that I hope?"

294

"I do sir, so does the rest of the fleet".

President Morgan Mansfield smiled and ended the call. He looked up at the office walls *"We have nothing to fear, but fear itself"*, *"We choose to do this not because it is easy but because it is hard"*, *"Success is not final, failure is not fatal: it is the courage to continue that counts"*, *"Courage is what it takes to stand up and speak, courage is also what it takes to sit down and listen"*, *"Courage is the first of human qualities because it is the quality that guarantees all the others"*, *"War is mainly a catalogue of blunders"*, *"The only thing necessary for the triumph of evil is for good men to do nothing"*, *"Our Patience will achieve more than our force"*.

Those words were why humanity would survive this, and prevail.

CHAPTER 38

VIGILANCE

Chief Carollio had kept the arrival of the cutters quiet, only telling the Commodore. These ships were fast, indeed much to his amusement they were so quick, he'd arrived ahead of the ship carrying Mr Athanasios by about two hours. He couldn't help himself and went to the security centre to check up on everything.

His early arrival shook some of the staff just how he liked to. He made it clear he was just in to check messages and would be back in the office the next morning. He waited long enough to see Athanasios arrive, saw him pass through ID control and then, right then and there, the officer whom he always seemed to conveniently have on hand, pulled him to one side and took him through a secure door into what the chief knew was a back corridor used only by security staff and maintenance crews. Athanasios had completely bypassed any real physical scrutiny.

Why? What was he doing that he needed to avoid being securely scanned? Tracking him was now impossible without being obvious. Where was he going in the station? Carollio needed more people on this, he just couldn't do it alone. He'd have to pick at least two he could trust one hundred percent and they needed not to have any relationship with the staff who let Athanasios through.

He chose two of his best female officers, not because they were women, but because they were shorter, looked less threatening and considerably less obvious than the men he would normally choose to trust. Linda Bryant & Marie May were both discreet, and given a wide respect in the darker places of the base like the bars and the casino, because they were honest but not too pushy, and the bar owners especially knew they could go so far but no further.

"I appreciate you both agreeing to do this, but I cannot stress how important it is you don't discuss this with anyone, and I mean anyone, other than me".

The two officers looked at him mildly quizzically but were actually grateful they were being allowed to do something other than keep the smarmy bar owners in line.

"What's this guy done sir?" asked Bryant.

"Nothing, yet. And that's the problem, we seem to be unable to pin anything on him, but he's been assisted through security screening, seems to have easy access to almost anywhere on the station, and spends a lot of time travelling backwards and forwards to Mars and the outer systems for reasons we simply don't know. He's been flagged as a security risk, but seems to have some attachment to the Mars Colonial Government, though nobody there seems to know who he is either".

Carollio decided it was simply better to give them some background and make them understand the purpose of their mission was more than just a regular counter-criminal operation.

"You think he has some connection to the Martian separatists?" Asked May, extrapolating beyond his description.

"We don't know, I mean the separatists are all but history, but they're not gone altogether, he may be working on something to bring them back, or its something else, just find him and as discreetly as only you two can, find out where he goes, and who he sees, but don't ask questions, he mustn't get suspicious, and we don't want anyone even suggesting to him he might be under surveillance of any kind".

The officers left and Carollio hoped it would be enough.

++

The Nemesis was back at the station, each cruiser was taking it in turns to get into the repair dock, so Nemesis went first. It wasn't that their weren't enough docks, their were two, but Baylin didn't have enough ships to risk two of three being caught off guard. Repairs needed were light, it would take just a few hours.

297

What he needed now was to draw up plans and he hijacked the main briefing room from Commodore Tan, gathering all of the Captains and senior officers from each ship to work out what they did next. The Presidents direction had been clear enough for him, go back to Luyten 789 and seize the system.

The discussions were interesting, for one Baylin found himself with a heavy contingent of troops, not just a few marines but an entire division. And they had a Major General Shorter in command - and his rank equalled Baylin's, but the President had made Baylin commander of the entire operation, putting him a step above.

Shorter was actually shorter than almost everyone, at just 1.62m in height, and was proud of his reputation for being so, a 'cookie cutter' general. If there was a mould, he was cut from it, just smaller. He was a by-the-book type and had seen some combat in his more junior days during the Vega Suppression. He'd also been on the front lines during the Indo-Pakistani nuclear confrontation twenty five years before, as the Alliance tried to separate the warring sides on the River Chenab, averting a total nuclear exchange by just minutes. Those days were far behind him, but he remained the most experienced senior field officer in the Alliance. There had been little in the way of wars to fight.

Shorter attended the meeting virtually, as he was still five hours out.

Baylin laid out the general idea for the plan to take Luyten-A-1, and in doing so secure the system.

First, the fleet would enter, the warships would ensure the planet and the system were clear, and make sure the jump gate close to the planet was guarded. Nobody wanted the enemy coming through un-announced.

Once the planet was secured from space, the Midway and Akagi carrying the marines would land a contingent at the site previously known to be occupied by the enemy, provided the radiation had died down enough.

If it had and there was a structure to occupy, that would occur, meanwhile another larger contingent would set up a military base from modules aboard the Akagi, establishing a perimeter defence and then bringing down heavy surface-to-space defence systems.

It was all straight forward enough. Once they were in and established the Amundsen would begin full scale exploration of the trinary system.

The plan was agreed. Any enemy incursion would be dealt with depending on how it happened, if it was early on a battle would immediately begin, if it was later, the troops would need to be either able to evacuate or be installed deeply, and quickly enough, to be able to fight as part of a combined defence.

In the coming days tensions ran high, the hyperspace jump was particularly worrying because nobody could be sure the enemy didn't pass them going the other way to Procyon, now almost undefended. Travelling right past another ship in hyper space was easy, a twenty klick gap and the chances of seeing them or sensing them in the gravitic currents of hyperspace, still so little understood, was barely one percent.

Doctor Branson had now had plenty of time to study the genetics and the few samples salvaged from the conflicts, on the first day out he gave a briefing to the Admiral and command staff, relayed to the other ships.

"Admiral, we have the images, and we've all seen the physical size of the aliens. I've managed to work out several key things about them. We knew they were CO_2 breathing, a gas they use in the same way we use oxygen, but they seem to prefer, and their genetics would indicate, they need almost an exact mix in proportions of CO_2 as we need Oxygen, in fact if you swapped the figures over, there's less than half a percent difference".

Lieutenant Kagala also stepped in here, "Sir it's even more fundamental than that, we've found on all of the colonised Type-A worlds, those with multiple life forms, that the same correlation seems to exist within around 2%, once it varies from that range the numbers of life forms drops exponentially".

Branson continued, "They're basically what they look like, which without sounding crass, is a typical reptilian, highly carnivorous, with genetics not entirely dissimilar, at their core, to Earth species like the alligators, but their length of evolutionary development must have been far, far, longer. They're almost what you might have expected to develop on Earth if the Great Extinction Event hand't wiped out the dinosaurs".

"So", asked Science Officer Marilyn Gold, "what do we take from this genetic profile? That we're basically up against hyper-aggressive intelligent lizards?" There were sniggers from some of the others in the room and online.

Branson wasn't amused, and for that matter neither was Kagala. "You may joke Lieutenant-Commander, but we're talking a massive 120kg, exceptionally muscled and physically powerful warm blooded reptilian, with a natural predilection for aggression and viciousness so profound that it's likely to go beyond anything we can conceive".

Lieutenant Kagala stepped in again, "It's even more fundamental than that. From what we've seen of their tactics and their approach, their behaviour in general, they're vicious bordering on reckless. They'll do the most violent thing they can conceive of if they think it will overwhelm an enemy. They like surprise, if they have the luxury of time, but would rather simply fight it out face to face in the open as a preference.

Their ships show they want and expect a face on battle, subtlety and tactical finesse are not their strong points. Massive overwhelming fire to inflict the maximum damage, to destroy, is their way of doing things".

Markus Obishka couldn't help but tease Kagala, "and you got all that from a DNA strand?"

Admiral Baylin cut in, "Come along everyone, play nice, we may have beaten them twice now, maybe three times if you count the action with the Ramorra, but what we can't ignore is that by now they'll have learnt something about us too. They'll adapt, and the thing I worry about them adapting to most, is the one real advantage we have right now; the fighters. They seem to have no idea how to deal with them, like the concept of small combat ships in space has never dawned on them".

"I agree, came in Captain Andros, the fighters have proven effective, our main weapons seem to be far less effective than I'd have expected".

Dr Branson was quick to make another point - "Physical damage on their ships is hard to make, but they have one weakness as badly as we do, and they may not even have experienced it before; they're highly sensitive to neutron radiation".

300

Captain Harris came in, "That may be so but using weapons that create massive doses of neutron radiation is simply barbaric, didn't they have this very argument on Earth during the 1970's?"

The Admiral and Dr Branson were shocked that he knew such a piece of history, both of them were quiet, private students of Earth history, all of it, not the more sanitised official versions written post-climate collapse to point out the error of everyones ways before the tragedy. For once the Admiral felt that admitting he knew was a positive thing and he said so, "Yes, you're right Captain, President Carter was pressed to deploy them to kill Russian tank crews if they invaded Western Europe in the Cold War era".

"So why didn't they?" asked Markus.

"They did make them, under President Reagan, but it was seen as the ultimate capitalist weapon, killing people, without destroying property, and they were never used anyway, the Soviet Union collapsed".

"Look I hate admitting what kills anything, I'm a doctor, not a weapons advocate, all I can tell you is neutron radiation, if it becomes necessary, well it works on them". Branson hated talk of weapons and radiation killings, it was barbaric and mass murder in his eyes, but the fact was the enemy would do it to humans in an instant and they had to be stopped. That he knew was fundamental and that's what kept him in the Fleet.

Admiral Baylin continued, " I spoke directly with the President yesterday, and explained pretty much what you've told me again here. We're up against a ruthless and warlike enemy. Only our speed, our fighters, our electronic warfare capacity and our tactics have kept us from being blown to kingdom come. This offensive action is to set up a forward operating base in what they will consider their territory once they find out we're occupying their old outpost. And they will find out. So let's be ready for them, more support is coming from Earth and one of the Amundsen's sisters is meant to be coming in from a mission. She'll give us more warning time and counter measures power. We're going to fortify the Luyten system and put it between the enemy and Procyon".

"Admiral"…

"Yes, Captain DuBret?"

"What happens after we secure the system?"

Baylin hand't actually thought that through himself yet. Strategy for this war was all about forward defence so far, but what did come next?

"I suspect Captain, we'll be taking a little bit more of this war to the enemy, but we must be vigilant, our forces are small, one major defeat and Earth is finished".

CHAPTER 39

WRECKS

Chief Todd Carollio had barely put his head on the pillow when the cabin door buzzer sounded. It was Officer Bryant, she asked to come in. Carollio, instinctively told his cabin cameras to record - he was always very wary of one-on-one meetings in his cabin with junior officers, you could never be too careful.

He got out of bed, quickly pulled on some joggers and a shirt and answered the door. Bryant looked like she was worried someone would see her, she was clearly stressed.

"Chief, somethings going down, I don't know what, but the suspect has gathered a group of at least a dozen heavies from around the station and they're leaving on a light freighter around 0130 hours".

"OK, tell me, slowly how you found out, but keep it concise, skip low level detail". As he said it he looked up at the clock on the screen wall, it was 2345 hours.

"We've been keeping out of sight for three days, just doing what we do, always keeping him at arms length, making sure he had plenty of time with neither of us around, then about five hours ago, he left his usual haunts, mostly the market, the malls and the coffee shops, he seems to meet people there. He took a call, Marie May saw him get up and go to a quiet spot. After he took the call he, for him, because he never does anything quickly, nearly bolted, he rounded up two of the locals he speaks to more than most and they started to gather a group of the most unsavoury heavies at the entrance to Kalinda's Bar, and you know what sort of place that is. It was odd because he never goes anywhere like that normally.

I saw him address them all and picked up the time, Marie, Officer May, she's trying to find which dock they're going from".

Carollio went to his terminal, accessed the dock database - something the junior officers couldn't do, and found a small freighter, the '*Echoshine*', due for departure at 0145. Registered in Procyon to a Tutankh Clan operator by the name of Pietr Orgel, it worked out of Dendera.

Once again Athanasios was dealing with the Tutankh's, and Carollio really wanted to know why. He'd read Captain DuBret's reports, but the clan had registered her sisters death only as docking accident, even though it clearly hadn't been. The question was why did Athanasios need to go there again, and with such a bunch of heavies?

The Chief was feeling that the new police cutters might prove useful, but he didn't want to raise an alarm bell by using the one that was docked.

He called up the captain of the one patrolling the approaches to the base, "captain, can you quietly approach the base, and meet the shuttle I'm coming out on at 0100, details to follow. Do you have a boarding squad on board or do I need to bring one?"

"Er, we have have a half squad sir, which is normal for light patrols, we only go full up when its essential".

"Well this is essential, so quietly Captain, and I mean very quietly, have the other half of the squad meet me at the security shuttle dock, but don't have them arrive there in their combat gear, they can suit up when they reach the bay, not before".

"OK, yes sir, but why all the secrecy?"

"It's secret, thats why all the secrecy Captain".

The captain got the message, he wasn't going to make himself look an idiot by asking any more questions, OK sir we'll be there in around 14 minutes".

Carollio looked at the somewhat bemused Officer Bryant, "OK, I want you to tell Officer May to disengage, and go back to her normal duties, we've got this covered, you too, we'll debrief you when I get back".

"But sir…"

"This depends on everything looking normal, you two need to do the rounds of the bars and casino, if you don't someone will pick up you were missing, and our cover is blown". It probably wasn't that serious, but it gave them a purpose and kept them out of the way.

Bryant left, and Carollio buzzed the Commodore. She too was asleep, and not especially pleased to be woken, but she quickly paid attention; "Commodore, the Immortal Project has just stepped up a notch, there's some activity that needs my attention right now. I need an arrest warrant for a freighter, the '*Echoshine*'"

"An arrest warrant needs some grounds Chief, and I handed over the civil justice operation to the Procyon Judge Advocate literally a few hours ago. He's going to want a reason".

"Tell him its people smuggling".

"Is it?"

"Well, in the broadest sense of the term, yes".

"I know I should ask more questions, but I don't want to hear the answers, so I'll have it for you in an hour or so Chief".

"Thanks Commodore, it's just keeping things on the level".

She signed off, and Carollio realised he must be way behind on station briefings., Judge Advocate eh? One more bureaucratic hurdle to over come every time he needed to get something serious done.

****

On board the Task Force flagship, Nemesis, the crew went about their briefings and drills, they were just one hour out from the Luyten's jump gate. Nobody knew what to expect, nothing was impossible.

For a while Markus and the Admiral spent around twenty minutes discussing the possibility of using the the Amundsen's jump generator with Captain Andros and their counterparts, but the engineering teams simply didn't have enough data on how to safely operate it to be sure all of the task force could get through.

For a while they considered the benefits of Amundsen and one of the cruisers jumping independently, carrying out a quick sensor sweep and the rest jumping in through the gate.

Everyone agreed it was an idea they might be able to use in future, but nobody was able to guarantee that the Amundsen could keep a jump point open long enough to let a ship as big as a heavy cruiser come through with it. Anything less would be too risky if the Amundsen jumped into an enemy fleet.

In the end the plan was simple, the fighters, all of them, would precede the cruisers and the gunships, followed by the Amundsen. Once the all clear had been ascertained, the assault ships would come through, and they would proceed to the planet.

Every ship in the task force was on edge, what they were doing was audacious and daring. They all knew it and Baylin made it clear to all in his pre-jump all-hands broadcast: *"I know what we are about to do is daring, I know that you, all of you, will rise to the occasion. Two centuries ago, a British Admiral, John Jellicoe, was described as being the only man who could loose the First World War in an afternoon. I'm not going to pretend, all of us are John Jellicoe right now. We are on the cusp of turning the tide of this war in our favour. We've shown what we can do, so let's do it again. Battle stations everyone!"*

***Carollio's shuttle with a half squad of police troopers docked with the new police cutter, UEAS Diligence, the first thing Carollio noticed was how cramped the ship was with a full squad now onboard and all their gear.

The cutter's commanding officer was a young Lieutenant-Commander by the name of Drake, who's nick name he'd already found out was Dede, on account of the fact his parents had named him Drake Drake. There had been a fashion for such stupid naming around 23 years ago, because of a legendary asteroid belt racing legend called Fred Frede. Drake Drake, initials D.D. Carollio found this type of thing childishly amusing, but couldn't help smiling even in front of him.

"Chief, if your grinning because they've told you my nickname, get it over with, I've heard it all, nothing shocks me".

306

"Dede? You've gotta admit its funny, I mean does anyone think..."

"...that I'm a woman?"

"You said it".

"It happens and then I smack them straight in the face".

Carollio laughed out loud. This was a guy he could deal with.

"So, Chief what's the mission, and why so urgent?"

"I can't give you the full details, but we have to follow a small freighter called the "Echoshine", she's carrying a bunch of heavies and, let's say, a person of interest".

Drake spoke to his helm officer, "Helm. Can you track the Echoshine, where does her beacon put her right now and what was her flight plan?"

The helm officer brought up the details, "Sir she's already deviating from her flight plan, she was routed through to the Farside-C processing facility, but she's off course, current heading and projection takes her through the inner belt. Sir the only thing out that way is Dendera".

Carollio must have said it out loud, the word "shit" was loud enough to get Drake's attention.

"Now I know why you wanted a full squad, if they're about to pick a fight with some of the Tutankh Clan, it's gonna get bloody, real fast".

Carollio simply couldn't understand what Athanasios was doing. Why take a goon squad to fight the clan, even heavily armed they'd never get out alive?

The helmsman made an announcement, "Sir, the Echoshine has switched off her beacon".

"Get a lock on her helm, active scans if you have to, a ship like that won't know we're tracking her".

Carollio wasn't so sure about that, but it wasn't his place to interfere. He watched as the ship tracked its way swiftly through the asteroids, on what was a clearly pre-arranged route. He could but prey they didn't know the cutter was there. "They cant' see us can they Captain?"

307

"No Chief, they don't have any passive sensor arrays, no active jammers, if they did it would have been spotted and questioned, besides that type of kit is expensive, it would be a waste on a ship that small".

They followed it for hours, eventually, it began its approach to Dendera, the cutter sat well away, outside of the clans detection system. They monitored the comms, something these cutters were specifically able to do. "Chief, Dendera control is letting them dock".

They waited, and waited. The *Echoshine* powered down. Clearly she was going nowhere. An hour later a much larger freighter left the Dendera docks. "Its unregistered, no beacon, and there are just sixteen life forms on board, enough for the crew of three with thirteen others, the same number who'd gotten off the *Echoshine, sir*".

Captain Drake looked at the Chief, raised his eyebrows in a "now what" and waited for the answer.

"Lets follow them".

"OK, helm, you'd better use passive sensors only, that ships a lot bigger and might see us if we're really unlucky".

****

The Nemesis and her group jumped. Baylin had a pit in his stomach, leaping as they were into anything, from nothing to a full blown trap.

Much to everyone's relief, it was nothing. Suspiciously so to Baylin and all of the rest of his captains and crews.

Amundsen powered up long range scanners and anomaly detectors. All of them looked for the tell-tale DeBroglie Waves that would show up a cloaked ship. They approached the planet, cautiously, armed, ready, waiting. Nothing.

Other than a reduction in the radiation levels from the nukes used, there was nothing, nothing at all that was any different. The Amundsen was cleared to come right up to the planet, focusing her powerful scanners and sensor arrays. She collected petaflops of data, but most importantly, she revealed that the structure under the surface the enemy had bunkered down in was largely intact from about 10m down. The nukes had been airburst so had taken off the top layers and destroyed the defence systems on the near surface. There was no sign of life.

"Dr Branson, from what you've got available, do you consider it medically safe to proceed to a landing?"

"Well Admiral, the radiation's down low enough environmental suits will be fine, but its going to be quite strenuous walking around, everyone will need to keep an eye on their oxygen levels. I'd like to volunteer to go into the structure".

"Of course you would, and from the number of faces staring at me right now so does half the bridge crew. Markus, work out a suitable survey team from across the task force, we need to include the other ships, coordinate it with them, and yes Doc, you can go".

Baylin knew what came next, the troop transports would leave their assault ship and the military engineers would get to work building the defence platforms.

He handed over the con and walked into his office, as he sat the yellow alert klaxons blared out across the fleet. He rushed back to the bridge, "Update me".

"The Jump Gate from the enemy system has activated sir, something's coming through".

"Here we go again, get the other captains on the line and bring us to red alert".

Bridge view screens displayed it all as the gate flickered on, then a black, smouldering, massive hulk of a warship hurtled through. It was out of control, spinning slowly over its own axis, small explosions were going off all over its superstructure.

"What the hell is that, science officer?"

"It's identical to the enemy battlecruiser we fought here sir, but it's totally disabled, crew is dead or dying, its power reserves are nearly gone, reactors, weapons, all off line or destroyed, sir its a total mess, radiation scars, massive energy weapon damage and unidentifiable energy discharge signatures. Sir, it's basically a wreck, and it's headed straight at the planet, around three days to impact, current trajectory puts it in the south polar regions".

Baylin had wondered what new surprises awaited. This though, was not one even vaguely on his guess list of what they might run into.

****

Chief Carollio hated not being in command, but let the Captain of the cutter do his work all the same. They were zig-zagging behind the freighter so that they were at maximum sensor range, loosing it one minute, tracking the next, it was heading out into deep space.

Carollio wanted desperately to know what they were doing, why were they all the way out here? Their course plotted them deep into the vast expanse of what was known to locals as "The Upper Eight". Procyon formed a figure of eight shape with its asteroid field, this was the hole in the top, smaller part of the eight.

Whereas the asteroids and planetoids and vast dust clouds were dense and dangerous for a ship at speed, in here, the space was clear, open, and as dark as space seemed to get.

They went on for hours. The freighter's course projection seemed to be heading for, well that was the thing, nowhere. Not even the most distant industrial miners had even gotten this far over here yet, it could be twenty years before it was commercially viable.

"Chief, how long do you want us to keep following him?"

"Until we find out where he's going, I have to know, because the further he goes the more and more mysterious this guy becomes. There's nothing out here, yet he gets a squad of armed heavies to..."

Carollio was interrupted by a bright flash almost forty thousand klicks ahead. There was no science officer on these cutters, the helm officer and the Captain effectively split the role.

Captain Drake was on it instantly, analysing the passive scans, it didn't take him long to have an answer. "Technically I would have said until a few weeks ago, this was impossible, but that was a jump point opening into the system, but I can't detect anything that came through it".

"How close was their freighter?"

"Under one hundred klicks and she's slowed right down, we need to cut speed or she'll see us".

"Don't bother, we're going in".

"Are you sure chief?"

"Just get us there, we're taking that ship and whatever it is they've got".

The freighter was taken totally by surprise. It wasn't fast enough to outrun the police cutter, it's captain surrendered despite protestations from the heavies on board.

Chief Carollio went on with the full squad, their shuttle met no resistance. The heavies looked eager to fight but they were outgunned and didn't have anything like the protective gear the police had. Carollio knew, from their body language and long experience, they'd been told never to fight the security forces. Anyone else they would have taken on, but not a full squad.

They quickly accounted for everyone, well all but one. To the chiefs fury, Athanasios was nowhere on board. Not a hint of him. He must have stayed on Dendera. Carollio found a quiet spot and got the cutter to patch him through to Security Control. It didn't matter who knew now, Athanasios had worked out he was being tracked. The chief just wanted to know where he was. He'd gone back to Procyon, and had already bought passage on the next days evening express flight to Titan and on to Mars. For two.

"He bought a second ticket? For who? I'll call you back". The chief was being called by Captain Drake.

"Chief you'll want to see this, you'll really want to see this".

The walked down a level and to the doors of an airlock into a sealed dock. From the observation port Chief Carollio could see a wrecked life pod of some type, he didn't recognise it. It was blackened and drab, but it was certainly a life pod. "What the frack is that doing out here? Is that what came through the jump point?"

"The registry on the pod isn't clear, but we'll be able to work it out once we get a closer look Chief".

The airlock alarm went off. Something was on the other side opening the doors, they rushed to the lock window, but the condensed air was like steam. The air cycled back in. A human male in a space suit was in the lock, his face unclear through the tinted glass of the helmet. He soon twisted off the helmet seal, and pulled the helmet over his head.

"Good afternoon, I'm sorry I don't know your names, I'm Professor Nelson Kagala".

CHAPTER 40

DISCOVERIES

"Chief, I have no means of preventing the professor from leaving Procyon. The medical assessment is there's nothing wrong with him, he reported the loss of the ship he was on, says he knows nothing about how he ended up in Procyon, nothing about how he got away from the explosion he claims destroyed the PlanExCo ship. He knows nothing other than he's glad to be alive. And I might add, Mr Athanasios has exerted Martian Colonial Government Diplomatic Privilege and extended it to the Professor, who is after all, a Martian citizen. So no, I can't detain him on grounds that you think "its all weird!"

Commodore Tan was fuming. Todd Carollio had exceeded his authority trying to detain the professor, Mr Athanasios had demanded to see her and complained about being spied on and the whole 'low profile' operation was blown.

Once again the Chief seemed to be like a dog with a bone, just not willing to give it up. She had no choice, "I'm ordering you to drop this investigation and drop it now. It's over. For god's sake Todd, this was supposed to be secret, not blow up in our faces. I've got the new judge advocates office making waves, desperate to prove his worth and show how much the military governor - that's me in case you'd forgotten, over reached in the system. Its a shit-show and you've turned it into one".

Carollio kept quiet. There was no point in making the commodore angrier than she already was. But he knew what he'd seen. There was no way that life pod made its way out of hyperspace on its own. How did Athanasios know where to find it? That was a pre-arranged rendezvous, it had to have been. No, there was more to this, much more.

Right now though, he'd have to walk on eggshells until he had evidence. But one way or another, he'd find out what was going on.

After his dressing down, he went back to his office, Athanasios and the Professor got on their flight back to Mars. The news networks picked up the professors return, but he said nothing, Athanasios kept out of the coverage.

++

On the Nemesis, Avode Kagala was stunned, he hadn't even known his father was missing. He couldn't reach him, and was advised to wait until the professor got back to Mars. He finally got hold of his mother who told him his father was off on the mission, had (not unusually) barely mentioned any details and told her it would be at least three months. She'd accepted all of this because it was how he'd always been, besides which she had her own job as a senior administrator in the city council.

She didn't know where he'd been, she knew no more than what she'd seen in the news feeds, and he hand't spoken to her, which upset her and made her angry, but again, it wasn't unusual behaviour for him.

The news channels were all chasing after PlanExCo, but all they did was issue a short statement regretting the loss of the ship, and they knew no more than the professor did and would have to debrief him on his return to Mars.

Many of the officers were watching the broadcast in the ward room, and Avode was torn both by anger for his supposedly empathic fathers insensitivity and his mothers anguish. Major Granding watched just behind him. As the PlanExCo statement was read out, he said out loud, "they won't wait until he gets back, they'll have their on-site station manager on him from the moment he sets foot out of his hotel room door".

Avode turned round to look at the major. "How do you know that?"

"Because that's what all of these big corporations do, they don't want to be sued or have any liability pinned on them".

"I suppose so. I just wish he'd be more open with us about things like this, he's always so secretive". Avode was clearly upset, but could do nothing. The major, clearly sensing his discomfort, asked if he could help.

"In what way could you help me major?"

"A friendly ear to listen, a shoulder to cry on? You choose." Major Granding smiled broadly, and Avode felt himself recoil slightly. "Major, are you trying to..."

"Who? Me? Just offering a friendly, human, sympathetic ear if it's wanted".

"Honestly, major, its not, I need to go, excuse me".

As he left, far more quickly than he usually did he ran into Marilyn Gold coming in, "hey, Avode what's the rush?"

"The major, he just tried to pick me up".

She laughed, "what a slime ball, those T-paths give me the creeps. Anyway you don't...you know...do you?"

"NO, what is it with being young and black and good looking that everyone thinks I'll just sleep with them for no reason at all?" He laughed, she laughed. "Good looking? Isn't beauty in the eye of the beholder?" she quipped.

"Oh very funny! Its just all this stuff with my father, its all so bizarre. Anyway are you coming down to the planet, we're leading a team going through the aliens old base, hoping to get some intel on them".

"I can't, I'm leading a team with Sam Carradine on how to stop the ship impacting the planet. The Admiral wants to see if we can prevent it hitting and get time enough to study it if we can get on board".

They went their separate ways, Avode would have preferred if she'd have been with them, but instead he had two officers who were sub-specialists in xenoarchaeology from the Pollux and Hercules.

When he reached the shuttle bay the two from the other ships were already there, and so was Dr Branson.

"Lieutenant-Commander Kagala, I'm at your service", the Doc bowed slightly in a semi-mocking tone, but Avode was used to him. The Docs' irreverence was a ship wide standing joke.

"Doctor, please remember we have guests from the Hercules and the Pollux, Ensigns…", he pointed at one, a pale white skinned ginger haired Irish European and she spoke her name, "Kate O'Mara, Hercules". And, as he pointed to the other, a young looking Taiwanese man, "Sun Jao Sen, of the Pollux".

"Well welcome to both of you, we've a couple of marines coming down with us but I'm reliably informed we shouldn't need them. Shall we go?"

They trudged, in full environmental suits, aboard the shuttle. Avode was sure he could see the Admiral in the launch control room. The marines boarded, equipped with enough weaponry to start a small war.

The shuttle launched quietly from the Nemesis, a feature the Doc quite liked as the Ramorra's old bay was underneath and it always felt like you were being dropped. This was much more sedate and civilised.

Avode chatted with the ensigns, whose specialisms were very different, O'Mara's was structural engineering and ship integrity, she ran the damage control operation on her ship. Sun was a medic, but as with all Fleet ensigns they were required to have at least one sub-specialism, and neither had ever really expected to use it.

The doctor listened to the young and enthusiastic if slightly apprehensive ensigns. Was he really that young once? He never felt like it.

The shuttle was rattling, harder. He looked out of the side window opposite and saw the heat flow from the atmosphere as the shuttle entered the upper reaches. It was only going to get worse, and it did. After around four minutes the bumping and rattling started to smooth out, and the shuttle slowed, slowly it hovered over the predicted landing site, then, alarmingly, seemed to drop and hit the ground harder than the doctor expected. But they were on the ground and in one piece. The marines were lowering the ramp door and out before he was really ready, but that was nothing new.

The four of them went round to the side of the shuttle and opened the cargo bay, two tracked multi function robots and a tracked multi-purpose

316

carrier rolled out. Their kit and sensor, medical and test equipment was aboard.

The area they'd landed in was a glassy, rough, pancake, the result of the intense heat from the nuclear air burst that had levelled the area. It was the first time any of them had stood in a nuclear blast site, and as they looked around, the eeriness of the place came across. The carbon dioxide heavy atmosphere gave the thin sky a yellowish tinge, and the reflected sky in the glassy surface gave it a strange watery effect. The star was bright but cool, not that they could feel the outside temperature, which was actually only around three centigrade, and this as Avode already knew, was the summer in this planets northern hemisphere.

The Marine Engineers had already used the data from the pre-strike scans to work out where the entrances to the enemy bunkers might be and located the most suitable to get into. They'd constructed a basic entrance and opened up a corridor into the underground labyrinth the enemy had occupied. They'd even put lighting in for the first 200m or so.

There was one thing they all felt, and that was small. Even in their full kit they were still small compared to the corridors and control panels, which were higher up than a human would find ideal. They'd long acknowledged the enemy was a large, reptilian type, but some of them must be considerably larger than expected.

With the sensorbot some fifty metres ahead of them, the scale of these bunkers became ever more obvious. Avode decided to launch the auto-drones. These small flying discs moved at high speed using lasers, echo pulse sounders, infra red, ultra violet and optical sensors to map out their environment, and they could do it a hundred times faster than just walking slowly in a full environmental suit. The data was relayed to the QuAC's on board the Nemesis and the Amundsen, which compiled a full 3D image of their findings.

For Avode, the thrill almost never stopped. Examples of control surfaces, alphabets, numerals, functions, soon became apparent. The QuAC's were able to decipher some of it within minutes, other areas they needed more contextual information.

Yet there was one thing missing, there were no bodies, certainly not up in the higher tunnels and their side rooms. There were no doors, none of the equipment seemed to function, which wasn't unexpected, because of the massive EMP the nuke would have generated.

The corridors descended in a spiral, short branches would come off them but essentially the long downed spiral of the corridor was the main thoroughfare. Ensign Sen suggested marking them off in 100m zones for research purposes and just to be sure they had a reference as to where anyone might be.

It took an hour but at just on 1.3 klicks things began to change. The spiral seemed less steep. As they reached the bottom it opened up into a huge open cavern. That's where the bodies were. Dozens of them, and around the walls of the cavern were laboratories, thirteen of them in all.

The Doctor was quick to take charge now, this was his field of expertise. He walked alone to the bodies, all of which seemed to have simply dropped dead on the spot. Some of them were nearly 2.2 m in height, they were physically huge, with massive tails. Yet their arms and hands were smaller, although the hands seemed to appear far less nimble. Somehow the doctor thought, they were more use than they appeared.

A cursory scan showed that all of them had been poisoned. Their blood systems were showing massive chemical contamination. Avode said it first, "is this, is this a mass suicide Doctor?"

Branson had reached the same conclusion, "Yes, yes it seems to be, they must have been willing, there's no suggestion of coercion here."

There were 37 bodies, some appeared to be female, but they were all quite dead. Branson contacted the ship, and asked for the Admiral.

"Bruce, its a mess down here, they all killed themselves by poisoning, some kind of alkaloid, I need a recovery team to get back some of the bodies to the ships labs. We need to preserve what we can. They're already decaying".

"Why would they do that Doc? What were they afraid of?"

"Well there are what clearly appears to be laboratories all around the bottom of the chamber here, we'll be having a look, but I'd say from what they're wearing, and from the machinery in the labs, this is some kind of research outpost. Maybe they didn't want anyone knowing what they do".

"Be careful Doc, those labs could have anything in them".

"Will do".

"Lieutenant-Commander, I've asked the Admiral to send down a team to extract some bodies, we need the samples before they deteriorate even further, I'm going to scout out which ones I want to preserve, you may as well recon the labs, but be careful, who knows what they were doing down here".

Avode was happy to do just that, but insisted the others stayed with him, "Nobody goes in these labs alone, we keep an eye out the whole time". Neither ensign seemed overly thrilled to be on their own anyway.

There was minimal light and power in the laboratories, possibly provided by a battery backup of some kind, and it was clear something unpleasant was being researched here. The universal need to protect and to access toxic materials or biological hazards was clearly something that required a similar approach. What the aliens used was different, but it was simple enough to extrapolate what most things did.

Ensign O'Mara was the first to recognise what they were dealing with. "I saw these signs up on the walls, symbols, circles with arms and flat heads, they looked mechanical, but I see it now, they're a general interpretation of a virus. This particular lab is a virology unit, I'm sure of it".

Avode was concerned, "is there anything on scanners to show contamination?"

"No sir, no, but behind that glass-like shielding, there are several genetically active signatures on the biology scanner, RNA and complex", she looked down at the scanner screen again, "yes its a virus, and its logging with the Amundsen's virology database - sir it's, it's a combination hantavirus, and the warnings are high mortality, highly infectious, the quantum analysis is - lethality to humans is high, in fact lethality to anything is high. Sir' I'd go as far as saying this needs to be destroyed right here and right now, it can't be allowed to get out of this lab".

The Doc overheard on the shared comlinks the group were using, and quickly made his way over to them, "show me ensign".

He looked at the data which was being processed by the Amundsen's QuAC - the lethality of this virus was 9.98. Since 2032 viral danger was rated on a ten point scale of exponential lethality. A VR0 of 2.0 would mean it was 2x2x2 so rated as an 8, but 9.8x9.8x9.8 was near as dammit 941 - so roughly 118 times more lethal. That would wipe out an entire planet of billions in a matter of 30-60 days. The QuAC's analysis was that it was transmissible in any known medium. It was by any means, a massively dangerous discovery.

They went to each of the laboratories, every one of them contained some kind of virus or bacteria, some were vaguely recognisable mutations, some totally new, but not one of them ranked less than a VR0 of 9.0 according to the computers analysis.

They all looked sheepishly at each other, worried for themselves and for what they had found. The Doc said it out loud as he spoke to the Admiral directly again, his voice deep, and somber, "Bruce, this is a bioweapons research facility, and there's nothing in here we should let leave this site, nothing. We need to destroy it, quickly".

Baylin was in his office aboard the Nemesis, listening to the doctor as he described the data that showed on his screens.

"What happens if we destroy them, but they've already got use of them? Would we be impairing our ability to build a bio-response, like a vaccine?"

"Look Admiral that's always a possibility, but if this stuff is in research, then they probably haven't deployed it, so lets…" the Admiral stopped him mid-sentence: "You see Doc that's the problem, *probably* isn't good enough".

"What do you mean? You want us to collect samples of this stuff and bring it back to the ship?"

There was silence, Baylin looked on a list of classified requirements that all ships captains on deep space missions were given. For the most part the directives were of cataloguing and analysis, with two exceptions. One was bacteria capable of being weaponised - any bacteria that the QuAC considered capable of being so. The other was any virus with a rating above VR0 3.0, a level that would cause a pandemic.

"Admiral, are you still there, Bruce?" the Doctor tapped his helmet in frustration.

"I'm here, I can hear you. Look Doc, I have specific orders, so does the Amundsen, any VR0 3.0 or above must be collected as a live sample for transfer and analysis".

"Are you out of your mind? That's ridiculous, its dangerous, we don't have the means of researching these things on board."

"Doctor, I'm giving you an order and its not up for discussion, get samples, and we'll place them in stasis, for transfer to a suitable facility back home. If you don't feel you can do this, you're relived of duty, and I'll get one of the doctors in the fleet to do it instead".

Baylin didn't think for a minute the Doc would let someone other than himself supervise something so deadly. The silence and anger the Admiral felt were being transmitted through the ether without the need for a comlink. But the Doctor did as he was asked, and the Admiral noted his strenuous objections.

But the breakthroughs weren't confined to their chilling discovery. Avode Kagala had discovered the aliens identified themselves as what seemed to translate as Kadressian or Kadres. There were references to militaristic mantras, conquest, just as the analysts had predicted. Feasting, blood rites, huge amounts of cultural background were slowly becoming translatable.

Yet, the one discovery that the Admiral and the Government all wanted most of all, was how their technology really worked. Of that there was nothing. There was no data, no functioning systems, and even when the QuAC had worked out a basic translation of system meanings on the control surfaces, which it did with remarkable ease in under three hours, there was nothing. One of the technology specialists on the Amundsen described it as, "it's like having a computer, but the entire operating

321

system, what makes it do what it does, it's missing. There isn't even a basic, underlying boot code, there's nothing, all of its been wiped clean, not a trace, no residual or forensic data traces, nothing. All of this is just physical material, inert, dead". Even more worrying they hand't the slightest clue how the system could be made to work even if they tried to backwards engineer it.

There was one possibility. The shipwreck, hurtling from the gate towards the planet. If that had enough live systems, maybe they could make this place come back to life by mapping its own operating system. There was though, one problem; a team was already failing to bring the huge ship under control and time was running out.

CHAPTER 41

THINGS THAT GO BUMP IN THE NIGHT

"Six hours....from...now!" That's all the time we have left to stop this ship from hitting the planet. Now we all know the planet isn't much to write home about, but it will cause a major localised trauma in the planet's south polar regions. More than that, we need to get it under control because it could be the intel find of the century. We've run simulations on no less than eight possible scenarios to slow it down and bring it under control, and this is the one rated as the highest percentage chance of success".

Markus Obishka looked around the real and virtualised briefing room, all 36 of the fleet fighter pilots were on the call. So were every shuttle pilot and the two gunship captains.

Putinova was the most senior pilot and squadron leader of the Nemesis fighters, 'SF66 *Vengeful Flyers*'. "Sir, you expect us somehow to grapple hook the ship with thirty-six separate fighters, bring in the two gunships and eighteen shuttle craft to do the same, then basically fly in the opposite direction to its current trajectory in order to slow it down enough to stop it, while the three cruisers fire low energy force beams at it from the front to slow it down?"

Markus looked right at her, unabashed, "Yes, that's exactly what I expect you to do".

The room, both real and virtual was silent.

"And what percentage of success do you think we have sir?"

"Engineering says around 31%, the QuAC estimates 34%".

There was an audible murmuring around the room, and Markus knew if it had been Putinova giving the briefing the noise would have been far greater, he could see barely restrained mirth from some of the pilots, so he decided to pick one out for himself. He wasn't afraid of their opprobrium or their attitudes. The Admiral had said to him this would happen, that's just what pilots were like.

"Bendix, do you have something constructive to say?"

Bendix could always be counted on to rise to the bait, and obliged, much to Putinova's embarrassment. "Yeah sir, I have an idea sir, why don't we tie a pair of Schmidt's tights to the alien wreck sir? You can't get them off and they'd snap right back in the other direction".

The room burst out laughing. Markus was mildly disgusted by the sexism, but Schmidt was more than capable of giving as good as she got, "Hey Bendix, are you admitting you can't get a woman's tights off? No wonder your face always look so weird when your stalking everyones quarters at night".

Once again the room erupted and Bendix went red. In his office Admiral Baylin quietly laughed as he watched on his monitor. It might be a little sordid but they needed this type of humour, it bonded them all, however inappropriate it might be. Markus knew it and handled it well.

"I'm delighted, Mr Bendix, that you're so full of positive ideas on how to make this operation a success, so I'm putting you in charge of working out how we get the grapples onto the target, seeing as you're knowledge of elasticity is so great and marksmanship so legendary".

Bendix looked mildly taken aback, but Major Granding, standing just behind Markus sensed Bendix react to the challenge, just as his profile said he might.

The meeting broke up after a few minutes on technical and organisation instructions. As they left, Markus turned to the Major, "tell me you didn't make him say that?"

"No need, that's Bendix all over, I just had a hunch that he'd react at some point to something, and I suspect you knew it too, Putinova certainly did".

"Will he do it?"

"Honestly from their profiles, he's the best choice, he'll get them all lined up and tell them how to do it right, he's rough around the edges but highly instinctive, he'll do it".

Exactly two hours later, the fighters from the three cruisers launched, engineering had scanned the outside of the ship and found as many points that would affect the slowly tumbling vessel that were viable, some sixty of them, but forty would be sufficient to bring it under control.

The fighters flew one by one towards their allocated points, not at the rear of the ship, but at its front end, the idea was first to stop the tumbling, which was slow, but uniform at one rotation every fifteen minutes sixteen seconds.

The fighters had to then rotate with the ship, not letting the grappling hooks loosen, but not exerting excessive force on the ship at the end of the 250m woven titanium-steel tow lines until they were all able to do so at once. It was a bizarre and skilful manoeuvre, and Bendix' plan for attaching them with accuracy worked in 33 out of 39 cases first time, with the other six on a second pass. The Admiral was impressed, so was pretty much everyone else.

As the ship tumbled forward, anti-clockwise as soon as the nose came round and was facing away from the planet, the fighters started exerting thrust back downward to slow it, it would they expected, take two rotations to reduce it by 50%, enough to get the shuttles close enough to add their strength. And it worked, at first slowly, but bit by bit, the rotation slowed to 20%, From the rear, now facing the planet, the gunships with the aid of drones launched their grapples at the top of the engine to pull upward, as the fighters at the the front pulled downward, slowly their combined force stopped the rotation, but the ship was still moving at a rate that would see it impact the planet in a little over two hours.

Now, the cruisers swept in from behind, the gunships moved away, the fighters were too improperly positioned to try a second round to pull it forward, although the six best placed did what they could.

The Nemesis, Pollux and Hercules lined up, with low yield pulse cannons and force beams, firing over and over at the engines and rear of the ship, slowly, slowing it down. All the Admiral wanted was another hour, one single hour.

The troop carrier Akagi had a pair of breaching pods, each capable of carrying a platoon into the ship, but this time it was not all troops.

Commander Marilyn Gold, science officer, two engineers from Sam Carradine's department, and a coder specialising in cryptography, were on board one of them.

The strange tube-like breaching pod closed with the alien ship, its tripod legs extended moments before it landed on the hull near the bridge section and the retros on them hard-fired to break its impact. If you'd never done this before, it was a shock to the system, even wearing special suits that absorbed and dissipated some 90% of the energy, it was still almost physically stunning, but the troops were used to it.

The pods nose used a combination of high-energy short burst laser cutters and micro-explosives to blast its way through the hull, the troops burst into the ship, gingerly followed by Commander Gold and her team. They heard the second pod, filled with more troops, break its way into the ship at a point pre-determined to be weak enough, about 60m further along the deck.

The smoke and fumes from the breach were thick and hung in the CO_2 atmosphere, but they soon moved through it, troops, moved through the huge corridor, weapons at the ready, in full battle armour. The ship seemed empty, yellow flashing lights, some sort of battle alert perhaps? Gold wondered aloud, but nobody said anything.

They knew where the bridge was from the ship that had blown itself up on the planet, bizarrely there was a great deal of dust, ash and what looked like organic powder, spread everywhere and floating in the air.

One of the engineers analysed the powder in a heavy pile, the data linked back to Doctor Branson's biology lab and the QuAC. Branson was back on to Marilyn Gold before a minute had gone by, "Commander Gold, that dust, that dust *is* the aliens, and its highly radioactive, its ionised, check your radiation levels".

"What type of radiation am I looking for? Our automatic detectors aren't showing anything above what you'd expect on a wreck like this with this much damage".

"It's a new type of radiation, some kind of sustained neutron energy, it'll go through almost anything metallic and decouple any tissue. The QuAC says its artificial, but who knows what created it?"

"Are we safe?" Marilyn was seriously worried now.

"It seems to be in the organic material, its not showing up on your suits as dangerous, it's there but almost like its inert, which it can't be, I don't understand it, yet, get more samples if you can".

They carried on up the corridor, the bridge doors were open, and Gold breathed a sigh of relief, as did the engineers, the bridge was functioning, systems were still live.

Their work was cut out for them, the engineer and the code specialist worked quickly, tracking down systems and trying to find a portal that would let them access the operating system. The breakthrough came with what the code specialist said was a navigation computer. That was ideal. Navigation was navigation, reference points they knew were the same as reference points we knew, and that meant it would make it far easier to crack meanings and purposes of parts of the software.

The portable computer drive system was designed to simply copy what it found, it didn't and couldn't make the software work, but it could copy every line of code no matter how unintelligible it might be right now. It was sophisticated, but as he told Gold, it did what it did, and that was pretty much comprehensible. It was different, we might learn from it, but his impression was it was no more advanced than our own, in relative terms.

Gold had already learnt that the basic systems were not dissimilar to Japanese in their format. There were characters at the base of an original language, but a secondary and tertiary language had been incorporated into the primary language over time to expand meaning, hence the vast array of characters, some 1,340 so far catalogued.

As the others did their jobs, she walked up to a dais that seemed like it must be for the commander of the ship, and then she realised something else, and couldn't believe she'd not noticed it before. None of them had. Their magboots weren't actually working. They were on the deck, they were being kept on the floor - by artificial gravity.

If only they had time to cut up a floor panel and take it out, or the kit to extract it, but that hand't been on the list of things they needed to do. As she wondered how to get hold of a piece of floor plate, Markus came on the line, "Commander how's things going? Because you've got five minutes before you need to go back to the pods, this ships starting to roll again as the gravity well drags it in toward the planet".

Marilyn checked with the engineers. They were done, one had downloaded data, the other had cut out samples of the hardware, including relays and what could be processors, but the were nothing like she'd seen before.

They moved back towards the pods, which were not really designed for extracting troops, just delivering them. It wasn't so easy getting back on board. She knew that the rotation of the ship before would have made it impossible to get what they had. There wouldn't have been the time and the stresses would have been too great. She praised the team on a job well done, as the seals slammed shut and the tripod arms let go of the hull, the booster's thrust kicked in and they were clear. Only now did she realise they were just moments away from the planets atmosphere. For the second time, she watched one of the alien warships as it caught the upper reaches of the carbon dioxide rich atmosphere, the incinerating heat made it glow in silent death, as it arced downward to the southern pole. Just two minutes later a brilliant flash emanated from the darkness of the southern polar night. A vast mushroom cloud smashed its way skyward, then the debris spread out like a pancake in the upper atmosphere. Before long it was over one hundred klicks across, some of it reaching into the sunlight further north, just as the sun was setting and the terminator line marched ever westward.

Even on the new Alliance base the flash had been visible, some 2,500 klicks away. The debris would soon spread around the planet's skies, leaving a strange, reddish hue to the normal yellow tinge of the sky.

Corporal Jorge Kessler stood sentry on the southern perimeter of the base. All he could think of as he looked at the spectacle from his watch platform, the darkness closing in as the sun went down, was of 'things that go bump in the night'. He smiled, it made him think of his mother, home on Earth, dozens of light years away.

CHAPTER 42

UNDERSTANDING IS A TWO-EDGED SWORD

Admiral Baylin was both delighted and impressed with the results from the operation to board the enemy ship. He and all of the Captains, science officers, chief medical and xenoarchaeologists shuttled over to the huge briefing and presentation room on the Amundsen, which was by far the largest of any ship in the small fleet.

He'd given them all twenty-four hours to come up with preliminary assessments and reports to present to as wide an audience as possible. He wanted a lot of people to know, so that there would be no way this information would be buried, for any reason, *any* reason at all.

The holographic suite in the Amundsen's presentation room was top of the line, designed for just this sort of expansive visualisation.

Each of the officers had worked on what was a slick presentation they'd integrated, because after they'd seen it, it was being sent to Fleet and The President.

They sat in an oval, the room pitch black, and the presentation began, voiced over by the Amundsen's QuAC which went by the name of Cynthia, because of the Captain's first wife, who was renowned for non-stop talking. The QuAC when first installed, had operated with an 'improved' interface, that would simply never stop explaining itself and had to be switched off.

Cynthia began, in her clear, perfectly enunciated voice; "In the past few days we have taken possession of an enemy base, and boarded a dying warship from that race before it plunged to its demise on the planet. This is what we were able to find out from visual recordings, peripheral and in-depth scans. It's top-line and merely skims the surface, much, much more awaits us as we study this new enemy".

The first thing that came up was a sudden full-life-sized (and far too realistic for some who visibly jumped), image of a 2.2m high lizard-like creature, dressed in a scaled armour. Its heavy tail balanced its weight, the tail was some 1.5m long and as the simulation showed, capable of being used with lightening speed as a weapon.

"This is the enemy. They are a highly advanced reptilian species, not unlike an Earth alligator in rough appearance, put with speed and agility closer to that of a velociraptor. They're carbon dioxide breathers, and based on silicon-carbon. And we now have a name for them, they call themselves the Kadre.

They are vicious, violent, motivated by anger and emotions, but with a practical and deeply instilled militarism that goes deep into their history and their psyche. War is a game for them, a reason to exist. Our initial analysis of some of the key data and information we have been able to find here on the planet, and in the ship and captured drone parts, suggests they are geared for conflict on a near permanent basis.

They operate what appears to be a physical caste system, there are different types of Kadre, different types of warrior, and females are clearly much smaller. Yet it is all geared towards combat, at all times.

However we have been able to ascertain that there has been nothing to fight, that they have made their conquests and for some reason become stuck. It's not uncommon with militarised societies, that they lack the economic and industrial base for change, that they become hide-bound by religion, tradition and factionalism. Eventually they turn on one another, one of the possibilities we have to offer is that the ship we obtained much of this data from, was attacked in a conflict with another of their own ships and lost, fleeing here to escape.

The behaviour of the Kadre battleship and its escorts at Procyon further supports this theory. The move was arrogant and a failure, and it suggests they simply couldn't comprehend of an enemy that was possibly their equal, never mind potentially superior in some ways.

Their behaviour towards us, the fighters, their lack of tactical foresight, it smacks of the unexpected. It's one of our conclusions that the Kadre have never fought anything or anyone on equal terms before. They behave with an arrogant stupidity that suggests over confidence born of easy victories.

Furthermore, their data was not security protected. Our QuAC networks on the four primary ships in the fleet were able to break open the data and read it in very short order. We believe we have ascertained enough to have an advanced idea of where they are, what they have in the way of assets and a worthwhile foreknowledge of what we're up against.

The Kadre have an empire. There are at least nine star systems, possibly as many as twelve, that they have direct control of, including at least one star system with what may be two or more conquered alien races, we suspect there are more. The alien located on the base by then Captain Baylin and the EAS Ramorra, is likely to have originated on one of these worlds.

A key item of knowledge we have obtained includes the key signals from the ship that locate and operate their jump gates."

As an image of a jump gate melted into the darkness, a new one, of a large star system appeared.

"This is where the ship we boarded came from, its a complex system with several planets, some of them heavily defended by very large orbital battle stations, though the details of those we don't have except for their physical scale. There are heavy defences in some areas, however we haven't been able to obtain the details, as the ship did not possess that information"

In conclusion, we have enough information to enter the system, we have an estimation that the weaponry and ships they possess would prove a substantial challenge to overcome, and that they outnumber us some five to one".

In conclusion we believe we should raid their system, carry out detailed reconnaissance and strike a target they would least expect, in an effort to draw their forces to the defensive.

We need to buy time, for fleet expansion and defence building, before we can hope to engage them on an equal footing, or to within a margin of acceptability. Thank you for your attention".

The presentation with its elaborate 3D graphics and data points faded away, and the lights slowly rose.

Dr Branson turned to the Admiral, "No mention of the research labs and the virus, and whose recommendation was that at the end, yours?"

"The labs data is classified, we don't want that in the public domain, and yes that was my recommendation at the end. The President wants a next move handed to him and that's what I'm giving him".

"So, you are playing politics eh?" Branson smirked, which Baylin found irritating, but decided now was not the time or place to argue with the Doctor. Branson started on about something else, but Baylin wasn't paying attention, he was watching Sam Carradine, his Chief Engineer, across the room. He was talking to the Amundsen's jump gate specialist. As Bruce watched, Captain Andros wandered over, "Admiral I see you've seen the love birds twittering in the distance?"

"Is it that serious? I knew he liked her, but, I mean has it gone that far?"

In a moment of comedic simultaneity that would have been impossible to believe had you not been there, both the Admiral and the Captain said, "I hope not I can't afford to loose someone that good". They laughed out loud, the Admiral said, "well it's true isn't it, but we can't stop them, well actually yes I can, but..." as the Admiral spoke, they watched as Sam got down on one knee, the old fashioned way and asked her to marry him.

"Well would you look at that", Branson had seen it too, "have they even had time to go on a date?"

"Sam's been back and forth on shuttles to the Amundsen more times than you or I have had hot dinners Doctor".

Admiral Baylin looked bemused, "how have I not known that?" Captain Andros shrugged his shoulders, "I suspect Admiral, that they didn't want senior officers to know".

Others in the room had now started to respond to what had happened, she'd obviously said yes, and congratulations were being proffered.

Baylin looked at Captain Andros, "well you're her military "father" so don't look at me if they ask for a shipboard ceremony, I'm just coming as a guest".

The Admiral went over to the couple and offered his congratulations, making clear he wasn't willing to loose Sam. But they had already crossed that bridge. Neither of the engaged couple had any intention of leaving their assignments.

As the Admiral and Captain Andros walked slowly down the Amundsen's corridor and back to the shuttle bay, Captain Andros said with all gravity, "you know Admiral, understanding is a two edged sword, we could just as easily cut ourselves as we could the Kadre, that information could kill us if we've interpreted it wrongly".

"I know what you mean. But we can't do nothing, we have to take the fight to them and show them we aren't to be scared or intimidated. Aggressors fear too, they fear being beaten, they fear not winning. Maybe that fear can be so strong they negotiate a way out, to buy us the time we need to get the ships we desperately need".

CHAPTER 43

RISK & REWARD

The Kadre star system of Kinkuthanza from the information obtained from the damaged ship, had one small planet amongst eleven larger ones, Kinkuthanzziax, to the humans it was Deneb-Kaitos-VI.

There was enough information to know it was small, around the size of Luna, rocky, no atmosphere and of little value; it seemed to have nothing more than a small mining outpost and it was undefended.

The Admiral had an idea, but it wasn't without risk. It would be an ideal target for the Amundsen to jump in, release probes and fighters, run some long range scans for enough time to recharge her jump system and leave. A total of around twenty minutes. There were other advantages too, the planet was out of alignment with the others, and appeared to be as far from even the closest, that only a chance patrol would see the jump point open that deep into the system. Even if they did see it, there was zero indication that the Kadre had ever developed jump engine technology, not because they were incapable, but the gates were there, the gates worked and the gates were defensible, so there was no need to. So if they did see it they probably wouldn't believe it until it was all over, and the Amundsen would be gone.

Captain Andros was surprisingly easy to convince but he wanted the gunships with him - which meant attaching them to the Amundsen before the jump. The Admiral agreed. They'd kept comms traffic to a complete minimum just in case they were being listened in on, not that Baylin though they were, but it was good practice. They held a planning meeting in the Nemesis briefing room and were just about to close, when Sam Carradine the Chief Engineer appeared, with a request for two of Amundsen's officers to join in on comms.

335

"Admiral, Captain, permission to bring in Lieutenant O'Neil and Commander Canetta, from the Amundsen?"

"OK, Sam, but we're pretty much done here, what's so urgent?" The Admiral was hoping some unexpected problem hand't just reared its head, and Captain Andros couldn't help let slip a smile; his jump specialist and chief engineer were tinkering with the jump programmes and the mechanics to open a point all the time. He just knew they'd done something.

Sam Carradine asked for O'Neil to explain it; "Caroli...I mean Lieutenant O'Neil, has been working on a theory to expand the point and make it larger, enough for more ships to go through, and hold it open while they do. Sir, I think with my suggestions and some of Commander Canetta's tweaks to the system, we've been able to to do it".

The Admirals attention, and that of the Captain were immediately focused. Baylin asked immediately, "How many ships can go through at once?"

"The QuAC simulation, says its 98% probable we can keep a point open for ninety seconds before having to traverse it, so if the ships are close to hand when the point is opened, they go through in a group ahead of the Amundsen, and she follows through, as the point collapses".

Captain Andros was baffled, "but how, the projector was only able to operate for long enough to open a point about five klicks in front of us, at the speed we are doing on entry its barely enough to keep the point open and get us through?"

"O'Neill here sir, the problem was we made certain assumptions when the generators were developed, and they've proven to be over generous. The protective magnetic 'slip field' that stops the point collapsing on us in transit, is almost 60% stronger than it needs to be, and that's with a ten per cent safety margin. I can explain the maths but it would seem counter productive right now".

She turned to Commander Canetta, "Sir's the Lieutenant is right, it turns out the field protecting us was grossly over powered and we didn't take into account the dynamics of a jump point that was self generated are different to a gates dynamics, where the gate structure controls the open-close procedure. By transferring the energy to hold the protective field into the gate projector, we can push the point out to fifteen klicks, and hold it open. In fact given time and some experimentation, we can almost certainly improve on even that".

Admiral Baylin understood the significance of this immediately, "So you're saying we could fly the whole fleet through the Amundsen's jump point, but she would have to be last through?"

"Aye, Sir, that's it exactly". Sam Carradine looked too pleased, and he wasn't looking at the Admiral, but in glowing pride at his fiancé on the screen.

"Well congratulations to the three of you, but you need to test it, and that requires Captain Andros to agree, it's his ship. Captain Andros, I'm leaving this project in your hands, call on anyone you need to make it happen, if we need to do a group jump in and out of local hyperspace, say the word. So do you three have a timetable?"

Commander Canetta responded, "We can field test it today sir, the modifications to the power flow are a programming issue and we've written the code with Cynthia, she's run over 300 simulations and is still running them, its good to go".

"Well in that case Gregor, it's down to you we'll take all three cruisers through, if that's what's needed for proof of concept".

The look on the Admiral's face was enough for everyone to know the meeting was over. This was going to happen.

As the others left, the Admiral went to his office on the bridge, he needed to brief Markus, but he hand't been sat long, reading his now well worn book, when the Doc Came in with Markus.

The Doc looked down at the book, "Is that a real book?"

"Yes, a very dear friend said no self respecting military man who aimed for a command rank should be without a copy, and I often re-read it".

"May I", said Markus, as intrigued at the Doc; neither of them had seen a paper book in more years than either could remember, outside of a museum.

"*Sun Tzu's The Art of War*?" Markus picked up the worn red hard hard back cloth cover, with large worn gold foil lettering on the front and spine.

"You know," said the Admiral quietly, "he wrote that nearly 2,800 years ago. He distilled down in basic language the core facts of strategy, military economics and tactics, and they're still true to this day. You can read any line, and extrapolate it to anything we're dealing with now".

As if to test the theory, the Doc took the book and opened it randomly at a page. It was number 65 in a chapter called *The Nine Situations*, that caught his eye, *"If the enemy leaves a door open, you must rush in"*.

Doc Branson flicked through more pages until another line caught his eye, *"the general who advances without coveting fame and retreats without fearing disgrace, whose only thought is to protect his country and do good service for his sovereign, is the jewel of the kingdom"*. Branson put the book down, his finger on that quote for the Admiral to read. "Is that you?"

"You know Doc, I sincerely hope it is". The Admiral took the book, noting that Markus looked a little discomforted by the way the Doc addressed him, he turned to the chapter called *Manoeuvring*. *"Number 19; Let your plans be dark and impenetrable as night, and when you move, fall like a thunderbolt"*. The Admiral looked squarely at them both, "so that's exactly what we're going to do".

CHAPTER 44

TALES OF THE UNEXPECTED

The test to open a jump point went exactly as planned, the Admiral fretted over the fact only the Amundsen had the capability, but he'd been assured the new cruisers all did. Indeed the practical data was relayed back to Fleet and the programming changes and testing would soon be implemented on all the new ships with the jump generators. Nemesis was in line to get hers within a month. The three officers received formal commendations for their contributions, a high honour, and in quick time, urged on by Baylin himself.

Three days later, they were ready. It was a 36 hour jump into enemy space at Deneb-Kaitos-VI, the accuracy of their arrival would be within 10,000 klicks of the planet, because they just didn't have the navigation refinement to be more accurate - yet.

The Admiral deliberately didn't use the jump gate to leave the Luyten system, fearing the enemy might have hyperspace probes or some ability to detect it had it been activated.

Every ship was fully armed, the idea was simply to arrive, scan the system, attack the planet if there was time, destroy the mining facility, and leave, having dropped a two-man listening pod onto Deneb-Kaitos-VI with a secure tachyon transmitter. That was a risky mission, but it would be able to provide unprecedented intelligence on what went on in the system.

Plans were made, everyone knew their job, what was expected of them. Now it was just a matter of time.

++

Dorinda Kagala stepped off the Express shuttle form Mars to Titan, more than a little discomforted and overwhelmed by what had happened in the past few days. Her name, her husbands name and that of her sons, Avode and Tikan, flighting with the fleet who knew where, had been all over the networks. People on the shuttle had given her strange looks, although one of the cabin crew had been kind enough to move her to a seat up front on its own.

The Titan Hilton was just a short vactrain ride, and it had its own stop. As the doors opened, the press were all over her. Lights, in her face, recording drones hovering above her, behind her, in front of her. Pushy journalists doing what they had done for decades for the networks, after any sensationalism they could stir up, and most of them with a narrative and spin of their own. They didn't want truth, they wanted gossip.

The staff at the Hilton were used to such things, they quickly cleared a path for her and saw her safely into a private reception room, so that she could check in without hassle.

The porter took her things and said he'd take them to her room. She shyly asked where she could find her husband, "He's in suite 650 Mrs Kagala, would you like me to let him know you're here?"

"No, no I'd rather you didn't, if you don't mind".

"I'm sure it'll be a wonderful surprise for him to see you Mrs Kagala, he's had an interesting week or two it seems".

She smiled, wishing Avode or Tikan, preferably both, could be there with her, but she hand't troubled them with the fact she'd traveled to Titan, what was the point? She'd had quite enough of Nelson Kagala and his treatment of her. She was fed up with the way he ignored her feelings, didn't even have the common decency to inform her of anything, not that he was even on Titan. That she'd found out from the newscasts. She'd tried to call him, but it just got backed up in messages that were never even listened to.

She got out of the elevator, walked the short distance to the steel door and buzzed it. She jumped slightly, it opened far more quickly than she imagined it would, as a hotel maid pushed out a trolley with some uneaten food on it, she walked in.

Nelson Kagala was standing in the huge panoramic window, his back to her, seemingly unaware of her presence. She wondered how he'd gotten such an amazingly expensive suite, this was just about the best in the hotel. She straightened herself, standing tall, with a great deal of trepidation she spoke his name, "Nelson!" It came out far louder than she imagined or intended.

Nelson Kagala turned, slowly, there was something different about him, she took a step closer, "Nelson?" This time she sounded questioning, uncertain. He looked, well he looked ten years younger, the grey was gone, his eyes were bright, but humourless. He looked right at her, right into her soul she felt, and it made her shudder, then he spoke, "I'm sorry, do I know you?"

+++

The jump point opened up 9,460 klicks from the planet, a remarkable achievement and the navigation crews who'd worked hard on plotting the course were justly proud.

The entire fleet deployed according to plan, fighters, everything, around the Amundsen. She instantly began to scan the planet, the system, and the Pollux launched the listening post module with its two man crew aboard.

Bruce Baylin and his command staff waited for any sign of the enemy. The first reports on the planet were coming through, "Admiral the mining facility is, Sir, its gone, totally gone..."

"What do you mean gone?"

"Sir there's a crater so smooth and so huge that it must have been some sort of energy weapon, its just gone".

Then the reports started flooding in, one by one, more and more, rubble, devastation, lack of communications traffic, wreckage. The Amundsen with her powerful scanners was able to gather most data, and with no enemy visible, Baylin gave permission to push the scans of all ships to full to widen the search.

Nothing, the ships deployed more widely, all they could find was devastation. The giant orbital battle stations were nothing but lumps of wreckage, reflecting sensor scans back without inhibition. Planets were ablaze. One planet, once protected by the largest battle station, had a human-habitable atmosphere, but the planets surface was scorched to oblivion.

Baylin was shaken, every sinew told him this wasn't right, something was very, very, wrong. He knew never to ignore his gut instincts; "Markus relay to the fleet emergency departure procedure, get us out of here, get us out of here now".

They'd practiced the protocol for a hasty exit. Captain Andros' crew relayed the departure pattern, the jump engine capacitor was online. "Helm, initiate jump sequence".

The Amundsen's Faflof Ion Drives accelerated her, the jump point opened up, around 20 klicks ahead of her, its welcome blue-white-red swirl felt as if it were drawing her in. As per the plan, the gunships went first, then the Pollux, the Hercules, and then Nemesis.

As Nemesis entered the point the Amundsen's scanners detected an anomaly, "Captain, there's something coming up behind us, a large vessel".

"Comms relay the information to the Nemesis".

"We can't sir not in transit, once we're through we can..."

From some 1000 klicks behind the Amundsen two balls of intense light flashed past her, Amundsen was accelerating toward the open jump point, only then did Captain Andros realise what was happening; the ship hadn't fired at them, it was firing at the jump point, trying to collapse its threshold, stop them from jumping, but it was too late, Amundsen was at 39 klicks a second, she would hit the threshold, but it was too compromised by the weapons fired at it to transit. There was nothing they could do, but it didn't stop him shouting out, "cut acceleration, turn sharp left ninety degrees, NOW!"

342

The Nemesis was already through into hyperspace. The Admiral, curious to see the Amundsen come through behind them, was watching on the main bridge screen, though it seemed shockingly distant already as hyperspace catapulted them forward. The Nemesis cameras relayed it all, there was a bright flash, the jump point seemed to flicker, the Amundsen seemed to be turning, then to his dumfounded horror, and gasps from the bridge crew, she exploded, Baylin jumped up muttering, "No, no, not like this…" The jump point behind the Nemesis quickly collapsed, he saw it, all of them saw it, the Amundsen was gone.

++

Mr Athanasios sat in the huge warehouse on Mars, behind the desk that stood alone in the middle of the empty floor. The two chairs in front of him were occupied. "They'll assume it was a jump point accident of course, so they won't use that method again in a hurry".

"You're misguided Athanasios", said the figure on the left, they're already deploying more ships with the capability, all you have done is slow them down by at best, an Earth year".

Athanasios was ready for that argument, "that's all we need".

THE END OF BOOK 1

Book 2: VOID is already under way!
Follow updates on our Facebook page
@SonsOfEarthSaga

ABOUT THE AUTHOR

JON CHAMPS is older than he'd like to be but wise enough to appreciate how lucky he is.

An aviation enthusiast, all round geek, this is his first science fiction novel, but his fourth book.

Jon likes to travel (a lot), and has been all over the world, with a fondness for Japan and California, especially San Francisco. He's renowned for his military and political knowledge, especially of the 20th Century.

He described his most profound experience, visiting Nagasaki and Hiroshima and meeting and talking with atomic bombing survivors, as 'simply extraordinary and deeply moving".

He's married and lives in England.

Printed in Great Britain
by Amazon